Rosalind Miles has worked as a writer, journalist and broadcaster in the UK and throughout the world. A contributing editor to *Cosmopolitan* magazine, Rosalind Miles specialises in the lives and careers of women, and has written award-winning non-fiction including *Women and Power, The Women's History of the World* and *The Rites of Man*. She is also the bestselling author of *Return to Eden*, based on the successful television series.

Also by Rosalind Miles

FICTION
Return to Eden
Bitter Legacy
Prodigal Sins
I, Elizabeth

NON-FICTION
The Fiction of Sex
The Problem of Measure for Measure
Danger! Men at Work
Modest Proposals
Women and Power
Ben Jonson: His Life and Work
Ben Jonson: His Craft and Art
The Female Form
The Women's History of the World
The Rites of Man

Act of Passion

Rosalind Miles

HEADLINE

First published in 1993
by HEADLINE BOOK PUBLISHING PLC

10 9 8 7 6 5 4 3 2 1

ISBN 0 7472 3922 3

Phototypeset by Intype, London

Printed and bound in Great Britain by
HarperCollins Manufacturing Glasgow

HEADLINE BOOK PUBLISHING PLC
Headline House
79 Great Titchfield Street
London W1P 7FH

For Alex
Wherever His Spirit Walks

Chapter 1

Outside the bright country was calling her as it did every morning. High above, the burning sun was promising yet another perfect day. And the same thought surfaced once again as it did so often now: *I can't go on like this*.

She smiled bitterly. How many women could live in such perfect surroundings and still be unhappy? And how many women wherever they lived in the world told themselves, *I can't go on like this* and still carried on, day in, day out, just the same?

All around her the old house seemed to be watching and listening, waiting for something to happen. She drifted down the long cool hall onto the wide sweeping verandah outside. Before her the outback stretched for mile after unforgiving mile into the secret heart of Australia, the dead red heart buried somewhere out there, centuries away. Under the blistering eye of a sun that had scorched this hidden continent for half a million years, the land lay secret and forbidding, powerful, brooding, withholding all that its fearful inhabitants needed to know simply to survive.

Just like Phillip, she thought. *Withholding all I need*.

Farther down the well-kept roadway, beyond the outbuildings and away to the side of the homestead there came a gentle stir. Slowly the group of Aboriginals sitting in the dappled shade of the clump of silvery eucalyptus trees began to rouse themselves, stand up and wander

1

forward, their eyes fixed on the horizon.

How did they always know when the men were due back from the muster? The same way they knew everything, when the spirits who forewarned them of the nearness of things breathed their knowledge into the souls of those wise enough to hear their whispers. They always knew beforehand how the muster went, even who would be returning with it, and who would not. Something clawed at her heart, and with it the same familiar tug of anxiety and grief. For like a million million other women in the history of the world, Helen did not know what she would do if her husband came back this time, and she did not know what she would do if he did not.

'Mrs Koenig?'

She had not heard the silent pad of feet coming out of the drawing room behind her. It was the housekeeper, Rose, a tiny, wiry woman born on the station and mistress of Koenigshaus since time immemorial. No one now even knew her real name: Phillip had obliterated her Aboriginal identity when he nicknamed her 'Rose' on the day he took her from her people as a young girl, to keep house for him in his own early days as the first unmarried master of Koenigshaus in the station's history of almost two hundred years.

Unmarried then – but not for long. Ancient gossip murmured that Rose had kept more than the master's board for him all through the years before he had returned from America with a glamorous, unknown bride. *Rose was here then, she knew Trudi, she must remember her*, Helen thought for the thousandth time, *she's seen us all come and go. You were really the first wife though, weren't you Rose?*

The burning black eyes brushed aside the question, and fixed themselves on Helen's face. Helen stifled a sigh. She could guess what was coming. 'Yes, Rose?'

Rose's grizzled head moved emphatically up and down.

'Men been mustering need a good dinner, Miz' Koenig. Not some fancy new restaurant food.'

She might have known that Rose would not be happy to change the slightest detail of the ritual. She sighed. 'A good muster dinner? Same as always?'

Rose nodded again. 'They been out there all these weeks, bringing up the cattle for the road train, they want come back to a good dinner same as always.'

There was a silence. Rose's sharp old eyes took in the dejected droop of the still-shapely body, the sideways angle of the fair head, and knew that she had won. Helen waved a tired hand. 'Just as you like, Rose. Give them what you want.'

Why had she tried to change it? Phillip wouldn't want anything different from the routine he had established for the last forty years, king of his own kingdom since the first muster he led on this land. And neither would Jon, she knew. He adored his father, prided himself on being a chip off the old block, and would never question anything Phillip chose to do.

But he's my son too! she thought with a twist of pain. Of course it was only natural that as he grew to manhood Jon would get closer to his father, striving to become like him when the time came to step into his father's shoes. *But does he have to grow away from me like this? Isn't he a little bit like me, still mine just a little bit? Or am I moving away from him as I move away from his father, changing out of all recognition?*

She had to pull herself together. Rose was still standing there, her eyes watchful in her gnarled brown-black face. Helen tried to smile. 'Whatever you do, it'll be fantastic like always, Rose,' she said warmly, reaching forward to squeeze the older woman's work-worn hand. 'As long as there's plenty of everything, like Mr Phillip likes. Just give us one of your specials, and we'll all be happy.'

Rose shook her head angrily, gesturing towards the

kitchen. 'Only if that Ellie girl shape up! She don't come this morning till nearly lunch, blame that drunk husband of hers alla time. But she can be late by herself, no problem! She getting worse and worse.'

Helen looked at her in silent sympathy. Both women knew that however sulky, lazy and slovenly Rose's supposed help-mate around the house was, Ellie was safe from either of them. Only Phillip could hire and fire on Koenigshaus, and a maid like Ellie, who was clever enough to keep on his right side, had a job for life. She was sexy too, even a woman could see that, with her indolent, inviting eyes, her lightly-parted mouth, her lean, childish body strangely at odds with the pert, full, experienced breasts. And Phillip always had to have women around who called to the raw man in him.

Rose must have been like that once. But nature was cruelly unfair in her treatment of women. Aged beyond her years, all Rose had now to console herself was the odd secret nip of beer or sherry and the worn pack of cards she liked to mumble over in the evenings: it was the younger woman's turn to vaunt herself now. 'Mr Phillip likes things to stay the same – and Ellie's been helping in the house since she was a child, hasn't she?' was as near to saying all this as Helen dared get.

Rose laughed harshly. 'Call it helpin'? She first come hangin' round here before Jon born, and then she just stay. She older'n she looks. She come when Alex still here. When—'

'Thanks, Rosie.' She loved Rose, but she couldn't take any more now. With a half-nod, Rose took her dismissal and turned away.

Was it easier for the Aboriginals, Helen wondered as she watched the small fierce retreating back, to be so in touch with the past that those who had gone away were as real as those who were still around them every day? Among them, both their spirit ancestors and those still

4

waiting to be born all had a name, a face, and a place in their hearts as secure as that of anyone on earth. Or did it make it harder that the past was never dead, that the undead walked, that the mistakes and sorrows of years ago were never buried but lived to haunt the survivors till the day they died too?

Down by the trees the waiting men had drifted together into a purposeful cluster all staring out into the hot and sandy haze. She knew they could feel the approach of the muster, however many miles it still had to come. She watched them keenly, leaning on the verandah rail. They could feel Phillip, for sure – none of them had known Koenigshaus without his larger-than-life presence, without his spirit dominating all this sunburned land.

And not only his. Generations of Koenigs had carved their fortunes out of this endless space, imposing their unbreakable will to build out of its vast nothingness the greatest cattle station in the Northern Territory. Not for nothing had it earned its name of 'the Kingdom', so dubbed by the locals from the moment they first learned that the English meaning of the old German 'Koenig' was the same as 'King'. Phillip's great-grandfather had built the church at which their children were baptised as Christians, his grandfather had built the school at which they had learned the white man's words and ways. They would all feel Phillip and his unbending force, see his large, hard, stocky body, brutal hands and arrogant head, hear that loud commanding voice rapping out the orders that spoke his will, until their dying day.

She shivered, despite the sun glancing obliquely on the back of her sunbrowned hands, her unprotected head. She knew they felt Jon too, but in a different way. Open as daylight, straight and true, Jon did not have an enemy in the world. To most of the men who knew him he was still simply 'Phillip's boy', man enough to take charge of the muster when Phillip was away, but still lad enough to release his boyish high spirits in larking with the stockmen at the end of the drive.

The women of the Territory, and especially their daughters, tended to look differently at the tall well-made young man in his early twenties with the hard horseman's body and loose athleticism of one born in the saddle. They saw too the gentleness slumbering within his thoughtful nature, a sensitivity unsuspected by those who took the manly frame, dusty fair hair, untroubled blue eyes and cheerful smile at face value.

But it was this gentleness, not the streak of toughness that he took from his father, that spoke to the Aboriginals in their own language. And Jon was the first generation of Koenig males ever to attend school with the children of the station down in the Aboriginal's camp, where in the course of Australia's unending summers he had formed bonds with those who now worked with him side by side as men, bonds that would never be broken. Yes, they felt Jon. They felt him in their hearts.

And they felt her too, Helen knew that. Like them she was born to the land, an ordinary girl working for her living on the next station till the dynamic Phillip Koenig had suddenly decided to take the shy, sturdy eighteen-year-old and make her his own. For twenty-five years now she had lived on this land, serving Phillip and Koenigshaus in every way she could.

And it would have been any woman's life work, she reminded herself half in anger, half in tears. Within this green oasis lay not just an outback homestead but almost a small village. It was home not only to the great old colonial-style house where generations of Koenigs had struggled, fought and died, but also to the houses of the stockmen, the Aboriginal's camp, the office building from which Phillip ran his extensive business interests, the stables for his much-prized string of horses, and not least the stone chapel which the first of the Koenigs, a fierce

6

Lutheran, had built as soon as he had finished putting an earthly roof over his head.

Not that his was the only head that counted for him. Old Johann had cared passionately for that of his unbending, blonde-plaited German wife and the seven little angel-faced Koenigs who had made the journey from the old world with them. Within the year, six of those children had found their last resting-place in this quiet earth so far away from home, and only the seventh had survived to justify the blood and sweat that had been poured into this terrible endeavour. That Koenig's son had survived too and thriven, and so had his son after him. Then came Phillip, and now Jon.

Jon.

My only son.

Strange, she mused. Lusty between the sheets, the Koenigs were never lusty breeders.

But all you need is one. You only need one son to pass it all on to. Only one man to inherit, one man to rule. Only one king of the kingdom, one Koenig at Koenighaus. That's all you need.

And she had given them that. She had given them Jon, who was one of them, who was theirs in a way no other Koenig had ever been or ever could be, just as she had given him her own sunlit hair and wide, trusting blue eyes. And he would be a good man for this land when his time came. That was her work. She knew she could say she had earned a place in the Aboriginals' scheme of things that they called their 'Dreaming'.

Did they still dream her rival too, after all these years? Trudi and her son, her only son too, just like Jon—? Or was it only the second wife who was doomed to dream forever of her predecessor, dream in vain that God had given her that slender body white as a Madonna lily, that story-book hair as black as ebony and lips as red as blood, those long elegant hands, that air of languid confidence

7

and worldly assurance she had seen on the portrait of Phillip's wife the first time she came to the house – the portrait that had disappeared by the next time he had brought her here, never to be seen again . . .

Enough! Helen wrapped her arms around her body to stop herself from shuddering out of control.

What is this? she castigated herself. Get a grip! Phillip and Jon and all the men would be coming in from the muster in a couple of hours and expecting a royal welcome, the helicopter from Sydney was due any minute with its own waggonload of complications, and she was standing here catching flies?

Overhead a lone currawong flew in great flashing circles with its harsh crying lament, like an abandoned child. She ran a hand through her still-blonde thick shoulder-length hair and tried to think what she had to do next. *Shape up!* she scolded herself. *Pull yourself together, get going!*

But still in the dusty heat she shivered and grew cold. On the horizon the faraway mutter of rotor blades heralded the distant arrival of the helicopter. But when some time later its black shadow passed at last with a sinister clatter like a bird of prey over the rambling sprawl of the gracious old colonial homestead, the slim, sturdy fair-haired figure was still standing hunched on the verandah, a million miles away.

Chapter 2

Five miles from Koenigshaus, wave upon wave of the sleepy, sand-brown cattle snuffled with satisfaction as they picked up the scent of home on the evening air. At the head of the endless column, one lone horseman, aloft in his stirrups, shouted a challenge as he broke away from the pack.

'Race you to the house!'

'Hey, hold on!'

Dad's as bad as a child, thought Jon delightedly as he fixed his gaze on the flying figure ahead and clapped his own heels to his horse's side in a vain attempt to catch up. He'll be shouting 'Last one back's a cissy!' next, he laughed to himself. Godsakes, how long has he been mustering on this land? Must have been almost every one of his sixty years!

Yet he's still as keen as ever – still as fit, as hard, as lean, as good in the saddle, as fast with a rope, as quick with a branding iron, as slow to give way, or back down. I'm going to be as good as him when I'm that old, he thought. And in the meantime, I'm not going to let the old bastard get away with this!

Whooping with delight he threw himself into the chase. Behind them lay all the immensity of outback Australia, on all sides the hot red earth under the vast pale dome of the heavens running flat and straight to the stark black line of the endless horizon. With the end of the day the shimmering heat had melted into heart-piercing shades of violet, blue and indigo as the sun tumbled down the sky, and now the sudden tropical night was not far away. All over the evening world, those still at large, the wanderers human and animal, were running for their homes.

'Get on! C'mon, boy, come *on*!'

Ahead of him the taut hunched figure spurring forward and bellowing at the white stallion quite belied the years that Phillip Koenig was supposed to have lived on this earth. God, he could ride! Jon conceded with reluctant admiration. And Kaiser would do anything for him, bloody-minded nag that he was for anyone else! 'Still, we'll show 'em, Butch, won't we?' he whispered, leaning forward in the stirrups to pull his horse's ears and urge the sweating gelding on.

In response his horse quickened its stride and leaped on towards the cluster of buildings ahead with renewed vigour. In the centre of a grey-green sprawl of eucalyptus and saltbush, surrounded and protected by a darker mantle of cypress, cedar and rhododendron trees, the two tiers of wide red roofs as ornate as a Chinese pagoda swept magisterially down to the long iron-wrought verandahs which surrounded the gracious old mansion on all four sides. Within their sheltering shade, wide sash windows and French doors looked into low, spacious rooms lovingly furnished over many years with the best of everything that the Koenigs of each generation could afford. Yet it was still a home where people had lived, loved and died, and where he had grown up, and Jon loved it with his soul.

Yet he loved too the world outside the homestead, that little patch of green painfully carved out of the huge wilderness all around. That was the true kingdom for him, not just the homestead, fine as it was. For thousands of miles out there the earth ran like the terrain on Mars, a world of red earth, burned vegetation and opal-brown sky. There the human soul could be free in a place as spacious as itself. He knew he could never leave here, never survive anywhere else.

'I'm going to leave you standing!'

The deep cry floated back to Jon just at the moment when he started to feel his striving horse was gaining ground at last. 'Don't be too sure!' he yelled back.

Now he could see Phillip's great-striding stallion slackening off as he saw the stables ahead and knew he was almost at home. Neck and neck they turned into the stable yard and almost in unison pulled up their mounts as they raced towards the rail, Jon's horse just nudging into the lead. 'I won!' he cried.

'Not yet!'

With the rashness of a twenty year old Phillip threw his leg forward over his horse's ears and vaulted to the ground to touch the first upright of the verandah, his other hand reaching out in a violent rugby hand-off to floor Jon, who was trying to do the same thing. The large sunburned face of the older man flushed with success as he straddled Jon lying full-length on the ground. 'I beat you, boy!' Phillip cried.

Jon could hardly speak for laughing as he picked himself up. 'You cheated!'

'I won, didn't I? Nothing in the rules against cheating!'

'You *cheated!*'

Phillip's answer was another rough push which sent Jon sprawling to the floor again. 'Y'got to be quicker on your feet, boy! Still, you pressed me a little bit there, I'll give you that!'

From the kitchen Helen watched the by-play between her husband and son with fear in her heart. *He won. To him that's all that counts. He even needs to beat his own son. But as long as winning is everything, what about anyone else?*

Her heart turned over as it always did now not for her

husband but for her son. God, he was so beautiful! And so trusting, so open to being hurt.

Yet Phillip loved Jon too, he always had. Why was she so obsessed with the fear of what he might do to their son? She was just being stupid again. *Stop it!*

Forcing a smile, she nerved herself to push out through the mesh-covered door to greet them, into the still-throbbing heat and dust outside. 'Welcome back!' she said as gaily as she could, opening her arms to embrace them both. 'Good muster?'

Phillip bounded up the low flight of steps onto the wooden verandah and swept her into a cruel bear hug. 'The best!' he announced loudly. 'It gets better all the time. Like—' he laughed his great rough laugh. 'Like—?' he said tauntingly, in a voice heavy with meaning.

Like sex, she knew he meant, and prayed he wouldn't say it, not in front of Jon. From the malicious crackle in his eye, she knew he read her fear. He wrapped his arms round her again and squeezed her to him. His body was hot, and the rank smell of him after weeks in the saddle rose up to her so strongly that she could taste it in the back of her throat.

Phillip felt her draw away, and clutched her even tighter. 'Like – like what would you say, Hen? Like—? Come on!' he drawled, his eyes never leaving her face.

'Oh – I don't know, Phillip—'

Jon shifted awkwardly. If only Dad wouldn't tease her like this! Didn't he know women were a bit sensitive about these things?

But Phillip was impervious. 'Don't know?' he boomed. 'What d'you think I'm on about? It's like life, that's all I meant – like life!'

Another boisterous laugh. He scrutinised Helen minutely, enjoying her discomfort. 'So, did you and Rosie fix us a good dinner? Especially as we've got guests.'

'Guests?' Jon was taken completely by surprise, Helen could see.

12

Phillip grinned again, more wolf-like than ever. 'Yeah,' he said casually. 'We've got your uncle Charles here from Sydney, didn't I tell you he was coming? And old Ben from the city office, I had the chopper pick 'em up this afternoon when I knew we'd make it back tonight.' He paused. 'Things to talk about. Interesting things.' He nodded meaningfully at Jon. 'Very interesting things. You're gonna see.'

Why does he do this? Helen thought wearily. There was a time when she had found it fascinating, wonderful, sexy even, to be kept on the hop like this, at the mercy of Phillip's sudden decisions which seemed so spontaneous, but which in reality often sprang from deep and secret plans.

But nowadays – she could see Jon struggling with his surprise. 'Charles is coming? And Ben?' He shook his head. He looked awkward and wrong-footed at not being given such a simple piece of information, puzzled and even hurt at finding the easy family home-coming he had looked forward to after weeks in the outback suddenly turned into something else.

And something important, if his father's elaborate charade of casualness was anything to go by. Helen looked at Jon with all a mother's pain. He'd been so happy when he arrived. Now he seemed tense and concerned, suddenly five years older. Oh, why does Phillip have to do this? her heart cried.

Phillip turned to her, his grey hawk's eyes sharp and dark. Not for the first time she felt the fear that he could read her disloyal thoughts. 'They radio in from the chopper yet?'

'They didn't need to. They're here. They arrived an hour ago.' She took a breath. 'We have another guest too. Ben's brought Geena. She's just come to the end of her term at college and he thought she could use a weekend in the country. He did ring to ask. It's such ages since we've seen her I couldn't wait to say yes.'

'Great, that's fine! The more the merrier! Let 'em all come!' Phillip slapped his broad hands together in approbation. 'OK, kid!' He punched Jon on the shoulder. 'Since you lost, you get to take the horses in, see that everything's ready for the last muster tomorrow. I'll shower and see you inside as soon as you're ready.'

In silence mother and son regarded each other as the burly form trod heavily away. 'You did win, Jon,' Helen said quietly. 'He cheated. He just had to beat you, he had to win.'

'Yeah,' Jon nodded, and shrugged uneasily. 'But Dad's only fooling, you know that. You don't want to take him too seriously.'

She knew what he was saying to her, and kicked herself for even opening her mouth. Now his face wore that tense troubled look again, and this time it was her fault, not Phillip's. You may have fallen out of love with your husband, she scolded herself mournfully, but that hasn't changed anything for anyone else. Phillip's still the same man. And he's still the father your son has hero-worshipped for the last twenty-odd years. Don't spoil that for him. You mess with that at your peril. Because you'd better hang onto something good in the desert of your life right now!

Chapter 3

Through the polished glass of the French windows, heaven and earth were meeting in a wall of solid black, as dense as only a moonless, starless night in the huge unpolluted bowl of the Australian sky can be. Inside the room, clusters of little table lamps threw golden pools of warm inviting light around a dining table set for six with full silver service for the Koenig household and their pampered guests.

In the drawing room beyond, Phillip Koenig stood with his son at his side and mentally reviewed the evening ahead. Erect beneath a forbidding portrait of his founding ancestor Johann, legs astride in front of a huge open fireplace glowing at this time of the year with vivid greenery and wild flowers, Phillip locked his hard hands behind his back and permitted himself a secret smile very different from the expansive welcome he wore on his lips as the first of his guests entered the room.

'Charles!'

Striding forward, Phillip grasped the hand of the tall slender man approaching him and wrung it vigorously, roughly punching his brother's shoulder with a hard swing of his fist as he did so. 'Good to see you, mate!' Swiftly he extended the same greeting to the man who had entered behind. 'And Ben! Where's your lovely daughter? What have you done with her?'

Ben Nichols smoothed down the thinning hair above

his broad, rather impassive face, and tried to raise a smile. 'Geena's upstairs with Helen. Girl talk. They'll be down soon.'

'Hi there – Charles.' Jon had not stopped saying 'Uncle Charles' for quite long enough to feel entirely at ease with the shorter form. And the lean, reserved Charles Koenig had nothing of Phillip's brash expansiveness, always seeming to Jon to be a man who kept his own counsel and made sure that all his real thoughts remained locked away deep inside the well-shaped, still handsome head.

How different two brothers could be, Jon thought, Phillip so broad, bluff and larger than life with his huge frame, great red-gold head and animal grin, Charles dark-haired, slim and elegant, even saturnine tonight. But there was no doubt of the regard he felt for his father's younger brother, and he tried to pull all of it into the firm hand-shake he now offered. 'Welcome to Koenigshaus. And Ben – good to see you again. How y'doing?'

'Drinks, boy!' ordered Phillip expansively. 'Chas, the bar's open! What'll you have? And Ben? Name your poison. We've got your favourite hangover already lined up for you, mate!'

Neither of the two men made any pretence of returning the social jollity. Charles held Phillip's gaze with eyes as grey and cold as his own. 'I think we'll all feel better when we've got this business wrapped up. We've got nothing to celebrate till then.'

Phillip's bonhomie vanished. 'That's the trouble with you, Charlie boy,' he murmured dangerously, 'and it always was. You've got no nerve. Your big idea, and you're just going to bottle out again like you always do, aren't you?' There was a painful silence. 'Well, aren't you?'

What the hell was going on? Jon stared from his father to the others in bewilderment. Charles's lean dark face

16

furrowed with anger as he tried to hold onto his temper. 'It's not a question of nerve,' he said harshly. 'It's a big decision, the biggest in the company's history, you know that. It can't just be treated as a formality.'

Phillip laughed unpleasantly. 'That's nice.'

I must get a grip here, Jon thought. 'Drinks, guys?' He forced himself to play host with the cut-glass decanters and crystal tumblers on the laden trolley standing to the side of the fireplace until each man was clasping a reassuring slug of something good. Then he said as casually as he could, 'What's all this about? What's not just a formality?'

Phillip cocked a black, mocking eye at Charles. 'Your uncle's had a brainwave. A big idea.'

'It's not just my idea,' said Charles doggedly.

Phillip snorted in derision. 'You telling me it's Ben's?'

Ben visibly quailed. 'Look, Phil, you know I'm just the hired hand when it comes to these financial decisions.'

'I wouldn't call one of the country's smartest business accountants "just a hired hand", Ben,' Phillip said easily. 'And as my financial director for forty years, born on the station and practically one of the family, you've got every right to put in your twopennyworth. In fact for what your salary costs me, I expect a lot more than twopennyworth out of you!'

Jon felt as if he were watching a tennis match without having been taught the rules. Tensely he surveyed the three men still standing on the hearth-rug, Charles and Phillip facing each other like antagonists, Ben the pig in the middle. When he spoke, he knew his voice was rather too loud. 'Give me a break, guys. What are you talking about?'

Phillip did not miss a beat. 'Selling Koenigshaus.'

There was a terrible silence. Neither Charles nor Ben looked at Jon. Jon's reaction seemed to come from some unknown pit of his soul. '*What?*'

17

Phillip turned to him with elaborate show of surprise. 'Oh, didn't they tell you?' he said innocently. 'Your uncle Charles and our financial wizz, old Ben here, want to sell Koenigshaus.'

Only he knew just how much it was costing Jon to speak. 'Sell Koenigshaus?' Unconsciously he reverted to the station's local nickname. 'Sell "the Kingdom"?'

'That's the property we're talking about. The old place has got to go! Go, go, go! Yoho!'

Jon laughed too, with a hysterical note of relief. 'Oh, come on, Dad! That's a lousy joke.'

'Yeah!' Phillip laughed uproariously. 'Yeah, I knew you'd think so!'

Slow recognition began to creep over Jon. Still he resisted it. 'Not funny, Dad.'

'I'm not joking, son.'

Jon froze – 'You mean—?'

Charles stepped a pace toward Phillip, his face a mask of distaste. 'Oh, cut this out, Phil!' he snapped. 'I thought you were going to tell him.'

'I was.'

'I mean tell him today!'

Phillip grinned more broadly. 'I have told him today. Just now.' He turned to Jon. 'How do you feel about it, son?'

Jon had gone very pale. 'You know how I'd bloody well feel about it!' he ground out. 'It's not possible! You just can't do this, Dad!'

'Oh dear,' said Phillip sardonically. 'Seems I've dropped something the dear boy can't cope with.' He looked round the room. 'You were right, Ben. You warned me our Jonno'd be a mite sensitive on the subject. Can't imagine why.'

'*Why?* Dad – I—'

To his hot shame and fury, Jon found himself fighting rising tears. Ben rushed uneasily into the breach. 'Look,

Jonno, the company's in trouble. Phillip's known about this for a good while now. We've been through the figures again and again, and there's only one way they add up.'

Charles nodded. 'And Koenigshaus, the cattle end of the business, is the weak link. The international beef market is failing everywhere, our sales are dropping year on year—'

Phillip took up the refrain. 'And ranching as we know it's a thing of the past. So according to Chas and Ben, Koenigshaus has got to go! We're going to have to sell, boy. They're going to kick the kings out of the kingdom!' He laughed even more uproariously now.

He seems to be enjoying this, Jon thought dully. I must do something. 'Look, Dad—'

As he spoke, two female figures appeared in the elegant archway that separated the drawing room from the wide hall and stairs. In a classic gown of sea-green crêpe de chine that subtly echoed the silvery lights in her fine blonde hair, Helen had a rare quality usually hidden by the shirt and riding jeans that were her everyday wear. In the bloom of the table lamps she lost at least ten of her forty-odd years, while her light step and gentle carriage banished another ten. Only her innate shyness prevented her seeing what an impact she was making on every man in the room.

But it was the girl at her side who caught every eye. Half-Aboriginal, she had drawn the best of the beauty from both sides of her heritage. The large, delicate, liquid brown eyes in the glowing deep golden skin gave her all the vulnerability of a bush baby, but the well-shaped nose and fearless chin argued a strength beyond her twenty or so years. Slim as a marble column in a simple sheath of white silk, she moved like a dancer as she stepped shyly into the room under the scrutiny of all the men.

There was a general murmur of welcome. Only Jon did not speak.

19

'Jon?' said Helen, prompting him. 'You remember Geena, surely?'

Remember her?

Of course he remembered her! She'd been at school with him, only three or four years below. Then when the business expanded and old Ben had had to move to Sydney four or five years ago, she'd gone to live with her family in the city. He knew she'd lost her mother a couple of years back, and that she and Ben were now on their own. And he'd gathered from family conversations at home, not that he'd ever paid much attention, that she'd started college a while back too, and was going to finish her studies soon.

But that was Geena, the little waif so protected by her Aboriginal mother, Ben's unexpected choice of a wife, that none of the boys were ever allowed to play with her. That was the ugly little waif with the skinny, starved-looking body, legs like sticks and eyes too big for her face.

That was . . .

Not this!

Outside in the hall an unseen hand sounded a gong and Rose appeared with Ellie at her heels. Phillip laughed and clapped his hands together in loud report. 'Dinner!' he roared. 'Christ, I'm hungry!' His eyes were gleaming. 'It's great the way a good bit of business works up an appetite for your tucker, isn't it, mateys?'

Chapter 4

In the wide oak bed that had made the journey with the first Koenigs all the way from Saxony, Helen lay awake and listened to her husband's heavy breathing. If just thinking about it hard enough could do it, her heart cried, half the women in the world would kill their husbands *right now, this second*!

She tossed and shivered in the velvet dark. Jon's face came back to her as it was when she'd walked into the drawing room last night, bruised round the eyes like a young prize-fighter, the expression on his face that of a bull on its way to the slaughter.

She knew she could never argue business with Phillip, he had never even considered taking her opinion, and he would not now. Still she had presided at table, dispensing food and wine and good cheer and all the while trying to nerve herself up to chime into the conversation, 'Look Phillip, if the rest of the company is supporting this place, then can't we make change elsewhere and keep Koenigshaus on – for – for—'

For Jon, she wanted too say. *For my son. Your son. Your heir. The only one you've got left now, don't you remember? Or don't you care, now Alex has gone? Has Jon always got to be second best?*

Of course she had said nothing. Everyone else round the table had been silent too, Charles in the fury that always seized him when Phillip began to play his games,

Ben cowed, Geena clearly troubled by the tension in the atmosphere and Jon apparently struck dumb by the attractive young visitor's presence.

Yet Phillip had seemed delighted with the occasion, waxing more and more full of himself as the night wore on. As ever he had eaten and drunk at least twice as much as all the other men. Then at the end – she burned and twisted in the overheated bed to recall it – he had seen fit to put a public seal on the last of the night's entertainment. Pushing aside the remains of the sweet dessert wine, the nuts he had been cracking still in his hand, he looked down the table and caught her eye in a hot stare that excluded everyone else in the room. Then he leaped to his feet.

'Hen!'

In the silence that followed, he strode down the room to grasp her by the arm. As he pulled her to her feet, he ordered *Come – now!* in a way that left no doubt in the minds of anyone where he was taking her, and why.

In the bedroom, more orders: *'This way – no! Like this! Again! Harder! Now!'*

He had always been dominant in sex, rough and impatient, urgent to plunge, to penetrate, convinced he carried all before him by the force of his thrusting manhood. As far as Phillip was concerned, if he was satisfied, then she must be too. She used to smile to herself when she read articles in women's magazines earnestly urging readers to convey their sexual desires to their men, educate them in foreplay, 'show them what you like'. In Phillip's world, foreplay consisted of his decision to have sex. And women could have no likes apart from the desire to please their men.

And she had gone along with it. At first his rough haste had excited her, his hand down her dress while she was still raising her face for his kiss, her skirt round her waist even before someone leaving the room had fully closed the door. She could still remember their first embrace, the very first time they met. Arriving at the neighbourhood station where she worked, he had first seen her when he reined up to ask where her boss was to be found. Later he had sought her out in the feedstore where she was checking the cattle grain and supplies. 'Come to say goodbye,' he announced casually. 'Got a feeling I'll see you again.'

She knew he was going to kiss her from the moment he walked through the door, and her body set up an insistent throbbing while her mind was still struggling to decide whether she wanted him to or not. But when she closed her eyes, she felt not a 'getting-to-know-you' brush on the lips but a hard hand on her breast, an electric bolt through her frame from the rough fingers probing her nipple, her body claimed as if he were her longed-for lover returning famished for the feel of her after a month away.

From that first touch he had made her his: she was unable to resist him. And their sex together always followed the pattern of his rhythms, his drives, his desires. He liked his sex like fast food, hot, quick and often. He liked to try different relishes and garnishes, just to see how they tasted or felt.

'For tonight, Hen,' he would announce, throwing a package on the table whenever he returned from Sydney or one of his long business trips overseas. She had been flattered, years ago, when a visit to France had produced the ultimate set of Parisian lingerie, including a fancy corset with suspenders and black lace frillies that would not have disgraced the Moulin Rouge. Germany had yielded a pair of boots that Marlene Dietrich might have sported in The Blue Angel, London by contrast a school-girl gymslip in white cotton. 'Marks and Spencers,' he laughed, showing his sharp white teeth. 'I told them they were for my little girl!' Phillip was nothing if not Catholic in his tastes.

But latterly his demands had been more extreme, and

her satisfaction more elusive. Once she had loved him enough not to care if she came, to feel the surge of power and joy at the end of love-making simply from having the strong weight of a man lying spent and defenceless across her breasts. Now when he bought her lacy knickers, he expected to bend her over, rip them down and deal her half a dozen brutal strokes across her buttocks too. He never kissed her now, almost always preferring to take her crudely from behind, bundling into her like a dog, his huge hands grinding uncaringly into the tender tissue above her hips as he strained her body against his until he reached his climax.

If she cried out and protested, it only seemed to excite him more. Now he did things she was sure were meant to make her flinch and squirm, groan and shrink away in the vain attempt to escape the swelling torment. Any resistance stimulated him to crush her down. She knew she was locked into his dream-world, the dominance fantasy of an increasingly sadistic man bent on her humiliation as a necessary factor of his own satisfaction. Numbed and brutalised, she could not now remember when it had started. And for the life of her, she could not imagine how it would end.

Tonight she submitted quickly and completely to his demands, hoping as ever to hasten his climax and shorten her own ordeal. And as she did so, tonight as usual, a little piece of her died inside.

And then he was finished, sprawling on the bed, brutally spent. But for her, the nightly torment of inquisition had only just begun. When had she stopped finding that violent abrupt tumbling sexually exciting or even attractive, and begun to crave for something gentler, fuller, slower, something mutual?

When had she stopped loving him?

She shifted frantically beneath the light sheet, vainly seeking a cool place in the hot itching bed with its still-lingering smell of their sex in all its sourness. When Phillip first claimed her as his, she had been so proud to be his wife she did not care if the whole world knew of their love-making. Now the shrewd appraisal and mute sympathy that she saw in Charles's eyes as Phillip led her like an animal from the room scalded her like boiling oil.

Charles . . .

He too had spent his life in the shadow of Phillip, his strength unvalued against Phillip's piratical flair, the injustice of his life hardening now, she felt, to a bleak place of great bitterness deep within him. Yet he was as bright and hard as any of the Koenigs, given half the chance.

Charles . . .

Would she have been better off with him?

Around the edge of the heavy mahogany window-shutters the tropical dawn was painting its morning symphony of purple, red and gold. Not another bloody wonderful day! What hope of another hour or two of sleep when she could find no peace of mind?

Would she have been better off with Charles? Without Phillip?

What kind of a question was that? Her whole life seemed to be reduced to an endless, pointless questioning these days. When had that started? And when, oh when would it end?

As the sun burst like a ball of fire over Koenigshaus, Jon finally abandoned any attempt to sleep, and slipping out of bed, pulled on jeans and shirt and quietly left the house by the back door into the yard. For the first time in his twenty-four years he felt a torment so great that he refused to approach it head on, instead crawling around it like a wounded beast.

Sell Koenigshaus? Leave the Kingdom? How could his father even think of it? He stood on the kitchen verandah

25

and his eyes raked the homestead and all the land around. Land his people had fought over and died for.

But it was more than that. Jon turned softly into the early morning air as it arose fresh and sharp from the damp earth in the effort to cool his burning face. He loved this land, loved it with passion that lay too deep for speech, too deep even for tears. Dimly he knew that none of the rest of his family cared for Koenigshaus and these dry sandy acres, the unyielding miles of dead red earth, in the way that he did. Yes, Helen loved it, he knew, but she had not been born there – like all children, he had never stopped to wonder where on the earth his mother had been born – and besides, his father had always been her greatest love and the centre of his loyalty.

Charles? Jon tried to put himself in the place of his tall, withdrawn uncle. It can't have been much fun to be the much younger brother – no wonder that Charles had so early in life fled Phillip's broad shadow to try his fortune in Sydney. There he had built up a thriving business until Phillip, over-flush with cash after the booming beef-years of the seventies and eighties, had staged a board-room coup and bought his brother out.

That had been the start of Phillip's business empire, which he had immediately hired Charles to run. So Charles had found himself stripped of his business like a bankrupt, yet in the same move, given it back and given even more and bigger toys to play with, for Phillip would act on any recommendation he made for business expansion. 'You've got a great deal going for yourself there, young Chas,' Phillip was fond of assuring him. And Charles had never thrown back in Phillip's teeth the bitter reproach, 'Sure mate, except that none of it is mine!'

Was this move now to sell Koenigshaus, to break off the jewel in the crown and throw it away to strangers, Charles's revenge on Phillip for all that he had done? Such thoughts were alien to Jon's nature and he instantly shrugged the suspicion off. Yet he could not believe that Koenigshaus had to be sold, that there was no other way. 'I've got to do something!' he muttered desperately, like a child. 'There's got to be something I can do!'

At the base of a great gum tree, a tiny grey nocturnal creature ran like a little spirit away past him in the swiftly-rising light. Over the distant mountains ringing Koenigshaus in their eternal stone embrace, the first kites and hawks lazily rose to ride the swelling thermals as the sun began its work.

This land is mine.

With a new passion Jon surveyed the cluster of buildings around the beautiful old house and its orderly run of stables forming the neat yard behind. Almost in a dream, he circled the old mansion till he stood at the front.

Now the whole homestead lay before him, the land sloping gently away to the great water-hole miles away in the bush, the well-kept driveway with his mother's favourite roses and palm trees lining the road as far as the highway, the stockmen's quarters, the office building, the guesthouse where Ben and Geena slumbered even as he paced the ground outside.

Geena . . .

But even that strange and pleasantly painful thought could not dislodge his mind from its deepest track, the vein that ran through the centre of his being.

Koenigshaus is mine.

He promised it to me all my life. He always said I would have it, he promised me. How can he take it off me now?

Suddenly the front door of the guest house opposite opened silently and a slender figure in white slipped gently out, descended the little flight of steps from the verandah, and began to cross the wide circle of grass towards him. Geena! He was robbed of his tongue. Even at this distance, she seemed to catch his shyness, for although she set out from the house confidently enough, by the time that she drew near, she seemed to be tongue-tied too. After a quick glance of greeting, she dropped her eyes to her golden brown hands and began to twist and plait her long fingers as she spoke. 'I saw you,' she volunteered awkwardly. 'From my window. I wasn't asleep. I always wake up early.'

'Yes.'

An agonising silence fell. 'Sit down,' he said desperately. 'Why don't you sit down?'

Ensconced side by side on the old stone steps leading up to the mansion's front door, they did not have to look at one another and immediately the tension eased.

'I just wanted to say,' Geena began tentatively, resisting the urge to search him out with a sideways glance which she knew would show off her large liquid eyes to their full effect, 'that I could see you had a bad surprise last night. It seems a bit sudden, this sale of Koenigshaus that my dad's been working on, and I don't really understand it.'

The comfort she offered made him realise how sad and alone, how abandoned he had been feeling, and he grasped at her sympathy like a starving man snatching crumbs. 'Neither do I!' he blurted out. 'We've got the best cattle station in the Northern Territory here, probably in the whole of Australia, I've heard Dad say that a thousand times. We've got over three thousand square miles, thousands of head of the best cattle money can buy, we've spent a fortune making them sound and healthy and free of every disease you can name, and just when Dad could think about winding down and sitting back to enjoy it, he's planning to sell up!'

'Is he, though?'

'What do you mean?'

Bewildered, Jon turned to look into the thoughtful brown eyes. Geena shook her head. 'I don't know. And I don't know your Dad. OK, I've known him all my life.

But he's always been a remote figure to me.' And a terrifying one she thought privately. Sooner you than me taking him on now, Jon!

Jon seemed to pick up on her thoughts. 'But you've seen something? Noticed something?'

Geena nodded. 'For all the talk last night, he hasn't signed anything, has he? They're talking about this Japanese company your uncle Charles has lined up to buy the property, but they don't seem to have gone very far down the road with them. There's no contract. And as long as there's no contract, there's no sale.'

'But why would he do it? Dad, I mean? – talk about selling up like this if he's got no intention of going through with it?'

Geena studied him carefully, trying to work out how much she should say. 'To wind you up, maybe? Keep you on your toes, keep you guessing? My dad says he always promised you Koenigshaus – that you'd inherit it, that it would be yours.'

'Yeah,' he said. He knew he sounded bitter. 'He always did.'

'Well, you're the son and heir!' She smiled at him. 'There's your mum too, of course, but I shouldn't think she'd want to run it.'

Jon shook his head. 'No, that's got to be true. And Charles – my uncle – he's no rancher, he's only interested in business, he wouldn't want it anyway.'

'And there's no one else, is there?'

Jon paused and took a deep breath. At school, the Aboriginal boys used to say that when you told a lie, the Great Snake in the sky stretched out his neck and tail, unfolded his terrible huge body, and prepared one of his great coils for you, to snatch you away to the place where liars went.

But it was only a lie if you knew for sure that it could not be true. He did not have to think at all before he

29

made his answer. 'No,' he said firmly. 'There's no one else – no one who wants Koenigshaus the way I do.'

Geena shivered. 'Well then,' she said as simply as a child. 'It's yours, then. And you'll have to fight for it – you'll have to keep it.'

A sense of powerless rage took hold of him. 'But they say the business is doing badly – that something'll have to be sold.'

'Maybe.' Her husky little voice was suddenly very clear. 'But it doesn't have to be Koenigshaus! Maybe some of the interests in Sydney could be sold off, so Koenigshaus can be just as it always was, before your father got into any of that stuff in the city.'

Oh God, if only, Jon thought. A wave of gratitude swept over him that she'd offered him this ray of hope, that she'd made it possible for him even to talk, come forward to be with him in his loneliness and pain. Almost imperceptibly he moved closer to her soft gentleness and with infinite care allowed his shoulder to move towards hers until the lightest possible contact had been established between them.

They sat in the opal morning light as the first of the kookaburras laughed and chattered overhead, neither daring to move, in a light trance of fragile intimacy and tender, nervous contentment. And from the master bedroom above, a pair of hard grey hawklike eyes looked down upon the young couple and unhesitatingly resolved that whatever they thought lay ahead for them, it was not going to be allowed to happen.

Chapter 5

Predictably enough, breakfast that morning was a grim affair. One by one the family assembled at the massive oak dining table under the stony gaze of other long-dead Koenigs, and tried in vain to pretend that this was just another day.

With the taste of Phillip still in her mouth, Helen knew she could not even keep down a piece of dry toast. *I can't go on like this*, she thought. Opposite her Charles was pulling a bread roll to pieces while Ben chewed mechanically through a plate of bacon and scrambled eggs, avoiding every eye. Jon and Geena sat together, apparently not hungry, but not speaking either. It's like a wake! Helen thought. Or perhaps now we've heard the death sentence announced, we're all just waiting for Koenigshaus to die. Already, even at this time of the morning, the sun was beating against the glass. Suddenly it seemed too hot even to breathe.

Only Phillip, seated as always in his great carved throne-like chair at the head of the table, was on his usual ebullient form. Despite his excesses at dinner last night, he was now consuming vast quantities of bacon and eggs, fried bread and toast, washing it all down with cup after cup of coffee brewed just as he liked it, black, hot and almost unbearably strong.

'Good coffee, Rose!' he informed the old housekeeper as she moved among the guests with the pouting Ellie in tow. 'Share it round, good and hot, they all look as if you need to put something strong and dark into their bellies this morning. 'Give 'em all another cup of coffee, Ellie!'

'Sure thing, Mr Phillip!'

With a glint in her cat-like brown eyes and an over-ready smile, Ellie hastened to obey. Rose would have died for Phillip, but her loyalty did not extend to joining in with his games of power. Nor did she intend that the useless Ellie should be allowed to get above herself like this. 'Coffee for the master is all, Ellie,' she instructed loftily. 'That's enough!' Then she turned on her employer. 'You leave 'em be, Mr Phillip,' she snapped, 'and think on yourself. What else are you having for breakfast today?'

Sulking furiously, the hot-eyed Aboriginal girl fell back, still trying to get Phillip's attention. But he was impervious. 'Whatever it takes to go mustering!' he laughed. 'Last muster today! We've got two thousand of 'em within a day of the homestead now, there'll only be one more night outside. We'll get 'em as far as the water-hole at Devil Rock tonight, then tomorrow we'll have 'em on the road train and away. And another successful season for Koenig Cattle! For Koenig Holdings too as a result, wouldn't you say? Eh?'

He fixed Ben with a quizzical glare. Ben's broad, flat face suffused with embarrassment. 'Phil, you know it's not as simple as that—' he began placatingly. 'In the framework of the business overall, it's a question—'

'Questions, questions!' interrupted Phillip roughly. 'I pay you for answers, mate, not questions!'

Charles took a breath and leaned across the table to intervene. 'Listen, you can shout all you like, but it won't change anything! There's no way we can continue to run the station here and everything else as well.' He threw a glance at Jon. 'I admit that the cattle and this place don't mean to me what they've meant to you guys.' His eyes narrowed. 'But don't you think I hate the idea of having to sell anything, having to split up any part of the business?'

Phillip smiled dangerously. 'Hate? You don't know how to hate! You don't even seem to know you're a Koenig any more, little bro – if you ever knew what Koenigs are really about. Why don't you change your name to "King" like Dad always wanted us to do, then you needn't even pretend you're one of us any more!' He paused, to give the words that followed a sarcastic emphasis. 'Koenigs buy land – we don't sell it! We live on our land, we draw our strength from it, our way of life, our reason for living. *We never let it go!*'

What's he doing now? thought Helen in rising panic. Last night he was telling Jon that Koenigshaus had to go!

Charles was staring at Phillip with open disbelief. Clumsily setting down his knife and fork, Ben rushed blindly into the breach. 'Phil, there are good financial reasons, I promise you—'

Phillip laughed in his face. 'Your promise! You're just out of your depth, running scared with your shit down your legs! You'd say anything! Give me one good reason why I should take your word, mate!'

Christ in heaven, what had come over Dad? Some men'd kill you if you treated them like this, Jon thought wildly. He leaned urgently into the debate. 'Dad – you will sell, you won't sell, or what? You can't! Look, we've got to hang on—'

Charles threw him a look of fury. 'Let's keep this between the grown-ups, shall we? Face it, Phillip, your precious Koenigshaus is nothing but your pet indulgence! It's become a luxury, and one we just can't afford! Tell him, Ben!'

Caught in a searchlight of attention, Ben struggled to speak. 'Till '87 we could afford it,' he said desperately. 'But since the crash, we've just been digging ourselves deeper and deeper into the recession. Now it's over. We're about to go bust – we're on the point of bankruptcy. We've got maybe three months left on cash reserves. It's sell now – or go under.'

Phillip had turned to stone. Jon recoiled from them all in horror. 'Why didn't anyone tell me things were so bad?' he gasped. 'I have a right to know!'

Charles's eyes were lethal. He flicked a contemptuous thumb at Phillip. 'Ask him. He's known for years the way things were going. He was supposed to keep you in the picture. As the son and heir.'

'The son and heir . . .'

Charles ignored Phillip's ominous murmuring rumble and confronted his brother head on. 'My end of the operation, Koenig Holdings,' he said, emphasising every word, 'is keeping this cow of a cattle station afloat just so that you can go on posing as an outback hero, the Clint Eastwood of the Northern Territory! Well, it's over!'

Helen saw a moment of blind fury in Phillip's eyes.

'Don't think I don't see through your little game, Chas,' he said pleasantly enough. But his colour had risen with sudden violence, and his face had taken on a waxy, unnatural sheen. 'I know what you're all up to! You want to sell my land and pension me off!' He laughed, a harsh, mocking cry. 'Put me in some bin, eh, along with a lot of other geriatric old fools, and then you can really all get your fists in the cookie jar up to your elbows!'

Jon felt a jolt of fear. What's he talking about? He's losing it, he thought, the old man's losing it! 'Dad,' he began urgently, 'that's not—'

But Phillip was beyond restraint. Sweating and pounding the table, he bore no resemblance to the self-satisfied and jovial host who had sat down to breakfast not half an hour before. 'Get this!' he hissed, 'get this, all of you. I won't sell this land! I had it from my father and he had it from his, all the way back to old Johann who rode out here all the way from Germany with his gun and his axe

34

and a bag of flour and a waggon load of children, and every one of them a mouth that had to be fed! *Just like all of you!'*

Not a breath stirred in the room. Phillip ranted on. 'Children – that's what you are—!'

Suddenly he faltered, and lost his thread. Again Helen felt the cold breath of panic. *This isn't Phillip, this isn't the man I know. I haven't loved him for a long time. Will he make me love him now?*

But he shook his head and stumbled on. 'No, not children. Figures! You tell me figures? The figures have been bad before, and they'll be bad again. They were terrible in the 1930s! Before that too, in the 1890s, when the whole of Koenigshaus nearly went under before it was more than a few seasons old. All figures go bad sometimes. Then they come good again!' His eyes roamed wildly round the silent table. 'I defy any of you to look me in the eye and tell me that isn't true! Because I'll look you in the eye and call you a liar!'

There was an almost unbearable pause.

Then Charles shook his dark head and rose stiffly to his feet. 'It's your decision, Phillip,' he rasped. 'It's your land. But it's my business you're going to ruin to keep this place afloat for a few months longer, and it's my credit and my business life that will be finished while you'll still have this place to live on even if all your precious cattle have gone.'

In spite of himself, his low voice was gaining power now, rising with passion as he faced the glaring Phillip, both breathing heavily like men in a fight. 'But you don't care, do you? You've never given a damn for anyone else. Just as long as you get your own way, you don't care if you trample on any man alive.' He threw a deep, impenetrable glance at Helen and she started at its force. 'Or woman. Human beings are nothing to you. Their whole lives can change and you don't even notice.'

Oh Charles, Helen thought wonderingly, *you've noticed – you understand?*

Phillip gave a mirthless laugh. 'I don't have to listen to this!'

'Indeed you don't.' Charles was beyond fury now, somewhere in a deadly region of his own. He pushed back his chair and rose to his feet. 'I'm leaving. I'm getting the chopper back to Sydney this morning. I don't think I'll be back. You'll find my resignation on my desk in the office. *And it will still say that we should sell!*'

Every eye followed Charles's progress to the door. Only Phillip was brash enough to break the silence that followed. He glared mockingly at Jon. 'And what says the son and heir – did I do OK? Or do you think this pair are right – should we sell?'

Jon leaned forward and took a pinch of salt from the salt-cellar before him, gripping it between his finger and thumb. He knew he was trembling, but he had never felt more confident in his life. The sense that Geena beside him was concentrating on him with all her force only lent strength to his words.

'If I owned this place,' he said with deliberate emphasis. 'I wouldn't sell as much as one grain of it! I wouldn't sell—' he clicked his fingers and the salt scattered through the air in a million sparkling grains – 'that much of it, if they offered me a million dollars an acre!' He paused and looked Phillip stonily in the eye. 'That's what the son and heir says. *If I am the son and heir!*'

He never would have dared to do it before last night, Helen reflected. But the sudden threat to Koenigshaus had catapulted him from unselfconscious childhood to that cold lonely place where you know you can't trust anyone, not even your own father. Now at last perhaps Phillip would learn that when you start playing games with people, some will play back, and pay you back too.

'My son and heir?' Phillip's voice sounded strained and

unnatural. 'What are you talking about? Of course you are. Put it in my will, haven't I?' He laughed again. 'The latest one, anyway!'

'The latest one?' Grim-faced, Jon was not to be fobbed off. 'How many of the bloody things are there?'

Phillip laughed again. 'Only one that concerns you, boy! Leaves you Koenigshaus and everything in it.' He looked at Helen for the first time. 'If I die, this place is going to need a man to run it. A man, not a woman. And I don't mean Charles.'

He had them all in the palm of his hand, and he knew it. 'I'm talking about leadership,' he said softly. 'A man's leadership, not rule by committee of mom and uncle.' His look was almost brutal now. 'Young leadership – not a couple of people who've had their chance.'

And made nothing of their lives, that's what he means, Helen knew. *That's what he thinks of me and Charles, he despises us, he probably always has*. She forced herself to pay attention again.

'—someone who hasn't been corrupted by city life and all that crap brother Charles believes about his bloody "business". Someone who can see past the next fast buck and "investment opportunity" to what really matters.' He was staring at her again. 'You and Charles, Hen – you'll get what's fair, incomes for life. Jon gets the land and all the capital.'

Ben's eyes flared with alarm in his troubled face. 'Phillip, that's not what Charles has a right to expect! And a wife has rights too, under the law, Helen has rights! A will like that could be challenged!'

Was it affection or contempt in Phillip's eyes as he grinned in her face?

'Nah,' he scoffed. 'This wife won't argue, will you, Hen? Jonno won't have any trouble. And I will have my way!'

Again the great fist beat the table and sent the china

clattering. Now the hectic flush had risen to Phillip's cheeks once more under his outback tan. 'I know what's best for Koenigshaus, alive or dead! You'll all see! You're all going to see! Alive or dead, *I know*!'

Chapter 6

'He made us a promise, Helen. And now he's going back on it.'

Heavily the four-wheel-drive bumped over the rough surface of the bush track, the sandy, stony going as heavy as her heart. All around them the air was already liquid with the heat, the ghost gums on the horizon shimmering like dancers as they dissolved and re-formed under her gaze. Beside her in the jeep Charles spoke with his usual calm control but with something new in his voice, a danger that she had never heard before.

'And you've always forgiven him,' the level tones continued. 'Are you going to this time?'

Helen took one sticky hand off the blistering driving wheel to push the thick straight hair out of her eyes. 'Oh Charles . . .'

She concentrated on the road ahead in the attempt to hide from him some of what she was going through. Her voice trailed away. 'He promised us an income . . .'

'Helen, there won't be any income!' Charles burst out in exasperation. 'And even if there was, that's an insult to both of us! After Alex—'

She drew in a sharp breath. He bit his lip and started again. 'Before Jon was born, it was going to be a two-way split between you and me. Even afterwards, Jon was going to get Koenigshaus, and you and I would share the rest. Now Phillip's going to destroy the business by hanging onto Koenigshaus and refusing to do anything about the cash-flow problem. And anything that's left after that goes to Jon too!'

She knew she was sounding stupid, but she had to say it. 'If he's right about this muster, it might all come round again. And what he's leaving us in his will, it'll be a good income, he says.'

'Income!' Charles almost spat the word. 'Income! That's not capital! Not land, or property. It's a word, that's all. Written on water, like all Phillip's promises!'

Helen took a breath. 'I know what he thinks. He thinks if he left me a share of Koenigshaus or the business, I'd be incapable of running it sensibly. He doesn't believe that women have minds of their own. He thinks I'd do just whatever you or Jon told me to.'

For a moment his face softened, and a tired smile crinkled the lines around his eyes. The back of his knuckles brushed the side of her thigh with a fleeting downward touch. He did not look at her. 'Do whatever I told you?' he said quietly, almost under his breath. 'You stopped doing that a long time ago.'

They were both silent. Then the old anger seized Charles again and he was away. 'God, when I think of it! He was just playing with us all!'

Out of the corner of her eye she could see the tall figure beside her now rigid with fury. 'It's his way of keeping us all off balance, out of control. You, me, even poor old Ben, above all Jonno. Think, Helen! Even if you can put up with it for yourself, can you stand it for your son?'

That was the only question that counted. 'Charles, I don't think Phillip means to'

'He does it deliberately!'

Stiffly he turned and stared unseeing at the parched flat landscape all around, the outback dirt-track ahead running straight and true to the landing strip where the helicopter waited. 'He let us all think last night at dinner that he'd agreed to the sale. He must have given Jon one of the worst nights of his life.' He paused. 'Let alone you . . . what he's doing to you . . .'

He knows, she thought dully, *he knows everything that Phillip does to me now. Even the worst things?* she shuddered. *Yes, even those. He's a man, and all men know those things. They may not do them, but they know them. God, he must despise me . . .*

Her face was burning and she could feel the start of rising tears. But the voice at her side was huskier now, not harsher. 'You chose the wrong man, Helen. If he ruins the business too, he's taken from me everything I ever cared about. Before, I couldn't stop him. But I can now!'

He struck the side of the car door with his fist, startling her with the sudden hollow boom. She had a violent impulse to stop the car and take his hand, stroke his arm, his face—

'We're both in this together, Helen, you realise that?'

She spun the wheel as the jeep bounced wildly out of a deep rut and juddered like a wild thing. 'I think we always were.'

He nodded savagely. 'Because we've never stood up to him! Never successfully, anyway.'

'I've tried – but I've never got anywhere.'

God, did she have any idea how it went through him when she said that? Charles thought dimly. Or how beautiful she still was, even with that frail frayed look she wore every day now? He resisted the urge to touch her again, but his voice thickened in spite of himself. 'You've always been more worried about keeping everyone else happy – 'especially him! their minds cried in unison – 'than in being happy yourself.'

She felt a spurt of vicious cynicism. 'Isn't that what a wife's supposed to do?'

'As long as she loves her husband, maybe. But you've

done it out of guilt. You've always felt guilty, ever since Alex—'

'Charles, please.' Her voice was stronger than she expected. 'Don't let's do this. I'm not asking you to excuse me – or anything. I was guilty then. I still am!'

He shook his head. 'That's rubbish, Helen, and you know it. And even if you were, how long are you going to go on paying for it?'

As long as it takes.

The unspoken answer lay accepted between them. She veered away onto another tack. 'Charles, d'you think Phillip's changing at all? Or is it only me?'

She could see she had startled him. 'Changing? What d'you mean?'

'Oh, the sudden switches of mood that seem to seize him nowadays – suddenly angry, in a vile temper, suddenly all smiles again – these games he's been playing – the delight he takes in keeping us all on the wrong foot— and then laughing at us'.

A thin smile distorted Charles's well-shaped mouth. 'He's always been like that! And the bastard can only get worse!'

A silence of cold recognition descended. Helen's heart sank under the weight of it.

'Unless . . .'

She had never heard that note in Charles's voice before. 'Unless . . . ?'

But she could read his thought. *Unless we do something.* And in spite of herself, she thought *Yes.*

The airstrip was just ahead now, the helicopter with the pilot already in position waiting in its white circle in the centre of the bare, dusty strip of land. From left to right in a straight line half a mile long marched the double row of powerful electric lights that equipped Koenigshaus for night landings. Behind it stood the station's executive jet kept for longer flights, parked in the shadow of the hangar and radio control tower which formed the station's life-line with the outside world. She could hear the pre-flight call-sign crackling through the hot, dust-laden air: Papa Kilo Lima calling Koenigshaus Station, Kilo Hotel Sierra . . .

Slowly she drew the jeep to a standstill, killed the engine and dragged on the brake.

'Unless we do something,' Charles said aloud, very calmly.

She did not want to ask *what*?

But she did not have to. He seemed to be thinking aloud, oblivious of her presence. 'Sooner or later we're going to have to take the law into our own hands. Phillip's not immortal, even though he thinks he is. He's nearly twenty years older than both of us, it's another generation now. You know that, Helen.'

Suddenly he reached across and gripped her by the shoulders, forcing her to look into his face. 'I've spent my life in brother Phillip's shadow. I've never had anything I haven't had to fight him to get. Most of what I got, he managed to take away from me, just as he took you.'

His eyes were very black, and small gold flakes of fury danced around the darkened pupils. She felt her own tears, never far away, pricking the back of her eyelids.

But he was not seeing her now. He stared out into the melting haze as his voice went softly on. 'And now he's going to destroy everything I've done, everything I've ever worked for, just on a selfish whim of his own. And I'm supposed to stand by and let him do it? Oh no, big brother! Don't think I'm ready to put up with your idea of brotherly love for another second!'

Let them all go!

Watching the dust-cloud of the jeep on the far horizon from his vantage-point at the French windows of the dining room, Phillip was indifferent as always to any needs or desires outside his own. Hen could drive Charles to the airstrip, the mood she was in lately that was all she was good for! He shrugged his heavy shoulders and stalked away to follow Jon to the stable yard.

Left alone in the dining room amid the remains of the breakfast, Ben and Geena stared at one another like the survivors of an earthquake.

'Is he always like that?' Geena asked in a low voice.

Ben shook his head in total bewilderment as he stood up, and his misery went straight to her heart. 'I don't know what's got into him! Oh, he's always been an old bastard, and he always had to have his own way, regardless of anyone else. But he hasn't had such a great life, you know – the way his first wife went – and then afterwards–'

Even now Ben felt bad, he couldn't pretend to find it easy talking about all that – still less about Alex . . .

Ben broke into a light sweat. The complications if Alex was still around – God Almighty, it didn't bear thinking about! Hastily, he drove all the dangerous old memories back to their lair.

She was asking about Phillip.

And he was the one that counted!

'Yeah, he always was a hard man, and a mad old bastard. But there was always method in his madness till now!' He pushed back his chair. 'Come on, let's get out of here.'

Together they walked through the cool arched hallway down to the open front door and out onto the shady verandah. Outside the sun was making harsh patterns of shadow under the great trees around the house, and the raucous red and white rosellas overhead were in full, clattering flight.

Ben grasped the rail and looked out. 'Beautiful, isn't it?' he said simply.

Geena looked at the familiar face with its broad fea-

44

tures, deep-set eyes and heavy, impassive stare. However little he showed his feelings, he had been born round here, Geena knew. She felt a tug in her heart. 'Dad – has it got to go?'

He sighed. 'Koenigshaus will be sold, Geena. If not by us, by the receivers.'

'Is it really that bad?'

He nodded. 'The station has been a drain on the business for years. We got over-leveraged in the '80s trying to keep up. We've been literally fighting off the creditors since '87. Phillip's known all about it. In his saner moments he understands the whole thing. But his heart just won't let him sell.'

The next question was inevitable. 'What'll Jon do?'

Ben scratched his thick grizzled head. 'When the crash comes, you mean? Take what's left and run, if he's got any sense. He'll probably try to find a place of his own, no matter how small. Running cattle is the only thing he can do.'

In the distance a group of the station Aboriginals were getting ready for the last day of the muster, their calm unhurried ways contrasting strongly with the vigorous activity of the station manager, a young Australian around Jon's age. If worst came to worst, Henry would go with Jon and work for him, Geena decided. He'd been at school with Jon too, as they all had. He'd throw in his lot with the Koenigs wherever they went.

Jon . . .

Don't even think about him, she told herself. High and mighty Koenigs didn't bother with Abo girls, except for one thing. *Put him out of your mind, or it'll only end in tears – your tears. Think of something else.* 'And the people? Mum's people? What'll happen to them?'

Ben was startled, even shocked, and his face showed it. 'Well – whoever buys the place will need stockmen, station workers, help around the homestead. They'll be

OK.' He paused, and looked away. 'Look, I didn't think you thought about Mum any more. She's gone, and you've got your life to lead. You're a city girl now, have been for years. And when you finish that course of yours, the world'll be your oyster. You'll be able to teach dancing anywhere in the world.'

Where they won't hold it against you because you're a Koori, Geena knew he meant. Where they'll think your name is just a modern way of spelling Gina, not short for Nungeena, the Woman Spirit of All Things. The name you had from your mother who was full Aboriginal. Who pined and died as soon as she was uprooted from the land and transplanted to the city. You don't have to suffer like that. There are places where people will find you beautiful, exotic, special – where no one has ever heard men say they should have kept all them blacks on the other side of the rabbit-proof fence, those squaws'd cock it up for any man, and old Ben, why, he dipped his wick in the tar bottle long ago and then he was stuck with it, caught by the short and curlies . . .

Ben loved her, she knew. But he had been powerless to shield her from any of that, and he couldn't live her life for her now. 'I'm going down to the camp, Dad,' she said levelly. 'Just to say hello, see if there's anyone there who remembers Mum.'

'Yes, well—' Ben was unsure, she could see that. But he had always bent before the prevailing wind. 'Well, I've got to go through the books here before we can leave. Maybe it'll give you something to keep you busy while I'm working.'

'I was hoping I'd be able to take care of that!'

They had not heard Jon approaching round the side of the house. Clad in a blue shirt the same faded denim as his eyes, worn chaps and cowboy boots, he was clearly ready for the last day of the muster, the final push to bring the cattle home. 'I thought you might like to join the muster today, Geena, while Ben's busy,' he said, his eyes bright. 'I'll have to spend the night at the water-hole with Dad and the rest of the mob, but one of the men could see you safely back. And it's not too far to ride on a day like this.'

'Join the muster?' She could feel the colour in her cheeks. 'What a great idea!'

'Join the muster? No way!'

They had all seen Phillip emerge from the stables on his great white horse and set off towards them at a rapid trot. But they were as ever unprepared for the force of his interruption as he reined up and leaned aggressively out of the saddle. 'Geena doesn't want to do that! You can't drag a young lady out into the bush among a pack of roughnecks like Dusty and the lads!' he roared.

He doesn't want me anywhere near his son, Geena realised in one bleak instant.

Jon looked troubled. 'Oh, Geena, I'm sorry, I just thought it might be fun . . .'

'It would be,' she said firmly. 'And I'd love to come. I'm not worried about rough-necks, I've known Dusty and the rest of them all my life!'

Jon's eyes lit up. 'That's OK then! I'll just look out a ride for you—'

'Don't be in such a rush, Jonno.'

Phillip's voice was like granite, and the expression in his even harder. 'Sorry, Geena, not today. We've got a lot to do to get the mob up to the water-hole, we'll only just make it by nightfall. And it disturbs the cattle having a woman around – let alone the men!'

Jon turned to his father in disbelief. 'Dad, what are you talking about—?'

'Sorry, Jonno. That's it, mate, final.' He rounded on Geena with a glittering smile. 'But I'm sure you can entertain yourself round here, young Geena. Why don't you try the Blacks' Camp?' *Where you belong!* hovered unspoken in the air. 'Show 'em some of that dancing you've been learning in the city.'

Geena put all the feeling she was capable of into her reply. 'They don't need me to teach them how to dance. They've been dancing for millions of years.'

'Yeah, well, you can learn from them then. Basic moves.'

Her face tightened. 'Mr Koenig, I've been studying dance since I was eight years old.'

Phillip laughed. 'Yeah, I remember. I went to one of your concerts once. In the school. Or was it the Blacks' Camp?'

Christ, what was he *doing*, going on about 'the Blacks'? Jon winced at the offence in Phillip's words. What was wrong with him? Not daring to look at Geena, Jon was fighting down the urge to intervene. She wouldn't thank him for fighting her battles!

Beside him Ben let out a harsh breath he had clearly been trying to restrain. On the verandah rail before him the older man's fists were bunched like a boxer's, veins and tendons standing out and throbbing for violent action. This is his daughter you're talking about, Dad, Jon tried to signal, his *wife*, for god's sake, *lay off*!

Geena could feel herself losing control. 'Well, now I'm with the Dance Theatre of Sydney, and we have black dancers there.'

'When you say black . . .'

He was playing with her she knew, but she couldn't help herself. 'Koori. Aboriginal. Some from the Islands, all colours. And some like me, *choc-ices*!'

Phillip gave a roar of genuine delight, unsettling the horse, who danced nervously away from the sound. '*Choc-ices*?'

Geena knew she was trembling. 'Yeah. Dark outside, white inside. Born black, brought up white.'

Phillip snickered. 'Best of both worlds for a dancer, eh?'

Ignore him, she told herself. She turned to Jon. 'So now I guess I'll spend the day getting to know my mother's people – and maybe learn their dances, maybe teach them some of mine, who knows?'

Phillip carelessly pulled round the head of his sweating horse. 'Then straight back to Sydney, eh? Smart thing like you, you don't want to bury yourself out here.'

She knew that Jon was listening keenly for her answer. 'You do. Jon does.'

Phillip waved a massive hand. 'We're men. Cattle men. A cattleman's got to be with cattle. You're a dancer, and there's a big world out there. You could work in London, Paris, New York. Lot of black dancers in New York, from what I hear.'

She took a deep breath. 'Sure.'

Phillip stilled the restless horse and looked down hard into her eyes. 'If money was a problem, we'd be happy to help out, wouldn't we, Ben? How about a scholarship to study somewhere, anywhere you like—'

As long as it was far enough away from here. Away from your son. In case he gets too interested in a girl from the Blacks' Camp . . . ?

He's vile, she thought, and the words simply followed that thought. She did not look at Jon as she stared his father in the eye. 'Mr Koenig. Are you saying that you'll pay me to go away?'

Phillip opened his arms extravagantly, the reins hanging loosely from one hand. 'Geena! With an imagination like that, you should be a writer, not a dancer! It's horses for courses. Cattle men for cattle stations, dancers for theatres. How many theatres d'you see round here? Think about it. And think about Paris, New York. Good fun, so they say, New York!'

And with a cry he was gone. Hunched, shrunken and brooding, Ben stared after him into the bush.

Jon put a hand on Geena's arm, and felt her tension. 'Don't take all that too seriously, Geena,' he said with an unconvincing attempt at lightness. 'Dad's a born leader, he likes to try to help. He thinks he should control things.'

'Well, he's not going to control me!'

Leaving the two men standing, Geena walked rapidly away in a frantic effort to gain the shelter of her room before she burst into tears of shame and rage. *If someone doesn't murder that man before long*, she sobbed to herself, *there's no justice in this world!*

Chapter 7

Not good.

It was not good.

Seated at the kitchen table, the remains of the breakfast cleared away, the kitchen cleaned till it shone and the useless, poisonous Ellie packed off back home for the day, Rose shifted her thin frame uneasily in her chair, took a long pull on the bottle in her hand, and tried again.

Out there with the rest of their people, those who answered to 'Dusty', 'Slim' and 'Frank' though they were not their real names, all those who worked on Koenigshaus as stockmen or hired help and went home to the bush camp at night, they had better ways of speaking to the spirits and asking what they wanted to know. They didn't need the stuff that came in bottles to see their way ahead, or to get them through the night. But she had to make do by herself, with what she had.

And she had for decades now turned to her ancient Tarot when she felt the spirits walking – when she felt bad things brewing for the land and those that she called hers. Like now. But not like this before. Many bad things over the last fifty years with Mr Phillip and Koenigshaus, she thought, but never bad like this. Diligently she shuffled the worn cards in small black hands twisted like tree roots, and tried again.

Again she cut and shuffled, dealt again, cut and came again.

And again they came, the bad cards of her battered pack, all the faces she dreaded to see appear, one by one. She started unblinkingly at the unholy trinity of impending doom: the Falling Tower, the Hanged Man, and the old Skeleton with the Scythe, Death himself.

Side by side but a million miles apart, father and son rode towards the distant muster lying a few miles further off in the path of the rising sun. Already the stockmen had the mob on the move under the direction of Dusty, the Aboriginal foreman, and they would catch up with the drive soon. For the last few miles Jon had been wrestling with an emotion he had never felt before: blind anger with his father.

Phillip was the first to break the silence. 'Don't you be sulky with me about last night, when I was playing on about selling the place, Jonno,' he said warningly. 'I never meant to sell, I was only feeling 'em out. Just like to keep them on their toes, that's all.'

He hasn't got a clue, thought Jon bleakly, he really hasn't got a clue. Out loud he said, 'Maybe. But that's not the way to do it.'

Phillip's temper flared at once. 'So you think you could do better, eh?'

Jon stared ahead. 'Since you ask, yeah. I'd try to deal with the cash-flow problem instead of just ignoring it, for a start. And I wouldn't go round pissing off men like Charles and Ben, who are going to save things for us if anybody can.'

He knew without looking at Phillip that the older man's eyes were bulging, his face suffusing with rage. But the retort was dangerously quiet. 'Anything else?'

'Yeah.' Jon's stomach was in knots, but he had gone too far to turn back. 'You're wasting your time trying to frighten Geena off me. She's got too much about her for that.'

Phillip let out a bellow of fury. 'She can be as smart as she likes, blast her! But she's a Koori, for Christ's sake!'

'So?'

'So if y'like 'em, mate, you fuck 'em, you don't marry 'em! I'm telling you, you'll never marry that while I've got breath in my body!'

The horses had picked up their riders' tension and Jon's mount whickered quietly in distress. 'Easy, boy, easy.'

Leaning forward, he patted the satin-soft brown neck while he tried to work out what to say. He glanced at his father and in the tension of the moment found himself almost laughing at the glaring eyes, the flushed red face, the very caricature of heavy Victorian fatherhood.

It made it easier to say what came next. 'It's a bit premature to talk about marriage, Dad, I don't even know what Geena thinks about me, for a start. But I'll tell you one thing. When I find the right girl, I'll court her for keeps, not just in the hopes of a quick jump!'

He drew a quick breath, and went rushing on. 'And about Geena – there's something you ought to know. Maybe Mum never told you. But when I was a kid and had my eyes tested at the school clinic – turned out I was colour-blind. And I still am!'

And standing up in his stirrups, he put his horse into a rapid gallop towards the slow-moving mob of the great muster ahead.

Stark on the horizon an ancient baobob tree, old when the world was young, black and grizzled against the westering sun, stood as a landmark for the weary mob of cattle and riders as the muster drew near. Monster more than tree, an ancient, twisted thing with the hide of a rhino and the girth of a giant, it darkened the landscape with its huge branching arms and twiggy, grasping fingers and lent an air of undefined menace to the livid evening.

But things are only bad if you make them bad, thought

53

Dusty, as he turned his horse and patiently guided another wayward straggler back into the herd. Boss could do with a drink of the baobob flower juice the way the women made it, sweet and healing, soothe his bad spirits, calm him down. Bad mood all day and badder still now. His serene brown eyes took in the brooding Phillip riding furiously away to his right, tearing the head of his great white horse around and spurring mercilessly to and fro as if he had a lump of meat between his legs and not a living thing. Dusty shook his head. Any minute now that stallion gonna show him he won't take any more, and do us all a good turn!

Over the brow of the hill rising ahead lay the watering-hole, a place of strange unnatural beauty in the middle of the dry whispering bush. From the harsh desert plateau of broken boulders, dried-up creeks, forbidding outcrops of rock and wind-whipped bottle-trees all leaning at strained angles, the land dropped swiftly down to a gentle hollow lying at the base of a towering wall of sandstone. Across its primeval face, Aboriginal artists now sleeping the sleep of millennia had painted the most sacred secrets of their tribe. Time and the elements had joined in the art-work, carving and whittling the layers of soft red stone into strange undulations and curious sculptures of erosion and decay, caves and hiding-holes, yet still the rock endured like the secret face of God, undisturbed by time.

At the base of the rock wall, the water-hole lay like a sheet of platinum mirroring the torn and cloud-wracked sky. Around the edge clustered a frieze of water lilies in thick, waxen white and indigo so deep that it looked black, while at a distance grew dense clumps of great soaring ghost gums glimmering silver-grey in the fast-fading light. Sacred to the people of the land for almost fifty thousand years, it was a place so ancient and so special that it never failed to bring a shiver to Jon's spine. Here in the very shade of the Great Spirit, the All-Father of All Things, it was impossible to escape a sense of the littleness of man.

Jon took a deep breath, and at once felt better. *Let's hope it works on the old man as well,* he thought grimly as he dismounted from his horse and turned the animal loose to graze, *we're going to need something like divine intervention to make him fit to live with tonight!*

But all through the thousand and one tasks of settling the muster down for the night, Phillip held aloof, taking out his temper on every man in turn and making no response to Jon's overtures except to administer a violent rebuff. Only when the cattle had been settled, the camp-fire lit, the evening meal finished and Phillip had stalked off to find a spot on his own to bed down for the night did the atmosphere lighten, and the men settle down to the kind of easy communion which passes between those who know each other so well they can almost dispense with speech.

Around the fire Jon surveyed the lean, hard features of the men he had known since childhood: Dusty, Slim, Frank and James, men without whom a muster simply could not take place. At his side sat Henry, the station manager, another school friend and contemporary for whom Koenigs were also a total way of life. But even Henry was thinking twice about how to broach the obvious topic of the evening when Dusty launched straight into it in his quiet, lilting drawl: 'So we lost the boss again tonight?'

Jon laughed, a little uneasily. "Fraid we lost him – or rather I did – a while back, before tonight, Dusty. Nothing to do with us snoring and scratching this time. He's gone off in a hump because he and I had – hell, a bad difference of opinion earlier. A real exchange of words, as you might say. And he's still chewing on it.'

There was a general silence of approval. If Jon had a fault as far as these friends of his boyhood were concerned, it was that he was always too easy-going and ready to give in to his father. But times were obviously changing.

Slim, a slight, mischievous figure with wild eyes and hair and a sense of humour to match, grinned impishly. 'He's not scared of the Bunyip, then?'

There was a burst of laughter at the mention of Australia's answer to the Loch Ness Monster. Jon grinned back. 'I reckon it'd take more than any Bunyip, even the Great Snake of the Water-hole himself, to finish off my dad!'

Only Dusty did not join in the merriment. Instead he looked across the campfire, across the still waters of the pool with eyes as old as time to the shadowy mass of the cattle softly milling and lowing in the deep black night. Stray whimpers and snuffles of distress that others did not hear never escaped his ears. James nodded in his direction. 'Dusty seen something though.'

Jon looked up, startled. 'Seen – what?'

Dusty gave a slow smile. 'Not the Bunyip,' he said quietly.

Dusty had taught Jon to ride, how to read the secrets of the sky and the bush, how to size up a bad stockman, a sick steer or a cow in calf, and almost everything else of value that he knew. And Dusty knew more still, more than he could ever teach a white man, his sense that came from the closeness of his communion with all living things. Jon could not remember a time when he had not relied on this second sense, almost second sight, of his friend. 'What then?' he pressed.

'The cattle,' Dusty said quietly. The flickering firelight carved his face into a mask of tragedy, the deep-set eyes dark pools of grief to come. 'Not good here. Cattle restless. Spooked.'

It was a word of fear to all who knew that Yowi, the spirit who warns of the coming of death, will often speak to the beasts when men's ears are too dull. Frank and

Slim exchanged a wide-eyed stare while James fixed his eyes on Dusty in mute appeal. Imperceptibly the atmosphere darkened and the cold wind of fear touched every man despite the heat of the fire.

'Hey guys, come on!'

Henry Suffolk, the station manager and the only other non-Aboriginal around the fire beside Jon, jumped to his feet and threw another log on the fire. Honest, down-to-earth and completely unimaginative, he could not take any more of this. A look of impatience passed over his firelit face as he resumed his seat. 'Bloody cattle are spooked because they know they're going to market tomorrow!' he laughed. 'And they know that means they'll walk in on four legs and come out as prime steak!'

Dusty closed his eyes and did not answer. Jon was unconvinced. 'Do they, though? Know they're going to die? How can they?'

Henry shrugged. Dusty sat on in the darkness as still as a statue and silent as the grave. Frank, quieter than Slim, nevertheless had his own kind of persistence. 'Something up, though. If Dusty see it, Dusty feel it, something up.'

A week ago I wouldn't have paid much attention to this, Jon thought. But now . . . 'Something bad?' he asked, trying to sound casual.

Only Slim did not feel the deepening atmosphere. He giggled loudly at the solemn faces all around. 'Maybe something good! Aboriginal women come here to get babies, so the spirit children in the water can enter them and find a home. Maybe you get a baby here, boss!'

Suddenly out of nowhere the thought of Geena seized Jon and pierced him to the core. *Geena – and a spirit baby – our baby—*

In that instant he knew that he had fallen hopelessly for the fawn-like girl who had walked unannounced into his house and his life.

He pulled himself up. In love, maybe, but not hopelessly. She liked him at least, he felt sure of that. Now all that lay ahead was to turn liking into love.

He stood up and moved abruptly away from the others in the dark, trading on the easy acceptance of the men. In a dream a bright future unfurled itself before him, Geena lifting up her little face to listen to his courtship, then unfolding to him like a flower to the sun. Then Geena as his bride, all in white with white flowers in her hair – he caught himself up, laughing at his own absurdity. She could turn up in white, or yellow, or sky-blue-pink, or in any colour she wanted, and dammit, she'd still knock spots off all the other women in the world if she got married in a plastic sack!

And then – and then—

Maybe the time had come for the old man to move over, he'd been acting so strange lately it was probably time for new blood. So – himself the master of Koenigshaus with Geena at his side, the city businesses sold and all the money worries at an end, only the land that was his and had been his since he could remember, land for him and his children, their children, the boys all as tall as him and his father, the girls all as golden, shy, tough and sweet as their mother . . .

In the black satin sky the stars were out now, blazing with pale fire. The scent of night rose to him from the still-warm earth and his soul was never more at peace. Suddenly he was aware of Henry standing quietly at his side. 'I could die happy here, Henry, you know that?' he murmured.

Henry was never comfortable with this kind of talk. 'You making plans to drop off your perch?'

Jon laughed and threw a retaliatory punch at his friend's shoulder. 'No fear, mate. You know what? You and me, when we're running this place, we're going to make it the best cattle station in the world.'

Henry grinned. 'You finally decided you're not cut out for college then, like your mum wanted?'

'Nah, I'd never make a scholar, when all I want to do is count cattle all day long! I belong out here, I couldn't live in a world of books and brick and concrete.' He paused. 'All I've got to do is let my uncle Charles sort out the city end of the business, then I can make Koenigshaus everything I've ever wanted it to be.'

Well, well – things have been moving underneath the surface of the water, Henry thought, concealing his surprise. 'Only one problem with all this, mate. What about your old man?'

Jon sounded almost careless. 'He's had a bloody good run for his money. It's my turn now.'

In the dead blackness of the night only the faintest dusting of the dying stars threw any radiance on the earth. Beside the embers of the fire the sleeping forms lay like the dead. Even the nervous cattle and restless stock-horses were quiet now, as all nature slept and the pulse of life itself slowed to the slowest beat.

Yet even now some of earth's creatures were alive and stirring, ready to make mischief, hungry for their prey. Through the fleshy stems of the wild lilies, a questing water-snake slithered down to the edge of the silent water, parted the gunmetal surface and was gone. And through the darkened bush beyond the small oasis of peace around the water-hole, all the night predators moved silently and purposefully about their business, closing the gap between them and their undefended prey with every step. And foremost among them came something heavy and dark, something that writhed and slithered and had its own evil being, carrying its own force of destruction coiled and ready to strike.

It was the work of a moment to pause on the rim of the valley and identify the small encampment with its huddle of motionless men lying round the camp fire. And any predator would single out the lone figure, large, heavy and imposing even in sleep who lay at a good distance away from the protection of the group all by himself, wrapped in a thick bedroll and lost to the world.

Moving like a ghost, the agent of death closed in on its chosen victim. A second later the long glittering forms of writhing snakes, each bearing a fatal shaft of death in its tongue, fell on the lone sleeper on the ground.

Phillip had been dreaming, a dream like all his dreams of victory and triumph, mastery and domination. Now he awoke to the worst of all nightmares, the feeling of being trapped in a body that cannot move, that will not answer the panic signals of fear and flight from the brain. Next came the blind sensation of the endless silent scream when an unseen force stifles nose and mouth, and he felt himself choking. From there he was catapulted with all the speed of dreamworld horror straight to a hell of unimagined pain, as uncounted pairs of bloody fangs sank themselves again and again into his defenceless face and neck.

Was he dreaming? Could any sane mind dream this? He could not move his legs for the weights holding them down, and his arms too were trapped and useless, pinioned at his sides. But the frantic twitching of his every muscle still enraged his assailants, and the maddened reptiles redoubled their attacks. Now the venom had entered his blood and he could feel himself sinking beneath their terrible frenzy, sinking beyond hope.

With one final effort he tried to shake off the weights clogging his arms and legs, break free of the suffocation blanketing his nose and mouth. As he surged upwards in a violent convulsion, he dreamed a face he knew as well as his own, and looked into a pair of eyes he only ever saw in dreams. *You*. He knew he was encountering the face of death and he greeted it without surprise.

Surrendering to a greater force than his own, Phillip

sank back to the hard ground and the mists of darkness rose before his eyes. Then he passed into the eternal dreamtime from which he would wake no more.

Chapter 8

How was it that she couldn't sleep when Phillip was here in bed with her, and she couldn't sleep when he wasn't?

All night long Helen had tossed and turned between sheets that were always too hot or too cold, pierced by the staring eye of a swollen fevered moon, a prey to unprecedented thoughts and fears. One army of anxieties laying siege to her peace clustered round *Phillip, Phillip, Phillip*. The other answered simply to the name of *Charles* . . .

'I'll call you', he'd said as he climbed into the helicopter, but almost absently, as if he had already said goodbye to her and his mind was turning away from her towards some task that lay ahead, taking him into some bleak cold region where she could never follow. And why did he say that now, when he had never said it before? They always communicated through Phillip, like any sister- and brother-in-law. 'I'll call you.' It was something lovers said.

Charles.

'You chose the wrong brother, Helen,' he said when she was driving him to the helicopter.

Oh Charles . . . You know as well as I do that I didn't choose, I was chosen!

She didn't say that, of course. Nor any of the rest of it as it boiled up inside with all the force of twenty-odd years of suppression. *OK, you saw me first, you saw me before he did, when I rolled up with my back-pack looking for work that muster-time on the next-door station. And yes, it was for you, for what we both thought we had going between us, that I stayed on after the muster was finished.*

But then . . .

But then he came . . .

Enough!

No point in re-hashing what they both knew, would remember until their dying day.

When he came . . .

As soon as Phillip rode over that day to do business with her boss, that tender, fragile boy-girl love between her and Charles had been trampled as if a whole herd of stampeding cattle had passed over it. Within a week she was installed in Phillip's house, in Phillip's bed, and within a month he had made her not his mistress but his wife. Charles, half-drunk and stunned with disbelief, had stumbled through the ceremony as Phillip's best man. And the next day he had left Koenigshaus to make his own life, his own business, as far away as he could.

The business . . .

She shrugged off the hot and twisted sheets, got up, and threw on the lightest shirt and jeans she could find. Charles and Ben were insisting that there wouldn't be any business if Phillip didn't face up to financial reality. That at least was something concrete she could check up on, something she could try to sort out.

It was not yet dawn and she shivered in the glimmering dark as she left the house. Crossing the rose-lined drive-way and the circle of grass which formed the focus of the homestead she made her way towards the office building. A low, red-roofed bungalow like the guest house opposite, it housed all Phillip's old business records and official documents, plus the most up-to-date computer system and all the telecommunications needed to run an international business operation.

Like all the buildings on Koenigshaus, the office was

never locked. When was the last time she had been in here? She couldn't remember, she never had any reason to come. Like everything else at Koenigshaus, the low square room, part-business centre, part study and gentleman's den, was a jumble of old and new. She stood on the threshold blinking a little in the sudden electric light, taking in the massive ancient iron safe, the heavy old oak desk and old-fashioned wooden filing cabinets, all strangely at odds with the advanced computer hardware, VDU screens, telex and quietly humming fax.

Along the wall Phillip had displayed a collection of old stockwhips, a pair of military sabres and a cluster of photographs of the past. Prominent among them were mementoes of the fancy boys' college of which he was so proud, the school he had pronounced Jon not good enough to be sent to. With a surge of the old defensive anger for her son, she stared at the images of Phillip in the rugby team, Phillip in the cricket team, Phillip on graduation day. In pride of place on the wall facing Phillip's desk hung his scroll of honour: *PHILLIP JOHANN KOENIG, HEAD BOY, ROCKHAMPTON COLLEGE, 1948–49*.

On a second desk in the corner, Ben had been at work and his papers and folders still lay on the surface, loosely stacked beside his computer terminal. Phillip's desk by contrast was completely bare, all his pressing concerns cleared before the muster. But from the hunting rifle and stock-whip in the corner to the photographs of her and Jon alongside the cigars on the desk, the room was heavy with his presence. She took a deep breath. God, it even smells of him in here — it's as if he could walk in at any second.

But even the sense of Phillip's outsize personality could not deflect her from what she had to do. And even with computerisation, she thought, there must be some evidence of how well things have been going – or how badly.

She crossed to Ben's desk and opened the first folder on top of the pile. The black typescript and red figures danced accusingly before her eyes.

This sum has now been outstanding for . . .

Unless your account is settled forthwith . . .

We wish to advise you that we are now placing the matter in the hands of our solicitors . . .

There must have been forty or fifty of them. In a panic she turned to the folder below. One glance at the description of its contents in Ben's neat accountant's hand, and she did not need to read any further: *judgements for default obtained against Koenig Holdings, January-March, April-June.* Beneath that lay *Judgements Pending* – God in Heaven, did they owe money to everyone in Australia?

What had Phillip been doing? What had he been playing at? In a rage she took the space between Ben's desk and his in three powerful strides, and sat down in his great carved leather chair. Furiously she tore open the drawers one by one.

In the top right-hand drawer lay a large manilla envelope she recognised, for he had shown it to her years ago and told her where to find it – *to be opened in the event of my death.* She tossed it aside. Beneath it lay pens, pencils, and all the debris of a businessman's desk, with a couple of things that spelled Phillip alone – a formidable Swiss Army knife, a bull-worker and a heavy-duty hand-gun. She pressed on. She did not have to look very far.

Invoices, invoices and bills – bills, bills, bills. Charles was right then – Phillip had known all about the financial problems of Koenigshaus and had chosen to ignore them. Indeed the division of responsibility could not be more clear between his desk and Ben's – the dates on the documents showed conclusively that the information had not even been passed on to Charles and Ben until things had reached the point of no return.

Oh Phillip. What have you been doing, what have you

been thinking of this last year and more? With a heavy heart she reached the last drawer down on the left hand side. Unlike the others it was sticking badly, and she had to yank at it to get it free – when had it last been opened? One glance at the faded contents, and she knew.

The headline on the top leaped out at her as vividly as it had done the first time she saw it twenty-five years before.

KOENIG WIFE IN BUSH TRAGEDY, WOMAN KILLED IN FALL FROM HORSE.

With fingers so cold that they had lost all sensation, she picked out the flimsy bundle of cuttings and spread them on the desk.

She did not need to read the story below, she could remember every word.

In a tragic accident this week on Koenigshaus, the wife of the 3000-acre station owner Mr Phillip Koenig is reported killed in a fall while riding.

Mrs Koenig (33) is said to have died instantly when her horse bolted upon encountering a King Brown snake far out in the bush. Her husband was riding with her at the time, but was unable to avert the disaster.

Mrs Koenig, better known as Trudi to her many friends in the area, was a popular figure in the Northern Territory since her marriage to Phillip Koenig fifteen years ago. A native of America, she came from an old-established and wealthy family of the Deep South, and her Southern Belle charm never deserted her. A gifted hostess and a sparkling guest, she was an adornment to the life of the Territory as well as a brilliant consort to one of its leading figures. Had Phillip Koenig embarked on the political career which he has recently been considering, there is no doubt that Trudi Koenig would have seized the chance to shine on a wider stage and made an unforgettable mark on Australian national life.

Beneath the cuttings lay a photograph, the hand-coloured flesh-tones still vividly alive though the edges of the cardboard mount were cracked and battered with age. Framed in the doorway of Koenigshaus, a woman was half-turning to the camera, laughing with confident assurance, her face lifted towards the sun.

Despite the burning sunshine, the slender body in the off-the-shoulder sun dress was as pale as a Madonna lily, and the long slender fingers on the jamb of the door spoke the same quality of delicacy and breeding, the pedigree of centuries. In the mellow light of the verandah her large dark eyes, glossy hair and full red lips took on an almost unnatural glow, and her whole body was imbued with the same beauty and vitality. At her side a young boy clung to her waist, his gaze fixed on her as adoringly as she seemed to regard the man behind the camera.

Helen's eyes fell on the last line of the newspaper report. *She leaves a son, Alexander, now thirteen . . .*

Was that why she had first loved Phillip twenty-five years ago, for the sake of that child, left motherless in an afternoon?

No – for even then the lost child had bitterly rebuffed all sympathy and struggled as only young boys can to become a man overnight. A hard enough task for a lifetime: impossible in a month, in less than a month. And he never made it.

Her numb fingers searched the newspaper cuttings: she knew it was there.

*NEW BLOW FOR KOENIG FAMILY,
SON LOST IN WAKE OF
MOTHER'S FATAL ACCIDENT.
Hopes are fading for the safety of the son of Phillip*

Koenig, missing in the outback for the last five days. Alexander Koenig (13) was reported to have been behaving strangely after the death of his mother in a riding accident three months ago. Last Wednesday he said goodbye to the Aboriginal housekeeper, Rose, took a horse and rode into the bush. He did not return. Extensive searches have since failed to reveal his whereabouts.

Police sources are indicating that the search will now be called off. It is understood that Phillip Koenig will continue the search for Alexander, his only child, by private means. Alexander's sudden disappearance casts a new shadow over recent plans for the tragic family to find fresh happiness. Last Tuesday Mr Koenig (35) announced his engagement to Miss Helen Jackson (18), who has been working in the area for the last few months. The wedding had been expected to take place shortly. Mr Koenig had no comment to make last night.

Alex.

There was no respite, it was still an open wound.

Why had she been so sure that once they were married, she could win the boy's love and trust, bring him round to accept her? Why had she been so caught up in the madness of Phillip's wooing that she had allowed herself to ignore the loss, the pain, the fear, the accusation in those bright burning child's eyes?

Because of her, the boy had gone out in the bush to die. And then the madness of Phillip's loving had turned to a madness of grief that only she could cure. That was her marriage portion in place of simple love – the sense of a man so strong, so powerful, being brought down to this, along with her knowledge of his wound, his anger, his pain, and the lethal cocktail of his need, his desire . . .

Phillip.

She felt him now so strongly it seemed he was here, here, now—

Her heart swelled with pity and pain – pity for his pain, pain for his pain.

Oh Phillip, why did it have to be like this? I know you went through so much with Trudi. But I shouldn't have had to suffer to make up for it. No woman should. Sorry, Phillip, but it's all over now.

The door opened and Rose came silently in. The ripe, rancid smell of booze came in with the housekeeper's small black shade as it always did after a bad night. 'Light on,' she said abruptly. 'Light in here two, three times late at night – never anyone here.'

She's dreaming, thought Helen wearily as she groped for a tissue and tried to dry her eyes. Or else it's the drink. Aloud she said huskily, 'I just came in to look for a few things.'

Rose's stare took in the cuttings, the photograph and Helen's face in one comprehensive sweep. 'Foun' her anyways, whatever clse you look for,' she announced in a low liquid mutter. 'She in here, still in here.'

'Still here? Who?'

'Miz' Trudi. She never gone away.'

She's right, Helen silently acknowledged. We've never got rid of her, Phillip and I.

Nor Alex.

If ever spirits walk, theirs do.

Maybe they had found each other, mother and son? She dismissed the idea at once. If only I could believe that Trudi and Alex came together at last, joined forces to comfort each other, wherever they walk now. If only.

Rose was still muttering on. 'Coming back. Today.'

She couldn't have heard properly. 'Rose – what did you say?'

'Come back,' Rose said in a flat guttural that was never-theless alive with conviction. 'Miz Trudi come back now.'

A slow fear congealed the marrow of her bones. 'Come back? What for?'

But she knew the answer already. There was only one thing – or one person – that Trudi would come back for.

Rosie let out her breath in a harsh extended hiss. 'She come for Mr Phillip.'

Chapter 9

They had him back within an hour after that, a slow cortège of riders with the heavy, twitching frame suspended in a makeshift sling between the strongest of the horses.

Yawoma, yawoma yaldeenie nongoma murtanna, ouraka mantenekin. wana ma nanudagabalaria . . . come back, O come back the wife cries to her husband, wait, wait for me, why didn't you wait for me . . .'

Rose's desolate cry as she launched into her chant of lamentation was the first and only warning Helen had before dropping into her own free fall of terror and grief. As she raced out onto the verandah, as she watched them lift blind-eyed, jerking and crying Phillip from the makeshift stretcher, she could not believe how fast her whole life was blowing away, exploding in a storm of pain and blood.

Oh –

She had always known it would hurt, and like any younger woman married to an older man, she had often tried to rehearse the pain, to anticipate it even just a little.

She thought she had prepared herself in advance. Now she knew she would never have been ready, even if he had lived another lifetime.

'Mrs Koenig?'

It was Dusty, the understanding in his age-old eyes

startling in a man so young. He gestured awkwardly towards the fevered shape on the crude litter. 'Where shall we . . . ?'

'In here,' she said. 'Bring him in here.'

Beside the heavy form of his father Jon stood mute and wild-eyed, his tall, broad-shouldered body that of a man on guard, his eyes those of a lost, bewildered child.

'It was a snake bite,' he said thickly. 'Must have been a King Brown. Henry's radioing for the flying doctor.' Their eyes, their minds locked on the same thought. *But it's too late now.*

Don't scream, she told herself dully. It won't do any good. But she could not stop the tears welling from a deep pit of grief where she seemed to be all melting, all dissolving inside. *Phillip, oh Phillip. . .*

She seemed to suffer twice, as a wife for her husband and then again as a mother, for her son. Jon looked as if he had been taken from his death-bed too, his face blood-less, his whole body only just hanging on to life and strength. He could hardly force out the few words it took to tell her what had happened. Then he broke down completely. 'I've lost it, Mum,' he whispered hopelessly. 'I don't know what to do.'

Outside in the shimmering haze the dead red outback slumbered relentlessly on. What was another death, she knew, after fifty, a hundred, two hundred thousand years? The spirits of this land had seen so many come and go. *But not like him*, she wept, *not him*.

'Bloody bad business, this!'

The brisk little flying doctor had seen his share of death, and like all medics recognised its place in the grand scheme of things. At the end of a long life, for instance, lived to the full and easily relinquished, or as a door opening to release a tormented sufferer from the torture house of pain, death could be accepted, even welcomed.

But not like this! A man in his prime, taken out like a sitting duck, and in such a bloody bad way too, vocal chords paralysed, eyes turned inside out in his head, muscles screaming like steel ropes as he thrashed around as if he was still trying to fight off his attackers—

Angrily he confronted the drawn and hard-faced men surrounding the still-twitching outline of the burly figure laid out upon a trestle hastily fetched in from the cattle shed.

'Phillip Koenig's been out in the bush all his life,' he demanded. 'How come a King Brown got him now?'

There was no answer.

Only the throaty rattle of the dying man, which in its own time, came to an end.

He was really lovely, that's what he was, just one beaut, gorgeous bloke. And if only he'd follow up on that smile in his eyes, then there's no knowing what a girl might do . . .

Sighing, the room-maid closed the door of the motel bungalow and trekked disconsolately away. Of course he knew that the motel didn't really do room service, what motel ever did? Well, maybe in some fancy places. But not out here in the heart of the Northern Territory, so far off the map that travellers were glad to find anywhere to put up. And whatever the Happy Valley Motel (prop. E. G. Gibbons) laid claim to be, it wasn't the Sydney Ritz.

And he knew she was only the maid; he'd seen her cleaning the next door bungalow when he arrived and said 'Hello!' with that brilliant smile of his. So he'd know it wasn't really her job to knock on his door this morning and say, 'Y'had breakfast? It's all in with the room-rate. C'n I getcha anything from the bar?'

But she just had to see him again. And when he'd opened the door and seen who it was, he didn't seem surprised. In fact he'd chuckled to himself and those bright dark eyes had stared at her so quizzically she'd felt all her neck going red till she had to drop her gaze.

'Get me something?' he said, his eyes travelling up and down her body. She stood there feeling his gaze coursing over her like scalding water in the shower. 'Y'know, I don't think there is anything,' he went on, running a lean brown hand through his thick dark hair. He grinned. 'Except maybe . . .'

Maybe. The way he said that one word just made her melt inside. Whatever it was that some men had that made you want them, he had it, squared and in triplicate. Just like Phil Gibbons didn't have it, she thought miserably, remembering the sweaty hands, short legs and bulging beer belly of her current swain.

'*Except . . . ?*'

She couldn't believe she'd said that, and looked straight into his eyes at the same time. Coming on to a customer, getting fresh like this was enough to get her the sack straight off, quicker than a blue duck, the way that old ratbag Gibbons ran the motel, and him as straitlaced as his son was randy as a 'roo in rut.

But this one was not just any old customer! A dream of a body, both loose and hard at the same time, broad shoulders and the neatest backside in the smartest pants she'd ever seen, he seemed to live in himself with an easy grace that at the same time had a charge of powerful arrogance too.

And he had plenty to be cocky about. Dreamily she took a mental inventory of his charms. Sun-streaked thick shining hair, fantastic profile, classic jaw and chin, eyes as fierce and smoky as a hunting falcon's, lightened by amusement but with something darker smouldering in their depths, hard, businesslike hands . . .

She almost groaned, she could feel them on her breasts . . .

'Except . . . ?'

He laughed again as he said it. He knew exactly what she meant, he knew she was offering herself to him on a plate, she could see that in his face. She felt it too from the swift squeeze he gave the fleshy part of her arm as they stood at the door. 'Oh yeah,' he said. 'Except my bill. I have to go.'

She hardly heard the rest. He was leaving now, here on urgent business, had to keep a very sad appointment, come a long way to be here, good old Qantas, if it weren't for Australia's premier airline he'd have missed the whole thing, wouldn't do to be late now.

Through the door she could see the well-cut sober suit laid out on the bed, beside it a white shirt and black tie. She nodded mournfully. Maybe if he'd come earlier . . . if she'd had more time . . . if he could have seen her all pooned up and not in this stupid overall and dirty white pinafore . . .

Maybe.

Still, at least she'd have something else to think about tonight when Phil Gibbons heaved his short fat bulk on top of her and floundered away uselessly, snorting and jerking and sweating like the pig he was. She could think about the mystery man and make out it was him instead. And he was a mystery, all she knew about him was his name, he hadn't even given an address when he registered yesterday, only 'passing through' . . .

'My bill?'

His eyes, burning as black as fire now with those little glow-worms sparkling in their depths, were fixed on her face in frank amusement. Blushing furiously, she pulled herself together. 'Sure, yeah, your bill – I'll tell them straight away. It'll be ready for you whenever you want to leave, Mr King.'

God Almighty, when was the last time he had worn a

suit? Cursing and swearing, Jon struggled into a jacket that together with its formally-tailored trousers made him feel as if he had been strapped into a strait-jacket, however well-cut. Already the stiff collar of the white shirt was slicing into his neck till it felt as if his head was coming off. Knotting the black tie seemed only an incidental torment on top of all the others.

Now he thought he knew what weightlessness was, he felt so strange as he left his room. Descending the wide staircase, his feet automatically made a left towards the back of the house, he could not face the people already assembling in the front drawing room. The funeral guests were coming in from all over the Territory, by car, helicopter and light plane. It was only natural that they'd all want to pay their last respects.

But his soul cried out against it. If I'd had my way, Dad, he vowed, tears in his eyes, it would have been just Mum and me and Charles and Ben and Geena and Rose, and we'd have made you a resting place out there on the land, a high place where you could sleep out on your own under the stars like you always did. I wouldn't have had you shoved away under the floor of that bloody chapel with all the rest of the old bones!

As he left by the back door the stable block confronted him with another great reproach. Hanging his head heavily over the edge of his box, Kaiser, Phillip's huge stallion, looked as sullen and sick as only a once-great, neglected horse can be. Even his glowing white coat looked harsh now, his eyes dull and his temper, from the vicious flare of his great yellow teeth and laid-back ears, savagely deteriorated in the week since Phillip had died. I must get him out, Jon thought, and give him some exercise, he'll just go mad locked up in there. He'll probably throw me and half-kill me, he's such a brute. And he's so used to Phillip he'll probably turn out to be a one-man mount. But I owe it to both of them to try.

He knew better than to approach an evil-tempered horse to fondle it, and with a last few words, drifted around to the front of the house to wait for the funeral procession to emerge. As he did so, he was just in time to see Helen hurrying out of the front door and down the steps, then across the central driveway and into the office building. What was she doing? Silently he padded after her over the grass and entered the bungalow.

She was standing against the far wall behind Phillip's massive oak desk and heavy, carved chair, huddled tensely in front of the safe, alternately wrestling with the knobs and trying to hear the fall of the tumblers inside. She was so absorbed in what she was doing that she did not hear him come in. He was almost upon her. 'Hi there.'

She whipped round, her face a mask of guilt, the hand at her mouth choking back a scream. 'Jon! I thought you were up at the house!'

'What's up?' She lurched unsteadily on her feet and he caught her by the arms. 'Hey, what's the problem?'

Helen made a huge effort to pull herself together. 'No problem, darling, none at all. Everyone was busy up at the house and it seemed like a good moment – I just thought – well, as Mr Carey is coming in from the bank I thought we ought to see if there's another copy of the will – or anything else we ought to have ready—' Her voice trailed away.

Jon shook his head in puzzlement. 'But surely if he's the executor, he'll have the will.'

She nodded brightly. 'Oh, sure. But I just wondered if there'd be any others – you know what Phillip was like . . .'

Poor Mum, he thought. It's all been such a strain, she's losing her grip. 'But you know Dad said there was only one that counted,' he said gently.

She nodded in quick relief. 'The last one, yes – leaving

everything to you. Oh, I'm sure we've got nothing to worry about.'

Awkwardly he patted her shoulder. 'Look, if you want to get into the safe, the number's probably with the note of the bank accounts and all that, in the envelope he left in the desk to be opened after he died. It'll be a six-figure number, all those old safes are the same. It's in my room. You can have it any time you want.'

'No, no, darling, that's fine.' She squeezed his hand reassuringly. 'I'm sure Phillip didn't keep anything of importance in there, it probably hasn't been opened since his own father died. Everything's on computer now anyway, with a password and everything, and Ben and Charles are the ones in charge of all that.'

Together they turned and left the office to rejoin their guests.

You've got nothing to worry about, Helen told herself doggedly. *Phillip must have taken care of everything, he always did. And you've learned something you didn't know before, it's a six-figure number you're looking for. But that was a stupid mistake, you've got to be more careful next time!*

Chapter 10

Outside in the baking heat and dust of midday, the Aboriginal inhabitants of Koenigshaus had gathered to make their last farewell to their master, and to ease the passage of Phillip's spirit wherever it wandered in the Great Dreamtime which was now its home. Raising her hands to her head, one of the old women began a musical chant in her liquid guttural and one by one others took it up.

'*Ninnana combea, innara inguna karkania* . . . O Great Spirit, All-Father of All Things, the swamp oaks sigh and weep, the gum trees shed tears of blood and mourn, for darkness has come up on one of your creation . . .'

Inside the house, all those who had known Phillip had come to pay their last respects. In a dream Helen greeted them all, they seemed to pass before her like swimmers under water. Local farmers, cattle men, stockmen, those he had dealt with in the local town, she never knew how many people Phillip was friendly with, or how many had cause to thank him for what he had done.

'He was a beaut bloke, Mrs Koenig, one of the best,' observed a large, heavy-set figure clad in the light khaki of the local police. 'Me and Roscoe here, we'll always remember how generous he was. To us all, and to the Force – he never passed up his Christmas donation to the Police Widows' and Orphans' Fund, did he, Roscoe?'

His companion nodded mournfully. 'Like George says, we'll miss Mr Koenig, he always liked us to keep an eye on the place, not that there was ever any trouble, the way he ran it, was there, George?'

'No trouble, Roscoe, never any trouble, no, not with Mr Koenig.'

'Thank you, George . . . thank you, Roscoe . . . Oh, thank you . . . you're very kind . . . so glad you could come . . .'

It seemed the torture would have no end. But at last the signal came that the service was ready to begin. In heavy silence the mourners left the house in a sombre procession of twos and threes, crossing the pathways and grassland of Koenigshaus beyond the office building and the guest house until they reached the little stone-built Lutheran chapel behind. Already the sun was striking hotly through the high narrow windows to make the dust motes dance around Phillip's coffin where it waited in the glancing light inside. But at the end of the stone-flagged aisle the small altar lay cool and aloof, its pure white altar-cloth and plain wax candles of a simplicity that Luther himself would have recognised and approved.

Before the altar, beside a wreath of white lilies and camellia, half a dozen of the flagstones had been lifted to expose a dark vault gaping beneath. At the head of the procession, his mother clinging to his arm, Jon felt his heart catch at the sight of it. You don't belong here, Dad! he cried in silent anguish, we should be burying you out in the bush, under the stars!

Beside him Helen approached her last sight of Phillip with a soul so full she could hardly move. On the same trestle where he had breathed his last, Phillip Koenig lay in a handsome silk-lined coffin, to all intents and purposes, in the phrase of the local funeral director, 'at peace'.

But the sightless, upturned eyes of the dead man had refused to close despite all the undertaker's efforts, and even the magic of the morticians' cosmetic arts had failed to obliterate the venomous purple-red puncture wounds that vividly disfigured the waxen face and neck. Like all the other men present, Phillip was clad in an unaccustomed suit and tie, and his great hands, white and heavy like his face, were crossed on his breast. *This isn't Phillip!* was the only thought in Helen's mind, *this isn't the man I knew!* Her gorge rose at the sanctimoniousness of it all. *What have they done to him, now he can't fight back? He never would have crossed his arms like that in his life! He wasn't a believer, he was his own God and his own Satan!*

Moving down the aisle on Jon's arm she stopped beside the coffin and feeling the eyes of all upon her, leaned down to kiss her husband's face. Phillip's cheek was as cold as she had expected, but somehow clammy too. It seemed filmed with moisture or sweat, dank as a rock face underground. She fought fiercely to repress a shudder. As she raised her eyes and broke away, she caught the eye of the dying Christ where the great carved old oak crucifix hung above the altar. He seemed to be regarding her with infinite compassion, infinite contempt.

Oh, where was Charles?

She had given him the news herself, overriding Jon, overriding Ben and also the station manager, who had been doing sterling work helping with the cruel chore of spreading the word of Phillip's death around the neighbourhood. She had been happy enough to delegate those phone calls or telegrams that she thought could decently be given to someone else. But Charles she knew that she alone could call.

'What? How?'

His voice had sounded very flat, as if the news held no surprise at all. He just can't believe it, she said to herself.

'A snake. Snake-bite.' She began to cry.

'Don't cry,' he said urgently. 'Oh, don't cry, Helen, please. There'll be masses to do here – but I'll come as soon as I can.' Now he sounded distressed. But it was because she was crying, she knew, not for Phillip's dreadful end.

Now he was here on her other side, dark-suited like Jon and grim as death himself. No one today would call him handsome, all his good looks were lost in the air of savage abstraction he wore along with his mourning suit, and he had hardly said a word to anyone since he arrived from Sydney in the Koenig helicopter a few hours before.

Across the aisle knelt Ben with Geena at his side, his head buried in his hands, heavy lips moving as he tried to pray. Grey-faced and drawn, he had aged ten years in the last week, burying himself in the office and avoiding all contact with any other member of the household. Geena in black looked golden, gorgeous and untouched by everything around her, Jon noticed with a lurch. As soon as all this was over, it would be the time to start thinking about that . . .

At the front of the church the flying padre, the overworked man of God responsible for this vast tract of God's forgotten land, came forward to greet them.

'When you're ready, Mrs Koenig?' he said quietly. Stepping back to allow Charles to enter the front pew then assisting Helen to her place beside him, Jon gave a curt nod as the signal to begin. Moving to the centre of the aisle, the minister had no need to refer to the old gold-lettered Bible that he carried open before him supported on the palms of both hands. His low but sincere tones carried the familiar words to every ear in the chapel.

'I am the Resurrection and the Life, saith the Lord. Man that is born of woman hath but a short time to live, and cometh soon to the time when the secrets of all hearts shall be laid bare, when all things that are hid shall be revealed, and our souls shall stand naked as at our creation before you, O Lord our God . . .

. . . before the mountains were born or the earth and the world were brought to be, from eternity to eternity You

alone are God. You return the Son of Man to the dust from which he came before the Serpent smote his head and consigned him to death everlasting. You say unto him, "Son of Adam, turn again to the Lord your God, till he breathe into you the life eternal of all that know, love and follow Him . . .'

Suddenly the even, flowing voice faltered and broke off. At the same moment Helen felt the almost tangible heat of eyes on the back of her neck, scalding through the white lawn blouse she was wearing with her black linen mourning suit. Slowly she turned to follow the line of the padre's startled gaze.

At the back of the congregation a black shape filled the doorway, the dark figure of a tall, well-made man outlined against the burning light outside. The thick glossy hair springing away from a classically sculptured face with a light bronzing of city tan, the strong jaw and clear, unselfconscious gaze were those of a man who could have made a living as a male model. There was something almost professional too about the easy grace, the relaxed stance as he stood in the doorway of the chapel silhouetted against the light. Behind him the flaming rays of the midday sun formed a demonic sunburst behind his handsome head. He looked like Lucifer before the Fall.

In this part of the Northern Territory where strangers were as scarce as hen's teeth, and at this ceremony, where there was no one who had not known Phillip Koenig and all the others there all their lives, he might have been a Martian. Every head in the chapel had swivelled to follow the minister's eyes and Helen's blank and stricken stare. Now one thought filled every mind, *Who the hell is he?*

Into that vast question-mark the stranger advanced with a friendly apologetic smile. Helen could not move. He seemed to speak to her alone. 'Sorry to disturb things like this, folks,' he began in a light pleasant voice. 'But I kinda lost my way getting out here from town. It's a while since I've been this way, y'see.'

Helen felt the dread of dawning recognition. In the pew behind, Rose drew a breath as deep as a groan. Beside her Charles was staring as if he had seen a ghost.

The newcomer gave another winning smile. 'And I had to come.' He paused. 'I'm—'

'We know who you are.' Helen was completely calm as she rose to her feet and moved up the aisle. She had dreamed of this moment for so many years, and always before had cried to awake to the truth that it was only a dream, nothing but a cruel delusion. Now at last it was real, it was true. She stepped up to him and took his hand. 'Welcome.' She gathered all her strength. 'Welcome home.'

Chapter 11

Welcome home, Alex.

The voice of the pastor murmured on. 'For man is born to trouble as the sparks fly upward. He comes forth like a flower and withers in the sun: he passes like a shadow and does not stay.'

Legs braced and feet apart, his hands clasped behind his back, Jon stared at the ivory Christ on the carved wooden crucifix and tried to keep the blasphemous phrase from surfacing in his mind.

Jesus Christ!

Lose a father and gain a brother, all in the same week? What was it – some kind of cosmic black joke?

Beside him Helen was trying to comfort a sobbing Rose and at the same time still the tremulous joy and fear surging in her own heart: *Alex!*

Rising above the turmoil all around him, the padre went serenely on with the service. 'In the midst of life we are in death—'

And in the midst of death, new life.

New Koenig blood.

Jon almost laughed in disbelief. A blood brother, when he'd been an only child all his life. It was ridiculous, it couldn't be happening!

'The days of man are but as grass, he flourishes like a flower of the field and when the wind passes over it, it is gone, and the place where it grew will know it no more.'

The padre bowed his head, concluded the service and fell back. Solemnly the bearers shuffled forward and with practised skill hoisted up the heavy coffin, carried it a pace or two up the aisle and swinging it over the aperture, lowered it into the void. Mechanically the family gathered round to cast the symbolic handful of dry red earth onto the place beneath.

'Earth to earth, ashes to ashes, dust to dust: in the name of Our Lord Jesus Christ, world without end, amen . . .'

At last it was over. Slowly the mourners, all trying to maintain a decent reverence but unable to suppress their excitement, made their way back to the house. There it fell to Jon to take the decision that Helen was still too numb to deal with. Facing the chattering throng in the drawing room, he cleared his throat and began.

'Folks, I'm sure you've all picked up on what's happened. Dad's former son—' he checked himself in confusion. 'I mean, his son by his former wife – sorry, his first wife – has turned up out of the blue to be with us today. I'm sure you'll all appreciate we've got a lot of – of catching up to do. So there'll be plenty to eat and drink, just help yourselves, but I hope you'll excuse us if we adjourn to keep Dad's wake as a family. Thank you all for coming. Thank you very much.'

'You did well there – if you don't mind my saying so . . .'

In the family den off the kitchen, Jon was aware of the newcomer moving towards him past Helen and Charles, hand outstretched. 'Look, I know this isn't easy – the way I turned up and all,' he said awkwardly, but with an undeniable charm. 'But I saw Dad's death in the paper, and I just couldn't think of another way to do it.'

In the background Rose was keening. Charles laughed rather oddly. 'There aren't any rules for this sort of thing. We'll just have to make them up as we go along.'

Helen stepped up to him, her eyes unnaturally large. 'Where were you? Where have you come from?'

'I was in France when I read about it – Paris – I always get the Aussie newspapers wherever I am. But I had to come back to London to get a flight – only just got the last seat on the plane as it was, and I practically had to buy up half of Qantas to get that.' He gave a rueful laugh.

'But before that,' Helen persisted. 'Alex, where have you *been*?'

Telling the story took a long time. Rose's coffee helped, and a slug of something stronger for the men as the housekeeper hovered around, her attention fixed on Alex as if he would disappear again if she stopped watching him. But the stranger had no problem holding his small audience. Sometimes laughing bitterly, sometimes simply amused, sometimes with his head in his hands, he pieced together the story of his flight and the missing years.

'I rode farther in one night than anyone would have thought a kid of that age could,' he said. 'Then I gave the horse to some old galoot on condition that he kept it hidden for a few weeks and played ignorant if any questions came along. Then I hit the road.' His eyes were very bright. 'Australia's a beaut country to get lost in. Plenty of orphans out there. Didn't take me long to figure it out.'

'Figure what out?' asked Jon in bewilderment.

Alex laughed, and gave a careless shrug. 'How to survive.'

Well, he certainly knows how to get the sympathy vote, Charles reflected coldly. And whatever he's missed in his twenty-five years on the lam, he's certainly learned how to handle the female of the species. Alex Koenig; Lady Killer to the Gentry, and Orphan of the Storm. He's all we fucking need!

Strained beyond belief, Charles threw a glance at

Helen. God, she was hanging on his every word as if he were her long-lost son as well as Phillip's! Maybe in a way he was. But he was going to have to do more than this to earn his place in this family! He couldn't just walk in from the bush looking like a grown-up version of the kid who disappeared, with no other claim on anyone's sympathy – no, be honest! with Trudi's eyes, Trudi's striking colouring, Trudi's smile and the young Phillip's body – and say 'Cooee, folks, I'm home!'

He coughed dismissively, and stared at his newfound nephew. 'How to survive? Seems to me you've done a lot more than that, by the sound of things. Paris? London? What's all that?'

Alex looked back with a frank open stare. 'I went into the travel business,' he said simply. 'Seemed like an obvious thing, if I wanted to keep on the move myself – as I did.' He dropped his gaze away from Charles's hard challenging glare. 'And it's worked out pretty well,' he said modestly. 'So far at least.'

Helen looked around. Jon was gazing at Alex in fascination, mesmerised, she could see, by the newcomer's well-tailored suit with its subtle accent of European styling, the fashionably-cut hair, the indefinable sense of something special that the newcomer conveyed. And he had to like him as a person too, he couldn't help it, Alex was trying so hard to be nice!

'Look, I want you to know,' Alex said suddenly, 'that I haven't come to upset anything here. I just wanted to pay my last respects.'

He looked down at his hands and seemed to be struggling with what he had to say. 'I always meant to come and make it up with Dad, you've got to believe that.'

He raised his eyes to Helen's. 'And with you too. I never thought he'd – that it would happen like this. I thought there was plenty of time.' His voice was husky now. 'I didn't want to come back till I'd made my first million. I wanted to impress him. I wanted him to be proud of me.'

Jon leaned forward impulsively, offering his own hand. 'And he would be, mate,' he said abruptly, 'I'm bloody sure of that!' The two men gripped hands in a warm handshake.

'Listen mate,' Jon went on. 'I don't know anything about all this stuff about the past, 'cos I wasn't there. But I know that Dad never got on with his brother, and went on making his life a misery right up to the end – right, Charles?'

If Charles's nod of acknowledgement was both sardonic and distant, Jon did not notice. 'So I'm telling you I'm not going to have any of that with my brother now I've got one! – half-brother anyway. We're going to start with a clean slate, and this time, we'll get it right. Anything you want on Koenigshaus, you've only got to ask. Or just help yourself!' He lifted his head and stared round the group in an unconscious echo of Phillip at his most powerful. 'And as long as I've got any say in what happens round here, that's the way it's going to be!'

There was a general silence of approval.

Only Charles again seemed to strike a discordant note as he nodded at Jon. 'Before you take over for good, don't forget Carey's here.'

They had all forgotten. Helen stared at him. 'Carey?'

'The bank manager. From town. About Phillip's will. He's probably ready to see us by now.'

'Him in the dining room,' Rose intervened. 'Him in there one hour, two, maybe more.'

A general laugh helped to break up the tension. 'Well, we'd better get in there too!' said Helen firmly. 'And you'd better come along, Alex. You're family now!'

God, he hated this!

He'd signed on to be a bank manager, not to do

people's dirty work for them, still less to be head washer-woman when all the family's dirty laundry was coming out! Still, there was nothing for it, Carey reflected as he mopped his brow for the hundredth time. Phillip Koenig had been a good customer of the bank for forty years, a bank whose very existence in this part of the world was dependent on Koenig cash. And so it would always be. What did it matter which of the Koenigs held the reins as long as Koenigshaus went on?

They were all round the dining table in front of him now, the widow Helen, smart as ever even in mourning, he noted approvingly; Phillip's brother Charles, young Jon, the worried-looking accountant – Nichols or whatever his name was – that Aboriginal girl of his, though what right she had to be here God only knows, and the mystery man himself, the long-lost brother. Carey had not even been in the area when that old tragedy had taken place. But no one could live in the Territory for any length of time and not know the story of the little lost Koenig lamb.

Or perhaps we should say black sheep, he thought to himself as he scrutinised with interest the dark, handsome, slightly raffish-looking man of what – thirty-eight? forty? who lounged at the head of the table with all the confidence of a man thoroughly at home.

Carey pulled himself up with a start.

At home?

Well, come to think of it . . .

'Mr Carey, I think you know everyone here.' Helen's voice was always easy on the ear, Carey thought, you could listen to her all day. 'Except my – my stepson, Alexander Koenig.'

She did that well, Alex told himself, with just a touching hint of newness, and a really fond glance at the Prodigal himself, yours truly. Seems like a nice woman, after all.

And still a looker, too. He did not need to check out

Helen's body, her long, slender legs, firm breasts and full hips, he already knew what they looked like. Y'know she's not bad at all, mate, he told himself. Forty-ish OK, but no one'd kick her out of bed. The old man always did well for himself, whatever you said about him, no one could criticise his taste in women! Shouldn't be too hard to get plenty of sympathy for the long-lost boyo from her. And I'm overdue a bit of the old home comfort at Koenigshaus. This place owes me, they all owe me . . .

A movement across the table caught his eye and he smiled to himself. But the other one now, the little choc-ice – sssshhit! She sure was a horse of a different colour . . .

Carefully he veiled his scrutiny of Geena under an open smile, friendly, but not too familiar. A moment later he rearranged his features into respectful attention as Carey began to speak. 'If we're all ready?'

Helen nodded. 'I think we are.'

Carey cleared his throat. 'Are you all sure you want to proceed with the will today? With these recent develop-ments, after all—'

Helen looked at Charles in indecision.

He reached across and briefly squeezed her hand. 'I don't want to push anyone here, but I think we're all under a bit of strain about this. My feeling is that it's better to get it all over with and then get back to normal life as quickly as we can.' He turned to Jon. 'Agreed?'

Jon did not need to consider his response. Poor old Charles! Any man who was about to be cut off without a shilling'd want to get it over as soon as possible. Let's do it then, if that's what he wants. He nodded. 'Agreed.'

Carey picked up the document lying on the table in front of him and began to read. 'This is the last will and testament of Phillip John Koenig—'

'Sorry to interrupt.'

It was Jon, passing a hand over his face and shaking

his head. 'But we've all had a lousy day. Can you cut out the legal bits and just give us the gist of it?'

Carey pursed his lips. 'It's customary to read the will in its entirety, especially when the estate is as big as your late father's. And he made several wills, you know, in the course of various changes in his life and fortunes. Only recently did we get this final version of his will delivered to us at the bank, though we knew he was reconsidering his whole business situation following some – er, rather disappointing business indicators for Keonig Cattle and Koenig Holdings – he'd rung several times to discuss these with me. But the will we have today certainly represents his most recent considerations, indeed he returned it to me by special messenger only last week. But since you ask . . .'

He resettled himself in his chair and stared at the will. 'In brief, to his brother Charles is left the business control of Koenig Holdings. To his widow Helen is left an equal share of all the liquid assets in the form of cash and securities, along with her son Jon, whatever those sums shall be at the time of his death. To Helen Koenig and Charles Koenig he also leaves an income for life from the revenues and increments of Koenig Cattle and Koenig Holdings.'

He took a breath. 'To Ben Nichols, in recognition of his faithful service to the Koenig business, is left a share allocation of 10 per cent in Koenig Holdings, plus the sum of 500,000 dollars.'

Ben shook his head and buried his head in his hands.

'To the housekeeper Rose for her faithful service to Phillip Koenig, the sum of 100,000 dollars.'

'And finally—'

He might as well have said 'End neeow, the moment you've all been waiting for!' like a game show host, thought Jon hazily. And all he's got to do is just wind it up the way we all know it's got to go. But what's wrong with him?

Jon paused in sudden anxiety. Hesitating, sweating, you'd have thought the bank manager had come here to foreclose on the mortgage! Carey looked like a man who had bad news to give, not the word he now felt he had been waiting for all his life. 'Get on with it, man!' Jon commanded roughly. 'We all know what Dad intended. But it isn't mine till you say it's mine! *Get on with it!*'

'And finally—' Carey swallowed and mopped his head again as he spoke, 'to my son Jon I leave the station Koenigshaus fully and unreservedly in his sole possession and ownership, trusting that he will continue to honour the traditions of ownership established on this land.'

The King is dead.

Long live the King.

In that moment Jon felt he grew into the space that had been prepared for him all his life. He was the rightful owner of Koenigshaus, he knew it. He would give it his whole life, his life's blood. He would not fail.

'Congratulations, mate!'

Alex was beside him pumping his hand, overflowing with good wishes, his face alive with delight. 'Good luck to you, it's fantastic—'

Jon grinned broadly. 'Thanks!'

But Carey was still speaking. 'Gentlemen, gentlemen please, the will is not finished.'

A ragged cloud of fear eclipsed the sun of Helen's content. All eyes turned to Carey.

Sweating heavily, the bank manager plunged headlong and gabbling into the silence that followed. 'Mr Koenig sent for his will the last time to make a number of changes he had not previously incorporated before – in the event of the pre-decease of Mrs Koenig, of Mr Charles Koenig, or of the death of Mr Jon Koenig if and before he comes to marry and produce offspring who would themselves inherit in their turn. His mind was turning towards the subject of death, in other words, and the rights of the survivors. And perhaps that explains it.'

By the time he reached the end of his sentence, Carey's voice had risen to an unnatural squeak. Helen looked at Charles, but he was concentrating on Carey as if he held the secret of the universe. Across the table Alex seemed to have picked up on the tension and was staring at the bank manager with alarm and suspicion.

But in Jon's eyes was a hurricane of distress growing darker every second. *He knows!* Helen's mind shrieked, he's seen something bad coming, something terrible, worse than anything so far.

Carey was prattling almost hysterically now. 'And with these new dispensations Mr Koenig inserted a new codicil to his will. It is dated last week and hence represents his latest intention with regard to his estate. In the event of the discovery of his son Alexander John Koenig alive and well, this supersedes all previous testamentary dispositions. In this event, the said Alexander becomes sole heir of Koenig Cattle, Koenig Holdings, Koenigshaus cattle station and all cash, securities, holdings and investments whatsoever.'

Chapter 12

'Mr Alexander Koenig is therefore the owner of Koenigs-haus cattle station, Koenig Holdings and all Koenig assets whatsoever.'

The voice of the bank manager died away into the frozen silence. In a kaleidoscope of nightmare impressions Helen took in the white, set face of Alex: Charles, rigid with shock: Ben's twitching mouth: Geena's huge frightened eyes and the sweating Carey mopping his brow.

She could not bear to think what this would mean for Jon. But she forced herself to lift her eyes, turn her head, and look at her son. His face was blank but naked too, stripped of all defences along with all feeling. He rose to his feet.

'Well, that's it, then!' he announced with a forced grin. Stiffly he advanced on Alex, tensely watching his approach, and stuck out his hand. 'That's it, then,' he announced again, vigorously shaking hands. Then, moving like a man in a dream, he turned and left the dining room.

Helen was the first to speak, but had to try two or three times to find her voice. 'Jon and I – we'll – we'll be out of here as soon as we can. When – when would you like us to leave?'

Running madly through all the rooms of the ground floor, out of the front and around the house, Geena found Jon at last in the stable yard. Fumbling the bit into Kaiser's snarling yellow mouth, he had bridled the great stallion and was leading him, plunging and rearing, out of his box. 'Jon!' she cried.

He did not seem to hear. She ran towards him at full pelt as he vaulted into the saddle and turned the horse away from the buildings in the direction of the sun-scorched bush. 'Jon!'

He reined up mechanically, working to settle the over-excited horse. All her love and sympathy choked in her throat. 'Jon, I – I don't know what to say.'

'There's nothing to say.'

She clenched her fists. 'It's just so awful, that's all.'

'Awful for me. Awful for Mum. Not great for Charles. But not awful for the new son and heir.'

As if mimicking his rider's mood, Kaiser gave a sudden savage buck and shouldered frighteningly towards the slight figure on the ground. Jon looked down at her with detachment. 'Gotta go. This fella's getting restless.'

She looked up at him and tried to put her heart into her eyes. 'I'm so sorry.'

'Yah, well—' He stared unseeingly at the horizon. 'Thanks.'

Forcing herself not to be afraid, she came as close as she dared to the huge animal and put her hand up to the reins. 'Look, if there's anything I can do—'

He did not answer. The smell of the wild, sweating horse enfolded her and she wanted to be sick. She knew she was losing him. 'Where are you going?'

He laughed, unnerving her still more. 'Still got those cattle to muster. And I don't think Alex is going to get the hang of how to do things straight off, just 'cos they're his cattle now.'

'When will you be back?'

'Can't say really.'

'When you come back—' she drew a deep breath – 'come and find me?'

'Oh Geena—' His eyes, huge as moons in his bleak face, seemed to see her for the first time. 'What can you do? What can anyone do?'

'He said he'd be happy to give Jon a job, keep him on, we could both live here as long as we want, we mustn't feel any pressure to leave!'

'Oh Helen!' With difficulty Charles resisted the impulse to brush back the heavy fall of silver-gold hair from the tear-stained face beside him, and pushed back his chair to a safer distance from the dining-room table. 'Can you really see Jon as Alex's manager, playing second fiddle all his life? To a city boy, a total stranger? And on land he believes is his own?'

Helen shook her head mutinously. 'Alex wants to do the right thing! He was shocked as we all were when Carey broke the news.'

'OK, he looked shocked at first, I'll give you that.' In a cold fury Charles stared through the dining-room window towards the office building where Alex, Ben and the bank manager were just mounting the steps. 'Didn't take the bugger long to get into the saddle, though.'

Helen leaned forward. 'Charles—'

She mastered the catch in her voice and tried again. 'Charles, it's not Alex's fault that this has happened. Phillip obviously felt so guilty that he'd driven his son away by marrying me that he felt compelled to make that gesture, even though he must have known his chances of ever seeing Alex again were slim.'

He was listening, she knew. She could see his hand tensed in anger on the table between them, and for a wild second longed to stroke it, kiss it, lift it to her breast.

She tried to steady her voice. 'And whatever else it means, that codicil he made shows he never gave up hope that Alex was alive. He just didn't live to see it, that's all.' She was crying openly now. 'I suppose it's fair in a way. But if only Jon didn't have to pay for it!'

'Helen—' He leaned towards her urgently. 'Look, it may turn out better than it seems right now.'

She shook her head hopelessly, trying to crush away the tears with the back of her hand. 'How can it?' It was hardly even a question.

He passed a hand over his eyes and tried to will her to feel better. 'Like this, maybe. Alex is no cattle-man, he admitted it straight off, you heard him. "I'm a city boy, what am I going to do with a 3000-acre station?" – that was his first reaction. I don't know what kind of business-man he is yet either, but you know I had some buyers lined up when I was trying to persuade Phillip to sell Koenigshaus.' He paused, and his eyes raked her face. 'With me so far?'

'So far. Go on.'

'OK, try this. If I can persuade Alex to sell, I'm pretty sure I can make a good deal for him, get a good price. Then when we free up the cash from the sale of this place and get Koenig Holdings up and running again, I can tell Alex that he ought to do something for Jon, considering what the lad's lost. At the least, I could try to get him to invest in a new station that would be Jon's alone – it'd be much smaller than Koenigshaus, but probably more profitable too. And it'd be somewhere where Jon could start up slowly as his own boss and, over the years, pay back the investment if he wants and make it his own.'

There.

Charles sat back and congratulated himself. Not bad for an on-the-spot analysis and instant business plan. *And surely she'll see that I'm doing it for her?*

But if he expected Helen to be grateful, he could not have been more wrong. 'Sell Koenigshaus?' she blazed with sudden fire. 'Straight after his father's death? – when he couldn't stand the thought of it even when Phillip was alive – and in his present state of mind – what the hell do you think that would do to Jon?'

'Helen, for God's sake! Jon's a man now, he's not a child! You can't protect him all his life, and you can't protect him from this!'

'*Tell me about it!*'

She was raging with fury. Jon betrayed and dispossessed, Charles the one man who might have been on her side, and all he could do was bleat about the bloody business and selling Koenigshaus! 'Go on, tell me! Is this the speech that begins "This place is bleeding us white, the station eats money, we're going under, we've got no option but to sell"? If that's the best you can do, Jon's better off with Alex. At least his brother cares what happens to him, he wants to look after him, do the decent thing!'

'No, I've got another one, if you'll only calm down enough to listen to me.' He was white with anger too, and they confronted each other in naked aggression like enemies. 'This one's by way of a Bible reading, there's some great lessons for modern life in the Good Book. Ask yourself, Helen, what d'you know about the return of the Prodigal Son? What exactly do they know for sure about the wandering boy in the family, when he shows up again after all those years?'

Her eyes flared the question before she spoke. '*What do you mean?*'

He laughed. 'Oh, I'm not questioning the fact that this is the lad himself, Koenigshaus's very own Prodigal Son. I practically grew up with Alex, remember? Coming on the scene so long after Phillip, I was more the kid's big brother than his uncle. I can still remember Alex as if it were yesterday.' From his veiled eyes she could see that Charles was looking straight back into a past that he did not seem to remember with any affection at all. 'I remember him then, and I'm remembering a few things now. He hasn't changed.'

What was he on about? 'Such as?' she challenged.

'Such as.' He rose and leaning forward pulled her to her feet, drawing her firmly towards the window. 'That, for instance. He always liked to talk big, spin a good tale.'

'What?' Around the front of the house, scattered along the drive and around the parking circle which formed the centre of the homestead was a handful of cars, the station 4WD, Jon's pick-up and trail-rider, the bank-manager's runabout and a few other vehicles which must belong to the last of the visitors and guests at the wake. 'What am I supposed to be looking at?'

'That.' Charles pointed a cold finger.

She stared at the dun-coloured, totally ordinary two-door saloon he was indicating with such scorn. 'What about it?'

'It's the car Alex came in.'

She turned to read his face. 'So?'

'So is this the car of a great businessman – on his way to his first million, didn't he say?'

'Charles, it's a car!' she exploded. 'How many Mercedes or Porsches d'you think they have for hire round here?'

'That's not the point.' His smile was very bleak. 'Time for Bible class. Why did the Prodigal Son go home?

'Why?' She could have hit him. 'To see his father! Because he knew his father would want to see him before he died! His family, his mother—'

'Uhuh.' He shook his head maddeningly from side to side. 'Selfish bastard like that, he didn't go to all that trouble to make his old dad happy – still less any grieving little step-mum! He went home because he ran out of money. And because he knew they'd be a soft touch.'

She was listening hard now. He pushed on relentlessly. 'Don't forget what Confucius or some other clever dick said: home is the place where, when you have to go there, *they have to take you in.*'

102

He paused to give her the chance to speak, but she couldn't think of a way to interrupt the relentless flow. 'Oh, I admit young Alex got lucky with his homecoming,' he went on, his voice heavy with sarcasm. 'If he came on the chance of getting his hand in the cookie-jar, he couldn't have dreamed he was about to drop into the whole pot! But listen, Helen.'

He grasped her by the arms and turned her to the window again so that he could look into her eyes. 'Let me ask you something else now. Suppose Phillip hadn't changed his will, and Jon had come into the whole thing, cash, Koenigshaus and all. If Alex had shown up now, at Phillip's funeral and touchingly confessed that his great business wasn't doing too well and in fact he was on his well-heeled uppers, wouldn't you and Jon have felt sorry for him? And wouldn't you have felt a responsibility to take care of the poor lost and abandoned laddie, pretty comfortably as well?'

Helen held his gaze defiantly, 'Yes!' she shouted. 'Yes, we would! We would have looked after him! And generously as well!'

Inside the office building there was a thoughtful silence. Ben, grey-faced and badly rattled, hastened as ever to fill it with a laboured summing-up. 'So there it is, that's the story of Koenigshaus. The main group, Koenig Holdings, needs capital, the station has drained us of every red cent. Even in the best of recent years, it's only been making about one per cent on capital. Lately, it's like an open vein.'

Alex looked up reflectively. 'Heavy borrowings?'

Ben nodded. 'Every day that passes the interest bill gets heavier.'

Alex drew a breath. 'And the meter's still ticking?'

'Louder and louder.'

Carey nodded importantly. 'I can confirm that, Mr

Koenig. The bank here is inevitably party to the station's capital flow, and my area manager has been on to Mr Koenig—' he corrected himself hastily, 'Mr *Phillip* Koenig – for years to sort things out, or sell.'

'Sell?'

Maybe he'd make a good boss, Ben thought grudgingly. He really looked as if he was listening, giving you his full attention when he fixed his eyes on you and asked questions like that. Amid all the misery of recent events, the thought surprised him with its sudden beam of hope. 'Yeah, sell!' he said strongly, encouraged by a chance to sort the whole thing out at last. Maybe at last he could be free, they could all be free . . .

'OK.' Alex shifted his weight, resettled himself on his perch on Phillip's desk, and nodded warmly at him to continue.

'Charles was looking around for a sale before we came out here from Sydney,' Ben went on. 'There was a lot of interest, but the front runner was a Japanese business consortium—'

Alex's eyes gleamed. 'And they've got the cash?'

Ben laughed awkwardly. 'She has.'

'She?' Business women were not large in Carey's world. 'Who are we talking about?'

'Mrs Matsuda.'

They had not heard him come in. The folder of sale offers that he had prepared for Phillip dangling from his hand, Charles stood in the open door surveying the little group of men with an impenetrable look on his face.

Alex smiled widely and opened his arms. 'Just in time, Charles, come in! Now who is this lady you've lined up for us?'

Charles sauntered in, perched himself on the desk opposite Alex, and took him time before replying. 'Head of a consortium founded by her late husband. Tokyo-based, but with world interests in a chain of fast-food outlets. Burger bars. Very big in America.'

Alex still wore his look of bright-eyed anticipation. 'So why does she want to sink a few of her millions in Koenigshaus?'

Ben grimaced. 'Hamburgers.'

'What?'

Charles stared sardonically at the puzzled Alex. Calls himself a businessman and can't figure out something as easy as that? 'A chance for what we call "vertical integration" around here. Means she controls the entire product chain from hoof to hamburger.'

'Cuts out the middleman.' Carey was not going to be left out of the big-business-talk. He nodded knowledgeably. 'Shaves costs to the bone.'

'And steers, I guess!' Alex laughed infectiously. 'What does she do with the bones?'

You had to hand it to him, he'd got a sense of humour, thought Carey admiringly. There was more about him than Jon, no doubt about that. And it'd be better for the station – or for the company, depending on what he decided to do – to have a man of his age in charge than a lad in his twenties like Jon. Well, who'd have thought it? Maybe that old devil Phillip had got it right after all!

Suddenly Carey was aware that the dark eyes of the new owner were now fastened reflectively on him. 'May I ask your advice, Mr Carey?' Alex said politely.

'Why yes, certainly!'

'What are my legal responsibilities to the Koenig estate?' He flashed a hesitant smile. 'I don't want to rush anything, and I hope I didn't offend any of you guys, laughing like that just now. I haven't forgotten we only just put Dad into the ground. But I kinda feel there's going to be a fair bit of tension till everything's sorted out. So I just want everyone to know where they stand and see that I'm not here to do anyone out of anything they're entitled to.'

Even Carey noticed that the atmosphere had picked up, that the two men beside him were staring at Alex with added interest. He rose to his moment. 'You must act with all due concern at all times in the interest of the estate,' he began pompously. 'But the situation is pretty much as the late Mr Koenig outlined it in his will.'

Alex leaned forward attentively. 'Yes?'

'Oh yes,' said Carey firmly. 'And once the will has been proved, as I have no reason to doubt that it will be, my duties as executor are over. At that point you become the sole proprietor of all that Phillip Koenig called his. And with me out of the way,' he laughed unnecessarily, 'you're the king of the Kingdom.'

'And that means—?'

He's grinning like a dingo, Charles thought violently. The bugger's eyes are shining! As well they might! Suddenly he lost patience with the whole charade. 'And that means,' he said with taunting emphasis as if talking to a half-wit, 'that – you – can – do – anything – you – bloody – well – like!'

Chapter 13

PHILLIP JOHANN KOENIG, HEAD BOY, ROCK-HAMPTON COLLEGE, 1948–49

Seated at the desk across from Phillip's, Ben lifted his eyes blindly from the flickering VDU and found himself staring at Phillip's school photograph with something like real hatred. What a fool he'd been to think that with Alex at the helm, things might somehow work out!

He might have known that Charles wouldn't take this lying down. He'd been under the cosh of the old man for too long to put his head willingly into a fresh noose now. He may have got used to the idea that he'd have to step aside for Jon. But for the Man from Nowhere, an unknown quantity, with the business in crisis and everything he'd worked for all his life hanging by a thread? No way.

Not after all they'd been through to get this far—

And Alex was ready to give battle if he had to, there was no doubt about that. Smiles or no, he was no pushover. Oh, he'd been pleasant enough, and when Charles threw down the gauntlet, he'd gone out of his way to keep the peace and turn the other cheek. But it could never last.

Groaning, he buried his head in his hands and gave himself up to his confusion and distress.

Bloody Phillip!

Leading them all up the garden path with his constant

talk of 'the son and heir', giving them all the promise that Jon would inherit Koenigshaus whenever the time came, and now this!

OK, so it might have been just a sop to his evil bloody conscience, and quite right too, because marrying Helen wasn't the half of if! Ben reflected savagely. Twenty-five years was a long time. But he could still remember plenty of occasions long before Helen came on the scene, when Phillip had treated Alex as a kid not like a son of his at all, but like some drunken, thieving roustabout he'd found on his property and was determined to teach a lesson. Yeah, Alex didn't only run away because his dad decided to marry again with less-than-decent haste!

But even if Phillip was trying to salve his conscience by including Alex in the will, he must have known there was at least a chance that the lost boy might turn up. They'd never found a body, after all. And the old bastard could reverse everything he'd put in his will without a second's hesitation, without a thought of what it would do to Jon, the kid he'd never brought up to be anything except a cattleman, the kid he'd never even allowed to go to his own old school? Jesus Christ, he deserved to die.

Jon – Ben's thoughts took a more painful turn.

Whatever evil demon had made him entertain even for a second the idea that a future might have been unfolding there for Geena? With a lone father's unerring love, Ben had seen instantly that Geena cared for Jon. And though like any father, something inside him died when he thought of having to give up his first place in her heart to another man, still he knew that young Jon was the only one fit to come within a mile of the brave, beautiful, girl-woman who was his daughter.

And he'd allowed himself to hope that it could ever be? More, that it ought to be? As if it ever would!

Bloody Koenigs!

They were all the bloody same, why should Jon have been any different? All they ever thought about was themselves and Koenigshaus, and everything to do with them went wrong! He should have got off this station as soon as he was old enough to walk, left the whole bloody pack of them behind! Instead of giving his life to hold their hands and wipe their arses, letting them fool around with the best thing he ever had, and then find himself condemned to go on doing it till the day he died!

Christ, it was hopeless, even with the old devil himself out of the way. No matter what he tried, there was no escape now, nowhere to turn. Charles and Alex and Jon were going to scrap it out, step by step, and good old Ben was going to be playing pig in the middle, so that even when he tried to break out, whatever he did went wrong.

A light sound outside the office drew him sharply round. He turned to see Geena flitting rapidly up the steps with her bird-like, skimming glide. He punched the dead screen alive again before him, and pretended to be immersed in the tables of figures flashing up. Another pace and she was through the door. 'Dad?'

Her arms were round his neck and he thought he detected a dampness on the cheek next to his. 'Yes, love?' he said huskily. 'Seen Jon?'

She drew back sharply. 'Yeah,' she said evenly as she slid round to sit on the side of the desk before him. 'He's gone off mustering. To lick his wounds.'

To his surprise he found himself defending the man he had been cursing only seconds before. 'Well, when you think what the old bastard Phillip has done to him—'

'Oh, I know.' He looked up, distressed by her tone. Her soft, bush-baby eyes were glistening with tears. 'Oh Dad, what are we going to do?'

He laughed mirthlessly. 'Short of bumping off Alex, there's nothing we can do. And even then, given our luck, he'd probably prove to have a wife and fifteen children in Sydney.'

He looked up at the little figure silhouetted against the

light. 'Best thing we can do is get out of here back to Sydney as quick as we can. We only planned on being here for the weekend anyway, and we're already overdue. There isn't much more for me to do, the paperwork's pretty much under control. Well—' he shifted uneasily. 'Just a few things I need to – double-check. And Alex has asked me to get him into the computer system, teach him the ins and outs so that he knows where everything's at. But that won't take long. We'll get the chopper out of here as soon as I've finished. Unless you want me to ask Alex to fix a lift to get you back before?'

'No, Dad.'

'That's settled then.' He gazed into space. 'Where are we today, Wednesday? Another good day should see the whole thing through. With a bit of luck, we'll have our feet under our own table by Friday night. That suit you?'

'No, Dad.' She slipped lightly off the table and moved away from him to stand by the window, looking out. 'I said "no" the first time, and I meant it.' She turned to face him, her eyes determined and her chin set. I'm not leaving here until I've sorted this thing out with Jon – seen him, talked to him properly and not while he's still in shock.'

Sorted out what thing with Jon? he wanted to shout. He instinctively knew that Jon would never offer Geena marriage now, now he was dispossessed, disgraced, lower than a hired hand on what was once his terrain. And Ben desperately feared that Jon would see no reason to resist taking advantage of the consolation offered him by a sympathetic young girl . . .

He could still remember the advice given to him when he fell in love with her mother. *Stone the crows, mate, if you want 'em, you fuck 'em, you don't marry 'em, what are you, a gin-burglar, a gin-jockey?* Someone had probably already said that to Jon. And if he was like most men, he wouldn't need to have it said . . .

He tried to cover his anger with a bout of forced coughing. But Geena was not looking at him. 'It's not only Jon,' she said slowly. 'You know I've been going down to the Camp, getting to know Mum's people. It's an amazing place.'

'They're amazing people.' Phillip's gibes came back to him from the first morning that Geena's visit to the Aboriginals' Camp was ever proposed. 'Done any dancing?'

She nodded. 'Right from the first day. A few of them were asking what I did, so I started to show them. Then they started sharing some of their dance moves with me, and it's gone from there. I'm really learning from them.'

'And them from you, I daresay.'

'Yeah.' She frowned. 'It's the first time I've played that part, being the one in charge. I rather like it. And working down there'll give me something to do until Jon gets back, and I can talk to him.'

'Geena, love—'

She shook her head, dismissing the appeal in his voice out of hand. 'Dad, I'm going to do it. I don't care how long I have to wait. I know they're staying out tonight, they still haven't got the cattle away from the watering-hole, they're all still where they were after Phillip died and everyone had to come back to the house. I don't know how long the muster will take either, it could be days. But I'm not going back to Sydney till I've spoken to him properly – if only once.'

Ben felt a helpless sense of things taking a predestined course, slipping out of his control into dark and dangerous paths. He could have wept with fear. 'I just – don't want you hurt.' Christ, he had to do better than this! He pulled himself together with a great effort. 'I guess you owe it to him.'

'No, Dad.' Suddenly out flashed her first smile of the day. 'I owe it to myself.'

So far, so good!

Re-entering the cool of the house from the stinging sun outside, Alex forced himself to contain his excitement. God, he was really getting into the swing of this! After the meeting in the office, first of all he'd escorted that pompous pillock of a bank manager, Carey, or whatever his name was, with every courtesy to his prickmobile of a car, and shown absolute fascination with the little dickhead's idea of coming into town to have lunch with him one day soon.

Bloody good going!

Then he'd returned to a truculent Charles and made him a happy chappy in one move by agreeing that the Japanese lady Mrs Moneybags should be 'coptered in immediately, if not sooner, to see about the sale. Finally he'd cheered up that pathetic old wet fart Ben with a few gracious bromides about good work and loyal service and left him to carry on with the donkey-work. So now he could fix himself a drink, look around, and simply take his ease, lord of all he surveyed!

Fix himself a drink? As he strode down the wide shadowed hallway to the kitchen beyond, Alex laughed aloud. Old habits die hard, boy, he scolded himself. Remember you're not a nobody any longer! When you're not just a Koenig *but* the Koenig, the lord and master, you don't keep dogs and bark yourself! 'Rose,' he began, pushing open the door, 'how about—?'

But the woman listlessly scouring the work surface with unconvincing sweeps of a cloth was not Rose. Alex's eyes narrowed as he took in the slim hips and skinny legs of the figure before him – from the back she could be a boy or just a kid. But when she turned – Jeez – from the front there was no mistaking that this was what he was looking for. The familiar excitement began to prick at him, and he smiled in anticipation. 'It's Ellie, isn't it?' he said easily, moving in towards her.

Her answering giggle began as a squeak and cascaded

down the scale to a low delighted gurgle. She stared at him with teasing, knowing eyes. 'Mister Alex, you playing games? Don't say you forgotten me?'

The ripe breasts moving freely, the pout was deliberately provocative, any man could see that. But even if it was obvious, it was sexy too, he could feel the old black magic starting to work. 'Forget you?' he grinned. 'Impossible! But you aren't the Ellie I remember, you're far to young.'

Amazing how that line never failed. Look at her now, he thought with amusement, bloody whimpering with delight. A few more like that and she'll come in your hand. 'I was a li'l, li'l girl when you went, Mister Alex,' she giggled, 'but I been here since, I doan forget you!'

'Well, there you go.' He pretended to cast his mind back as his eyes raked her body. She stared at him hotly. 'And you doan forget me!'

He frowned in mock-puzzlement. 'Yeah, I can remember a terrible skinny little ratbag kid, ugly as sin, who hung around the kitchen. Not you, surely, Ellie? You turned into this?' He laughed again, low in his throat. 'You sure have changed, Ellie. You didn't look like that then.'

Ellie was not laughing any longer. 'Well, I wouldn't, wouldn't I?' she whispered. She took a step or two nearer and challenged him with an upwards, sideways stare. 'Times change, Mister Alex. I'm a woman now.'

Inside the kitchen the late afternoon air was very still. The tension between them grew till it seemed to hum, to throb like a piano wire stretched from her taut expectant body to his smiling, waiting form.

Alex stood quietly, his whole body still. Like every natural Casanova he never had to do all the work. From the age of sixteen, when he had first awoken to his own attraction, he had revelled in the sense of mastery it gave him to know that women wanted him. Other men wept into their beer and talked endlessly of 'pulling the birds'. It always made him laugh. If you knew what you were doing, you didn't have to 'pull', you didn't even have to raise a hand.

Well, maybe one. Through the flimsy fabric of her cheap blouse he could see her nipples pricking to attention under his amused gaze. Following his stare, she dropped her eyes, but did not move away.

'So, Ellie?' he said teasingly, moving a pace nearer. She backed away, only to come up against the work-top she had been cleaning. She craned back from him, suggesting reluctance but in reality throwing up her breasts almost under his nose. He moved in on her.

As he did so she threw back her head and gave a long, slow, seductive moan, half pleasure and half fear. 'My husband not gonna like this!'

He smiled back. 'I'm not doing it to your husband. You're old enough to please yourself. I've got a feeling I know what you like.' As if all women didn't like the same thing when it came down to it, he grinned to himself.

She pouted. 'You doan' understand! He's violent, he's very jealous!'

He placed the tip of one finger to the side of her cheek and began to trace the line of her jaw along to the cleft of her chin, running it on down her neck towards the valley between her breasts. 'Well then,' he said. 'Let's give him something to be jealous about, shall we?'

With tantalising slowness he reached out and began to undo the top button of her shirt. The second his hand touched her body she responded like a bush fire, instantly surging to a level it took some women hours to reach. He could see the tips of her breasts, already erect, hardening for his caress.

One button – and the next—

Her eyes were opening and closing, she was breathing hoarsely. A small clutching brown-black hand reached out for his trouser belt and he lightly swung his lower body out of harm's way. Can't have her here, he was thinking with the part of his brain that was always, always ice-cold even in the heat of any climax.

So where?

It's gonna be the perfect finale to the perfect day, he mused with cold glee, if the Wandering Son returns home, buries his dad, inherits the kingdom, collects the loot and to celebrate his triumph, rounds it all off by satisfying himself with one of the slave girls by way of *droit de seigneur*. Fantastic! And no more than he was entitled to – after all he'd been through, everything that had happened to get him this far . . .

So where?

'Ohhh – c'mon, ooohhh—'

Christ, he'd better get a move on, if she was already moaning in the aisles like this, rolling her eyes up and bubbling like a pot on the boil. 'Hey kid,' he began, 'Ellie—'

The door opened and Rose entered from the dining room, a fistful of silver clutched accusingly in her hand. 'You think this cutlery clean enough—?' she began aggressively. Then she took in the tableau before her and was instantly immobile, like an animal, watching and waiting to see which way the master moves.

Alex turned away. He did not spare a backward glance for Ellie, flushed and foolish-looking as she fumbled to do up her shirt. Nor did he look at Rose.

'I'm going up to my old room in the Tower now,' he said casually. 'I reckon I'll be moving back in there. You'd both better come and see to it, help get it fixed up when I've decided what's got to be done.'

He paused in the doorway, one hand resting on the side of the door. 'Oh, and when that's done – one of you can bring me a drink.' He paused. 'Ellie, it'd better be you.' He favoured Ellie with a blatant smile. 'Fetch us a whisky – and make it a double, eh?'

How had he ever thought this God-abandoned country beautiful? But before this, had he ever really thought at all?

Under a fading, pale-washed sky drained of all colour like his broken dreams, Jon surveyed the land around the water-hole and wished himself anywhere else on the face of the earth but here. Around the dull sheen of the still sheet of water stood the same clustering, whispering gums, behind reared the same impenetrable wall of primeval sandstone hallowed by the mystical Aboriginal communion of millions of years, overhead the last tern of the day ran for home in a flash of smoky white, crying her eternal sharp one-note lament as she fled down the path of night towards the first low, wistful star, and everything was as it had always been. But he had changed beyond reach of all these things.

However could Dad have disinherited him like this?

And it wasn't only him, it was Mum too, where would she live, what the hell was she going to do? God Almighty, she couldn't manage on her own, she'd never even had to sign a cheque!

How could Dad have done it?

Yet what else could he have done?

Alex existed. Sooner or later he'd have come back to his birth place. And probably better now if it had to happen, than in years to come when he'd have been fooling himself for years that he, Jon Koenig, was the boss of Koenigshaus.

No point in even thinking about it.

Just get through this muster like always, get the beasts sorted out and off on the road train and then he'd be able to decide what he was going to do with the rest of his life.

Except for one thing.

One thing he didn't have to think about any more, that decision had already been taken for him.

His face set like a mask, Jon dismounted from his horse in the falling dusk and stood for a moment cradling the gelding's huge bony head and pulling at the rough woolly ears. Except for Geena.

Geena.

The thought, the very word, was a sharp and special pain quite distinct from the rest of his misery. When he had dreamed of making her his wife, he had dreamed as the incoming master of Koenigshaus, a man with a future as big as the Northern Territory and hopes as high as the stars.

And now?

Now he was less than a hired hand – because he didn't even know how to hire himself out, how to work for any other man, *how not to be boss*. And if I'm not the boss here, what am I? his inner voice cried out.

Suddenly out of nowhere Dusty was drifting towards him, distracting his staring gaze from the new-risen moon.

'Hey, boss,' he said gently, as if he had read Jon's mind.

He probably has, thought Jon distractedly. Well, there's no secrets from Dusty – none I'd want to keep anyway.

On his other side Frank appeared and silently relieved him of his horse's reins, leading the weary animal away to a well-earned rest in the nearby corral. They're looking after me like I'm sick, like I'm not all there, he noted with detachment. Well, maybe they're right.

'Grub's coming up, boss.'

With a gentle push Dusty shepherded him towards the camp fire where a light-handed Slim was coaxing the logs into flame. 'Beer?'

Thankfully Jon accepted the proferred can and tearing the ring off, downed the contents in a few savage gulps.

Without comment Dusty passed him another, then came to squat down by his side.

A light evening mist was swirling round the base of Devil Rock like the incoming tide of a phantom sea. From here the cave in the weather-beaten face that had been his boyhood den and hiding-place was nowhere to be seen. Farther off, Henry was overseeing the last manoeuvres involved in settling the sleepy, reluctant cattle and the rest of the men were going through the familiar motions at the end of the day. The air was full of the friendly presence of the lowing, scuffling beasts, and their sweet rich smell reached him on gusts of warm air wafted by the light evening breeze. A tiny corner of his injured soul revived. He hugged his knees like a boy as he spoke.

'Dad loved this place, you know. If he could have chosen anywhere, I think he'd have wanted to die here.'

Dusty absorbed this into himself with his usual ready acceptance, feeling no need to answer.

'We used to come here a lot when I was a kid, camp out here in the gorge, sleep in the cave, just the two of us.' He brooded for a moment. 'He was at his best out here, close to nature.'

Dusty nodded. 'All men best out here.'

Jon found himself suddenly fighting back tears. 'I just can't believe he's really gone. Where is he now, Dusty? Why did he have to die?'

Dusty considered his answer. He had asked his own spirits the same questions and was still asking. A deep unease with the second part of Jon's demand made him concentrate firmly on the first.

'Boss gone home,' he said simply. 'Back to the All-Father. He don't die, he just gone into another room. We'll meet him there again one day. An' he'll be right, just like he always was.'

Just like he was before . . .

Suddenly Jon saw Phillip as he had first remembered him, a hard man always, and one whose technique as a father owed more to the lion with his cub than any more sensitive human model. But still a man full of gaiety and life and strength, a man who was, within the limits of his character, always reliable, always predictable, always pretty fair.

He sat up, startled.

When had Dad started to behave so oddly, succumbing to those unexpected rages and equally wild flights of humour, tipping over so often into cruelty as he had done with Charles, with Mum, with Ben, with Geena—?

Geena.

There it was again, the stabbing memory like a blow crushing his chest, bursting his ribs. This is what a heart attack must be like, he thought. He threw back his head and tried to breathe deeply and calmly in the fresh night air. Ahead of them Henry was approaching the camp fire, behind him trailed the other men in straggling ones and twos.

With a sudden revulsion he knew that he could not handle their company tonight, the rituals of beer and cigarettes, the routine grumbling about the cattle, the talk about women. He jumped to his feet.

'Listen, mate, I'm not hungry,' he announced abruptly. 'Tell the boys not to take it the wrong way but I'm going to do dad's old trick tonight. I'll make my bed over there, on my own.' He gestured awkwardly at his friend. 'I'm not much company tonight anyway.'

Dusty nodded. 'That's fine, boss.' His smile said, no need to explain. He knew it was the right thing for Jon tonight.

He knew too he did not need to issue any warnings: look after yourself, think of the danger, watch out for those bloody King Browns. Dusty had already asked his spirits to look after Jon and he felt in his heart that whatever had killed Phillip had no designs on Jon. Each man had his time, and Jon's was not now, that was another thing he felt as surely as he knew there was a Great Rainbow Snake in the sky. He cocked his head on one side interrogatively. 'Need any help?'

'No, I'll be all right.'

Jon half-lifted a hand in farewell and moved off. Grabbing a bedroll from the pile where they had been off-loaded from the pack-horse, he set off up the swell of the valley towards the sheltering bowl of the ridge which gave access to the water-hole. Striking off the track about half way up, he found a small hollow between two large rocks just big enough to accommodate a man's body, and running gently downhill at just the right angle for sleeping in.

He could not be sure, of course, in the glimmering dark. But as he made his preparations and bedded himself down for the night, he felt a strange confidence that he had in fact found the spot where his father had passed his last night on earth, and the thought comforted him.

He lay awake for a long time, sometimes grieving in pain so fierce that all he could do was lie still and wait for it to pass, sometimes almost trance-like in quiescence like a child waiting to be born. What was it Slim had said about the spirit children living in the water-hole, dwelling there till their time came and they could come to life, join us in the world? He stared up at the great frame of the Southern Cross and Milky Way beyond blazing with white fire. Maybe something is waiting to come to life here, even in this place of death . . .

At last he slept, though he passed in and out of his strange drowsiness so often that he could not have said which moment he was asleep and which awake. As the night grew colder his sleep became more troubled, and he knew he was sliding in and out of dreams, unable either to sleep properly or to wake himself up.

Now he felt the grey and swirling mist of the early evening washing across his brain, blanking out his mind's eye so that his gaze could not pierce the all-blanketing dream-fog. Clouds washed away the moon, and still the mists drifted, thicker and ever thicker, across the rocky broken ground. Yet in and out of the fog flickered a shimmering, shifting pattern of little dancing lights, pin-points of brightness in a vague floating world . . .

And suddenly it was gone, as curtains sweep away to the side of the stage when a play begins. He saw himself lying on the ground, a tall, strong body huddled in a bedroll, face muffled against the cold. A pale light – the moon? – bathed the still figure as it slept in blissful peace.

Across the valley the same light picked out a pale horse, a great white stallion. Not my horse, he thought with the slow puzzlement of the dreamer, not the old gelding I came on, but Kaiser. Why? Now he could see all the men asleep round the camp fire, each one rolled up in his blankets peacefully asleep. In the dream he counted them: Henry, James, Dusty, Slim, Frank, and Jon—

But if Jon was there, who was the sleeper here?

With nightmare slowness he turned to look again at the sleeping figure alone in the hollow of the rocks.

Alone, but not alone – now there was another figure behind him, a dark figure quietly approaching with all the stealth of the predator who has sighted its prey. Behind came two others, shrouded like the first in darkness. In the silence they moved like animals in a pack, and seemed to communicate without words. Then from among the three of them came three strange long writhing shapes, three hideous, hissing forms, making for the sleeper on the ground.

Just as his father had before him, Jon tried to scream his horror, tried to scream himself awake. But he could not break through the muffling veils of sleep, he could not rouse the still figure on the ground.

In the dream he lunged forward in a frantic attempt to reach the helpless sleeper, grasped his shoulder and shook it violently.

Slack-jointed, in the horror of slow motion, the sleeper rolled over like a puppet onto his back. As he did so two or three huge snakes reared up from beneath his body, struck out in venomous terror and then vanished into the bush.

The head of the sleeping man lolled back horribly into a shaft of moonlight. His mouth was open in a silent scream, his eyes open too looking his death in the face and staring through it to eternity. Now from behind his neck came the head of a snake, tongue flickering its attack, jaws open like a trap, razor-sharp fangs primed and ready for action. Hissing like a scorpion it sank its jaws in the sleeper's face, neck and chest, striking again and again, the puncture wounds with their springing carmine death-spots joining those where its fellow-killers had already done their work.

Behind in the swathing darkness he could see the human killers fading away into the night, yet still with their eyes fastened on him as if they could not bear to lose a moment's drama of their evil work. Jon's eyes were fixed on the ring-leader, the last to leave, the last to fade away. *I know that face*, Jon's dream-voice screamed, *I know who that is*!

He knew with the pure conviction that comes only in dreams that if he could just make the effort, try harder one last time to pierce the ghostly wraiths of night that drifted so tantalisingly to and fro, he could see what he was now compelled to know before all else in the world, the face of his father's murderer. But he awoke the same second with nothing but the knowledge that Phillip had not died by accident as they had all thought – that his father had been murdered, done to death in as cruel a way as his killers could devise – and that he, Jon, would have no peace now until he tracked them down and brought them to justice for this terrible crime.

Chapter 14

From a distance the 4WD was no more than a cloud of swirling dust. Slowing down as she approached the camp, Helen turned carefully through the archway of woven ghost gum boughs and nosed across the dusty compound to bring the vehicle to a halt near the largest of the huts. Resting her hands on the hot plastic of the driving wheel she stared out at the scene that met her eyes.

It was a timeless image that might have been life anywhere in Australia before the white settlers arrived. In the centre of the settlement a lofty eucalyptus towered over the clump of smaller trees sheltering the camp fire. Nearby nestled a cluster of small and some larger huts, and farther off other family dwellings of the kind Aboriginals had lived in since time immemorial. Only a clutch of battered vehicles and the well-stocked horse-yard beyond made any concession to the twentieth century.

In the centre of the compound a group of naked, laughing children was playing an age-old children's game. Silent and impassive, the elders of the tribe were watching from their vantage point around the camp fire. Sprawled in the shade, their backs against the huts, some of the younger men lounged about drinking beer, while around them a rabble of half-starved dogs foraged the dust for scraps. Only the women were working, making food, nursing crying babies or rescuing over-adventurous toddlers, hanging out washing or fetching it in, greeting each other with cheerful raucous cries like parakeets as they passed to and fro.

Helen killed the engine and turned to Geena. 'OK, then? All set here? What time shall I come back for you?'

Geena smiled. 'Oh, around six-ish, I should think – in time to get back before dinner and clean up?'

Clean up. Helen smiled in mute understanding. With Jon due in from the muster tonight, she had an idea that Geena wanted to do rather more than just *clean up* before she saw him again.

Well, never mind.

None of her business.

Yet if there could be anything between these two, Geena and Jon, how would she feel about it anyway? she suddenly wondered. She knew the answer before the question even took shape in her mind. If anything could make Jon happy again – *anything* – or anyone . . . let alone this sparky little thing with her lovely big, sad eyes . . .

Oh for God's sake, she chivvied herself, stop building castles in the air!

You can't protect him for ever and you can't protect him from this, Charles had said.

She'd hated him when he'd said it, but he was right. Jon was a man, not her little boy any longer, she couldn't live his life for him. Unconsciously she stiffened her back and squared her shoulders. So be it.

'OK, then,' she said as casually as she could. 'See you later. Have a good day.'

Geena watched the squat vehicle bumping away down the track and wished again that she'd had the courage to say something, anything! The more she was with Helen, the more she had a feeling that she was desperate for someone to talk to, somewhere to turn.

With a resolute lift of her chin she turned in towards the centre of the compound and approached the scampering, tumbling children playing in the sand. 'Hey, mate!' she said, ruffling one tangled little head. 'How y'going? OK?'

'OK, OK!' laughed the child. He raised his arms to her to be lifted up and she swept him up into a hug. 'Wow, what a big boy! You got bigger since yesterday! Soon you'll be a big man, big enough to get married! You want to marry me?'

The little boy giggled with delight, burying his head in her shoulder with tightly-squeezed eyes, then popping up again to play peep-bo. 'Marry me, marry me!' he chortled. 'Marry, marry, marry!'

There was a loud laugh from behind them. 'You don't wanta get married, girl like you with a life of your own! You carry on teachin' dance like you do here, you have a good life, and no kids!'

Geena turned to see Dora, one of the young women of the camp – about her own age she knew, or younger, but her broad face already looked five or ten years older than she really was. For already she was burdened with two or three babies and a husband whose charms, whatever they once were, had long since faded in her eyes. But Dora was always happy, she never seemed to resent her lot. 'You stick to dancing, you're good at that,' she chuckled, relieving Geena of the child. 'They're all ready for you up the compound, you find them there, give'em a good time!'

'Thanks, Dora!' Turning, she sped up the compound towards the group clustered higher up under the shade of a great ghost gum. Her heart lifted as it always did at the sight of the villagers she had already started to think of as 'her' dancers, a good mix of talent from some of the youngest boys and girls to several of the best performers in the tribe, large, burly men with strong, athletic bodies. At the centre of the little gathering squatted an old man playing the didgeridoo. Around him the others, old and young, were singing along in high, wailing tones or keeping the rhythm with drums and clap-sticks.

Geena paused on the edge of the group, drawn in as always by the unerring, eerie rhythms of the Aboriginal music and the power of the songs which seemed to speak to her very heart even though she could not understand any of the words. The sun was racing up the sky now and the thin plangent whine of the didgeridoo seemed to hang trembling like glass wind-chimes in the hot seething air.

'*Wija narani, jilalan, nagugari*,' sang the old man. '*Koppi unga, allinger yerra-ballama*.'

'You know what he's saying?'

It was Timbo, one of the first of the villagers to show an interest in her when she arrived. A handsome boy of eighteen or so with a natural dancer's build, short and well-muscled, he had also proved to be a mine of information on the traditional dances of his people, and had shown a friendly keenness to work with her, swapping dance moves and ideas.

Geena smiled and shook her head. 'Haven't got a clue.'

She listened carefully. The didgeridoo continued its hypnotic yawing up and down the scale, the primeval instrument sawing and sighing like a live thing as the player subtly laid back the rhythm off the beat.

Timbo cocked his head. 'It's the lament of a dying man,' he said softly, 'he's taking farewell of the one he loves. He says "Now I go, I go on a journey, I have to leave you, give me some water for the sun is setting . . ."' He broke off. 'It's an old story of the station, what happened here long, long ago.'

She was instantly intrigued. 'Tell me.'

He looked at her curiously. 'You like sad stories?'

'I don't know,' she said slowly. 'Until you tell me.'

The boy shifted his position, and looked out away across the compound at a distant line of trees, black, stark and dead-looking like an army of gallows silhouetted against the phosphorescent sky. High in the tree overhead an unseen bird coughed and cried like a baby, and with an answering chuckle the old musician coaxed a cascade of wild calls and sounds from the hollow centre of his didgeridoo in response.

Timbo glanced back at him detachedly as he went on. 'You know Kooris been here a thousand thousand years.'

It was not a question, but she hastened to offer him her answer. 'I know the archaeologists keep pushing the date of the first art-work here back and back – forty, fifty, sixty thousand years—'

As she spoke she shivered; she seemed to glimpse the aching beauty and silence of that old, unpeopled world.

'Yeah.' Timbo's eyes were coolly accusing now, but not of her. 'And they could live here because they had water – before the white man came along.'

'Along here? To Koenigshaus?'

'Here,' he affirmed. A bleak smile twisted his lips. 'But not called Koenigshaus then. Not till Johann.'

'Johann.' Jon's great-grandfather. She nodded. 'Go on.'

'He came here because there was water, good water at Devil Rock, plenty of it. But he came to make the land his, his and his son's. He came to make a kingdom. To him the water was like gold, not a thing to be shared.'

If she knew anything about her mother's people, it was that Aboriginals shared as freely as the first family in the Garden of Eden, with no thought of 'mine' and 'thine'.

Timbo's level voice flowed on. 'He took the water-hole, bring in his cattle, drive off the kangaroos and kill them to make room for his cows. Now the people had no water except what they find in little water-holes, and no food because no kangaroos. All starving. Then the oldest man had a dream, and in the dream Karora the Great Spirit who awoke from the first water-hole back in the Dream-time, told him that the cattle were only 'roos who had been born again in a new shape. They were all the 'roos the men had killed before, spirit 'roos come back as cattle to feed the starving people. And so the warriors could kill them so the people could eat.'

'Oh no!' She felt she knew the story, she could see the tragedy taking shape even as he spoke.

'So the young men went out and killed the cattle they needed to keep their women and children and old ones alive. And Johann came with his men and his guns and whips and fought the people and killed the warriors and drove all the rest of them over Devil Rock to die.' He paused. 'That's why we call it Devil Rock, because the old devil killed the boys and little girls, all the people, to drive them off their land.'

The age-old music was groaning and crying now, keeping pace with the story as it reached its bloody climax. The drums coughed like old men gasping their last breath, the clap-sticks cracked like a hundred children's bones. Now she could see trembling ancients hurled off the savage red-rock cliff, mothers with babies leaping to their deaths, as the heart-beat rhythm endlessly repeated its lament like the cycles of the earth. In Timbo's far, staring gaze she could see the dun-coloured surface of the water stagnant with rotting bodies, the dark earth streaming with red-black blood like rain.

God, how did she think she could get off a plane from Sydney and become one with these people by a sheer act of will? Like the deep canyon where the ancestors of these people died, her life was split by a great chasm, the divide marked 'black' and 'white'. Was she a complete fool to think of bridging it by her own efforts, against a past like this?

'Y'getting a history lesson, teacher?'

The loud, jeering voice could not have been more discordant with her mood. She steeled herself to turn and face the speaker as pleasantly as she could. 'Hello, Mark,' she said levelly.

He was drunk already although it was nowhere near lunchtime, and from each hand dangled an opened can which he lifted turn and turn about to swig. 'Hist'ry lesson,' he repeated triumphantly as if he had said something very clever. Then his rambling thoughts took a new and darker turn.

'Y'come from the house?' he demanded truculently. 'Y'seen my wife?'

Already Geena knew better than to answer this query. Of all the marriages in the Aboriginal village, that of Mark and the Koenigshaus kitchen maid was by common consent the stormiest and most unhappy. On her first visit Geena had been a witness to a brutal scene of the drunken Mark beating his wife because Ellie insisted on going to work up at the big house.

Yet if she stayed at home in the village compound, he was as likely to beat her for being idle and not earning the meagre salary which kept them both. Older than Ellie, idle, drunken and vicious, he was a living nightmare of a man. Geena did her best to avoid him whenever she came down to the camp, but clearly she had not succeeded this time.

And equally clearly, Mark was spoiling for a fight. He stood before her in his torn singlet and filthy shorts, swaying on his feet, his small eyes as swollen and suspicious as a pig's with too much liquor in the heat of the day, reeking of beer and years of body sweat.

He would be a terrifying opponent, Geena shuddered. No woman would have a chance in a fight against him, especially when he was drunk.

He saw the look in her eye and his smouldering anger caught fire. 'Why you look at me like that, you bitch?' he howled. 'You can't look down on anyone, you just nothing, you less than nothing, just a bastard bitch! You bugger off back to the big house where you belong, see what your big daddy done for you when the other throw-

131

out got his chance at last, got what they owed him, what was his at last!'

Suddenly the fire left him and his rambling assault collapsed into drunken maunderings. 'Your daddy – your dad – that's what you think – what they all think—'

'Hey, c'mon, c'mon, Markie!'

A couple of the young men had shouldered up, alerted to the crisis by Mark's shouting. Now they took the opportunity to manhandle him away, dragging him back through the compound to his own hut where they deposited him gently enough in the shade, propped up against the wall.

Geena turned to Timbo in puzzlement. 'My big daddy?' she frowned. 'What did he mean by all that?'

Timbo shrugged. 'Dunno,' he said indifferently. To him all adults were crazy, and none more so than drunken old washouts like Mark. 'You don't want to give a toss for him.' He laughed. 'Worry about us if you want someone to fuss over. We can take all the time and energy you got to give!'

Where was it?

At least now she had the chance to look.

Charles had been 'coptered out to Sydney to bring back the prospective buyer of Koenigshaus to look the place over, Jon was out mustering, Ben in the office as usual and Geena safely occupied at the Aboriginals' camp.

That left Alex, and he'd be kept busy all morning. He'd gone straight back to his old room after breakfast in what he called 'the Tower', the square brick two-storey addition built on to the house by some long-dead Koenig which gave its occupant the illusion of being lord of his own territory and, with its high windows and jutting balcony on the upper floor, lord of all he surveyed.

'The Tower.'

She and Phillip had hardly even spoken the words since Alex left home. She knew he would find everything there

132

pretty much as he had left it when he ran out on them twenty-five years before. Apart from such trivial tasks as stripping the bed and emptying the waste-paper basket when it became clear that the lost child would not return, she and Phillip, by tacit consent, had left the room untouched.

How would it be now?

The thirty-eight-year-old Alex could not possibly need the clothes and possessions of his thirteen-year-old self. But he would be kept very busy sorting everything out and making the room fit for his occupation now. And in any case, he would have no call to come looking for her upstairs in the main house.

OK, now's the time. And there wouldn't be much more spare time today if Charles made good his promise to bring the Japanese buyers back with him from Sydney. That would mean dinner to organise, guest rooms to prepare, the whole house to spruce up – get going, then! Why are you wasting time?

With renewed purpose she mounted the wide stairs from the hall, and turned down the passage to Jon's room. From the doorway she could see at once what she was after. Lying on top of his chest of drawers among the usual sparse clutter of manly bric-a-brac was a brown buff envelope, the same she had seen in Phillip's desk in the office before the accident, *To be opened in the event of my death*. He had shown it to her years before when he had first prepared it, while Jon was still a child.

'Everything's there, Hen,' he had announced, 'bank accounts, administrative details, the lot.'

That was before Koenig Holdings had been formed in the wake of Charles's success on the city front, before the business had been computerised, before Koenig Cattle had grown so big that it had gone international, so she doubted that this one envelope would contain 'the lot' today.

But the very same safe that stood in the office now, the

massive dark green, brass-bound monster with its lead-weighted floor and lining of steel had stood there then. The same combination had worked it then, it must have – old safes were stuck with one set of numbers, they could not be reprogrammed like modern devices. And whatever Phillip kept in there, he must have left a note of the number for his successor.

A few hurried steps took her across Jon's room to the chest and she pounced on the envelope, up-ending the contents on the bed in her haste.

Six figures, Jon had said, all those old safes were the same. Feverishly she rifled through the surprisingly meagre contents – a few sheets of bank details and account numbers, a few names and addresses, a few trivial instructions – and nothing at all resembling the combination number which would open a safe.

She must be wrong, it must be here somewhere! With a sense of panic she began again more carefully, scouring the papers before her line by line. She was conscious of feeling frantic with heat even in the cool of the low, west-facing room – it must be later in the morning than she thought. *Keep cool*, she told herself, *keep calm, he must have left a record of the number, it just doesn't make sense*.

Perhaps he had hidden the number somewhere among these sets of figures. Anxiously she returned to the top and started again. But each line of digits seemed to correspond to the number of a bank account or a sorting code, and those would have been established by the various banks maybe a hundred years after making of the safe. The date maybe? But even as she stared at May 29 1972 she had a gnawing conviction that she was barking up the wrong tree.

Don't give up so easily, she scolded herself, biting back tears, *it's here somewhere, you just have to keep trying*!

Making a metal note of the date inscribed in Phillip's large, florid handwriting just in case that might prove to be the missing set of numbers, she restored the documents to the envelope then carefully placed it back on the chest of drawers, lying face up just as it had been when she came in. Why she did so she could not say – except that she did not want Jon to know that she was searching with increasing desperation for something she dreaded to find . . .

Leaving the room, she carefully placed the door on the latch just as she had found it, and padded softly down the landing to the elegant suite that she had shared with Phillip. Running the length of the first floor of the house, in prime position above the porch and equipped with its own wide, white balcony giving out over the immeasurable Koenig acres rolling away on all sides, the master bedroom suite was a fitting reward for the senior Koenig of the day and a welcome haven of retreat from the pressures that went with the role. Soft white walls, natural woodwork and a clear apple-green carpet together with the pale blossom-sprigged wallpaper covering one long, sloping wall, gave the impression of waking in an English attic, on a sweet morning of an English spring.

But nothing to do with Phillip could ever be sweet for long. The huge old dark oak-framed bed with its European half-tester and swagged canopy and coverlet, the solid reclining chair and old oak table-top desk announced his dominant presence in the room with the unmistakeable aura of a gentleman's smoking room which Phillip so readily created as his atmosphere of choice.

The desk drew her like a magnet. This would be the place where he would have kept it – if it existed. In all their time together, from the first moment she had moved into what she had thought of for years as another woman's bedroom, the desk had been locked.

'Security, Hen,' Phillip had said easily when she had questioned it at the time, and she had accepted that. Over the years too she had managed to make the bedroom hers, gradually and she hoped subtly weeding out all traces of 'her' taste. She rarely referred to Phillip's first wife by name. Redecorated, re-organised, the furniture relocated and a table added here, a bookcase there, the bedroom had come in time to feel truly hers and Phillip's at last.

But sometimes her ghost still came between them, as she strongly feared it was about to now. Rose had been sure Trudi had returned, she remembered with a shudder, come back for Phillip. Could it possibly be true?

Crossing to the bedside table she fetched the bundle of keys that had accompanied Phillip's body and which in life had never left him, even in the bush. Ruling out all the large, bright, modern specimens, she came by trial and error to the one she sought. With gentle pressure the lock on the desk drawer eased open, and its contents were laid to view. From within the shallow drawer the face of a long-dead woman stared up at her, even in the flat black-and-white image still vibrantly, beautifully alive.

Trudi.

Why, of course. Who else?

She almost whispered a greeting – or a curse.

For here at least was the solution to one twenty-five-year-old mystery: what had become of the striking portrait of the vivid beauty who had been the first Mrs Phillip Koenig, sighted on her own first time in the house, in this room, the first time Phillip took her to his bed. By the time of her second visit, Trudi had disappeared. She knew Phillip must have hidden the beautiful studio portrait somewhere, it was not the kind of thing you'd ever throw away. But as a new bride she had had the sense not to go looking, and over the years she had almost forgotten its existence. And never for one second in all that time had she dreamed that she had been here all along, here in their bedroom, a party to all their most intimate secrets, all their recent most shameful deeds.

A wave of nausea seized her, she wanted to throw the

picture from the top of the Snowy Mountains and see it crash into a thousand pieces, or tear it up and flush it down the lavatory. Carefully she forced herself to lift it out and lay it on the bed. Time enough to decide what she was going to do with Trudi when she had found what she was looking for. And she was no nearer now than when she had begun.

Like all locked and secret drawers, Phillip's was a blend of the valuable and the worthless. There were old-fashioned sets of gold shirt-studs and matching cuff-links set with diamonds and mother-of-pearl, a heavy onyx seal carved with a flourishing Gothic 'K', another in garnet and bloodstone, gold signet rings engraved with intertwined initials, and various solid gold gentlemen's watches of the sort designed to be worn across waistcoats, complete with fob and chain. Phillip had had no time for such things, he despised men who wore what he called 'jewellery'.

Alongside the antique valuables lay a jumble of nick-nacks, some from his everyday life, some that he must have kept since he was a boy. A block of red sealing wax and a box of matches, some old keys, a broken Scouts' penknife, a post-card or two from long-forgotten friends, all these she cast impatiently aside. Beneath them lay a jumble of letters, some official, some clearly personal. Carefully she examined and sorted every one. And what she discovered was the last thing in the world she would have wished to know.

At the bottom of the drawer lay a jumble of ordinary-looking mail, typewritten communications in nondescript business envelopes.

Dear Mr Koenig, began the first official letter from an address in Sydney, *This is to confirm your appointment with Mr . . . on . . .*

The second was more explicit – *to let you know that arrangements have now been made for the radiological tests and X-rays suggested by Mr . . .*

The story had its own dynamic, its own inexorable progression – *appointment herewith to discuss the results of your recent tests . . .*

What the results had been became very clear from the last cluster of increasingly angry communications.

– cannot impress upon you too strongly the import-ance of taking immediate action in this case. Though the prognosis is far from hopeful, as you have insisted on being told, nevertheless with modern drugs and treatments there is much that can be done to retard the progress of the tumour and ensure an extension of useful if not active life.

In the case of brain tumours such as yours, especially those situated on or near the pituitary gland, it is also true that surgery will almost certainly leave you with restricted speech and movement, possibly in a wheelchair.

But without treatment you may expect not only increasingly severe pain but an increasing derange-ment of your normal life, with a marked alteration in behaviour and in the pattern of your previously-established moods.

Cancer.

He had had cancer.

Numbed beyond feeling, she looked at the date on the first letter. Almost three years ago Phillip had had cancer, he had had a brain tumour and he had refused all treatment.

He had done so in the knowledge that it would mean undergoing damaging surgery, and in the fear that this would leave him less than the man he was. And he had borne all this alone, determined to keep going to the very last as the Phillip he had been, refusing with all the fight in his body to go gentle into that last goodnight.

Precisely, mechanically, she replaced the letters in their envelopes and laid them back in the drawer. Then she closed and locked the desk, restored the keys to their place on Phillip's overnight table and lay down very carefully on her side of the bed.

She stared at the ceiling for a long time as the fierce fingers of the noonday sun forced their way in through the Venetian blinds and drew tram-lines across the rough white surface, lines that moved a long way as she stared unseeingly towards the light. And then at last, with a bursting heart and a grief so deep that she never wanted to lift her head again, at last Helen Koenig wept for the death of her husband.

Chapter 15

Jon.

She must speak to Jon.

And she must stop crying, stop these endless, useless tears.

Was she still grieving for Phillip?

No, she was crying now for her failure as a wife.

She was weeping for the woman who had stood by and watched her husband walk up to the gates of death without going with him, hand in hand, as far as she could along the way: without offering him, for all their years together, a second's help or a single word of comfort as he drank that bitter draught to the very dregs.

And she was weeping for the woman who had lost an exceptional man – who had lost him years before he died too, so that her final memories had to be of that cruel usurper, that doppelganger who had come to take the real Phillip's place and poison their last years.

What a relief to be able to tell Jon the truth about his father now, to explain what Phillip had been going through. That the rages, the vile bursts of evil temper, that last madness of changing the will against Jon had been the product of the black growth inside him.

What was she saying, then?

That Phillip was mad?

Groping for a tissue, she swung her legs off the bed and sat up swiftly, too distressed to lie still. Surely it would be worse for Jon to feel that he had lost Koenigs-haus through his father's sickness and insanity, rather than through Phillip's belated desire to do the right thing, settle a debt of honour with his last act on earth?

A new and terrifying thought struck her, stopping her in her tracks. In the mirror of her dressing-table she could see a face white with shock, the mere ghost of the woman who greeted her there every morning. *His last act an earth.*

Phillip had known he was dying. He had refused surgery or any kind of treatment because he did not want to become a hopeless invalid or even a vegetable before he died. Yet if he had lived, he could not have escaped that slow degeneration, the inevitable decay. Knowing the man he was, could it be that he would have chosen the long walk alone into the bush armed with a shotgun that was a time-honoured way out for any cattleman? Of all of them, Phillip would be man enough to do it.

Would he have taken his own life?

Yet even if he had not, death would have claimed him soon enough, without assistance. His tumour was advanced and inoperable, his condition terminal. Though he had walked and talked with all the appearance of his normal vigour, fought with Charles and Ben and insisted on sex with her, he was a dead man, his fate was sealed.

The thought took root and grew. Surely no man would choose to die that death, even if he had resolved to end his ruined life? Yet even at the end there was no escape for Phillip from the death rushing forward as he neared the final act. And if the Koenig of 'the Kingdom' had chosen a King Brown to speed him to the kingdom that is not of this world, was there not a terrible, final logic to that too?

'Thanks, Charles. That's fantastic. See you all around six then. Great stuff! 'Bye.'

Thoughtfully Alex racked the handset on its battered stand in the downstairs den and, grabbing a piece of paper, began to make a swift plan of action.

So Charles had pulled it off, he had succeeded in persuading Madam Butterfly to come out to Koenigshaus to take a look around before she flew back to Tokyo? Good on Charles! He let out a brief whistle of approval while his mind turned to the logistics of it all.

The whole entourage would be here in time for dinner tonight, staying over at least until tomorrow. OK, brief Helen they were coming and on their way, have her organise the domestic arrangements, then go down to the kitchen, sweet-talk old Rose into one of her major dinner specials and make sure that Ellie was going to be around to lend a hand with serving it . . .

Ellie.

His lips curved in a reminiscent smile. You can always pick 'em, tell 'em a mile off, can't you, boy? he congratulated himself, you can spot the real goers, feel out the hot-pants brigade? Christ, she'd do anything for you – and she had done! Glad to see the old hand has lost none of its cunning!

Who'da thought that skinny little body would go off like a catherine wheel the second you wound her up and let her go? And who'da thought that those tits, amazing as they looked through her skimpy blouse, would have proved quite such a glorious handful in the flesh?

Flesh that was made to handle, a deep glimmering brown, glowing like bronze yet warm as melting butter to the touch. Yet flesh that had already been handled by rougher hands than his.

He frowned. Ellie's body, as he had seen when they made love, bore the marks of beatings that now made her come-on line about her jealous husband look like more than just a married woman's way of spicing up her bit of extramarital fun. Christ, what a drongo that drunk

143

Abo must be, if the only fun he could get out of a body like that came from knocking it about!

A body like that . . .

And not only a body.

Those hard little hands, with their wiry, grasping fingers, her teeth, sharp and white as a cat's, even her ears, so sensitive that one touch almost blew her away . . .

He could feel her touch now, here, right *now*, he shivered with sensual abandon. And Christ, could she go! She was insatiable, she'd do anything, try anything, she just couldn't seem to get enough . . .

He could feel the familiar stirring between his legs, the solid promise of a mighty erection seconds from now. Behave yourself, boy! Business before pleasure. Keep your eye on the ball. There's one little lady rather more important to your future happiness right now, and that's Mrs Fujiyama or whatever she was called, She Who Must Be Made One Happy Jappy before the night was out.

And not through what you do best boy, sad to say, but that's the way it goes. OK, what's the drill? Speak to Jon, he primed himself, gotta speak to Jon. Crucial to have him on line. Mrs Whatserface will never open the moneybags if she thinks there's a disgruntled, disinherited younger son hanging around all ready to throw a spanner in the works, start making trouble, even sue!

No, get it right. Get Jon lined up, make sure Helen's feeling sweet too, see she's got her nosebag full of candy, have a word with Charles. Then make the sale, collect the loot and straight off into the sunset again, melting away back where he came from.

Well, not exactly where he'd just come from. Alex's handsome face darkened with shame and anger and he ruthlessly drove the memory back into the past. Just bad luck that they'd caught up with him, that's all. An administrative error, he wouldn't slip up like that again.

And even in – *that place* – he wouldn't name it to

himself, even now – he'd learned things, made a few useful contacts. Oh, very useful, indispensable you might say. So it all came around.

Anyway, that was history, it was over, gone. He'd paid his dues, with interest! And it wouldn't happen again. Once this was over, he'd be right, he'd be set for life.

And then . . .

And then, Australia was a bloody big country, a bloody big beaut of a country to get lost in. And a boy who was lost once before could get lost again any time, no worries.

All set then.

With the happy sense of having done a good morning's work, Alex lifted the handset and switched to the house intercom. 'Oh, Rose, hi there, who's my best girl?' he smiled down the line to the kitchen. 'Fix us a whisky, will you? Yeah, a double.' He smiled again. 'I'm in the den. Why don't you have Ellie bring it along?'

Jon.

Soon she could talk to Jon.

Oh, it was a nuisance that the Japanese woman and her accountant were going to be there at dinner, as Helen had told her when she picked her up from the Aboriginals' camp. But the visitors wouldn't want to spend the whole evening with the family, surely? There must be a chance that she'd get some time alone with Jon. Always providing that he'd want to spend time alone with her.

Oh God! If only she knew what he was thinking! Geena sighed heavily, and stretched out her tired limbs as she wriggled deeper into the warm water of the bath. All she wanted was a few minutes with Jon on his own, was that too much to ask . . . ?

Only a few minutes?

Honestly?

Truthful to the core, Geena squirmed at her own self-deception. No, not just a few minutes. If I'm honest, a whole lifetime – or at least the chance of one, anyway.

Was it complete madness to think of him like this? she asked herself anxiously as she sat up and slowly reached for a towel. You've hardly spoken to him, you don't know him, he could already have a girlfriend, he could be engaged to someone from another station, he could find you totally physically repulsive, he might think you're the last girl on the face of the earth that he'd ever dream of marrying.

He could, said one small voice in her ear.

But he doesn't! declared the other with total confidence.

She sighed heavily. Well, one way or another, tonight she'd find out. As soon as she saw Jon.

He could see the chopper coming from miles away through the pale, clear air, circling in the hollow golden bowl of the sky like a mosquito, and buzzing like one too. To his fury the pilot brought the aircraft low over the cattle clustered beside the road-train where Henry and the others were loading them on board, doubtless to show the prospective purchasers what fine steers they might find themselves the owners of, if they decided to buy. But the beasts hated aircraft, the noise terrified them, and when they got frightened enough, they just ran.

And he might have expected Charles to remember that! Unless he was so desperate to make this bloody sale that he didn't give a damn about anything else! From his vantage point outside the stables where he had left his horse, Jon cursed violently, though as he knew, fruitlessly too.

'Thanks a bunch, you selfish bastards!' he yelled, 'and bugger the lot of you! You could've spooked the cattle, we could have had a stampede on our hands. Lost the lot of them! And how much would your precious holding have been worth then?'

Still cursing, he swung away and, avoiding the back door of the house, stalked on until he reached the small stone chapel where his father had been buried such a short time before. Throwing open the double doors before him, caught like an avenging angel against the light, he threw down his mustering gear and whip in the dirt beside the entrance and strode in.

The flowers on the flagstones above the vault where Phillip lay, lilies and white gardenias in a laurel-leaf frame of glossy green, were still sweet and fresh, their delicate fragrance greeting him as soon as he came in. The grave itself was still unmarked, he noticed with a fresh access of distress.

'Christ, Dad,' he burst out, 'we haven't even had enough time to get you your brass plate yet, and already they're selling off your bones! Yours and all the Koenigs!'

With a spasm of self-punishing hate he raised his eyes to the crucifix, and the outsize ivory figure of the twisted, suffering Christ. 'Did you hear that?' he attacked the Christ passionately. 'D'you see all this rubbish that's going on? If you do, why don't you do something about it? Or don't you bloody well care?'

The cold echoing silence was his only answer. 'Oh God,' he cried, and falling to his knees, tried to collect his thoughts, tried to pray. But ever since last night, he knew, he had been in a state of frenzied tension bordering on madness. 'Dad was killed!' was his only article of faith now, the only creed he clung to in the desert of his despair.

For he really believed that he had been visited by a true dream last night, when he had lain down by the water-hole.

He was convinced of it, in every fibre of his bones. Now at last it was clear to him why Phillip, experienced bushman as he was, had not heard the great snake coming, had not saved himself from the approach of the

147

King Brown. The killer had had two henchmen, who had set three of the venomous creatures onto him in case one failed, bringing them up silently so that he would have no chance to hear their approach, wake and defend himself. That was the secret of his father's death and he alone could bring it to light.

Yet if he tried to tell it, who would believe him? What proof did he have, what facts, except his dream? What kind of evidence was that? Could he imagine himself before a judge and jury: 'Yes, Your Honour, I know my father was murdered, I saw it in a dream.' He'd be laughed out of court!

And who would he accuse? Who were the killers? Three of them for sure, one the ringleader, two others the strong-arm men. Men? he did not even know that. The wraithlike forms shrouded in darkness could have been male or female, it would not require masculine strength to release three snakes upon a sleeping figure on the ground. But who would want to kill Phillip like that?

He tried to think if anyone had left the station recently on bad terms. A drunken roustabout who tried to bully Rose for food and shelter, and was roughly sent packing without either. A surly misfit of a hired hand dismissed without notice, both driven off the station by Phillip's none-too-gentle orders, which they had disobeyed at the cost of feeling the boss's stock-whip backing up his commands. Yet would they kill? And if not – who?

Jon had never in his life thought ill of anyone. Now his wounded mind shied like a frightened horse away from other, darker thoughts – someone on the station, someone in Koenigshaus itself . . .

No! It couldn't be!

Yet it had to be someone – someone close at hand.

Someone he knew.

Round and round went his thoughts like rats in a trap till his mind was crying like a child, *I don't know what to do, Daddy, Mummy, tell me what to do*!

And still all he could hear was the cold echoing, punishing silence of the chapel, the silence of the tomb.

Tell me what to do . . .

Impotent, terrified and exhausted, crouched in the narrow pew, he lifted up his voice and wept: *O God, tell me what to do!*

Chapter 16

The descending helicopter whipped up little twisters of
dry red dust as it settled to the earth. A safe distance
away, Helen engaged gear in the 4WD and drew the
vehicle up to the landing strip to greet the new arrivals.

The hatch in the side of the white 'copter cracked open
like an egg and a little flight of steps unfolded from its
belly to help the passengers to dismount. First out was
Charles, his eyes searching her with one oblique glance.
'Hello, Helen. How y'doing?'

'Fine,' she murmured mechanically, 'just fine. You?'

He turned. 'Can I introduce you to Mrs Matsuda, and
her financial adviser Mr Buckley?'

'Yoshiko, please.'

The woman climbing out of the chopper must have
been forty, Helen thought, but it was impossible to tell.
An ageless Oriental beauty, she also bore at every point
the unmistakable imprint of heavy money, and with it all
the class which does not necessarily go with ready cash.
Her skin, the classic porcelain complexion of the Japanese
woman, had clearly been tended in the world's best
beauty salons, her glossy raven bob spelled Paris, her
stone-washed linen safari suit said Beverly Hills, her fine
tan shoes and bag breathed Rome. Even her briefcase
could have come from that bloody place in London where
they were still making umbrellas for Queen Victoria,
Helen thought with a sinking heart.

151

She tried not to feel jealous. Yeah, the very rich are different from you and me, she told herself without amusement. For a start they last longer.

Too bad for the rest of us!

Against the immaculate chic of the well-groomed newcomer, Helen felt old and faded, unstylish, too big, as clumsy as a horse. Mentally she compared herself with the fragile Yoshiko as they must have looked to Charles's eyes, and wished they were both dead – Yoshiko first!

'Mrs Koenig? I was sorry to hear of the death of your husband.'

'Helen, please. Phillip? Yes, well, I – Well, as a matter of fact –' For God's sake! Surely she could think of something to say?

But Charles was there, covering for her, smoothly as always. 'Thank you, Yoshiko. Yes, he was an outstanding man, it's a great loss – for Helen and for all of us.' He turned to include the newcomer just climbing out of the helicopter, still doing the honours. 'And Helen – meet Mr Buckley.'

'Mr Buckley.'

She fumbled out her hand to receive the young man's firm, businesslike grasp as he greeted her politely enough but without even the ghost of a smile. His voice, suit, pale, polished face, button-down shirt and steel-rimmed glasses were all-American, he looked smart, preppy, and twenty-eight going on fifty years old.

'Buckley, Craig Buckley, ma'am,' the newcomer began in a light, New England voice. 'I'm Mrs Matsuda's financial assistant. It'll be my job to get into the figures here. Glad to know you.'

Suddenly with a flash of insight she saw what Jon would make of both of them, the steel magnolia and the humourless side-kick with his Nazi glasses and soulless determination to see Koenigshaus as no more than a set of figures, good or bad. Jon would loathe them.

Mrs Matsuda stared at her with jet-black, expressionless eyes. 'Mr Koenig – Charles – tells me you have a son, Mrs Koenig.'

'And a stepson,' she said weakly.

Mrs Matsuda gave an inscrutable smile. 'And a stepson. How lucky you are. I am looking forward to meeting them both.'

So far, so good, Alex told himself in his tried and tested formula of comfort in tricky times. The dining room was glowing with light that played on silver and white damask, the first course had just appeared as if by magic and looked and tasted magical, and the ice-breaking with the visitors was going along just fine. But no thanks to little brother Jon!

'More wine, Yoshiko? Craig?'

Smiling pleasantly, he helped the guests within reach of him to a generous top-up of a rather outstanding Shiraz he'd found earlier in his father's cellar, and taken the trouble to open in advance, to allow the rich blood-red liquor time to breathe. 'Helen? Charles? Can you pass the bottle down to Ben? Yes, it is good, thank you, Yoshiko, I'm glad you like it.'

What the fuck was Jon doing scowling away at the end of the table as if he was just about to be dragged off to be murdered? We have to pull this round! With a winning smile, Alex made small talk in a determined attempt to lighten the atmosphere. 'So, Yoshiko, have you been able to see anything of Australia while you've been here?'

She shrugged. 'Sydney, the Great Barrier Reef, Ayers Rock.'

Charles laughed. 'All the tourist traps! We should be able to show you a bit of the real old country, if you have time.'

Mrs Matsuda gave a glimmer of a smile. 'What I really want to see is the Koenigshaus ranch.'

'Station!'

Jon's interruption came like a bull in a china shop. 'Station!' he repeated loudly and truculently, swilling his wine carelessly round his glass. 'Americans have ranches in the Wild West. In Australia, we call them stations. Cattle stations.'

Thank you, little brother! The cold anger coiled deep inside Alex stirred viciously to life. OK, he hadn't expected Jon to cream his pants with delight at the thought of selling Koenigshaus, getting the buyers in to look over the old pile. But he had at least thought the kid would be civilised about it!

And since he knew he hadn't got a snowball's chance in hell of getting his hands on the place himself now, how come he couldn't even see the main chance for number one and get his bloody shoulder behind this sale?

"Cos when we get our hands on the boodle, Jonny boy,' he'd assured him magnanimously, 'you can be sure I'll see you right! Old Charles here has told me it'd be a good investment to shove a decent wedge your way, set you up with a place of your own. Let's just do the deal, then a station for Little Jonno'll be the first thing on the shopping list!'

He might even come through with it and all, Alex brooded, if Little Bro would only shape up and suck around Ma Moneybags a bit! But all the bloody kid could do was slump over his end of the table pouring down a first-class wine as if it was lemonade, looking as happy as a bastard on Father's Day!

His eye fell on the girl at Jon's elbow, neat and nifty in flower earrings and a pale pink cotton shift, and he could have laughed aloud.

Bloody Jon!

What a drongo!

Couldn't he see that his Rebel Without A Cause routine was doing less than nothing for the poor tart beside him, all pooned up and nowhere to go?

Not for the first time, Alex marvelled at the blindness of his fellow men. They could have a woman lying down before them in the street, ready to cock it up at the drop of a whore's drawers, and they'd still trip over her without noticing, lift their hat and walk away! Bloody amazing! And a smart little handful like this one too, she'd be a goer like Ellie given half a chance, if he knew anything about women!

Covertly running his eye over Geena, Alex became aware that Charles, conveniently seated on Mrs Matsuda's left, was busy doing the sales pitch. 'We've got a lot to show you, a lot I think you'll like,' he was saying smoothly. 'The whole place amounts to over three thousand square miles, but the homestead here is the centrepiece, of course.'

Mrs Matsuda cast her jet-bead eyes around the dining room with its dove-grey panelling, moulded ceiling and polished floor. 'Very old?' she inquired.

'Historic!' said Charles. He threw a meaningful glance across the table at Helen. 'Helen'll tell you about it.'

'Built over a hundred years ago,' Helen chimed up obediently, but her soul was in turmoil. *Caught between a rock and a hard place*, she mourned. *If I don't help this sale go through, Jon will get nothing; but will he ever speak to me again if I do?*

'It's one of the oldest properties in the Northern Territory,' she went on huskily. 'It's in all the records, it's been written up in all the local papers, it's pretty famous round here as a prime example of colonial architecture . . .'

Her voice trailed away, but the shoeblack eyes in the ivory Japanese face never left hers. 'But it's been your home. And now I want to buy it and live here. Does that make you sad?'

Did it? She didn't know. 'Not at all,' she said stiffly. 'Things change. They can't always stay the same.'

'Maybe you and your husband planned to retire?' Mrs Matsuda probed on. 'Hand over the running of the station to your sons and go round the world – visit friends – travel—?'

Helen wanted to burst out laughing. The very idea that he would ever retire was a sheer travesty of Phillip, just as the picture of a pair of Golden Oldies globe-trotting their sunset years away was a travesty of their life. 'No. He never said anything about that.'

Mrs Matsuda inclined her head gravely. 'I understand. He never talked business with you?'

Why did it humiliate her to have to admit it? 'No, never.'

A tight nod from across the table. 'My husband was the same before he died. Very old-fashioned, a traditionalist.' She gave a tinkling laugh. 'But then the men die, and leave the women to run everything.'

She leaned forward, her perfect ivory finger with its rose-enamelled nail tapping at the white table-cloth. 'My husband's money was my seed-corn capital. Since he died, and since I found the right help, the help I needed—' she threw an impenetrable sideways glance at the bespectacled young Buckley, hanging attentively on her every word— 'with some very good, devoted assistance, I have made that money grow ten times over.'

She looked at Buckley again, with a definite gleam in her eye. Her glance seemed to bounce off his glasses as he returned a challenging stare to the rest of the company. 'I like to think,' she finished, reaching for her wine, 'that I have played the part of a good wife in this. I feel that my success would have made Mr Matsuda a very happy husband.'

'You bet!'

It was Jon, unnecessarily loud and aggressive again. Mrs Matsuda eyed him with mild interest but her remark was addressed to the table at large. 'It's so beautiful round

156

here. I'm surprised you want to sell.'

'Yes, well,' Charles eased in, his lean strong profile at its best in the candlelight, Helen noticed with a pang, 'we feel that for Koenig Holdings—'

'I don't!' Jon interrupted violently, sprawling away from the table in a graceless lurch against the back of his chair. 'I don't want to sell! Buggered if I do! But you don't need to give a monkey's about me, do you? I'm only the kid brother, nothing I say counts!'

So shut the fuck up, or by Christ – the old anger he thought he'd left behind and buried ten miles deep when he shook the dust of Koenigshaus off his shoes awoke again in Alex and this time would not be trodden down.

But the steel butterfly had clearly weathered far worse squalls than this. 'Mr Koenig,' she said to Jon with a perfect white smile. 'Don't underestimate yourself. Your Uncle Charles had told me all about you and Koenigshaus and your skill with the cattle.'

Such a good-looking young man, she mused regretfully, with that dusty fair hair and blue eyes. And such a great body . . .

What a pity that these boys who were so beautiful, so desirable, were so unformed. It would be good to take this one to Europe, teach him about food and wine and – and all the rest.

Especially now.

Especially now Craig was growing so boring and middle-aged! Twenty-eight must be too old for her, she needed a younger man. Well, maybe afterwards. Let's see how the sale goes. She smiled at Jon again, discreetly veiling her gaze. 'It's good to know my first cowboy anyway.'

Was there a come-on in the way she said that? Alex wondered with rising excitement. And why not? This could be useful to us!

Like most men who gave even the slightest attention

to women, Alex did not find it hard to fathom their ways. Jon was a pretty lad, just the kind to appeal to an older lady of good taste. And if he knew what was good for him, he'd dump that sad-eyed kid Geena and be after Madam Yum-Yum like a rat up a drain!

If he knew what was good for him.

Was he too stupid to see, or just too drunk to care?

'Cowboy?' Jon was demanding thickly. 'Gimme a break! We say "stockman" here. Just like we say "station", not ranch. And this is my station, and that's why I'll fight this sale with every bone in my body!'

He leaned forward unpleasantly. 'You might get some idea of what I'm on about,' he announced drunkenly, 'if I tell you that all my ancestors are buried here! Ancestors. Y'know ancestors? Thought you people were very big on 'em!'

There was a glacial silence. At last Craig Buckley opened his thin mouth in a contemptuous smile. 'They're not all coolies and geishas and rickshaws and funny hats in Japan, you know, Mr Koenig. I think you'll find our consortium is pretty broadly international in its outlook. We'll be interested to see if we can say the same of the Koenig Holdings at the end of this deal!'

Jon laughed sardonically 'Be my guest!'

He's drinking far too much! thought Helen in a panic. Oh God, what's going to happen?

Mrs Matsuda pushed back her plate and dabbed at her mouth with a dainty napkin. 'We'll need to see the books and statements for the past five years,' she said as if nothing had happened. 'Certified inventory records, everything you have that will show us how the station works . . .'

'No problem.'

Charles nodded at Ben, seated silent and impassive at the end of the table. 'Ben's our finance director – he'll have all the information you need, he's at your disposal as long as you're here, OK, Ben?'

'Delighted,' said Ben, though he wouldn't have made the first cut in the Delight Olympics, thought Buckley sourly. Shit, what was wrong with these people?

Ben coughed uneasily behind his hand. 'You're here until when?'

Mrs Matsuda glanced across at Buckley and smiled. 'Oh, I guess we can spoil ourselves – we can take as long as we need. What d'you think, Craig?'

Like an automaton Buckley whipped a wafer-thin electronic organiser out of his breast pocket and began punching buttons. 'We'll probably get through pretty quickly – but a couple of days, say, will take us through to the 22nd,' he announced unnecessarily. 'Then we can still make the Beef Convention in Chicago on the 25th, if you want to go.'

'The 22nd?'

It was time for him to come in hard and strong, Alex felt, his face calm but blazing within with pale fire. He'd have to lead from the front now despite all his plans to keep a low profile, he'd just got to show all these bastards who was the real boss! These useless buggers couldn't tell selling from a bar of soap!

And as for Jon . . .

Still, he would pull it out of the hat, give them a lesson in how to do a deal. He smiled winningly. 'We can easily get all you need together before then. After all, Charles and Ben have been preparing for this sale for some time, so we're quite ready. We'll all do our best to help you—'

Noisily Jon pushed back his chair and stood up. ' "We'll all do our best to help you!" he mimicked in a savage impersonation of Alex's smooth tone. 'Sure, we'll kiss ass from here to Kyoto if it'll make this precious sale! All except one! This one! Don't count on me to bend over! If you're all set on tearing Koenigshaus to pieces, I'll do everything I can to stop you while there's breath in my body!'

His stumbling exit was marked with a painful embarrassment. 'I'm so sorry, Mrs Matsuda,' Helen said humbly. 'Jon's not normally like this at all. I don't know what's got into him.'

It sounded unconvincing even to her own ears.

But the Japanese woman merely smiled. 'Your son is unhappy,' she murmured with a shake of her smooth black head. 'And all young men get drunk sometimes. But business is business – if Koenigshaus is still for sale?'

Chapter 17

'Would you excuse me?'

As calmly as she could Geena got to her feet, bowed politely to the assembled company and walked out of the dining room. In two strides she had caught up with the lurching, stumbling Jon making unsteadily for the front door. 'Jon!' She clutched at his arm. 'Where are you going?'

'Out.' He reached for the latch, threw open the door and gestured slackly at the deep purple void outside. 'Out there.'

'Where?'

'Anywhere.'

How far would he get in that condition? And she'd been hoping for a quiet tête-à-tête, dreaming of getting close to him under a warm midsummer moon. She could have kicked herself, or him. But she would not let him go now, not like this. 'I'll go with you.'

'No point.' He was refusing to look at her, starting to move away. 'It's all over.'

She tightened her grip on his arm. 'What's all over?'

'Nothing. It wasn't anything anyway.' He swayed a little and put his hand to his face. 'Christ, I'm drunk! Take no notice of me, I don't know what I'm saying.'

'Oh yes you do!' She was fighting back the tears, but still the anger drove her on. 'Don't talk to me like that, you know there was something—'

She broke off, unable to control her voice. He looked down at her, his eyes full of pain. 'Something – between us,' she managed to bring out.

Behind them the sound of chairs being pushed back, a louder hum of voices and a buzz of activity indicated that the party was breaking up in the dining room and would soon be spilling into the hall. Jon shook his head as if to clear it of the drink. 'We can't talk here,' he said slowly. 'Come on.'

Taking her arm he drew her through the front door and closed it behind them. Outside a huge moon rode serenely in a sky thickly carpeted with stars. The night air, fresh and sweet, cooled her hot cheeks and seemed to bring Jon to himself. Moving much more soberly now he escorted her across the lawn towards the guest house, coming to a halt at the foot of the steps up to the door.

Something between us.

Geena could have torn her tongue out. Why did she have to blurt it out like that? The hot shame of loving a man who, however kind, did not feel the same way, filled her cup of misery to the brim.

She knew she should say something, pass it off, but she could not speak. When at last Jon broke the silence, he made no reference to her words. 'The Japanese lady, Mrs Whatever-her-name is,' he began. 'When she leaves, I want you to hitch a lift.'

'What?' Whatever she had been expecting him to say, it was not this.

He sighed. 'I want you to get a ride with her back to Sydney, get out of here.'

Was he trying to get rid of her? 'Why?'

'There's just no point in your staying, that's all.'

The flat, almost casual dismissal could not have hurt more, she almost gasped with pain. But she could not help adding to her own torment. 'There must be a reason. There's a reason for everything. Tell me.'

He stood towering above her small frame, his broad shoulders blocking out the moon. 'Nothing to tell. Just go.'

She found her answer. '*No*.'

Somewhere out of the dark there came a wild cry of mortal fear, then a long-drawn-out dying scream as one of the night predators claimed its unseen, unsuspecting prey. Jon gave no sign of having heard as he gripped the rail of the verandah in both hands and went on. 'Look – there's a lot going on here right now. Last night – last night out mustering, I had a—'

He couldn't bear to say 'dream', it sounded so bloody girly, like a teenager pining for a pop star. 'I had a kind of – of experience – an out-of-body experience if you like. Out at the water-hole. Where Dad – died.' He shook his head bemusedly. 'A crazy kind of dream.'

'About your father?'

'Yeah. I dreamed about the night he – and about the snakes, the three King Browns—'

The *three* King Browns?

How did he know how many there were? All they had been told was that Phillip had died from a snake bite. They hadn't even had the post-mortem results yet to confirm that, let alone any suggestion that there might have been more than one. She cleared her throat and fought to sound casual. 'Did you dream anything else?'

But something in her voice had alerted him to her alarm, and his reply was studiedly cool. 'Oh, nothing, really. Mist and clouds – the usual dream stuff – a few people, nothing I could be sure of, no one I recognised. I told you it was crazy.'

He contrived a laugh. 'Anyway, I gotta go. I'll tell Charles in the morning to hold a seat on the chopper for you when they all take off for Sydney.'

'Don't bother,' she said angrily. 'Just listen to me!' She took a step up on the low flight of stairs and then another, bringing herself almost up to his eye level. 'I'm not a child, and I'm not your responsibility, you can't tell me what to do. And I'm not an idiot either. You can't expect me to run screaming for cover on the basis of some half-baked dream of yours – which probably only happened because you'd had too much to drink, just like tonight!'

She had meant it to sting, but hated herself the moment the words were out of her mouth. A dark flush swept over his face in the moonlight and he looked at her properly for the first time.

'I wasn't drunk, if that's what you mean!' he ground out. 'There were other things in the dream – other people – bad things, things I don't know yet what they are, what they mean. Things so bad I can't talk about them yet, because it would look as if I was accusing someone of terrible things.'

Bad things, terrible things – what was he on about? He was rambling like a child.

But she held her tongue as he stumbled on. 'And until I can find out what it all means, if it's true or not, I want you out of here. Out of danger.'

'Why me? I haven't got anything to do with it.'

He turned to her, almost pleading now. 'If any of this is true, everyone's in danger, this whole place is dangerous.'

Dangerous for me and for anyone close to me, he was longing to say. But he knew he had not earned the right to make this claim. Still he ventured one last appeal. 'For my sake. Go with them when they leave, OK?'

There was nothing in the world more calculated to move her woman's heart to love than the sight of this man defeated and pleading, humbled to her will. Geena seized her moment. 'If you'll come with me!' she demanded softly. 'Then I'll go!'

'Oh God!' he groaned.

His unspoken response, *if only I could*, hung between them like a silent prayer.

She stood before him perfectly still, exerting every ounce of the power of her nature to cast her spell over him and make him love her. Surely he could see how much she wanted him, how much she cared.

Look at me, she willed him, *look at me, you great idiot, you beautiful, marvellous man, what have I got to do to make you look at me, see me, touch me, love me . . . ?*

He looked down at her distractedly, as if she were the first woman he had ever seen. The faint fragrance of her body rose to his senses, her eyes, her skin glimmering with its dusting of starlight, her little pink earrings glowing up at him like the petals of a rose. Feeling as clumsy as an ox he raised his hand carefully to her soft cheek. 'Oh Geena,' he murmured brokenly as his fingers brushed the warm inviting flesh.

The next second her arms were round his neck like ropes of silk, her body pressed against the length of his. With a gentle pressure under her chin, feeling as if he had been moving towards this moment all his life, he tipped her face up to his.

Her kiss was like coming home.

He felt he would never stop kissing her, that his spirit would never need any other sustenance. Folding her body into his, tucking her head into his shoulder where she stood just as high as his heart, he clung to her fragile frame like a sailor lost in a shipwreck who has found one slender spar to bring him through the storm.

'Christ, this is hopeless!'

Horrified she opened her eyes as she felt him roughly thrust her away and step to one side. 'I shouldn't have done that,' he said huskily. 'And it doesn't change anything. You've still got to go.' He was backing away furiously into the dark. 'I want you out of here as soon as you wake up tomorrow!'

'Anything you need, just ask Rosie or Ellie or any of us.

Rosie will show you across to the guest house, and make sure that you've got everything you want in your rooms. I do hope you'll be comfortable.'

And I do hope I don't have to play the charming hostess for a single second longer, Helen thought, or I'll run screaming out of this front door and I won't stop running ·and screaming till I reach Sydney.

'Thank you, we'll be fine,' the Japanese woman was saying. Together she and her young man were trooping through the door under the care of a silent, watchful Rose, followed by Ben, also bound for bed. 'Goodnight then.'

There was a general 'Goodnight'.

'Goodnight, goodnight all,' called Alex waving them off into the night. 'Well, that's it for tonight,' he continued, closing the front door. 'It seemed to go quite well, wouldn't you say? I think we've done all we can.' He yawned and stretched gracefully, like one of the great cats. 'I'll just have a whisky in the den before I turn in. No, no, don't bother, Helen, I'll get Ellie to bring it along.'

'Hmmn!'

Charles's eyes, always angry these days, Helen thought, followed Alex's easy, striding step down the hallway to the kitchen where Ellie was still clearing up. 'Going to give a hand with the dishes, is he? Proper little Boy Scout!'

She passed a weary hand through her hair. 'Charles, please.'

He turned. 'Sorry, I'm not quite at my best. It's been a long day.'

She nodded. 'For me too. I'm going to bed.'

He hesitated. 'Sure you wouldn't like a last drink before you go up? Help you to sleep?'

'No, thanks. I'm all in.'

Together they mounted the wide stairway. Ahead lay the master suite, and they paused for a moment outside the door.

Charles looked at her with eyes so like Phillip's but with none of their cruel glare. 'I won't be going to sleep just yet,' he said diffidently. 'If you change your mind about that drink, just give me a shout.' He indicated the door to his boyhood room across the hall. 'I'm not far away.'

'Thanks, Charles.' She gave another weary nod. 'Goodnight.'

Inside the suite the room lay in deep shadow and she felt herself merging into the blue-grey emptiness as if she had suddenly been stripped of her body. Suddenly what should have been a blessed relief after the pressures of the evening became a terrifying loneliness, too much to bear. Overcome by panic she backed out of the door. Charles was still standing on the landing, watching her with some interest as she turned in confusion to meet his quizzical gaze. 'Maybe I could do with that drink after all,' she mumbled.

He did not laugh. 'Why don't you go through on to the balcony?' he suggested. 'I'll see if I can find something from the dining room and bring it up.' His eyes glimmered with sardonic amusement. 'We don't want to interrupt the hanky-panky in the kitchen, do we?'

Her chin dropped. 'You don't mean that Alex would – that he and Ellie –?'

'What, our new young lord and master? I think he's quite capable of a lot more than screwing the hired help, especially one as screwable as Ellie.' He laughed. 'But they're both over twenty-one. Nothing to do with us. I'll just have to see what I can lay my hands on, without interrupting him laying his hands on her. Don't go away!'

He was back with a bottle of Chardonnay and a couple of glasses before she had even decided which of the long low recliners she would take. 'Why don't you sit here? And try this wine – OK?'

Gratefully she accepted the welcome glass of wine and thoughtfully sipped at the cool oaky liquid as she mulled over what he said. 'Charles – if Alex and Ellie – well, you know that husband of hers. I asked her once how she had got a bruise on her face and she wouldn't tell me. But I know he beats her up, Rose says so. She says he's very jealous—'

'Helen—' Charles's voice held a warning note. 'We mustn't get involved. There's nothing we can do.' He dropped down lightly on the lounger next to hers.

'Oh, I know.'

Above them the moon was dipping down below the mountains, low in the sky, its rays almost level with the blue-black horizon and the blood-black earth. She felt tired beyond sleep but somehow rested too as if she had passed beyond her body and was floating away out there, sailing with the moon. She heard herself speaking before she knew what she was going to say. 'I loved him, you know.'

His voice, infinitely sad, echoed her words. 'Oh, I know.'

'But I loved you too.' Where had she found the courage to say that?

His voice in the dark was light enough, but its razor edge of bitterness had been sharpening for twenty years and more. 'Not quite as much as I loved you.'

She had to ask him. '*Why did you let me go?*'

There was an astounded silence. 'So that was it? You were just testing me, is that what you're saying? To see if I loved you enough to fight Phillip for you, take you away from him, was that it?'

She was writhing in pain. 'No! That wasn't it!'

How could you explain to a man the power of men? How could she account to him for the drive, the ruthless

168

thrust of Phillip's will, which had robbed her of her own, robbed her of her self? 'I was eighteen!' she cried. 'What did I know?'

'More than you ever let on!' His voice held a surprising savagery now. 'Oh, you blew out of nowhere to take that mustering job, didn't you? No history, no complications. But no one ever knew where you'd come from – where you'd been before – or *who with—*'

She lay there numbly while it sank in. 'So you thought—?'

He laughed, a harsh cry like a mocking-bird's. 'I realised afterwards that you probably had designs on Phillip all along. After all, the Koenig family tragedy was not exactly a state secret! You knew he'd lost his wife, and you must have guessed that he wasn't the kind of man to stay unmarried for very long. And what nicer life for a girl from nowhere than to find herself mistress of Koenigshaus?'

'But if—'

She was still feeling her way round this, like a nightmare game of blind man's buff. 'But if it was Phillip I wanted all along, why did I love you? Where did you come in?'

'Elementary, my dear Watson!'

Again that cutting laugh. 'You told me you'd never made love before me. But you weren't a virgin, even I could tell that. If you wanted Phillip, you had to have some excuse for that, my dear brother was amazingly old-fashioned about such things. And who better than little Charles, who Big Bro had spent his life putting down? Did you know that? —women do know these things – or did you just take a gamble that as soon as he knew I'd had you, he would have to take you away from me?'

She was hurting so much now, all she wanted to do was to hurt him back. 'You were just jealous of him, that's all!'

She could see his head nod in the starlight, his lips

moving in agreement. 'Sure I was! Of course I was! I was jealous because he was all the things I wanted to be, and never ever could!'

'No!' she cried in anguish. 'You were different, that's all. Why should it have mattered?'

'Oh God, Helen – you know nothing about men if you can ask that!'

'Why? Was it so terrible to be you and not him?'

'Yes!' he said passionately. 'When it denied me all the things that mattered. Our parents' interest – they only cared about their precious first born! My identity and my place in the world – the respect I should have had.' He paused. '*And your love.*'

'Oh God, Charles, is this the time . . . ?'

He sat up and swung his legs urgently to the ground. 'When is the time, Helen? When will it ever be? I've loved you since we were both kids, too young to defend something so precious we never knew how good it was until it was gone.' He sprang to his feet and swung across to the balcony, staring out unseeingly over the moon-bleached terrain, bleak as a landscape on Mars. 'I've been waiting for you all my life. I never married because I never met another woman to compare with you – surely you knew that?' He turned accusingly to face her. '*Why did you marry him?*'

She could hardly speak, her lips felt swollen and bruised. 'I loved him, we were happy, he gave me every-thing a woman could want.'

His sarcastic laughter exploded in her face. 'God Almighty, Helen, spare us the woman's magazine crap!' He was straddling her lounger now, gripping her wrist. 'Made you happy? I know he made you cry!'

'Charles, I—'

But he would not be interrupted now. 'Did he take you special places like I did? Did he find water-holes where you could swim together like we did, naked like babies, stay there all day and never want to leave?' She could see tears standing in his eyes. 'Did he ever brush the hay from your hair in the morning and make breakfast for you after making love all night in the barn?'

She burst into tears. 'Oh Charles,' she wept, 'why did it go wrong? Why did it all have to happen the way it did?'

He reached for her other hand and crushed the two of them to his lips, covering them with grinding kisses. 'I don't know,' he muttered thickly. 'But I know one thing – now I've got that bastard Phillip out of my life at last, I'm not going to waste another second getting what I want – and that means you!'

Chapter 18

Tomorrow is another day.

Whoever said that, Jon reflected in the bitterness of his misery, had never woken up to the kind of tomorrow that he had to face today. He felt sick to his stomach and most of all sick with himself. But there was only one thing for it. Just walk through the door, and do it.

'Morning, everyone.'

Well, not quite everyone, Jon noted. Ben and Alex weren't down yet, if they were intending to come to breakfast at all.

But she was, and she was the one who counted. Taking a deep breath and fighting to quell both the swimming nausea in his stomach and the pain splitting his skull, Jon approached Mrs Matsuda as she sat at the breakfast table with the rest of the household on the verandah, and bowed his head. 'I believe I owe you an apology,' he began, cursing himself for ever getting into this position. 'I hope you don't think I meant to be rude last night.'

Mrs Matsuda smiled.

Well, well.

Perhaps the boy had promise after all. 'It's not necessary. A misunderstanding, perhaps.'

'Yes, well—' he plunged on. 'I behaved like an idiot, and I'm sorry.'

Mrs Matsuda fluttered a hand like a humming-bird, bright with nail varnish and jewels. 'Don't worry about it. No problem.' She smiled round the group.

'Good morning, Jon!' Helen said bright with relief. 'Just in time for breakfast!'

Rose was at his elbow as soon as he took his seat. 'What can I get you, Mr Jon?'

'Make it bacon and eggs, Rose,' Helen instructed.

Jon winced. 'Just coffee, thank you, Rose.'

He looks terrible, thought Geena, dreading looking at him but unable to look anywhere else. Almost as bad as Dad does these days, grey and abstracted and somehow furtive too.

And almost as bad as I do.

A sleepless night, a night of tears, was the worst thing for colouring like hers, she knew. She was only golden when she was happy, now she must look as if she had painted her face with ashes, sickly pale, her skin washed out and grey. Grey and hopeless, just like Jon. She wanted to cry.

Mrs Matsuda was smiling at Jon and patting his hand. 'I understand how you feel,' she said lightly. 'Mr Matsuda would never have sold a piece of land like this. You take after your father, he would have felt the same. And it is a very special place. That's why I became interested to buy.'

'If you're really interested . . .' Jon's expression quickened, 'maybe I could show you what I'm talking about – my Koenigshaus?'

Christ, that's all we need! Across the table the alarm bells were almost deafening an irritable, rattled Charles. 'Jon, there's a long day ahead for Yoshiko and Craig,' he began warningly. 'I don't think there's going to be time for anything else—'

'Oh, I can take a little time.'

Gracefully Mrs Matsuda rose to her feet. There had to be time for such a beautiful boy, or what was life all about, what had she worked so hard for? 'How about now?'

'This – this is what? – your own private church?'

In the little chapel the air felt stale and sick after the early morning sun. The lilies marking Phillip's grave in front of the altar had begun to fester, and the smell rose to Jon's throat, increasing his nausea. He nodded. 'All the old houses have them. The big stations were just too far from any churches in the olden days. So they had to have chapels of their own.'

From their vantage point by the door, they could see the huge ivory Christ looming sombrely overhead, dwarfing the human figures standing in the aisle. Behind the small neat figure of his employer, Craig Buckley shifted his feet, glinted behind his glasses, and coughed aggressively. 'We never did that in the early days of America,' he said with more than a hint of a sneer. 'It's all a bit British and outdated now, isn't it?'

Ignore him, Jon's good angel warned. Determinedly he pressed on. 'It's also a tomb. All the Koenigs are buried here.'

Yoshiko glimmered at him mockingly. 'Your ancestors?'

He nodded in embarrassed memory of last night's drunken outburst. 'Yes.'

He looked down, and gestured to the floor at their feet. Set into the old stones, leading all the length of the aisle from the door to the altar, was a series of brass plaques. Taking Mrs Matsuda by the arm he drew her towards the first, nearest to the doorway, virtually at their feet.

'Here.' Once a proud and ornate funerary plaque in the elaborate style of the nineteenth century, it was worn now with the passage of years and trampling feet, the Gothic black lettering almost trodden away. He knelt to trace out the name, and the name on the plate beside, its twin. '*JOHANN KOENIG 1850–1930*' he read, '*BEATE KOENIG 1870–1940*. She was his wife.'

'Oh.' The olive-black eyes widened as she took in the dates. 'Koenigs have long lives.'

'And do they always marry women twenty years

younger than they are?' put in Buckley offensively. He cackled. 'Trust a number-cruncher to notice that!'

Mrs Matsuda smiled to herself. So Craig's jealous of this Aussie boy? So he should be! And it would do him no harm at all.

But it never did to let men get out of hand. Without a sideways glance, she rode over him like a bug on the highway, addressing herself entirely to Jon. 'And he was the first Koenig to come here?'

'He founded the Kingdom.' He paused. 'Or invaded it, depending on how you look at it. He emigrated out here from Germany with his wife and children.' With a brief sign he indicated the little brass plaques dotted around their parents. 'He massacred a whole tribe of people for this land – Geena's people,' he added with difficulty. 'Lost all his own kids except one while he was doing it, too.'

'So.' She nodded, enthralled.

'This one.' Jon moved down the aisle. '*PHILLIP KOENIG* 1885–1917. He died in the First World War. Gallipoli. Johann had the body shipped back from Europe so that he could be here at home with us. And with his wife.' He pointed. '*SARAH JANE KOENIG 1887–1961*. They were my great-grandparents. The next Koenig here was John.' He pointed again. 'And then—' he stopped, and made sure his voice was in control. 'And then it was my father.'

Even Buckley was not crass enough to comment on Phillip's as-yet-unmarked flagstone, nor on the plate nearest to his resting-place: *TRUDI MARIA KOENIG 1935–1969*.

'So you see,' Jon turned and looked at Mrs Matsuda in deliberate appeal, 'why I'm having a problem when the others want to sell Koenigshaus. I can't— ' he gritted his teeth, 'I can't imagine life without the Kingdom. There are more dead Koenigs here than alive, it's our whole history. And we can't dig them up and take them with us when we go!'

Mrs Matsuda regarded him steadily. 'Everything,' she said, 'has a bottom line.'

He stiffened. 'Not everything.'

'Hey, buddy, listen.'

They were on Buckley's territory now and his sense of assurance boosted his right to chime in. 'From your own books, you guys are looking at less than a one point three return on capital here – and that's in a good year! You'd be better off if you simply shoved the cash in the worst bank in the world!'

Jon shook his head stubbornly. 'Some things aren't for sale.'

'Yeah, well.' The bully in Buckley took over. 'You're in a mess here that's gonna need some real sorting out, and you'd better get hold of that. Your people could have sold off some of the Sydney stuff, the motels, the Hong Kong trading companies, whatever they liked. And those are profitable, they'd have no problem getting rid of them. But this place, this precious station of yours is just a hole in the ground that soaks up money like blood. You're lucky to have a buyer. Which is us. And we do have a seller, it seems . . .' He flexed himself triumphantly in a sudden shaft of sunlight. 'It all seems pretty clear to me. I'd say game, set and match to Matsuda PLC as soon as we've done the sums, wouldn't you?'

'This coffee hot?'

Stiffly Rose levered herself up from her seat at the kitchen table as she replied. 'I'll make you some fresh.'

Helen shook her head. 'No, don't bother, this'll do fine.' Crossing to the stove she helped herself to a generous mugful. 'Just came in to tell you who'll be around for meals today.'

Lying on the table between them, half set out, were Rose's precious Tarot cards. Could they really foretell the future? If they could, did she really want to know? As if she had interrupted Rose in some intimate personal ritual, Helen looked away as she spoke. 'Mrs Matsuda and her assistant are leaving today, so they'll be off our hands. There'll be another one less for dinner tonight too.'

Rose had seen Jon and Geena leave the table together last night, and had not needed her Tarot cards to read the bleak faces at breakfast this morning. 'Miz Geena leavin'?'

'Geena? No.' Obsessed with Charles and Jon, not to mention Mrs Matsuda, Helen realised with a pang that she had not even noticed her other guest today. 'No, it's Alex – he's decided to hop the chopper to Sydney with them to take care of some business, so he'll be away for a couple of days.'

'OK. That all?'

The wary eyes were giving nothing away, Helen could see. She wished she knew what Rose was thinking: this woman knew more about Koenigshaus than anyone alive. If ever she decided to tell all she knew, it would fill a book.

A wild thought struck her. Did she know the combination of that blasted safe? God, if only!

No, it was ridiculous. Rose wouldn't have that sort of information. And she couldn't ever ask her, anyway. No-one must know she was even looking for it. And if she found it, no-one must know it had ever existed.

Still, if she couldn't get into the safe, couldn't find the combination, no-one else could either, she was sure of that. No-one on Koenigshaus.

Koenigshaus.

Another thread of the tapestry of her anxieties broke loose and fretted its way up to the surface of her mind. Should they go through with the sale?

Despite everything that Charles said, Helen was still not convinced it was all for the best. And after last night, she had no idea what she thought about Charles either:

she had left his room straight after his declaration, shaking and in tears, not knowing in her own mind if his promise to claim her at last was a love-pledge or a threat.

What should she do?

Did she love him, did she want him now?

How could she, so soon after her husband's death?

And what about Jon? He idolised his father.

How would he feel about a sudden replacement, and Charles, of all people. *Helen, he's twenty-four!* She could still hear Charles's scornful tones. *But I'll always be his mother! And how many sons want to think of their mums falling in love, making love, being with another man . . . ?*

God, she was going mad!

Still as a statue Rose was staring at her impassively but with a kind of understanding too – did she read minds as well? Between them on the table lay the Tarot cards, a bright splash of blue and yellow and red. 'Hey, Rose,' she said impulsively, 'tell my fortune, will you?'

Rose did not move. 'You doan believe that stuff, Miz Koenig.'

'I don't know if I do or not. Let's give it a try. Go on, Rose, deal!'

Rose's hands scurried like spiders over the cards, gathering them up, shuffling and dealing in one smooth sequence. She looked up to see Helen's eyes on the old tattered pack. 'Old cards the best,' she said defensively. 'Got most power.'

'How old are these?'

Rose rarely smiled, but her fierce face gleamed now as she replied. 'Mr Phillip brought me them first time he ever went to France.'

'The first time—?' Helen tried to work it out. France had always been a favourite of Phillip's, he had made several trips, some of them prolonged. 'That must have been over forty years ago.'

'Yeah, maybe.' Rose was concentrating now, feeling

for the cards she wanted. 'Alla way from France.'

Helen could not help herself. 'Was that all he gave you?'

Rose paused. She did not look up. 'Yeah,' she said at last. Another pause. 'From France. That time.'

'And – other times?'

Rose did not miss a beat. 'You knew Mr Phillip, Miz Koenig,' she said softly, staring her in the face. 'He always was all man.'

There was a clatter at the door and the sullen presence of Ellie was beside them, trailing a bucket and mop and the sulphurous fumes of her discontent. With a half-nod to Helen she spoke to Rose in a surly monotone. 'I done the verandah, clean up after breakfast, so what now?'

Rose looked at her with evident dislike. 'Get down the guest house, clean up there.' Disconsolately the girl went off. Helen watched her go.

Ellie . . .

And Alex . . .

On the table lay the first of the Tarot cards, pointed towards her. The Lovers. It had always puzzled her why this card showed not a happy, loving couple but one man and two women, the man caught in the eternal half-turn from one to another. Every man's sexual fantasy, she supposed, women on tap, their idea of bliss.

Like Alex . . .

And Ellie . . .

The next thought came like a sharp blow to the head.

Like Phillip.

And Rose.

Like father, like son.

Last night Alex had seen nothing wrong in taking his pleasure with the kitchen maid almost under the noses of important visitors, key business associates invited as his guests.

Phillip would have done the same.

Suddenly the half-formed fears and suspicions of years upon years crystallised.

OK, so Phillip had taken Rose as his housekeeper when they were both young and single – she had always sensed that 'housekeeper' meant more than just keeping house. But she had always thought that whatever there was between Phillip and Rose must have died the minute he married Trudi.

Yet why should it have done?

The attraction of a woman does not fade simply because the man who had loved her marries someone else. And Rose was always there, always on hand, always devoted to him. She lived with them, a part of the marriage as much as their own son.

And a party to its end. She would have made the breakfast that fateful morning that Trudi died, watched them ride together out into the bush . . .

And then he was a widower, with Rose still around.

Until she came along, eighteen, naive, and totally in his power.

He might have been having ten other women during their marriage, she now saw, and she would have noticed nothing, questioned nothing. Yet what kind of man would keep a mistress going all those years, through two marriages, running another woman alongside a young wife who adored him, who denied him nothing?

Phillip's kind.

A man of strong drives, and strong urges, sex for him was like eating, he could enjoy two, three or four good meals a day, every day. He liked variety too, and would have relished to the full the age-old spice of having one black body and one white. And to slip from the fragrant lady of the house in her blossom-sprigged boudoir to take her Cinderella sister below stairs, coupling in the kitchen grease and dirt, would be Phillip's idea of mastery in his own kingdom, Phillip Koenig all over.

On the table now lay the King of Swords.

She shot out her hand, arresting Rose's sweeping movements with the cards. 'What's going on, Rose?' she challenged.

The old woman turned to stone. 'Doan know what you mean.'

'You know everything! At least you know more than you ever let on!'

But the old woman would not budge. 'I only know what the cards tell me.'

'OK, ask them this.' If she was being unfair to Rose, she didn't care, this was one for Rose as well as for herself. 'What's going to happen to Koenigshaus, then? Will it be sold?'

'I asked already. They doan tell me, the future's all too dark.'

'They must say more than that!'

'They show the talk of it. But there's been talk before. They tell me Mr Charles for, Mr Jonny against, but not who gonna win it, who can stop it, stuff like that.' She looked at Helen, every wrinkle of her old face now a line of dark warning. 'We doan know, an' we can't tell. Now Mr Phillip's dead, anything can happen.' Her hands bunched up into fists, thumbs tucked fearfully inside like a child's. 'I never lived anywhere in my life 'cept here. If Mr Alex stay, he won't want me, he likes that dirty Ellie! An' if it's sold, who's gonna want me then?'

'I don't know.'

With great bitterness, Helen got to her feet, all the new love she had felt for Phillip after learning about his illness swept away by the pain of his old betrayal. 'Why don't you ask the cards? Ask your bloody cards!'

From the edge of the lawn, Sydney harbour sparkled in the sun, each little diamond-glinting wave a glittering reward for the owner of this ten-million-dollar view. From the historic Harbour Bridge to the legendary Opera House soaring triumphantly from Bennelong Point with the little sailboats plying up and down outside, it made a living picture that could never tire the viewer, however many times they stood to enjoy the scene.

Alex paused on the threshold of the elegant room. As he drank in the stunning vista sweeping away towards the picture window with the world-famous view beyond, he felt the sharp cocktail of envy, desire and awe bite with more than its usual ferocity. None of that, boy! he chastised himself. Get used to the fact that you'll soon be living like this too! Stop feeling so bloody insecure about your unexpected good fortune – you'll have a house and a view as good as this and better in just a few short weeks. Time to start living up to it!

'Mr Koenig!'

'Mrs Castlemaine! Please call me Alex!'

With a ready smile he turned to greet the hostess as she came sweeping through from the domestic quarters with a black-gowned, white-aproned maid on her heels.

'More champagne for the guests in the summer-house,' she ordered. 'And then take the canapes round again.' The girl despatched, she bustled forward, her face wreathed in effusive smiles. 'Welcome to my little party! How nice to see you up here in Vaucluse!'

That was always a safe enough line when welcoming total strangers, Lindi Castlemaine congratulated herself. At least she'd got his name right, he had to be the Koenig that Trisha said she'd bring along, everyone else was already here. Mmmmn. Wonder where Trisha found him – and with looks like that, what a pity she hadn't found him herself first . . .

'Lindi, please!' she laughed roguishly, giving him both her hands. 'I suppose you're looking for Trisha – this way, follow me.'

The garden, like the house, was a tribute to the vision

and planning of a more gracious and leisured age. On the long rolling lawn of vivid emerald green, women were dotted as brightly as the flowers which could be seen everywhere growing in natural clusters, not marching rigidly along flowerbeds in serried parklike ranks. Here and there other guests were gathered in the shade of well-established trees, admiring the ladylike ghost-gums and towering palms and bloodwoods, or wandering down gravel paths through drifts of sweet mimosa to the look-out point giving out on thirty miles of waterway, with beauty on all sides.

It was a place to calm even the most savage breast, but Alex was not at peace. Look at them, he thought, sick with disgust.

The world divides into people for whom a fashionable party will always brings a special thrill, and others who would rather spend their time at the zoo. Alex knew that he was welcome anywhere, that his ready smile, his good looks and charm would always see him through and ensure him a repeat invitation, especially from the women of any group. But assemblies like this of the seriously rich, the internationally idle and the 'I'm-beautiful-because-I'm-beautiful' brigade aroused a resentment and jealousy in him so violent that it almost made him ill.

'Freddie!'

'Polly darling, where've you *been*!'

'No, ask Josh, he was married to her before—'

'Yes, three hundred thousand, *that's* what they're paying him, would you *believe* it—'

'Of *course* she's looking good, the stuff she's had, she's pushing forward the frontiers of plastic surgery!'

Christ, what a bunch! Whyever did he agree to come here? He should have arranged to pick her up afterwards, or asked her to skip the party . . .

Skip the party?

What, Trisha, the original party girl, miss any kind of

thrash? That was the one thing she would never do . . .

The longing to see her now was as real as a hunger pain. Oh Christ, *where was she*?

'Louis!'

'Manny!'

'Sally!'

'Hal!'

Smiling politely on all sides, Alex followed the hostess through the packed gallery of Sydney types, the socialites, politicians and business men, the desperate older women and dumb younger ones, people on the way up and those trying to keep them down, all with their circling satellites of minders, keepers, walkers, talkers, toy-boys and sugar daddies, all frantically chasing all the fun of the fair.

Alex could feel the cold tide rising inside him.

Jesus, it's a fucking human zoo . . .

And by the time his hostess was bearing down on the last little group under a tree by the water's edge, he knew he had had enough.

'Trisha!' carolled Lindi Castlemaine, interrupting with the freedom of the hostess, 'Look who's here!'

And there she was. A slender back, a soft twist of golden hair at the nape of her neck, a pair of designer shoulders above a tapering dress, a white neck turning, turning, the voice he now heard in his sleep . . .

'Well!'

He found himself looking into the familiar tip-tilted eyes, pale, almost yellow, contracting at the sight of him to black slits, and felt again the stab of searing, trembling joy which was so near to pain.

'Hello, Alex,' she drawled. 'Let me introduce you.'

She waved a long black cigarette holder at four or five tanned, polished-looking people twiddling glasses of champagne, a representative selection of the Beautiful People and those who had worked their way into their ranks, become beautiful themselves by ministering to

185

their needs. He recognised Australia's top film producer, an actress now more famous for her memoirs than her work, a media baron, a fashionable shrink, and the hairdresser none of Sydney's leading ladies could live without. It was the work of a moment for him to detach her charmingly from their midst and steer her to a quiet arbour of pink oleander and drifting mauve jacaranda where they could talk.

'I don't know why I let you do this to me, Alex Koenig!' she exclaimed pettishly, pulling her arm from his grasp. 'For a guy I've only just met you take a lot of liberties!'

Only just met.

How long did it take?

With a derisive lift of his eyebrow, he let it go. He wasn't going to waste time arguing, she knew as well as he did that they were two of a pair.

'It's Koenigshaus,' he said, his eyes gleaming like a wolf's in the dark. 'I didn't just get a slice of the action, I got the whole pile. And now I've got a buyer, and it's just a matter of time till the gravy train rolls in. And while I'm waiting on the station, I need some company. Yours. Get yourself organised, we're flying back there tomorrow.'

Chapter 19

Not another bloody beautiful day!

As the brilliant sun burst through the window and drummed relentlessly on his closed eyelids, Jon woke for the second day running to the now familiar feeling of a swimming stomach and a sick, pounding head. He groaned. Surely he couldn't still be paying the price for one night of hitting the bottle? Or was it just the result of another night of broken sleep and tormented, reproachful dreams?

He knew he would never sleep again now until he had discovered the truth about his father's death. For his own peace of mind as well as for the duty that he felt to his own flesh and blood, he had to find out. Till then he was good for nothing, he could think of nothing else. Like a performing rat in a cage, his mind instantly slipped into its running treadmill of endless, circular thoughts the second he was fully awake.

If he wanted to unravel it, where was he to begin?

First things first, he instructed himself. Was he even sure that Phillip had been killed? Though he was no student of psychology, Jon knew enough to know that the brain played strange tricks. People dreamed the things they wanted to come true, or hoped were true. Had he wanted his father dead then, or even wanted to kill him?

'That's just Oedipal junk!' he told himself fiercely. In his uncomplicated world, he had loved his father, loved him unreservedly.

But suppose it was not just all mental junk, the voice of reason quietly went on, then Dad was killed, and some-one had got away with the perfect murder.

Then who?

A passing roustabout, or some other no-hoper? Hardly likely. Murder took planning and a cool intelligence, not the drunken fumbling of the kind of man who could not even hold down a job. And what of the other two who had been there aiding the killer in his dream?

The more he thought about it, the more Jon felt con-vinced that there had to have been more than one person involved. Even with the greatest care, the stealthiest approach, Phillip could still have been aroused and would have fought back. At the very least, he would certainly have woken with the very first snake bite – after which he would hardly lie back and take all the others necessary to make sure that his large, strong body got enough of the venom to kill him. Strong arms must have over-powered him, held him down and silenced him while all this went on.

How to find out?

This was the question that had been tormenting him, paralysing him for the last two days. Somehow he must shake off this weakness, break out now, today!

At least the Matsuda woman and her obnoxious side-kick had gone. And with Alex out of the way too, he could start to look around. If only he could have prevailed on Geena to take the same flight out, the decks would be well and truly clear. But he had cocked that up, that whole thing—

Geena.

Even under the stinging hot rain of the shower he shivered and grew cold. The next moment the memory of her kiss washed over him like fire and he wanted her savagely, hotly, *now*, he'd show her what a real man was, what women were for . . .

Oh God! Thinking like that, like the lowest bloody drongo, he didn't deserve any woman, let alone her!

For Chrissake drop it, forget it, forget her, he schooled himself in the desperate litany of the lovelorn male.

Clinging to these phrases like a mantra, he dressed, and avoiding breakfast hurried straight to the stables. From a hundred yards away Kaiser caught his scent and welcomed him with a wild whinny of glee. 'Yeah, I'm your man now, you noisy brute,' Jon greeted him with a firm slap on the neck. 'And you're my horse. Wanna go for a ride?'

'Hi Jonny!'

'Hey, Jon-Jon!'

'It's Mr Jon!'

He was always welcome at the Aboriginals' camp, it was the place he turned in times of trouble, and in good times too. Now from the old people of the tribe who had been ancient when he was a little boy, to the tumbling, wrestling larrakins scuffling in the dirt, everyone gave him a warm greeting, he was hailed on all sides.

'Y'come to see the dancing?' demanded Dora, waddling up with a child on her hip. 'Geena's up there, y'should see her, she's damn good!'

Glancing up the compound he could see Geena, in practice tights and a dance skirt, barefoot on the hard dry floor of the makeshift arena, busy with a group of the villagers. As she corrected a move by one young man, then was herself corrected by one of the older women in her turn, he could not tell who was teaching whom.

'What are they doing?' he asked Dora, mystified.

Dora gave her easy, happy laugh. 'They're working on a dance for the corroboree. Making a special show. Going to show everyone then what they been doing.'

'The corroboree!'

Christ Almighty, how could he have forgotten? When

was it, next month, surely not sooner? The most important event of the Aboriginals' year and he'd bloody nearly forgotten it! The one time when Phillip had always made a great fuss, held a big celebration barbecue up at the house, tried to honour the people and the work they did on Koenigshaus all year round. Now Dad was dead, it would fall to him, the tradition must be carried on—

Or would it fall to him?

Once more his loss pricked him, he was reminded of his drop in status and with it his right to care about such things, but he brutally crushed down all self-pity. *Someone* would have to keep up the corroboree, he'd tell Alex as soon as he got back. Hungrily his eyes fastened on the dancers, and the slight form in their midst. And he'd tell him that this year there was going to be a very special show . . .

'You gonna go up and watch?' Dora demanded.

'No, no, not now,' he said awkwardly. 'I came to see Dusty, is he around?'

'Here, boss,'

As always the silent approach of the small, smiling man took him by surprise. 'You wanna mount up, boss, go for a ride?'

'No, play with us, Jonny, don't go, don'go!'

Jon laughed. Popular as he was with kids, he could see that he would have no peace to talk to Dusty in the camp. He ruffled the nearest head. 'Gotta go, guys. Back soon, I promise. See ya.'

He forced himself not to look back at Geena as they left. Together they turned their horses out through the plaited archway of boughs, Dusty seeming to know where they were going, Jon content to let him lead the way.

High above, the climbing sun bleached out the sky and blistered the blood-red earth. On a distant bluff the drifts of powdery mimosa shaded from bright saffron through to an orange-red glowing like green fire. Black cockatoos and blue-bonnets flashed from the high branches, gaudy masks of white and yellow crested with sapphire. Jon's soul eased a little under its burden and he saw far ahead the fleeting hope of peace.

The Kingdom, he thought. Mine is the Kingdom. This at least no one can take away.

At last he felt he could speak, start to open his Pandora's box of griefs. 'Dusty,' he began abruptly. 'I know your people believe in dreams, Christ, you invented them in this country, you had the Dreamtime hundreds of thousands of years before we came along. But do you believe in evil dreams – in anything like Satan? The Devil putting evil dreams into our heads?'

Dusty took his time before replying. 'Always, always been evil, boss. Always good spirits and bad spirits, good animals and bad animals, good people and bad. But more bad evil in men than in any spirits. Always.'

'Dusty—'

Jon felt a strange excitement, sensing he was beginning to break through the fog of confusion and indecision that had kept him a prisoner since the night of the bad dream. 'Dusty, who lives at the water-hole?'

Dusty gazed straight ahead. 'Fishes, birds, lizards – and big snakes.'

'Snakes?'

'But it ain't only who lives there, is it, boss? Anyone can visit.'

Now he knew where they were going. 'Like we're going to do now?'

Dusty gave the ghost of a smile. 'Just like that.'

They rode in silence for a long time, as Dusty's reticence seemed to demand. Finally Jon could bear it no more. 'Were you coming out here this morning anyway? Or is this trip just because I showed up?'

'Oh . . .'

Dusty raised his eyes thoughtfully to the sky and tipped

back his hat. 'I guess I thought I might come on up here one of these days soon.'

Again Jon felt the stab of excitement. 'You've found out something!' he challenged. 'Or sensed it, picked it up—'

Dusty smiled ironically. 'This isn't Dreamtime magic, boss, just common sense. I heard something funny, that's all. You know out on the muster, we were taking it in turns to watch the cattle? Coupla hours before your dad died, it would've been Slim's watch. Slim told me he heard a plane that night. And no one come to the station and no one go anywheres I know of. So who? And why?'

Jon struggled to stay calm. 'Could have been flying over?'

'He says it didn't go over. Didn't come farther than the airstrip.'

'So a plane could have come in that night, landed, and gone out again without anyone knowing?'

Dusty nodded. 'Sounds like.'

'And someone—'

'Or someones—'

'—could have come quietly into the station and left again and no one the wiser that they'd ever been here?' Jon's mind was spinning. 'And from the airstrip to here – across country, even at night, on foot, how long d'you think it'd take? If they knew the terrain?'

Dusty had already worked this out. 'For a good healthy walker, no more than an hour. And boss—' he paused. 'Everyone round here knows the terrain.'

'Yeah.' Bitterness swamped him. Whoever had wanted to kill Phillip, it was becoming clearer and clearer that it had to be someone from here. 'So they could have been in and out under cover of dark?'

Dusty shook his head. 'If there was any "they". We gonna see.'

They were drawing near the water-hole now, and Dusty

192

insisted that they dismount and tether their horses to a tree high on the rim of the bowl sweeping down to the pool at the base of the rock.

'Enough walking round there already,' he said. 'Your Dad first, then all of us finding him and carrying him away, then you after – maybe we don't find nothing, maybe nothing left to find. You wait here by the tree. I gonna look. I find anything, I call.'

It was a long time before Jon's straining ears heard anything but the tiny living sounds of the bush. He sat so long silent and motionless under the tree that to the creatures of the land he became like one of them. Greeny-black bugs and gold-backed beetles scurried unnoticing around him as they went about their daily work, lizards scuffed his boots, and a small sand-mouse ran across his leg.

But at last the cry came. 'Cooee! Here! Over here!'

He stood up. Carefully quartering his way around the water-hole, Dusty had covered a series of ever-widening arcs sweeping out from the crack between the boulders where Phillip had stretched himself out for his last sleep. As Jon approached he was crouching near the earth, using his two hands as much as his sharp eyes to 'read' the ground. Now he parted a clump of low-lying brush and pointed with one accusing finger. 'See that?' he said softly. 'Three men, trotting.'

For the life of him Jon could see nothing except a few broken stems. 'Trotting?'

'Running light and fast. Jogging. Covering the ground.'

In a flash he saw it as clearly as if he had been there. 'Running. Getting away!' He paused. 'That must have been after – after they'd done it.'

Dusty straightened up and rubbed at his back, waving over to the left. 'They came down there. Round where your father was I lost them, too many people, too many tracks. But the same three that came down there went back up here.' He pointed again. 'Same direction too.'

'Yeah,' Jon nodded. 'Towards the airstrip.' He fixed Dusty with a glare of fierce enquiry. 'You're sure there were three?'

Dusty gave a nod. 'Three.'

'Men?'

'Three men, boss. Unless you know any ladies round here take size tens and elevens. And been in the army.'

'The army?'

'Or some men's outfit where they done military drill. Look.' He moved further down the bowl of the water-hole, towards the cleft in the rocks where Phillip had made his bed. 'See that track? They were on their bellies from there on in. Tiger crawl. Like this.'

He dropped to the ground and demonstrated a low, serpentine slither, legs and body stretched out behind slack and unmoving, pulling himself forward on his fore-arms. 'They used to teach them that in Vietnam, it's an old para trick from way back. Makes you sound not like a human, so it don't frighten anyone used to the bush. And it rubs out your tracks as you go, no footmarks, you could just be any big animal.'

Jon felt a wave of pain and anger so strong that he could hardly speak. 'Or a big snake.'

Was this how the old man used to stand as he waited for the household to come down to dinner, Alex wondered? Or maybe that legs-akimbo, king-of-the-castle stance was just too obvious for the kind of owner he was planning to be? Immaculate in his well-cut slacks and French blazer, Alex shifted his position on the hearthrug and tried again, trying also to suppress the worm of worry gnawing at his heart.

Why had he brought her here? He'd been doing fine till now. Adopted as the son and heir, waited on hand and foot, with even little Ellie on hand to provide rest and recreation for the troops, what more could a man want?

Except Trisha.

Ever since he'd met her, every minute of every day he wanted her. So the idea of a quick trip to Sydney to see her, to fetch her here, had seemed such a good one when the 'copter was going back. And once he had yielded to that fatal impulse, there was only one way it could go.

What was it about her? Alex ran a tense hand through his thick black hair as he grilled himself for the thousandth time. What did he see in her? Yes of course she was beautiful, super-model beautiful with that amazing body, thick clustering true gold, honey-gold hair, perfect bone structure, wide-set thick-lashed grey eyes and a mouth that looked far more generous than it was, than she could ever be. But Alex had never touched a less-than-good-looking woman in his life, he took that for granted, that was not her appeal.

Nor was it her sensuality, the call of the wild-cat in her, that fantastic body whose nerve-ends everywhere seemed to lie closer to the surface than other women's. She was all woman, sure. That too was no less than the all man in him would require.

All woman.

He took a sullen swig of whisky as that thought sank in and spread like a stain. All woman. Yeah.

All woman in her vanity, her self-centredness, her demands. Remorselessly he ticked them off in the familiar catalogue of her crimes. Jesus, her hairdresser, her manicurist, her aromatherapist were more important to her than he was! Because like the beautiful animal she was, she took exactly what she needed from life and then threw all but the bones away.

Only behave yourself at Koenigshaus, he'd ordered her. *And don't drink too much, there's no champagne lifestyle out here! These are farming people, decent people, they know nothing outside the cattle station.*

In reply he'd had no comfort but a mocking laugh: *well then, it's about time they learned!*

She'd only stay a few days or a week, she'd warned him, that would be long enough without her shops and salons, her fitness trainer, astrologer and masseuse, all the support systems that made her what she was, shallow, vain and self-absorbed. How they were going to work it out when he got the cash, God only knew!

If they were going to work it out.

He bit his lip. From the moment they met in that little champagne bar off Double Bay, she had shown less than no interest in his life, his past, his future, or anything except his body and his ability to pace her, step by step, in all her desires, pastimes and whims.

Yet it never did, in Alex's wide experience, to let women call the tune. They simply trampled on the good guys, while men who behaved like bastards could get away with murder. Trisha was not the kind of woman to take shit from any man. But she was exactly the kind to despise anyone who did not stand up to her.

Alex frowned in bitter awareness of the battles that lay ahead. One thing for sure, he was not going to join that silly circuit she adored, the party people, the Sydney jet-set she had attached herself to with such enthusiasm when her first husband died. An aged American, a retired mid-Western grain-trader of legendary wealth, he had hardly lived long enough to inconvenience her with his existence, or to break her stride between being the spoiled daughter of a wealthy doting father and the spoiled woman she now was, free to spoil herself.

And yet . . .

And yet . . .

Cursing under his breath, he broke away from his vantage point underneath the portrait of old Johann with its fierce hawk-like glare and all-encompassing frown, and poured himself another whisky.

And yet he wanted her as he had never wanted another woman in his life. Not that she held him off – on the contrary she had given herself to him as freely, he guessed, as she had always given herself to the men she desired.

And still he wanted her. She was an addiction.

And like any addict, he knew he needed money to support his habit. He had to have the cash from Koenigshaus as much to be sure of her, as to enjoy it himself. For women like her were expensive, they never came with less than an 'if-you-have-to-ask-the-price, you-can't-afford-it' tag around their necks.

So even with all your millions, even then, said the small cold voice of one of his private demons, will you ever truly possess her, ever really call her your own? Won't she be off again as soon as she tires of you, runs through your cash or finds another man with more money to his name?

Alex, could never use the term 'love', even in his secret thoughts. But however strenuously he avoided saying the word, he was beginning to fear that he had caught the disease, and in its deadliest form.

And where was she now?

Fuming, he paced the room. *Be down early!* he'd ordered her, *I want you there when the rest of them come in!*

Where was she?

His soul was aching, his whole body was missing her with an ache like the onset of an illness. How long could it take a woman to get dressed for dinner?

Where was she?

A light footfall in the hall had him turning with a broad grin towards the archway. At last! He kind of liked it when she defied him, because he could make her pay for it afterwards. Now he could tell her just exactly what he planned to do to punish her, when they were alone—

'Alex, dear, where's Trisha?'

She was a nice enough woman, Helen, Alex brooded, she hadn't stopped trying to make up for the past ever since he arrived. But this was one problem that she couldn't solve. 'Oh, she'll be across soon,' he said lightly. 'Probably still titivating, you know what women are.'

'I hope she'll be comfortable in the guest bungalow, we could have welcomed her up here in the main house if you'd wanted to have her here—'

In the Tower with you, in your room . . . her tone delicately implied.

'No, she'll be fine,' he said firmly. 'She likes her own space, she really needs it.' *And so do I*, he pledged himself. *We're two of a kind.*

He heard the latch lift on the front door as Ben and Geena arrived and a moment later Charles came down the stairs to join them. He seemed cold and withdrawn, he did not look at Helen, Alex noted, let alone gravitate to her side as he was always doing before.

Was that why Helen looked so washed out, almost as pallid as her ivory silk dress? Ben's daughter, Alex saw with irritation, listlessly accepting nothing more sociable than a mineral water, was another one who looked like death warmed up. What was wrong with all of them? At least the reason for her wretchedness was clear the minute Jon walked in – her eyes brightening, she moved at once to his side.

Just speak to him, Geena had been telling herself all day, you've done nothing wrong, he's the one who's all messed up, just speak to him, have it out! She was trembling with impatience as the hour for drinks drew near. Now she didn't care what anyone thought, she pounced on him as soon as he came through the door.

'Look, I'm sorry I didn't get the chopper out of here

198

and leave when you wanted me to,' she blurted hurriedly in a low voice, with a glance over her shoulder to make sure no one was in earshot. 'But I couldn't just walk out on everything I've been doing here – the time I've been putting in with the people up at the camp, the show we're working on—'

'I know.'

To his great surprise, Jon was much less embarrassed at facing Geena than he had expected. Things had moved on so fast, he felt a different person from the man who had capped a stupid drunken evening with an even more stupid pass at the girl standing before him.

Yet it was more than a pass, a small sweet trace of the memory scolded him. Still, after all he had found out today, been through, endured, that feeling, that kiss, came from another world . . .

He was in a dream, Geena thought, he just was not himself. No wonder, with this latest sign that Alex meant to be master of Koenigshaus, even down to flying in a mistress! 'Jon,' she demanded, 'what will you do now?'

'Do?'

'I mean, get your own place, or what? And where will your Mum go?'

He looked down at the concern in her eyes and wished with all his heart that he deserved it, or could hope to earn it. If only things had been different. God, she was such a great girl, such a lovely kid, if only—

No 'if onlys'!

'Thanks for caring,' he said haltingly, feeling his way around her question. 'Fact is, I don't know. I know I've got to think about it soon, but Alex has been pretty good about our staying here till we've sorted something out.'

'Yes, but now—'

Jon had come straight in from riding, Geena realised with a shaft of dismay, he hadn't spoken to anyone, he didn't know! She fumbled for words. 'I mean, now—'

'Now what?' He stirred with unease. What was that look in her eye?

Geena took a deep breath. 'Now that Alex's girlfriend is here—'

'Girlfriend?' Christ, what had he missed?

Suddenly the talk in the other group around the hearth faded away. Looking up Jon saw Alex's gaze fixed on the doorway behind him.

Turning, he saw one of the most beautiful women he had ever seen in his life. Almost as tall as he was, shaped like a goddess, deep-set dusky eyes glinting out from behind a cascade of hair that could only be called gold, she was encased in a dress of green-gold slithery fabric that made her look like some kind of gorgeous snake. Holding the pause like one born to the spotlight, she stood in the archway to the dining room and after briefly scanning the stunned and silent company, fixed her eyes on him.

'Well,' she drawled, moving towards him with the sensual swagger of a jungle cat, 'well, you must be the little brother.'

She came right up to him, ignoring the alarmed Geena and a tense Alex rapidly approaching across the carpeted floor. Her provocative glance was open and unconcealed. 'Well – nobody told me about *you*!'

Chapter 20

God, what an evening!

What a dinner! What a nightmare!

And that bloody woman Trisha! How could Alex bear her, surely he could have found someone nicer, someone *else*!

Oh, she'd give anything to be in bed right now, this second – she had to have time to herself—

'Helen!'

He was waiting for her when she came out of the dining room, although she had prolonged the clearing-up in order to give everyone time to go away and leave her on her own. Now the tall lean figure melting up to her out of nowhere at the foot of the stairs, shrouded in the half-dark of the hall, was more than her over-strained nerves could bear. She turned on him like a tiger.

'No more balcony scenes, Charles, please! I'm too old to play Romeo and Juliet!'

He drew back as if she had spat in his face. 'I wasn't going to try to get you up to my room for a teenage pounce, Helen, if that's what you think!' His face was pale with anger. 'If you say you're too old for any of this, you might at least pay me the compliment of thinking that I'm also a little past the stage of schoolboy fumbles and gropes!'

'OK, OK. It's just that – after tonight – the way it all was, and the way Trisha carried on – I've got to have some peace and quiet, I just want to wind down.'

'And so do I!' His face softened. 'Maybe we can do it together?' He paused. 'Look, don't go up to bed yet, let's take a walk outside.'

Gently he drew her down the hall and threw open the front door. 'It's a beautiful night. When was the last time you had a chance to look at the moon?'

After a moment's hesitation she gave in and moved towards the open door, passing through into the scented, murmuring night. Outside under the stars the whole night universe seemed alive with sighs and sounds and whispers and shy forays and kindly little scurries, the whole world more natural and real than anything they had endured all evening.

'I won't ask you what you thought of – of our visitor,' began Charles carefully, well aware from his first sight of her that Trisha was the kind of woman all other women instantly branded 'a bitch'. 'I just wondered what you think her arrival means for you and Jon.' And for me – for us, he might have added, but didn't.

'She doesn't love him!' said Helen passionately. 'Women like that never love anyone except themselves! If she cared for Alex at all she'd never have carried on with Jon like that. God, she was disgusting, flirting and batting her eyelids, she could see it was winding Alex up dreadfully!'

'Surely that's why she did it?' hazarded Charles as he shepherded her across the grass and down the rose walk leading away from the house. 'And would she bother to do that if she didn't care?'

And the whole performance was totally wasted on Jon anyway, he wanted to say. That boy's so unworldly that he didn't have a clue what she was up to, he wouldn't recognise a green light from a randy lady if it came thundering towards him mounted on a ten-ton truck!

Still, any man on thin ice with a woman, he reminded

himself just in time, does not make humorous cracks about her son. He held his tongue and waited.

But she picked up his train of thought. 'It's Jon I'm worried about,' she said. 'Where's he going to go?'

'What do you mean?'

'Well, we've got to get out of here, I knew that the second Alex radioed from Sydney to say he was bringing "a lady guest".' Her hand rose to her troubled forehead, pushing back her hair in that gesture he loved so much. 'Whether he plays the respectability game and puts her in the guest house, or spends twenty-four hours a day in bed with her in his own room, she's still his girlfriend all right, you can tell from the way he treats her. And if he's the master of Koenigshaus now, she's the next mistress.'

God Almighty, she'd got a long way!

Charles was grateful that the darkness covered his silent whistle of surprise. He had asked Helen for this night walk because he felt responsible for her, and never more so than after this new and quite unexpected development. But he had thought he would have to take her through all this, step by painful step, laboriously spelling out the consequences of what had happened. Now he saw that he had been underestimating her all along. 'You seem to have it pretty well worked out,' he ventured.

'Yes, well.'

When had she picked up that hard note in her voice, he wondered.

'I've been getting wised up about a lot of things recently!' she said sharply. 'Not before time, it seems. I've missed a hell of a lot that's been going on under my nose, and fallen for things I shouldn't have put up with for a second. God, I've been an idiot! And let's face it!' She gave a short unamused laugh. 'There aren't many prizes for being a stupid female in this day and age, are there?'

'What about Jon?'

She came to a sudden stop under a great cedar, her hands bunched into fists, her knuckles crushing her lips. 'Oh, Charles.'

Her whole body was shaking, she was fighting back great stifling, choking sobs. 'I can't bear it, I can't bear to think what's happening to Jon! I haven't dared take on board before what losing Koenigshaus must mean for him, because I never believed it till now. I can go anywhere, I don't matter, I've knocked around before, I can do it again if I have to. But he doesn't know anything in the world except this. What's going to become of him?'

Now, now they were all in bed and asleep, now was the best time.

Like all true country dwellers, Jon had no fear of the dark. Indeed, part of him loved the night bush even more than the day. The soft furry nocturnal creatures with their huge, night-adapted eyes swinging upside down from the trees to greet him as he passed were friends: he could decipher every cry, every whisper he picked up, every stick that cracked from a step not his own.

Tonight, though, he could not indulge himself in one of the midnight rambles that had been his delight since early childhood. His destination now was no farther than the office and its all-important radio link and fax machine.

Whoever slept throughout Australia, throughout the world, one breed of men were wakeful round the clock, he knew. And he needed to speak to them while all the rest of Koenigshaus was safely asleep. Slipping into the office building, Jon swiftly found the number of the air traffic control centre in Sydney, lifted the radio transceiver, and hit the 'transmit' button.

'This is Kilo Hotel Sierra, Kilo Hotel Sierra, Koenigshaus Station, yes, hi there. Can you patch us through to Flight Operations for the Northern Territory? It's an enquiry. A flight from Sydney airport, yeah, destination

Koenigshaus. Thanks.' He took up a perch on the side of Phillip's desk and waited, staring ahead.

From the wall before him, Phillip's schoolboy self, unlined, unsmiling, absurdly slim and arrogant as only a public schoolboy can be, stared back at him. Idly his eye travelled over the black italic flourishes beneath, *PHILLIP JOHANN KOENIG, HEAD BOY, ROCKHAMPTON COLLEGE 1948–49.*

Head boy.

Good old Dad. The start of a pattern of achievement Phillip had kept up all his life.

And yet to end up in a gully between two rocks, trapped like an animal, exterminated like vermin, by vermin, human vermin . . .

The now familiar bitterness of rage was welling up in him like vomit: I'll get them, Dad, I promise, they won't get away with it, I'll get them . . .

'Hello? It's Koenigshaus, yeah, hi mate, sorry to bother you at this time of night. Fact is, we've lost track of a flight plan from a week or two ago and the boss here's screaming blue murder. I was wondering if you could fax us out a copy of the details we must have filed with you when we logged the flight.'

He waited for the response from the other end. 'When? It was a week last Tuesday, the only flight we had all month, apart from a few 'copter shuttles. You will? Great! Thanks. OK, let me give you our fax, hang on, here it is.' Carefully he dictated the number to the unseen operator on the other end. 'You can let me have it now? Thanks a million, mate, you don't know what this means.'

Moments later he held the paper in his hand, its letters and figures jumbling before his eyes. *Light aircraft Victor-X-ray 4355 dep. Sydney 22.00 hours destination Kilo Hotel Sierra Koenigshaus Station ETA 00.10 hours. Return flight ETD 02.30 hours, arrival recorded 04.40.*

So there had been a plane!

He could hardly take it in, he had to force himself to decode the brief facts.

Victor-X-ray–4355—

Someone had flown here from Sydney at ten o'clock that night, arriving just after midnight. Then they had left at half past two in the morning and been back in Sydney just after half past four, so no one at that end need ever have known that they'd been away.

Two and a half hours.

On Dusty's calculations, that would have given plenty of time for anyone on foot to make the distance from the airstrip to the water-hole, strike down a sleeping man and get back to the plane.

Feverishly his eye scanned the page. *Passenger manifest: 3.*

Dusty was right, then.

Three men.

Oh, the bastards!

But who was the boss, who was the one in charge, *whose idea was it*?

His eye skipped to the final entry. *Aircraft registered to Kingdom Holdings PLC. Owner and pilot Mr I. A. M. Kingdom, prop.*

Oh, the bastard.

The bloody, bloody bastard.

He sat as still as a stone while the knowledge worked its way through his mind like veins forming in marble.

There was only one man on Koenigshaus who had been cheated out of a 'kingdom': cheated twice, once by the accident of birth, once when his businesses had been bought out from under him by an older, stronger man.

Only one man here might have been driven to kill to save the business empire he had created in the place of all he had lost.

Only one man had the bitter, sardonic humour which

would have led him to call the camouflage company by the name of his lost empire.

Only one man cool and angry and determined and motivated enough to kill.

To kill Phillip Koenig.

Charles.

It had to be Charles.

Uncle Charles.

Now another set of illuminations exploded in Jon's brain, bombarding him with danger signals unnoticed at the time but now spelling out a rising pattern of alarm.

Charles.

Charles close by his mother's side as they walked down the aisle at Phillip's funeral . . .

Helen turning instinctively to Charles as soon as she heard the will . . .

Charles using Helen to urge the sale on Mrs Matsuda and the influence he exerted over her then . . .

Helen's eyes fastened on Charles at dinner tonight . . .

No!

Whatever Charles was after with his mother, whatever he wanted, it was his responsibility to put a stop to it! He had to look after her!

Jon's conscience lanced him cruelly. If only he had tried to help Mum more through all of this, instead of slinking off like an animal to lick his own wounds. If only he hadn't insisted on getting drunk, fooling around with Geena – Christ, he'd left her terribly to herself, he hadn't looked after her at all! And into that vacuum had slipped dear old Uncle Charles, the new boy on her block, the man on the make!

No!

Not while he could still take care of her!

Crushing the flight plan into the safety of his pocket as he jumped to his feet, Jon took the space between the desk and the door in one great stride, switched off the lights, and left the office building at a run. Just check that Mum's OK tucked up safe in bed, then think this whole thing through again, he thought. Try to get a grip, get some more details, find more evidence, look after Mum—

Like all bushmen Jon ran lightly, soundlessly, covering the earth without disturbing anything or anyone within range. And the bushman in him always knew too when others were around, before they picked up his trace.

What was that?

Across the lawn, under the trees he caught a slight movement, but his light-accustomed eyes took a second or two to adjust to the dark. Then to his unimaginable horror he made out Charles and his mother standing close together, wrapped in the warm luscious night. He saw Charles take Helen in his arms and crush her to his chest, then kiss her passionately, protractedly, full on the mouth. Under the hopeless light of a cold futile star a million miles from home, he saw his mother lost in the hungry, deep embrace of the man who had killed his father.

Chapter 21

'Thanks for driving me over, Dad. I just couldn't ask Mrs Koenig to give me a lift this morning like she usually does, she seemed so – I don't know what! And with that – that *woman* on her hands, it's no wonder!'

So his daughter still had too much of her convent-school education in her to say 'that bitch!' Ben noted with a wry amusement.

'Trisha?' he queried grimly. 'Yes, she's not exactly good cattle-station material, is she? Can't see her settling down out here to make the Kingdom her home the way Helen did, not in a million years. The blessed spite of it all is, she'll still put Helen off the place, even if she never deigns to live here herself.'

'Yeah.' Geena's heart congealed with jealous resentment. 'And Jon, now she's here Jon'll have to get out too.' She put a hand on her father's arm. 'Oh Dad, you knew Mr Koenig – why did he change his will and disinherit Jon?'

'Search me,' said Ben heavily.

Mechanically he negotiated the last turn of the dirt track and swung the 4WD into the Aboriginals' village. In the centre of the compound stood a tall white figure earnestly engaged in deep discussion with a handful of the tribe's young men. Geena's heart lurched – Jon?

Ben nodded. 'Y'know Henry Suffolk, the station manager? Say hello to him for me, will you, I won't stop, better get on.' He forced a smile. 'I want to get all this done, get you out of here. I think we've both had enough of Koenigshaus and the Koenigs to last us a while, haven't we?'

Poor Dad, poor darling Dad.

With an ache in her heart Geena stood and waved Ben off, watching him go with a peculiar pain. Like all daughters of widowed fathers, she cared about him with a defensive passion all the fiercer for being completely unspoken between them. Poor old Dad. He tried so hard, but he always got slapped down sooner or later.

Were some men born to lose, she brooded, or did they just get defeated, worn down by time, bad breaks, not enough money, other men's aggression, other men's fights?

'Hi there – hello!'

She turned to see a tall, sturdy man approaching her, turning a worn cowboy hat in his hands. His pleasant, open face would have been handsome in the eyes of a woman who loved him, but his smile was his most winning feature, sweet and shy and somehow unsure, as if he did not get enough practice in having and sharing fun. 'Miss Nichols?'

'Geena,' she said with an answering smile.

'Just stopping to say hello,' Henry said awkwardly, regretting he'd stirred at all. God, when he'd taken it into his head a moment ago to have a closer look at the pretty little thing he'd seen floating about Koenigshaus, he hadn't imagined how tricky it'd be to follow it through! Too many nights with the boys and not enough practice with the ladies, he thought ruefully. And under the steady gaze of those outsize liquid eyes, eyes a bloke could drown in, he couldn't think of another thing to say.

'What are you doing here?' murmured Geena, softening as all women do to a shy man, especially one who hid his shyness behind a frame that would not have disgraced the young John Wayne.

'Just stopped by to organise the lads for the next muster. 'Course, Dusty does most of it. But I have to liaise with him to let Jon know what's going on.'

She choked down a sigh. 'You're lucky if you always know what's going on, Mr Suffolk. I wish I could say I did!'

Like a strip cartoon her mind replayed last night's wretched dinner. Why did it hurt so much?

He had been honest, he'd already told her where she stood.

There was nothing between them, and there never could be, he'd said that about as plainly as he could.

'If you'll excuse me, Mr Suffolk,' she said, 'I have to get on, as I'm sure you do. Give my regards to Jon when you speak to him.'

She hurried off up the compound to the improvised dance arena where her dancers had been gathering by ones and twos. Keenly awaiting her arrival was Timbo, now emerging as one of the most talented and dedicated of the troupe.

'Hey, Geena!' he began without preamble, 'you know you told us to ask the old folk if they knew any stories we could use for our show, for the dance we're going to make for the corroboree? I think I've got one for you.'

His eyes were shining and Geena could feel her own excitement rising in response. 'Great stuff, Timbo, what is it?'

For answer he encircled her wrist with his wiry thumb and finger and led her back down the hill to one small hut standing on its own. Pausing outside, he laid a finger to his lips. 'Don't talk, just listen. And no questions – she's very, very old, older'n the hills, she was taken as his woman by the first Johann, that's what they say.'

Geena gasped. 'The first Johann? Timbo, that's impossible, she'd have to be over a hundred years old—'

'Sssh!' Placing his finger on his lips again, Timbo beckoned her forward and led her into the hut.

Inside, a glittering gloom danced round an ancient woman seated cross-legged on a blanket in the centre of the dirt floor. Shards of broken sun pouring through slits in the roof, split and fragmented by dust-motes glancing up and down the shafts of light, played around an aureole of pure white hair and a blue-black countenance not merely wrinkled but carved and sculpted with lines deeper than time. Her eyes, two large globes full of milk, stared unseeingly upwards above a toothless, in-turned mouth, and her tiny wrinkled hands resting like crabs upon her knees.

The boy knelt before her, raising one of her hands to his face to introduce himself. 'It's Timbo, Gran,' he said clearly. 'I brought the girl. Tell her your story for her dance.'

In a chanting monotone the old woman began, as if she had been waiting for her cue. 'All-Father make men white, make men black, make women to match. Long time ago first Johann here have his own woman, white woman from his own country, and the black men here have theirs.'

Geena drew in her breath sharply. Timbo gave her a warning glance as the old woman went on. 'Johann come to take. Everything the people have, he take. He take the land, he take the 'roos they live on, he take the water-hole. But still want more. He see the wife of the head man of our tribe and he want her too.'

In the stillness nothing stirred. The old voice murmured on. 'He want her and he come for her. He come down the bush and he court her and she go with him. She thought she have him in secret, he be nice to all her tribe. But he want her all for himself, like the land, all for himself. So he close off the water-hole, drive the people away to die, put cattle there instead.'

She paused, crooning to herself. 'But their dreamers dream his new cattle just their old 'roos come back for them to eat. So they kill his cattle. Then he kill them. All 'cept the woman. When she see she can't save her man or her people, she save herself. She run away from the whips and guns, she run, she run, she run. But he come after her, and he find her. Then he keep her always as his black woman. And she stay his woman even though he killed her man, killed her people, took their land. And she never forget, never forgot nothing that happen. Aieee! Aieeee!'

Placing her hand to her head, she began to keen in a high, heart-rending wail. Timbo caught Geena's wrist and drew her out of the hut. 'So what d'you think?' he demanded.

Geena shook her head, almost too full to speak. Was she telling her own story, the old woman? Had she been the girl old Johann so desired that he had killed all her tribe to possess her? Or had she just imagined it, dreamed herself into that other young woman's place, reliving her tragic fate?

Geena gripped Timbo's hand in a welter of emotion. 'If she'll let us turn that story into dance – Timbo, I can't think of anything more powerful and more right for this place and this corroboree!'

God, it must be wonderful to be working on something soothing and easy like dance, Henry Suffolk thought in a moment of wild envy, instead of doing a rough job like this! Feeling strangely out of sorts, he watched Geena as she walked slowly back up the compound to rejoin her group of dancers with Timbo by her side. He turned back to the group of men all around. 'OK, that's the muster fixed. Now I know you're all on for it, I'll let you know as soon as we're ready to move.'

The ranks of heads nodded and the men began to stir in readiness to move off. 'Just one thing more before you go,' Henry resumed. 'Message from the boss – the young boss, Mr Jon, that is – no, look, I mean to say—'

He broke off in confusion, kicking himself. Christ, how long would it take him to get used to the fact that Phillip was dead? Come to that, how long would it take him to get hold of the even more horrible idea that Jon was not the new boss, but that city type Alex?

Henry cursed himself and fate violently, and tried again, covering his awkwardness. 'Look, Jon wanted me to ask if any of you saw anything, heard anything, the night the old boss died?'

There was a deep, reflective silence as all the men stared non-commitally ahead, avoiding each other's eyes.

Henry grinned. 'There'll be no trouble for anyone, I promise you, no matter what you've been up to. Jon just wants to know if any of you were awake and about that night on any kind of errand, if you saw anything unusual, that's all.'

A row of blank faces and shaking heads greeted his appeal. Henry gave up. 'OK,' he said. 'Well, thanks for listening. If anyone remembers anything – just let us know. It's just the idea of tracking down anything out of the ordinary that anyone happened to notice, that's all.'

'Well, boss,' laughed the mischievous Slim with a mocking gesture towards a shambling figure weaving by, 'why don't you tell him to have a word with old Markie there, Ellie's man? He's out of the ordinary, whichever way you look at it! Hey, mate!' he carolled, without waiting for further encouragement. 'Boss wants t'know, y'seen anything lately? Anything unusual going on?'

Like most drunks, Mark was quick to suspect an insult, and when baited, touchy in the extreme. Looking up now, the small red pig-like eyes seemed to fill with blood as Mark's powerful body swelled with sudden rage.

'Seems to me I should be asking the boss that!' he muttered furiously, bunching his burly fists as he spoke. 'Mr High and Mighty Koenig keeps my wife up at Koenigshaus every bloody waking hour these days! Morning, noon and night she's up there now, visitors, dinners, cleaning, cooking, I don't know what she isn't bloody doing! Now the bitch is giving herself airs and graces, she's too good for me, she won't have anything to do with her poor bloody husband!'

He was working himself up into a fury as he spoke, rapidly losing what vestige of control he had. Now he advanced on Henry, shaking his fist. 'You're all the same, you're all the bloody same! If it wasn't the old boss after our women, it'll be one of you young bastards, you just think you can have Koori girls on tap! Well, you tell your boss, if anyone up there's playing around with my wife, I swear I'll kill the cow. He can have a side of prime dead meat! I'll make him a little present! I'll kill the fucking cow! . . . fucking cow . . . kill her . . .'

The thick sound died away. Losing his thread, stumbling for words, still swearing and cursing, Mark fell to his knees and began to cry, his threats and oaths collapsing into each other till they became one long incoherent moan.

'Get him out of here, willya?'

Henry gestured to the other men as he surveyed the shambles at his feet with undisguised disgust. All piss and wind, he thought, like all these drunks. They never did anything. Oh, no one who knew the pair of them could believe that Mark and Ellie would ever settle down to be a happy couple. But she was safe from him, however much he mouthed off! As long as her loving husband went on drowning himself in the contents of a tin can, Ellie would safely live out the rest of her natural days.

Besides, he had other things to worry about now.

One thing, anyway.

It stood about five feet four in its bare, brown, muscular little feet, its head would just about have brushed the button on his breast pocket and it answered to the name of Geena.

Chapter 22

Only if it made Jon happy, that was what she had told Charles.

Actively happy, that is, genuinely pleased for her, for Charles and for himself, heartily relieved that he wouldn't have to worry about his mother any more – that was the only way that she could think of making a go of it with Charles.

Waking that morning feeling unaccountably happy, lying in a pool of sunlight, drowsy and warm, relaxed as a cat, Helen wondered for one wild moment if she was in love. It had been so long. Was this how it felt? She could have sworn it was . . .

And for more than a few moments then, she had allowed herself to dream.

It was a lovely dream.

Of having a man again, a man in her life, a man in her bed, a man of her own – for even this short agony of widowhood had taught her once and for all that she was not a woman who could go through life alone. Oh, some women prized their independence, adored their freedom, loved to take off when they pleased, answering to no one. But after a lifetime spent growing like a vine trained around the pillar that had been Phillip, she knew that she was not one of them. She needed a man.

And not just for the sex – though already she was missing that horribly. It was having a man to care about, to take care of in every little way. Someone whose welfare was more important to her than her own. Someone to organise her life around, to get up in the morning for, to look forward to seeing at the end of the day, to be together with in bed in companionship as well as in the hungry need for love.

All morning, as she got up and dressed, went through the motions at breakfast and found she couldn't eat a thing, her mind was playing and replaying last night like a teenager: the scented night, the two of them under the moon, the soft light of the stars . . .

Oh, Charles . . .

He didn't appear for breakfast, and like a teenager again, she could not decide if she was sorry or relieved.

And now she was sitting in her window dreaming out over the lonely, level landscape instead of setting about the thousand and one everyday tasks that she had to do.

Dreaming of Charles . . .

What did she feel about him? Could they hope to recapture that first love they had shared so long ago?

'We'll play it your way, Helen,' he'd whispered urgently as he held her last night, 'whatever you want to do, whatever you want to say to Jon, or anyone else. But I won't wait forever! I've waited far too bloody long as it is!'

And so had she, hadn't she?

Hadn't she been like Rose, a lady-in-waiting all her life – waiting for the hard-won approval of just one man, waiting on his convenience, his moods, his anger, his desires? She had made a god out of Phillip, she had thought he was God. And she had ended up well and truly trampled under his feet of solid clay.

Just like Rose.

She must get over this futile anger with Rose, she must stop blaming the housekeeper for what Phillip had done. What choice did Rose have? What choice did women like her ever have?

Well, now it was her turn to choose. The first thing had to be to speak to Jon. Where would he be?

Like Charles, he had not come down for breakfast, but that was nothing new, he often grabbed a coffee in the kitchen and began the day without stopping to eat. Pausing to check his bedroom, which felt as cool and empty as if no one had been in it all night, Helen made her way downstairs and set out to look for him.

She only tried the office as a last resort, to see if Ben had seen Jon, or had any idea where he might be. But here Jon was, seated beside Ben at Ben's desk, peering into the screen of Ben's computer, hanging on his words. 'So you see,' Ben was saying, 'once you've got into the system with the password, you can just choose what you want to call up. It's all there, it's all in there somewhere. The trick is usually to find it!' He laughed. 'Hello, Helen – come to join the computer class as well?'

'Jon!' exclaimed Helen in surprise, 'What are you doing here?'

Was it her imagination, or did he change colour at the sight of her? She could feel herself flushing, the memory of last night still hot on her lips, her face.

But Jon couldn't know anything about last night, she hadn't told a soul and she could have sworn Charles hadn't either—

God, she looks guilty already, Jon thought with distress. 'Just learning,' he said shortly, colouring a little, keeping his eyes on the screen. 'Learning a lot, thanks to Ben here.'

'Well, I think you've got the hang of it now,' said Ben. 'I'm just going over to the house for a coffee, anyone coming?'

Jon shook his head. 'I think I'll just play with this for a bit longer.'

Helen waved a hand. 'You go on, Ben, I wanted to have a quick word with Jon.'

'OK, see you at dinner, if not before,' Ben said, and was gone.

All the time she had been looking for Jon her confidence had been building, her excitement surging, her longing to share her feelings with him growing every minute. But now they were alone, it was strangely difficult to begin. 'You wanted Ben to show you how the computer works?' she ventured awkwardly.

'Yeah.'

He seemed deliberately offhand and preoccupied, he would not take his eyes off the screen. 'Just curious – about a few things. And I'm at a loose end till the next muster. That's if there's going to be a next muster, for us anyway.' His voice hardened. 'If the famous Mrs Matsuda gets her skates on, we might all be out of here on our ear before then!'

'That's – what I wanted to talk to you about, Jon, dear,' she began tremulously. 'We haven't had a chance to think about it till now – but whatever you decide you're going to do, I don't want you to feel that you have to worry about me.'

He flushed, caught her eye and quickly looked away. 'Worry about you? Of course I worry about you! You're my mother!' *And I don't want you falling in love with that bastard Charles!*

'Well, I have to look after myself now.'

He glanced at her strangely. 'Do you think you can?'

'Whatever do you mean?'

His eyes returned to the safety of the VDU screen and its flickering green hieroglyphics. 'Let's face it, Mum – hell, you've had a pretty sheltered life. You never knew any man except Dad—'

'That's not true!' she burst out. 'I knew Charles before I knew Phillip and he – he cared about me!'

Charles!

Well, it bloody would be, wouldn't it!

With a violent shock Jon grasped another piece of the jigsaw. Of course he knew that Charles had introduced Mum to Dad, that was just one of those 'how did you meet?' things that every kid finds out about its parents before it can remember even asking. But it had been more than just a casual introduction, he realised now – Charles had loved her, he could see it in her face!

And had she loved him? Enough to turn a blind eye to Phillip's sudden death and how convenient that was?

Did she love him now, was that what she was trying to say?

He had to stop her coming out with it, making it real. Wildly he carried on. 'Even so, Dad did everything for you, decided everything, took care of you – and there's people out there—' *and here, in here, here on Koenigshaus!* he wanted to scream— '—people you have to watch out for – protect yourself against—'

She looked at him in bewilderment. 'What are you talking about?

Fucking Charles, that's who!

The man who killed your husband!

The man I'm on the trail of now, getting into this computer so I can track down his shady business deals and crooked manoeuvres and find the way to bring him to book.

She was still staring at him, wide-eyed. He looked away hopelessly. 'No one special, I guess.'

Poor Jon, Helen thought, her heart overflowing with mother love, he's stretched to the limit, I shouldn't add to his strain. He's worried to death about his future and about Koenigshaus and everything, and here am I bothering him with all this roundabout rubbish instead of just telling him the truth, because I'm as embarrassed as a kid with her first boyfriend.

She took a deep breath. 'Look, darling, there's something I wanted to say – about – about the future. My future. Of course it's early days yet, but I'm terrified of the idea that I'm going to be on my own for the rest of my life. I just wanted to know how you'd feel about – how you'd feel if – how you'd feel about the possibility that I might find someone else – maybe even marry again—'

'Marry again?' He could not have looked more appalled if she had struck him across the face. *'Marry?* Christ, no!'

'Why not?'

He stared at her, shock, hurt and anger coursing across his face. 'God Almighty, mother, you're forty-two!'

'That's not old,' she said defensively.

'It's – it's—' He ran a hand frantically through his hair. 'It's not only that!'

'What is it, then?'

He threw her another horrified glance, then refused to meet her eye. He looked sick with disgust. 'After Dad – after a man like Dad – how can you even think of it?'

'Jon – look – you know I loved your father, but – he wasn't the only man on the face of the earth!'

He turned towards her, his whole body tensed in angry reproach. 'What is it, mother – can't you take the idea of not being the mistress of a big house any more? Or have you got your eye on a replacement for Dad already – before he's had a chance to grow cold in his grave?'

What could she say?

But Charles was not a 'replacement', for God's sake, he was himself, and if she loved him it was because he was so different from Phillip—

If she loved him—

'It can't be—' Jon broke off, flushed darkly and bit his lip. 'It can't be – physical, can it?' He looked tortured with embarrassment, but seemed determined to push on, no matter what it cost. 'At your time of life . . .'

At your time of life . . .

Was that what he thought?

She was consumed with pain, seeing herself suddenly through his eyes. 'No, of course not, I don't really want to – I don't know what made me say it, just forget it, pretend I never said anything, OK?' She knew she was babbling, but she seemed powerless to stop. 'Of course you're right, darling, I didn't mean it, forget I ever said anything.'

She was moving to the door as she spoke, wanting nothing now so much as to get out. Jon had turned straight back to the computer, his broad shoulders hunched against her and all the world, as if to shut out her presence and wipe away all trace of their conversation. She fled. Left alone, Jon buried his face in his hands and began cursing himself and her, but most of all Charles.

So the bastard had got that far already, had he? Christ, he was a fast worker! And Mum was so vulnerable, far too trusting for her own good, what did she know?

He could not believe she knew of Charles' part in Phillip's death, he would not believe it. Then an unwanted memory pressed in to stop him in his tracks: Mum trying to get into the safe the day of Dad's funeral, and that haunted guilty look . . .

No! It was impossible! OK, she didn't love Dad any more, the sharp realisation pierced him with sudden awareness of all the painful little signs he had seen and not acknowledged. But she wouldn't kill him – would she?

No, it was Charles, it had to be.

He'd have to warn her, tell her about Charles.

But tell her what?

What could he tell her, what did he know for sure?

Nothing, less than nothing!

A call this morning to the Register of Companies in Sydney had yielded no more information about Kingdom Holdings than he already possessed. It was registered at an office in Macquarie Street in Sydney's elegant business quarter, an accommodation address, no more: no one lived there.

With great persistence and the help of a well-intentioned clerk in the companies' registry he had succeeded in establishing that Kingdom Holdings belonged to another company, which itself was not the parent company, as the clerk had patiently explained. The whole thing was set up as a smoke-screen, and the killer could retreat behind it all safe in the knowledge that it would take another, even bigger crook to break through his cover.

Nothing for it then but to go after the man himself, and the tracks he had left.

I'll get you, mate, no matter how clever you are, no matter how much you bloody dodge and weave!

The greenish light from the screen played eerily over Jon's taut, grimly determined face as he tapped away awkwardly at the computer, the light clatter of the keys keeping an irregular accompaniment to the endless flow of his disordered thoughts.

Charles loved Mum, loved her before Dad knew her, must have loved her all along, men have killed for less.

He hated Dad, Dad had put him down all their lives, that's a reason to kill that goes back to Cain and Abel.

He was about to lose everything if Dad wouldn't move one way or the other to sort out the business, men have killed for that too..

Then bingo!

Dad dies, and he's home free and clear. And then Mum drops right into his hand the minute he's ready to pull the string.

Out of trouble and in control, getting your hands on the woman you love and the business you love too, that's motive enough for any man. He would have known I'd agree to anything to keep Koenigshaus going, not like Dad, I'd never fight him for all the Sydney stuff and Koenig

Holdings, he could have that on a plate. And he couldn't have guessed that Dad would have changed his will, that we'd both lose out in the end.

And he's a Koenig. Johann killed a whole tribe to get what he wanted. In Charles's place, I'd have been tempted too. Do Koenigs always kill then, when they find something in their way? Will I have to kill Charles now? Is that the way it's going for both of us, him and me locked in a mortal combat as our Koenig destiny?

Get a grip, mate, this is real life, not some Boy's Own adventure!

With a shudder Jon applied himself again to the computer. Motive was nothing without proof, he had to prove Charles was capable of malpractice, uncover some evidence that he had reason to turn on Phillip like the snake he was and take his life.

And finally he found it.

His eyes stinging, neck aching, head swimming, he knew at last he'd found what he was looking for.

PORTFOLIO OF HOLDINGS –

Grimly he peered at the screen and saw what he had turned up at last.

A new programme of make-or-break acquisitions.

Am ambitious set of ventures and purchases which had left the company overleveraged and stripped of capital, hopelessly exposed and heading for disaster.

The entire project handled by Charles Koenig, Operations Head of Koenig Holdings PLC – project name – Operation Kingdom.

Chapter 23

OK, she'd had her fun, now she could pay for it!

As far as Alex was concerned, it had not been a good start to the day.

'Hey, boss!'

Struggling up from a morass of bad dreams, he opened his eyes to a most unwelcome visitor.

'Yeah, you!'

Before him stood a tearful, truculent Ellie bringing a tray of morning tea and a mouthful of violent complaints. 'You bring that woman here, you don't want me any more!' was her opening salvo.

The fucking bitch . . .

The very sight of her triggered a violent nausea, he felt as if he had been confronted by a pool of his own vomit. 'You're right,' he replied coldly, eyeing her with disgust. 'I don't want you any more.'

Lucky for him she was too stupid to believe what he was saying in this rash outburst of truth.

'Aiee!'

With a scream of fury she threw down the tray and launched herself on him. So then he had been obliged to put a stop to that, put her in her place in the time-honoured traditional way.

Afterwards she had been weepy and full of self-pity, clinging to him in a way that simply provoked in him the desire to hit her harder, fuck her more cruelly. 'You do

227

something for me,' she wept. 'My husband knows about us, he threatening me, he gonna do something violent.'

He tensed. 'Knows what about us?'

They were all liars, Koori women, he reminded himself, you couldn't believe a single word the little slags ever said, *don't panic, keep your cool.* Sure enough, a shifty look crept into the angry burning brown eyes as Ellie replied. 'He think I spend too much time up here at the house for what I take back, he say I gotta get more money or he gonna—'

'Or he what—?'

She snuffled. 'Or he hit me—'

He laughed coldly. 'More than I do?'

She shrugged her child's shoulders pettishly. 'Not the same when you do.'

God, they were all the same, women, no wonder men hit them! He took her chin between his thumb and fore-finger as they lay in bed and twisted it towards the light. Under the dark skin of her face could be seen the clear contours of a ripening black eye. 'More than he does already?'

She began to whimper again. 'He gonna get me, he gonna kill me, he say I'll be dead meat before he let me be just another black woman for the bloody Koenigs to play with—'

Alex laughed again. 'Kill you? Him and whose army?' But his heart grew colder still.

'You gotta take me in here, Mister Alex!' she insisted. 'Plenty room out the back where Rose lives, I can live in, live here, help out like she does, and then I'm safe from him.'

Christ, have her here on the premises, snuffling round like a bitch on heat, with Trisha around, a woman who could sniff out another's interest in him a mile away—?

A hot flare of panic passed through him. 'And if I don't?'

But she did not need to spell it out.

If she spilled the beans, as she so easily could—

Christ!

Anything like this stupid affair, with its sordid whiff of scandal, a sexual imbroglio involving a surly, violent, cuckolded husband, that could not help stirring up the Aboriginals so near the homestead, was the last thing they needed if they hoped to close the deal with Mrs Matsuda. The Japanese were fastidious in these things: they had no respect for those who could not restrain themselves from mixing business with the lower forms of pleasure.

And who else would buy a well with the waters so thoroughly muddied by the last users?

And apart from anything else, Trisha was such a filthy snob that if she knew who her rival was, if she knew he was fucking the domestic help—

As he lay there with the little bitch still cooing in his ear, playing with his nipples and fancying herself well back in his favour, he had forced himself to stay cool, to assess it step by step. Then he'd given the girl a few sweet words and a few even sweeter dollars for her 'overtime', slapped her backside and sent her on her way. But Christ, she'd need careful handling for the future – she would, the whole thing would . . .

At least he'd had one fairly pleasant thing to welcome the day, a call from Carey to say that winding up the estate was proceeding smoothly, the will was being proved, and everything now would shortly be in his hands.

But even that was not enough to assuage the memory of last night. Alex burned again with cold fire as the humiliation returned.

Last night.

The night he had been so looking forward to, the night he would have Trisha back. And his lady friend had seen fit to devote herself to his brother *all night*, flirting with

Jon so violently, leaning forward and offering herself to him so blatantly that all night long she was in danger of overflowing from her none-too-generous dress and popping out naked on a plate, for all the world to see.

OK, fine.

If that was the way she wanted to play it, he had promised himself as soon as she began, for every moment that he had to sit at the table and watch her doing it, she would pay for it in triplicate.

Like right now.

Striding across the lawn towards the guest house, Alex was feeding a fury with Trisha that had grown ever colder for being kept on ice all night. He had refused to let her see then how much she had rattled him, he would never give her the satisfaction of knowing that she had him on the run, running scared.

No, he had escorted her back to her suite in the guest house after dinner like any gentleman with any lady, though no lady would have been so much the worse for alcoholic wear as the divine Miss Trisha was last night, tottering and giggling and mightily pleased with herself for all her bad behaviour.

Nor would a true top-drawer, genuine blue-blooded mistress of good manners have caught hold of his tie as he ushered her through the door and tried to drag him to the bed, grabbing him here, there, and everywhere else before he managed to free her clutching hands from the two-hundred dollars' worth of Armani silk neck-gear that had never been designed to take such punishment.

Punishment . . .

That could come later, he told himself as he deposited her firmly on the bed and disengaged himself. When she was sober enough to remember it.

So last night he had confined himself to salvaging his tie, and what remained of his self-respect. He had assisted her forcibly to lie down, made sure she was comfortable and bowed himself out. And this morning he was bowing back in with a vengeance to establish once and for all who was king in this kingdom – whose word was law and what happened to bad girls when they transgressed.

Geena and Ben had left after breakfast, he calculated sourly, Ben to his eternal wanking over his bloody computer in the office, Geena to her high-class version of the same down with her black chums. That meant they had the guest bungalow to themselves, which was likely to be necessary for what he had in mind.

Taking the shallow flight of steps leading up to the entrance in one lithe stride, Alex cleared the small hallway and entered without knocking through the first door straight ahead. Behind the closed pink satin drapes the midday sun bathed the whole room in a sensual glow. He dropped down heavily beside the sleeping form sprawled loosely across the great king-sized bed, fixed his eyes on the flushed face half-hidden under the tumble of shining curls, and waited.

It did not take long. Like all socialites, Trisha invariably knew when she had company. 'Urggghh!' she groaned, beginning the long climb up to consciousness. 'Who is it?'

What's the time, Mr Wolf?

'King Kong,' he said.

She wriggled lazily, like a small child. 'Uuurgghh! Whaddya want?'

Mr Wolf, what big teeth you've got!

He smiled, showing white teeth in a humourless grin. 'You're going to have to wake up to find out.'

She rolled over, still swathed in the crumpled sheets like a mummy, and tried to push the hair out of her eyes. 'Alex?'

He was building nicely now, he could feel his fuse shortening every second. Any moment now he'd be ready to go. 'Who else?'

'Well, if that's all you can say,' she grumbled hoarsely, 'get me a drink, or fuck off!'

'Drink afterwards, darling,' he said pleasantly. 'Time for a little fun first.'

'Fun? She managed to squint up at him through one eye and then two. 'Why, where's the party?'

All the better to eat you with—

'Here,' he said.

He wanted to kill her. Something in his voice made her eyes, still drowsy as morning cornflowers, snap wide open at the sound. Her hands rose to defend herself and instinctively she clutched the sheet tight under her chin. He laughed, chilling her still more.

With one swift move he leaned forward as he sat beside her on the bed and standing up, tore the sheet from her clutching grasp. Beneath it she wore a frou-frou of peach lace and satin, the sort of bed-wear whose size is in inverse proportion to its cost. A little rose made of silk, surrounded by a froth of satin bows, nestled in her perfect cleavage. Grasping the ribbons in one hand he gave a violent tug.

'You bastard!'

The tearing sound as the flimsy fabric disintegrated and came away galvanised her like an electric shock, and she surged upright, her hands flailing for his face. With a brutal shove he knocked her back down again and, gripping the neck of the garment in both hands, he ripped it down the middle.

'Christ, no!' she yelled, aghast, struggling for all she was worth. 'Alex, for Chrissake, I got this in Bloomingdales, it cost a fucking fortune, stop it, you bastard—!'

But with mechanical efficiency he pulled the remains of the garment from her recumbent form, and tore it to shreds.

She was lying now just as he liked her, tense and unnerved, her eyes dilated and her breath coming short, trying to work out what he was going to do and how far she would have to go to placate him. Standing at the foot of the bed he surveyed the lovely splayed-out length with a coldness that he knew she found far more terrifying than even the wildest lust. Slowly he straddled her on the bed, carefully studying the white-skinned body, ample and soft from sleep.

OK, she was ready.

And he was too.

With light practised strokes he caressed the full, soft breasts, brushing the nipples with upward sweeps of his thumb until they responded engorged to his touch – he wanted them awake enough to feel everything that was going to happen. His hands moved on down the rounded haunches and long white legs tapering down from the tender, tangled bush, and he could feel the violence of his longing for her as his cock strained at his jeans.

'OK, baby,' he whispered pleasantly at last. 'Hands behind your back.'

Her eyes widened still more. 'Alex, I—'

He leaned forward and gently took hold of the hair on either side of her face, then slowly crossed the two ropes beneath her chin and across her neck. Slowly, remorselessly, he bore down on her throat. Moments later, he was rewarded by the sight of her two hands slipping frantically behind her back. She closed her eyes and bowed her head to her fate.

'That's better,' he said, still in the same mild voice. 'Now you know what this is for, don't you?'

She nodded.

'I want to hear it, darling.' His hand found her breast and gave the nipple a less-than-gentle tug. 'I'm asking you. You know what this is for, don't you?'

She nodded again, her eyes tightly closed. 'Yes.'

'And you deserve it, don't you?'

Her voice was very low. 'Ye-es.'

'Let me hear it—'

'I deserve it!'

'That's a good girl. OK, here it comes—'

Steadying her body with his left hand he delivered two ringing slaps to her full, spreading breasts. The first blows raised red weals on the soft white flesh, but he did not stop.

'Because – I – don't – like – it – when – you–come–on–to–another–man,' he remarked almost conversationally as he worked rhythmically over her body.'

'Oh! oh! ooooh . . .'

Her low moaning cries served only to encourage him, the marks on her breasts, the swelling aureoles round her bursting nipples gave him the most exquisite pleasure which he felt must be like her pain.

'And I – can't – stand – it – when – the – bastard – in – question – is – my – little – brother!'

Breathing heavily, he paused and looked down. All over their satin surface her breasts were red as fire, their soft pink nipples dark and rigid with desire, thrusting for his touch. She was moaning hard between parted lips and a line of tears was welling along the rim of each tightly-closed eyelid.

OK, that was a start.

Loosening the heavy belt of his jeans, he toyed with the idea of turning her over and beginning on her backside as well. Warming that ice-maiden body, reddening her pale rump till she cried out for mercy, seemed to warm the chip of ice at his heart in a way that nothing else could do.

But his own urgency would not wait much longer, that would have to be for another day. Thrusting two fingers into the silky triangle at the top of her legs, he found her moist and weeping for him, and her readiness excited his. Shrugging off his clothes he drove into her and knew again that infallible sensation that only she could give, the wild ecstacy he never had with any other woman.

'You bastard!'

The second she felt him naked between her legs, Trisha came alive, alive and fighting.

'Christ, you bastard! You lousy fucking *bastard*!'

She was shuddering beneath him with a mixture of anger and desire. Almost of a height with him, she pitted her considerable strength against his as he rode her like a disobedient mare, mastering her at every turn. Her tears forgotten, she was laughing now with delight as he pinioned her or evaded her flying fists, thrashing arms and legs, and wild, white teeth, until he drove them both to a raw, bursting, orgasm. Then both lay sated in as near to peace as their stormy souls would find on this side of the grave.

Like all earthly peace, it did not last for long. As they lay post-coital, dazed and drowsing, there came a shuffle and a loud clanking outside in the hallway and the door was roughly thrown open with a deliberate lack of respect.

'Clean your room, missus?' came Ellie's voice. The next second she had taken in Alex entwined with Trisha on the bed, and her triumphant rudeness turned to a scream of jealous rage. 'You here – with *her?*'

'Don't you know better than to come barging into bedrooms when people are asleep?'

Before he could stop her, Trisha had reared herself up on one furious elbow and was glaring at the interloper with red, enraged eyes. 'What are you staring at? You can get the hell out of here this second, and don't you dare come back. Get your black arse out of here, you ugly cow! You're fired, you Koori bitch!'

'Jump in, I'll give you a lift!'

'Thank you – what a pleasant surprise, lucky for me you happened to come by!'

Luck, Henry reflected privately, had nothing to do with

it. He had 'happened' to find some rather pressing business at the Aboriginals' camp, and not 'happening' to find Geena there, and learning that she had already left to walk back to the homestead, he had happened to find some reason to set off in that direction too, which was how he was now pulling up alongside the slight figure trudging through the shimmering heat of the long afternoon. 'Yeah,' he said awkwardly, 'Lucky I was going this way. I'm surprised to see you walking back to the house? Don't you usually get a lift?'

She smiled ruefully, with an upwards, sideways glance that went straight to his heart. 'Oh, every day till now. But somehow everyone's at sixes and sevens since – since Mr Koenig's girlfriend arrived. And Mrs Koenig seems to have so much on her plate, and I know she's worried about Jon as well—'

'So you just thought you'd walk?'

'Well, it didn't seem so far when I set out!' She laughed, a delicious gurgling sound. 'Not till I tried it, anyway. But I sure was glad to hear the sound of this truck coming along, and to see you.'

Did she mean it? And how could he reply lightly enough? God, if only he had a bit more small-talk! There were so many things that he had wanted to say. Now, when he managed to say something at last, it came out all wrong. 'Tell me about yourself,' he blurted.

'About myself?' She had the unvarnished surprise of the genuinely modest. 'There's nothing to tell!'

'Well, what do you do in Sydney?'

'The same as I've been doing here!' she laughed, 'Dance! That's all I know how to do! That's why I've been working on this show with the people in the village while I'm waiting for Dad to finish up at Koenigshaus.'

'Oh yes, the show.' Why did she make him feel so terribly out of his depth all the time?

They were drawing near the homestead now, he would

not have her to himself for much longer. 'You're doing it at the corroboree, aren't you?' he asked. 'Pretty soon now, only another week or two, isn't it?'

'Yeah!' she nodded happily.

They pulled up outside the front door of Koenigshaus, and she hopped out at once, he noticed with a trace of sadness, she clearly had no particular desire to linger with him. As the car pulled up Ben came hurrying out of the office, where he had obviously been keeping a look-out.

'Oh there you are, Geena,' he began. 'I saw they were all so busy today that no one was going to come for you, and I thought—'

'I'm fine, Dad, don't fuss, I'm a big girl now!' She silenced him with an affectionate kiss. 'Anyway, I was in safe hands!' She rewarded Henry with a warm, flashing smile.

'Well, I'll be off now,' said Henry, feeling more awkward than ever. 'Bye, Mr Nichols. Bye, Geena – see you – see you round.'

They stood together watching him go.

Well, well, well, thought Ben, stealing a look at his daughter's unsuspecting face, Henry Suffolk, eh? Well, she could do a lot worse!

Chapter 24

Why was the weather always at its best when everything else was at its worst? Turning her face from the sun, feeling as if only dull grey skies and clouds swollen with all the sadness of the world would be in keeping with her mood, Helen paced the corridor leading to Charles's room. Now that she had decided, she had to tell him as soon as possible. She owed it to him – as the last consideration she would ever be in a position to show.

'Come in!'

He looked wonderful, she noticed with a painful sadness as she pushed open the door and stood hesitantly in the doorway. Just out of the shower, his newly-combed hair still wet, as sleek and dark as if it had been brilliantined, he was choosing a clean shirt and slacks from the wardrobe, clad only in a towel. 'Helen!' he said, his face lighting up with joy. 'Come in, close the door!'

'No, no,' she said awkwardly, 'I'm not staying. I just came to say that I won't – I'm sorry I won't be down to dinner tonight . . .'

He got it instantly, even through the feeble words of the conventional excuse. 'And you won't be having dinner with me here or anywhere else in the conceivable future, is that it?'

Oh God, why was it so hard?

She had thought about this, wept, prayed, tried to balance out her duty to Jon and the respect due to her long marriage and the man who had given her both her marriage and her son, with the new-old feelings for Charles which had resurfaced so powerfully now.

And at last she thought she had arrived at a decision. Whatever it had cost her she was there, she had found the path.

But now, seeing his face—

She felt like a murderer, killing his love, his hopes. His face, his whole body seemed to feel it like a blow; he was shaking, the hairs had risen all along his arm. He stepped towards her like a man in a dream. 'I don't believe it, Helen, I just don't believe you can send me away.'

'I have to,' she wept. 'I talked to Jon—'

'Jon!' His grief and rage came together in an explosion of bitterness. 'Helen, whenever did you hear of a son who would happily see his mother in the arms of another man? Especially a son like Jon, who idolised his father and thinks his mother is so simple he can't imagine how she managed till his father came along!'

'Charles, he's not like that, he—'

He gripped her savagely by the elbows. 'Helen, do me one last favour, don't talk to me about your precious son! I've told you before it's about time you let him grow up! In the real world women have sons AND lovers, and it's about time little Johnny cottoned onto that. But that's your problem – yours and his!'

He broke off and shook his head from side to side like a bull at bay, tortured by the picadors. Then he raised his eyes to hers with a pain she had never seen before. 'If you're telling me no, Helen, if you're saying that there can't be anything between us, have the guts to tell me for yourself. Look at me now and say "Charles, I don't want you, I don't love you, I want you to go away and never bother me again!" '

'Oh God, oh God,' she wept, 'I can't, I can't—'

'You can't say it!' He was shaking her fiercely now, she

felt like a puppet with broken strings. His body was very close, she wanted to smooth his chest and trace each outline of his ribs, she wanted to kiss the soft place at the base of his throat – 'and the reason you can't say it, is because *it isn't true!*'

She wanted to collapse on his chest, soak his shoulder with her tears, seek that enormous comfort of a man's strong arms and have him kiss every one of her griefs away. But if she took one step nearer to him, she knew she would be lost. 'You have to go,' she forced out through her tears. 'I can't marry you, I can't be with you, *I can't risk losing my son!*'

'And what'll happen when he gets a wife?' demanded Charles. 'Oh Helen, d'you think he'll have any time for his mummy then?'

'I don't know,' she cried hopelessly. 'But now – now, when he's just lost his father – I can't ask him to say goodbye to his mother too!'

'Helen, you're a fool.' He had withdrawn from her, armed with a new dignity, a new power of rebuke. 'You're sacrificing yourself and me and all that we might have had together, out of a misplaced sense of guilt. It won't make you happy, and it certainly won't make Jon happy. OK, so I don't count in your equation. But at least I won't be around to see the mess you'll make of it.'

He was staring at her now more like a priest, a confessor, than a lover. 'You've made your choice. I'll go, you can say goodbye to me now and I'll keep well out of your way until the sale's over, and I can go for good.' He paused, and even managed a glimmer of a smile. 'And it will be for good, my darling, because at our age, chances don't come round again. You don't keep finding the pot of gold at the end of the rainbow – especially when you've been mad enough to walk away from it once already.' His smile now held all the suffering of all the lost love in the world. 'I was fool enough to believe that we had found

241

our rainbow all over again. I was wrong, that's all.' He folded her in his arms and turned her face up to his. 'It would take a lifetime to say a real goodbye. Till our next lifetime – goodbye, my darling girl.'

Christ, she'd been in his room, they'd been together there for how long, he was kissing her goodbye, what the hell was *going on*?

Returning from a day of supreme frustration trying to get more than he knew how to find from a computer system whose workings he still hardly understood, Jon had been only half awake as he mounted the stairs. He'd give dinner a miss, he decided, and maybe give Kaiser some exercise or take a walk to try to clear his head. Then he could have another go at the computer to look for more information about Charles. Or he could call the Flying Doctor to check if the post-mortem had been carried out on Dad, he couldn't believe that was OK—

He had heard nothing as he entered the house. But he had made no noise either, since the heavy door was standing open as it always did on these hot afternoons. Now as he came upstairs, a flurry of movement on the landing caught his eye. Helen was coming out of Charles's room with her hand to her mouth in the unmistakeable gesture of a woman who has just been kissed. Her whole body spelled the aftermath of an encounter, and Charles was just closing the door, his eyes downcast, his face taut with emotion, clad only in a towel.

What the hell was going on?

Surely they hadn't—

Once again a black suspicion seized him, filling him with fear: did she know what Charles had done, had she encouraged him to get rid of her husband, even planned it with him?

Jesus, no!

He did not stop to think. A stride took him to Helen's

room, a brusque knock brought him through the door. 'Okay, mother, time we talked!'

She was standing just inside the door, fists to her mouth, shoulders drooping like a lost child, fighting back tears. 'Jon – what—?'

He stepped forward with murder in his heart. 'Is it him, mother, is it Charles you were on about? Is it him you want to marry? When you decided that "you couldn't bear to be alone for the rest of your life"?'

He was mocking her cruelly, taking off her every intonation, and she blushed with shame. 'Jon, what are you talking about?'

Her confusion only seemed to anger him more. 'What am I talking about? Just think, mother dear! Think! If you can think straight! And when you've finished celebrating your choice of a new husband, then maybe we can talk!'

'Jon, I—' She began to cry. 'I'm sorry if—'

He could not contain himself. 'You're only sorry I walked in on it! Or on the tail end of it, anyway!'

'For God's sake! What are you *talking about*?'

He became suddenly ponderous, like a court official. 'You, mother. You and Charles. Christ, I saw you just now! You were coming out of his room, leaving his room, and he was standing there in nothing but a towel!'

She could see it all now, and see too just what he had made of it in his overwrought state. A great despair seized her, she had no energy to fight back. 'You shouldn't have seen that.'

'Too damn right I shouldn't!'

'No, I – I mean – there was nothing to see!'

'Mother, please!' His face was wreathed in disgust. 'Do me a favour, I'm a grown man, not a child any more! You surely don't expect me to believe that?'

'Look, Charles and I' – Christ, it sounded so thin, she had to do better than this!

243

But he flinched away, he seemed almost ready to cover his ears. 'I don't want to hear about it!'

She tried to summon some strength. 'Look, you started this, you're going to have to hear about it!'

His eyes met hers. 'You're my mother!'

'But I'm still a person!' she cried. 'I've got a life to lead as well as you—'

'I never said you hadn't!'

'And Jon—' she was desperate now, or she'd never have dreamed of saying it, 'you don't know how unhappy I've been—'

He grabbed her hands, and wrung them painfully. 'Well, of course you're unhappy, mother, every widow is, every woman must be who loses a man like Dad!'

'A man like Dad . . . Jon, he—'

She caught herself up. Oh God, could she go through with this? Destroy his idea of his father just for some abstract notion of the truth, just for her own sake? And when she'd already lost Charles anyway? For his kiss had been a complete valediction, if they saw one another a hundred times a day now, he had made his farewell, he would not be back, he would never be hers again.

Jon was still running madly on. 'OK, so you've been feeling down, what makes you think that—' He almost choked, he could not bring himself to say the hated name. 'What makes you think that *he* could make you happy?'

'I don't know, I just—'

'But life goes on, is that it? Dad's dead, and you're alive?'

'Jon—'

'Isn't that what they say?'

'Jon, it's true! Life does go on!'

'Not for him!' His face was suffused with violent grief as he spoke. 'Not for Dad! He's six feet under and you're playing the bloody merry widow with fucking Uncle Charles! Well, fuck him! and fuck you too!'

He had never sworn in front of Helen before, much less at her like this. They stared at each other shocked into silence, two souls free-falling in terror. Suddenly, slowly, Jon's body was shaken with one huge, wracking sob. Helen reached up to brush his face and fought down the impulse to take him in her arms as she had done through all the sorrows of the past. 'Oh, my son, my son.'

'Christ, mother, don't!'

Furiously he brushed her hand away and with it the tears that were forming in his eyes.

But she felt calmer now. 'Just listen to me, OK?' she said huskily. 'Listen to me without interruption, then you can be as angry as you like. Will you listen?'

He hesitated, then gave a mutinous nod.

'Charles did ask me to consider if we could think of re-starting our relationship,' she began as steadily as she could. 'Because we – we cared for one another before – a long time ago – before your father came along. Charles always thought that Phillip took me from him. Now seemed like a good time . . .' she trailed off, losing confidence.

But he was still listening, his eyes, dark with emotion, fixed on her face. Wearily she resumed. 'But I told him no. What you thought you saw, whatever you suspected, an illicit assignation, a furtive afternoon tryst, was in fact a goodbye. When I spoke to you about it yesterday, sounded you out, I realised that this thing with Charles just couldn't happen.' She drew a deep breath. 'So I already did what you want me to do, blast you! I've already sent him away. He'll be gone as soon as possible, and I'll never see him again, OK?'

He was so ashamed now of his language, his suspicions of his mother, that he hardly knew where to look. 'Okay,' he mumbled.

Her heart, her whole being was bleeding, she felt as if an unseen sadist had opened a vein. Was it Jon, or

Charles? Think of Jon, she urged herself, he's the important one, he's the one you're suffering all this for! 'Look, forget about me!' she said angrily, 'think about yourself, you've got more options than you think you have.'

'Options? What "options"?'

'You know I always wanted you to go to college – try for university—'

'Oh, mother . . .'

He looked as if he could have hit her, she noted in numb fury. 'Look—' He was struggling for control. 'Look Mum, I know you've always thought I was the great undiscovered genius of the Northern Territory, but the truth is, I'm not a bookworm, I haven't got what it takes to be a scholar! I don't even want to follow the simplest course of study, they could burn all the bloody books as far as I'm concerned!' He sighed and lifted his head, his gaze unconsciously seeking the far horizon. 'I belong on the land. This land.'

'But now—'

'Now, with Dad gone,' he repeated stubbornly, 'I'm even more needed on the station.'

She could have screamed at his naivety. 'But the station's not going to be here!'

He treated her to a crazy, crooked smile. 'They're digging it up? Taking it away?'

'Oh, Jon . . .'

Don't cry, she was instructing herself fiercely, don't cry now, he's had enough water-works. 'Jon, you know what I mean.'

'Oh, yes, I know what you mean. You mean I've got to find a new life, stop playing cowboys. My real future can't be here any more, it's time I faced the facts.' He broke away in the grip of some powerful impulse that she could not read. 'Facts, mother, let's face the facts! If only we knew what they were!' He turned back to her 'Y'know, I'd kill to get some facts – get my hands on some hard

246

facts instead of all this – all this—'

'All this what?'

Helen was struck with a sudden anxiety. Was Jon OK? He'd been under such strain – and this thing with her and Charles seemed to have been the last straw. He'd always been sensitive and highly strung, ever since he was a little boy. Oh God, was he cracking up now?

He seemed to sense her fear, and let the strange elation that had seized him subside.

'Yeah, give me some facts, and I'll face them,' he said with an off-hand smile, more normally now. 'And don't worry, mum, I've been thinking about "the future" as you call it, and I know what I'm going to do. If Mrs Matsuda buys the property, I'm going to ask her for a job. She can't run it with that number-crunching finance idiot Buckley. She'll need a manager.'

She could not keep it back. 'Jon, that's demeaning! To work here as the manager on a place that your father–'

'That my father owned? And his father and his father, all the way back to kingdom come? Where did that get any of us, mother? And where does that leave me?'

A look of puzzlement crossed his face. Half to himself he muttered, 'Where did Dad leave me?' Then another violent mood swing swept him back to the black gaiety of before. 'They're sure to have plans for the old place, Mrs M and her new broom. Maybe when they turn the chapel into a disco I can get a job as a DJ!

'Oh, Jon—'

Suddenly he was his old sweet self again. 'Listen, I'll always love Koenigshaus, and I've made Dad – I've made myself a promise to take care of it till the next owner comes along. Alex can't do it, even if it's his now, he just hasn't got a clue.' His eyes were dark. 'Because it's a living thing, a station like this, it can't just be left to fend for itself any more than the cattle, or one of the horses. Every day it's not cared for, that's a day it's going backwards. We owe it to Koenigshaus to look after it now, the way it's always looked after us. And I'm going to do that for as long as I can.'

He paused and stared miles past her again through the open window. The low sounds of the bush rose to greet them on the thick, sun-drenched air. Jon's voice when he resumed wove in and out of the soft web of living sound. 'And after the sale, if I can find any way to carry on here, where Koenigs have always been, that's what I'm going to do. If not, I'll just have to find a way of setting up somewhere on my own.' He looked at her exactly as he used to do when he was twelve years old. 'Somewhere I can keep cattle. And look after you. Somewhere as near to Koenigshaus as I can be.'

Look after you—

He still had not understood, he hadn't grasped a single word of what she was trying to say, even after all this . . .

She found herself asking a question that she did not know she had been thinking. 'Somewhere with Geena?'

'Geena.' His face twisted. 'No, I don't think so.'

'Well, think about it!'

He smiled, looking infinitely old. 'You're a romantic, mother. You honestly believe that love conquers all.'

'Well, it does!'

'Mother.' He crouched down before her and took both her hands in his. 'Sometimes things go bad. Families. People. Like a dead animal in the sun. For a day – maybe two days – it could just be lying there asleep. But after a while there's no avoiding the rottenness at the core. It starts inside and no one can see it. But it's there, and it works its way out until no one can deny it. No love, no marriage can cure that.' He sighed heavily. 'And that's just what we've got to take care of on this station before any of us can think of anything else!'

Chapter 25

From its vantage point on the fiftieth floor of one of Sydney's premier office blocks, Matsuda PLC commanded the best business view in Australia. And that means the world, thought Craig Buckley with as near to happiness as his abacus of a soul was likely to get.

Oh, of course Madame had the corner suite with its ritual genuflection to the twin gods of Australian architecture, the Harbour Bridge and the Opera House nestling at its foot like a flock of seagulls resting in flight, both located firmly in the centre of her wall-to-wall plate glass. But his office next door had the same, only more. Because from his desk he could look almost sheer down into the concrete canyons of the finance district with its endless traffic of worker ants toiling incessantly in the floors below. It made him feel good, it was almost Wall Street, it was almost home. And when he showed Madame this latest turn-up in the Koenig books, he had a feeling they would be home and dry indeed.

'Craig?'

And here she was.

He had never got used to her habit of just walking in, he still craved the formalities of his rigid business school training. And it was so un-Japanese. But she was the boss. He jumped to his feet. 'Sure, ready!'

Attentively he ushered her to the seat he had just vacated, and stood beside her, his hand on the computer keyboard.

She crossed her silken legs and leaned back with a teasing glance. 'You said you had something to show me? Something interesting, I hope? Have I seen it before? Or are you planning to surprise me?'

He knew better than to rise to the bait in business hours. Carefully averting his eyes from the promise of what he knew lay beneath the petrol blue business suit with its mother-of-pearl buttons and the magnolia raw silk blouse, he punched up what he had been studying on the screen. 'This,' he said briefly. 'I thought it would interest you.'

He never needed to explain figures to Yoshiko, they were the first language she had ever learned to speak. He knew better than to expect her to show any reaction, but her eyes grew moist and bright as she read down the screen just the same way, he noted ironically, as they did during sex.

'So!' she said at last with a note of finality.

He nodded. 'Yeah, no matter what Charles Koenig says, Koenig Holdings is stuffed.' He jerked his head at the screen. 'In fact with some of the stuff they've got going on there, I'd say it was only a matter of time before the Australian Securities' Commission started sniffing around with a few unhealthy questions.' He grinned again. 'As accounting goes, creativity doesn't come into it! It's New Age stuff, it's off the map!'

'Yes.'

She always said next to nothing on these occasions. But he knew from her breathing how much she adored it when he could flay a potential takeover victim alive for her like this, dissect it into fragments and offer her the remains to do with as she pleased. Like a *meistersinger* giving a master class, he went on. 'Whoever was running the whole thing had just lost control. They were in an escalating damage situation, not even controlling the monthly interest rise. And going nowhere fast.'

There was a pause as she tested out what he said during a long and silent communion with the dancing orange screen. He waited patiently. At last she turned her sloe-black eyes away from the figures and onto him. 'You say "whoever was running the company"?' she said softly.

He nodded again, smiling at her in total harmony. 'I think that's it, that's the whole cookie secret, that's why it's crumbling.'

Tell me, said her eyes.

God, how he loved this! And her! 'They had a safe, conservative, well-run business for twenty-odd years until a few years ago. Then they ran into debt towards the end of the '80s. The banks threw money at them and they grabbed it with both hands. And then came October 1987, the shit hit the fan with collapse of the market and they've been dodging and weaving ever since.'

'And now?'

You know now, he wanted to say. But this was their ritual, he did not have the power to change it. 'Now they took another pasting with last year's Black Wednesday, and another plunge in the markets. They could have sold off the international and city elements of the business, cleared their debts, drawn in their horns, and agreed to make a modest living off the Koenigshaus Cattle station.'

She smiled like a cat who had just sighted an outsize bowl of cream. 'But someone did not want to sell, it would be a sign of failure. Someone did not want a modest living, and someone did not want to spend the rest of his life on Koenigshaus miles from anywhere.'

'Correct. So they got drawn into this mad spiral of over-leveraging—'

'And—'

He loved her when she played cat and mouse, it excited him like nothing else except money. 'And – though they've covered it up very skilfully for a long time, the weight of it's bound to drag them down sooner or later.'

'They?'

His turn to pretend he did not understand. 'They?'

She was happy now, the game was played out to her satisfaction. 'Finish,' she ordered.

He felt himself swelling, he could fuck her now within an inch of her life. 'You know who ordered it, who carried it out, and who covered it up,' he said softly. 'You knew all along, but now we've got proof. That means you've got Koenig Holdings and Koenig Cattle by the short and curlies. You can have every living soul in this outfit down to the fucking cows bend over for you right now and take it up the ass, if you want to.' He smiled a contented smile and punched the computer to print out. 'It's your move. Whatever you want to do.'

She glimmered at him. 'What do you want to do?'

'I want,' he said earnestly, 'for you to tell me your decision on our next move. Then I want to take you from here to that French bistro on Macleay Street and show you what real food is like, properly cooked.' He risked a gentle tease. 'None of your Japanese shit – even though I know that good stuff comes in little packages. And then I want—'

'Ah yes', she said vaguely, 'you want to eat at Daniel's? Where the guy is so nice?' She waved a hand towards the outer office. 'Have them book a table. And then—'

Now it was his turn to interrupt. 'Before that – Koenig Holdings.'

'Oh yes.'

It was the last move of the game. One of the reasons she loved Buckley, she decided, not for the first time, was that for all his less-than-prince-like qualities, he would always, just like Mr Matsuda, put business before pleasure. 'Mr Alex Koenig is on the phone every day now,' she said, 'pressing us to come back. Some corroboree they're having – a special show they're putting on about the history of Koenigshaus – a chance to see the station at its best, he says . . .'

He could read her mind, he was walking towards the outer office as he spoke. 'OK, I'll have them make the arrangements and phone Koenigshaus. We fly tomorrow?'

'Tomorrow.' She nodded once, then looked at him, her face expressionless. 'And bring your overnight bag to the bistro – you won't be back to your own place tonight.'

Why did he feel so bad when things were going so well? Irritably Alex pulled his all-but-empty briefcase from the front of the 4WD and hurried into the house. OK, so the lunch with that pompous prick of a bank manager had been a drag, a serious pain in the arse. But he'd got through it with flying colours, and finished up with the little fart pumping his hand in admiration as if he'd made a friend for life.

And the whole business was nearly over, that was what it had taken the rat-faced Carey a long lunchtime to tell him. Whatever happened when a will was 'proved', it was all happening now and in record time, Carey was proud to announce. 'It'll all be yours any day now, Mr Koenig!' he declared triumphantly. 'And as soon as it is, you may rely on yours truly here to be on the blower to you with the news in double-quick time!'

'Thank you so much, Mr Carey,' he had assured him warmly, returning the pump-action handshake as if Carey was his closest friend. 'I can't thank you enough.' He paused, then lowering his voice for effect, went on. 'I don't have to tell you that I regard this as the start of a long and mutually beneficial business relationship. I hope I make myself clear.'

He grinned to himself. In a rat's ass, that's where he'd go into business with Carey. But it never hurt to spread a little happiness . . .

So why couldn't he spread any for himself?

Well, part of it was this bloody shortage of ready cash!

Oh, he was the heir apparent, but so far it was all apparent, nothing real. OK he'd managed to stall the hire-car people when he returned that bloody awful Ford, and he was living as high on the hog as he liked here, rent free, but he couldn't lie around here penniless much longer, it was getting to him more and more.

And it was getting to her.

Whatever women were made of, Trisha was never cut out for the waiting game. Scowling ferociously he made for the den and checked out the time. Past two o'clock, so she ought to be awake by now. With the peculiar pain at his heart which she always gave him, he could not decide whether to go over to the guest house, or wait for her to surface and come to find him. Either way, better get her breakfast-cum-wake-up tonic ready first.

Dumping the briefcase which he had carried only for show, he shrugged off the jacket of his sober business suit and made his way down the passage to the kitchen. 'Afternoon, Rose!'

Rose was seated at the table with Ellie, he noticed briefly as he strode past. That was all right, then – yesterday's melodrama all over.

'Message from Matsuda,' reported Rose in a monotone. 'They're coming back tomorrow, they'll be here for the corroboree.'

Great!

In a second all his bad feelings melted and a wave of triumph took their place. She must be planning to buy Koenigshaus, there was no other reason to come back, a woman like Mrs Matsuda didn't waste time and money playing games! Now he had some good news for Trisha, and something to celebrate with her! He could tell her they'd be out of here before the end of the week, with the cash clutched tight in their grubby little fists! This called for that special bottle he had tucked away at the back of the fridge . . .

He was half-way out of the kitchen before he realised that the Aboriginal girl he'd glimpsed from the back sitting at the table with Rose was not Ellie after all. He tried to repress a flicker of concern. So it would take the stupid bitch a bit longer to get over being fired. Well, the sooner she reappeared, the better! She must have known she wasn't really fired, that Trisha didn't decide who came and went on Koenigshaus. And she certainly knew she was going to cause the maximum disruption when she had gone running out of the bedroom howling and shrieking, and hadn't been seen since. Belatedly he tried to cover his mistake. 'Afternoon, Geena.' Then he grabbed a bottle of white wine from the fridge and disappeared as fast as he could.

'Hmmn.' Rose put all her disapproval of Alex's action into the toss of her head that accompanied his departure, and had no need of speech. And to think, Geena marvelled, that she knew him as a little boy, she probably taught him his first words . . .

Deliberately Rose changed the mood, veering away from what they had seen. 'I jus' doan see why you're so bothered about this show of yours.'

Geena smiled anxiously. 'Well, the corroboree has come round so soon! At first it seemed ages away, now it'll be here in a few days.'

Rose stared at her unsympathetically. 'You done plenty of rehearsin'.'

'But it's still not polished,' pleaded Geena.

Rose slapped the table impatiently. 'As long as they can understand what's going on.'

'I'd just like to feel it's going to be a success.'

Rose reached out a hard black hand. 'Let's ask the cards.'

Geena caught her breath. She did not know if she wanted to hear from the cards or not. But Rose was implacable. 'Cut!' she ordered. 'And again!'

The first card answered all Geena's worries as far as

255

Rose was concerned. Triumphantly she placed it down, facing it towards Geena. 'The Queen of the World!' she breathed reverently. Her voice became an awed whisper and she eyed Geena with a new respect. 'She's the top of the tree, the final card, the last one of the major arcana. She's the best card you could have.'

Shivering slightly Geena studied the bold bright image of a woman crowned with flowing tresses, magnificently naked except for a drape across her Mount of Venus, balanced as delicately as a dancer upon a floating cloud. Above her an angel and a flying griffon supported a laurel wreath of achievement, while below her feet horses and lions nestled with adoring upward glances, submitting to her power. Geena raised her eyes to Rose's wide, shoe-buttoned stare. 'What does it mean?'

Rose laughed, a dry snapping sound like a cough. 'It means the world and everything that's in it is comin' for you, my lovely! It means success in what you're tryin' to do, an' a great ending to something you been workin' on. That means the show here – it's gonna be a great an' mighty success, though maybe not the way you think. An' it brings peace, this card, an' the satisfaction of something worked out to the end, something well done.' With a shock Geena realised that Rose looked as happy now as she had ever seen her, she lived through the cards and drew all her pleasure from them. 'You gonna do great things, good things,' she said fervently. 'This your first Tarot an' you get the Queen of the World? Let me tell you, missy, it doan get any better!'

Geena knew she should be pleased, grateful even to the old woman for such a lucky reading. But even as she struggled to find her thanks, a small thought broke through: *it isn't enough*.

Yes, of course she wanted success for her show, having cold feet today with the performance so near had shown her just how much she needed a good result, needed the reward for all her hard work. But that wasn't all – it wasn't everything – *it wasn't Jon* . . .

Rose was looking at her shrewdly. She crossed to the fridge and found herself a friendly bottle. 'Want to try a few more?'

She shivered again. 'Yes.'

He's a good man, Ben had said to her, *you could do a lot worse*. How could she say to him, Yes, Dad, but I want to do a lot better? In truth she hadn't even noticed Henry Suffolk till Ben had drawn her attention to the quiet young man. 'You know,' he'd observed thoughtfully as Henry had pulled away after giving her a lift, 'I don't think he wanted to go home.'

'Why shouldn't he?' she'd queried absently.

'And I don't blame him,' Ben continued.

'Dad!' Why was he being so exasperating? 'What are you on about?'

'Henry,' he replied simply. 'He likes you.'

'Oh Dad!' she laughed self-consciously. 'You're so biased, you think they all like me!'

'Oh, I'm not wrong about this, believe me.' He seemed very quiet. 'And I'm sure his intentions are—'

'His intentions!' She was instantly aroused. 'Dad, for heaven's sake, I've only spoken to him once!'

'I thought you said you saw him before, down at the village, talking to the men?'

'Well, twice then!' she said defensively. 'But for heaven's sake – look dad, back off will you?'

'Oh, Geena.' Taking her by the arm, he led her back into the quiet of the guest house. 'I promised your mother before she died that when the right time came—'

'—don't forget the right man!'

He smiled sadly, but rode over her sarcastic interruption. 'When the time came, I promised I'd see you settled

257

down with someone who could give you the kind of life that she'd have wanted for you. Someone who thought you were the sun, the moon and the stars.' He paused, then continued heavily. 'And I don't think that someone is Jon Koenig.'

She fired up at once. 'Why, what's he done?'

He looked at her with pitying love. 'That's just it, Geena. He hasn't done anything. He hasn't shown any interest in you, he ignores you! And I can see you eating your heart out for him, and it drives me mad! Any man who can't see what you are, what you've got to offer, is not worthy of you in my book!'

But he loves me, I know he does! she wanted to cry. But how could she convince Dad when she was so unconvinced herself?

'Now that young Suffolk, Henry,' Ben went on earnestly, 'he's a different proposition altogether. His family are good people, kind people, decent through and through.' *Not like the Koenigs*, he wanted to say, but didn't. 'He's steady – reliable—'

'And as dull as ditchwater!' Her angry face collapsed at the sight of him. 'Oh Dad, I'm sorry, I didn't mean to say that. But I don't love him, I'm not interested in him, he could be twice as nice and reliable for all I care—'

There was a pause. 'And you do love Jon?'

She flushed fiercely. 'I didn't say that!'

'Oh, love.' In an unaccustomed show of emotion he wrapped his arms around her and drew her to his heart. 'Oh love – you don't have to.'

'Now supposin',' Rose was still rambling on, lost in her cards, her divination assisted now by heavy application to the bottle at her elbow, 'now just suppose the Cavalier of Cups – that's this young man here, he a cavalier, that's a knight, a young prince in the Suite of Love – suppose

258

he get involved with the Queen of Clubs—' she stirred the cards together with her hand. 'The Queen of Clubs here, she an older woman with a bad temper, she likes clashes and fightin', men fightin' over her – an' she likes younger men—'

What was she trying to say? The young man – Jon?

'The Queen of Clubs,' Rose went on in her sing-song voice. 'No friend to other women, bit of a bitch you might say. Strong-willed, but flighty.'

The only older woman on the station apart from Jon's mother is that bitch in the guesthouse with us, that Trisha . . .

You don't have to be Gipsy Rose Lee to work this out, Geena thought with a sinking heart. 'Flighty?'

'Fickle.' Rose's eyes were owl-like now, swimming with drink and her visions of the future. 'Unfaithful.'

Geena's heart turned over. She would believe anything of that bitch Trisha. And she'd shown plainly enough on the first night that she fancied Jon. But would Jon let himself get involved with her? *Could* he? She would not believe it.

'She have to have her way. And the kings and knights are just putty in her hands . . .'

Kings and knights—

Alex and Jon?

In the heat of the evening Geena shuddered and grew cold.

Chapter 26

What was this nagging anxiety over Ellie?

And why did he blame Trisha for it all?

Christ, even first thing in the morning when other women were as frowsty as a dog's bed, she was beautiful, he thought with desolation as he entered her room. Beautiful and damned.

'Where's the drink?' she demanded aggressively as she came to life, as she always seemed to do these days. She was drinking far too much now, they both were.

'Here,' he said, handing over the smooth, chill bottle.

She struggled up in the bed, towsled, squinting, and still gorgeous. He sat down beside her, inhaled her rich sweet fragrance, and tried to recapture some of the good feelings he had had earlier. 'We're on our way!' he announced lightly. 'I've just heard that Mrs Matsuda's coming back, I'm pretty sure that means we've pulled it off, we've got the sale!'

'About bloody time!' she grumbled. 'Another week in this dump, and I'd have gone stark, raving mad!'

'Well, all you've got to do now is be nice to Mrs Matsuda, play hostess as only you know how, smile like the Queen of England all through the corroboree, and we're home and dry.' He paused. 'And don't drink too much, hey? Oh, and one more thing.' He grinned. 'I know that anyone who has the nerve to burst in on Miss Trisha in her post-coital state deserves to be strung up by the thumbs, with lighted matches driven under her toe-nails. But you don't just fire people on Koenigshaus like you fired the maid yesterday. Ellie and Rose are practically part of the family. Brace yourself. She'll be back.'

Her eyes glinted. 'Well then, I'll have to fire her all over again!'

He leaned forward and gripped her wrist, squeezing it very hard. 'You're not listening, darling. You don't hire and fire on Koenigshaus, I do. And when Ellie reappears, you'll take it in your stride and be nice to her, OK?'

A succession of emotions chased themselves across her face. 'You've been fucking her! That's why you don't want her to go!'

His voice stayed pleasant but his face set like stone. 'You'd better get it through your head, my love, that even for your humble servant, there are some things more important than sex. The sale of Koenigshaus, for one. And that'll only go through if we've all kept our noses clean – squeaky bloody clean! Who's going to buy a property stuffed with resentful locals, no staff in the kitchen and a general feel-bad stink about it?'

He paused, his eyes glittering. 'I don't give a fuck about Ellie or any other little tart like her, you ought to know me well enough to know that! But I'm not having her – or anyone else – making a scene now, just when the whole of Koenigshaus has got to smell like garden roses for Matsuda PLC! And that includes you.' He gripped her other hand viciously hard, and leaned forward with menace in every line of his taut body. 'Have you got it yet? Or do I have to teach you?'

Sitting in the office at the end of another fruitless day, Jon checked out for what felt like the hundredth time all he had done so far, and wondered why he was making so little progress. God in heaven, he knew his quarry, he had the bastard in his sights and still he could not find the way to bring him down!

He leaned back in Phillip's chair and watched Ben walk away from the office back to the house and get ready for dinner, as he soon must do himself. But he had to have something to show for another day's exhausting work, there had to be something . . .

If only he could find it!

Most of it was down to his ignorance of how to explore the ins and outs of the computer, he recognised painfully. His early crash course with Ben had only taught him how to get into the main programmes. Anyone who knew more than he did – and that meant practically everyone, he knew – could store what they liked in there and no one would be any the wiser.

He wouldn't find it, he was beginning to see that. If there was any 'it'. If the final proof that he was seeking existed, it was far more likely to be a web of tiny little clues which had to be taken together to spell out Charles's guilt. Those details would take more than careful searching to unearth, and that was all that he was capable of.

And as so often happens, he had had his big breakthrough at the beginning. When he stumbled on Charles's 'Kingdom' project, with its proof positive that Charles had been engaged in the over-ambitious buying that had brought the company to its knees, he had been sure he was within sight of his goal. But since then, nothing!

Yet why did he still persist in thinking that the key to it all was in here, somewhere here in this room, Koenigshaus's nerve centre, part office, part den, part gentleman's smoking room with its unmistakeable aura of old secrets and new schemes? Moodily he stared around from his vantage point behind his father's desk. He found himself sitting there more and more now, taking Phillip's antique throne of a chair without thinking. Was he trying out the role of the master of the kingdom for these last few hours before it all passed out of his hands? Because if Alex was right about the return of Mrs Matsuda, the sale of Koenigshaus was a foregone conclusion now, and there was not a damn thing on earth he could do about it!

With a mixture of emotions too deep to name he surveyed the strange blend of ancient and modern that was the keynote of Koenigshaus for him, the best of the old keeping pace with the best of the new. His random gaze took in the international hardware of modern technology happily co-existing with the old-world furniture, the heavy desks and chairs, the superannuated safe—

The safe.

Now why had Dad hung onto that all this time? He was a traditionalist but no sentimentalist: old things like that kept their place in his life only if they served a purpose, he never allowed anything to take up space just for old times' sake. What purpose did this serve?

There must be something in there that he would never commit to the computer, no matter how cleverly he could hide it.

A feverish excitement gripped him. So what had Dad hidden? And where, *where* had he concealed the combination of numbers that would open the safe? It had to be six figures, all the old safes worked on that set of tumblers. His mind racing, he stared blankly at the old school photograph of Phillip hanging above the huge brass-bound safe: *Phillip Johann Koenig . . . Head Boy . . . 1948–49—*

Oh, the clever old bastard!

Jon almost burst out laughing. Mum had been searching, he had been searching, who knows who else had been hunting high and low too, and there it was, all along! So plain, it would have bitten you on the nose if you'd got any closer to it! How like Phillip to have the last laugh on all of them.

1948–49.

Or *19 – 48 – 49*?

Slowly, serenely, Jon rose from his chair. He was supremely confident now. He crossed to the safe and, kneeling before it, reached for the central dial. It was stiff from disuse, but his fingers firmly guided the wheel where he knew it had to go.

19.

He did not have to wait more than a second before he heard the heavy tumblers inside the dial shift hesitantly, then drop into place.

48.

Again the satisfying light thud-thud.

49.

Thud-thud, thud-thud, thud-thud. Pivoting the bar handle, he swung the door open.

Nothing.

There was nothing there.

Whatever he had imagined, he was wrong. The deep shelves of the cavity, filling a space as big as a large fridge, were completely bare. He felt a wild anticlimax that amounted to outrage.

At the bottom of the safe was a shallow tray running underneath the lowest of the shelves. Listlessly he drew it open. Inside lay a couple of manilla wallets, worn, dog-eared and dusty with time. Probably Dad's father's bloody laundry list! he thought in impotent fury. He flicked the top one open.

REPORT ON HELEN GRACE WILLIAMS

At first he could not take it in.

Prepared for Mr Phillip Koenig of Koenigshaus by Neville Harvey, Private Investigator, Darlinghurst, Sidney— WILLIAMS.

It was his mother's maiden name. But he could not believe it, he could not credit the evidence of his own eyes. Dad had had Mum investigated before he married her? But why? Mesmerised, fearful, he began to read the faded typewritten pages.

Miss Williams is currently employed as a seasonal hand

*on the Golden Mountain cattle station next to Koenigshaus.
She is known there as quiet and reserved, a good worker
who prefers to keep herself to herself. Her only contact
seems to be Mr Charles Koenig, a regular visitor who has
been seeing her as her accepted boyfriend for over six
months now.*

Six months as Helen's regular boyfriend? And how long
had Charles known her before that?

Jon's mind flashed back to Helen's quiet words about
Charles – 'We knew each other before.' This was much
more than the brief and casual acquaintance he had
supposed.

*Miss Williams' whereabouts before this are something of
a mystery. She is reticent about her family, and workmates
have noted a reluctance to talk about herself. But she has
confided to a colleague that she left home to go travelling
because she did not get on with her father. He was apparently of a domineering temperament and believed that he
had the right to run the life of his only daughter.*

*Miss Williams has also been traced to other cattle stations
where she took casual work, and always gave satisfaction
before moving on. Several of her previous employers
would have been happy to employ her on a more permanent basis, but Miss Williams has always refused. She
wishes to travel, she says. She is apparently saving up to
go round the world.*

*A search has revealed no criminal or civil convictions
for any female by this name.*

Jon sat back on his heels, stunned. Suddenly the teenage Helen, quiet and true, but nursing her touching girl-
hood dreams of travel and escape came so vividly to life
before him that he could feel the tears starting to his eyes.

She had wanted to go round the world, and she'd got
no farther than Koenigshaus. She'd been running away
from a domineering father who ruled her life, and she'd
married Phillip, who simply took over where the old brute
left off.

And Helen – Helen with her open, trusting ways, her still-active schoolgirl faith in love and romance – she of all women to marry a man who could sink to have her checked out by a private eye? And the girl who had longed to travel had ended up tied to a man who left her at home, sometimes for months, every time he went jaunting off to France, Germany, to the USA?

Yet was she so innocent still.

Why had she been frantically trying to get into the safe, the day of Dad's funeral?

Was she looking for this? And what did she fear it might say? Or was she looking for something darker still, something that might incriminate her more, show she had a hand in Phillip's death? For now he saw the man she'd been married to, as if he were looking through the eyes of a woman who'd lost all love for him.

A sick feeling of dread crept over him. *Why did you do it, Dad, why did you need to have her raked over like this?* He was crying inside. *How could you do it, how could you even think of it? And to Mum of all women—?*

And not only to Mum. Even as he opened the second folder he knew whose life he would see lying there stripped down and dissected to shreds.

REPORT ON TRUDI MARIA KOENIG, nee FOSTER

The first wife. Well, it stood to reason, if you check out one wife, why not another? It was the same PI even, these private dicks must make a good living out of feeding the fears of suspicious husbands! Feeling sicker and sicker, he flipped through the contents of a file much thicker than Helen's.

Trudi Foster is the name by which Mrs Koenig was known at the time of her marriage. This however appears to be a name she picked up somewhere after leaving home, in an effort to bury her true identity . . .

. . . born in extreme poverty to an unsuccessful share-cropper, Trudi Koenig started life as Cindy-Lou Robards on a holding just north of San Carlos in Henderson County, Texas, USA. The eldest of a large family, she left home following a tragedy in which all her relations died. The father, who was known to have been a heavy drinker, apparently ran amok with a shotgun, killing all his family. Cindy-Lou survived through being out at work with a neighbour at the time. In the immediate aftermath of the shooting she left town and was never seen there again.

. . . next picked up as a teenage runaway in Los Angeles, California. Charges against her of prostitution and drug involvement were dropped for lack of evidence. Placed with a foster family, she was returned to the care of the Los Angeles Children's Department following complaints from the foster mother that the girl had offered sex to both her husband and her teenage son. Subject then absconded from Children's Corrective Faculty while awaiting a new foster home.

. . . next traced to San Francisco where she attempted a little modelling, a little stage work, with some success. No visible means of support but a good lifestyle, prostitution suspected. Two years later she appeared in New York as the companion of a well-known businessman whose legitimate activities were thought to be a cover for an illegal operation involving drugs. Through him gained the entree to New York social and charity-function circles where she made the acquaintance of Mr Phillip Koenig . . .

And the rest, as they say, was history.

His head reeling, Jon had to put down the file and lean against the wall to take it all in. He had no doubt of what he was reading, even wrapped up in the dry prose of the investigator's report. Dad had married some kind of a hooker! His first wife had been a good-time girl, an amateur prostitute, involved with drugs, and worse, mixed up with those guilty of peddling them too, if the PI was right about her last boyfriend!

How had she fooled Dad, why didn't he spot any of this the first time they met?

Yet how would he? Still young and thinking himself a lot smarter than he was, fresh from the outback, bedazzled by the American society lady, with no reason to disbelieve a word she said, he would be a natural to fall prey to a whirlwind romance and the thrill of bringing his beautiful bride triumphantly back to Koenigshaus to knock the socks off all the envious locals. That was how it had been, and all too understandable, too.

But he could not have known all this before he married her. A man like Phillip would never take a woman who had even played the field, let alone earned her living in the questionable way.

So that meant . . .

Hastily, he turned to the front of the worn and faded folder, searching for a date. *Report prepared and signed by . . .* come on, come on! *. . . by me, Neville James Harvey on this day, 12 June 1969—*

He'd have to check it, he knew. But he also knew without checking that Phillip had lived happily with his first wife for many years, years that had also given them their handsome little son. And he knew from the conversation at the time of Alex's recent reappearance just when the fatal riding accident had occurred that had left the thirteen-year-old motherless and a fugitive, in flight from his home.

1969.

Jon now knew, with chilling conviction, that Phillip had received and read this report on Trudi Koenig only a week or two before his first wife died.

Chapter 27

Feeling for his smile as other men feel for the necktie in their pocket to complete the attire before appearing in public, Alex hurried down the stairs from his room in the Tower, making for the kitchen. Outside the night was falling in a curtain of blue, purple, indigo and dense black, blotting out the burning red-gold of another tropical sunset, but he had no time for star-gazing now. The 'copter on its way down, and still no idea if the dinner would be ready on time – or if it would be any good even if it was ready – it was his idea of a nightmare.

Fuck Ellie! he cursed viciously. *Fuck* her for going AWOL tonight of all nights, when she should have been helping Rose all day! When he caught up with her, he'd take the greatest delight in making his displeasure with Miss Ellie felt, he swore to himself, in a wide range of painful and humiliating ways. And as he never strayed off flesh onto bone like her stupid husband, he'd make sure she had nothing to show for it but some very, very sorry-for-themselves soft tissues for a week or two to come . . .

Still, don't forget to smile for the troops . . . 'How's it going, girls?'

Around him Helen, Geena and a smouldering Rose were working frantically to prepare food, Helen dealing with a side of Koenigshaus's own prime beef, Geena chopping vegetables like an automaton, and Rose juggling

271

melon cubes, grapes, tomatoes, mushrooms and shrimps.

'Fine,' replied Helen mechanically.'

God, she looked awful since Charles had dumped her or whatever he'd done, Alex noted. Can't let her upset the sale, looking like that! 'Cheer up,' he said winningly. 'Find a smile for Jon, if not for Mrs M, he'll need you to keep cheerful tonight!'

'Oh, yes.' Helen nodded faintly.

'And how's my Rosie?'

She turned on him with a venomous gleam in her eye. 'How we managin' without that no-good Ellie, I jus'don'k-now! Las' night, didn't matter she didn't show, only fam'ly. But tonight! You gotta sack her now, Mister Alex, leavin' us in the lurch like this!'

Christ, they all had it in for the little tart! 'Don't worry, Rose,' he reassured her, 'she hasn't gone, she'll turn up soon, I swear.'

'She turn up now, I break her bloody neck!' pronounced Rose, returning furiously to her shrimps.

'So it's all going OK?' said Alex cheerfully, desperately willing them to agree, shape up, fall in line. 'And Charles has gone to the airstrip to pick them up? Good, great stuff!' He was suddenly conscious of behaving like a cheerleader, he might have been whipping up the audience like a bloody TV evangelist, the way he was going on.

Keep cool, boy, he told himself as he bowed gracefully out, just keep cool. All you've got to do now is get over to the guest house and make sure Miss Trisha is shaping up like you told her, and you're all but home and dry!

'Have a good flight?'

Mrs Matsuda smiled. 'I always have a good flight.' She gestured carelessly at the figure following her down the steps of the helicopter with his arms full of briefcases and files. 'And so does Craig. And you, Charles? Are you well?'

'Well enough,' replied Charles briefly. 'Let's get you in the car, shall we?' Hardly any luggage, he noted with the business part of his mind, that means a short stay, they've decided on their terms and they don't think we'll argue. Well, let's see their offer. Then we'll know if this is good news or bad.

'No Helen this time?'

Buckley was always onto everything like a fox terrier, Charles thought sourly, he might almost have sensed that the women were running round in flat panic trying to put together in a couple of hours what should have been done all day. Well, he wasn't going to get the chance to read anything into this!

'We always share the ferrying around on Koenigshaus,' he said easily. 'And as it's my turn to drive, I thought I might show you a bit of the station you didn't see last time. It's not much out of our way. And it's worth a visit, especially at nightfall like this.'

Making determined small-talk, he swung them into the path of the setting sun. 'I know you saw the water-hole when you came before, from the helicopter,' he said. 'But the cattle were on it then, it's very different when it's quite deserted. I think you'll appreciate it.'

He was drawing up on the rim of the great natural bowl as he spoke. In the glancing light, the strange trees, half alive, seemed gathered round the rocks like dancers at a big corroboree, shivering in anticipation. The great sheet of water lay like a mirror reflecting the vast wall and cave of ancient sandstone, and all the world seemed to hold its breath. Even Buckley seemed awed, and Mrs Matsuda drank in the scene in total silence.

'Want to get out?' Charles said.

Together the visitors clambered down from the 4WD and wandered a few steps into the bush. Overhead a flock of rainbow lorikeets scattered with cries of distress and from the water's edge rose the night-call of the clearwater frogs, so like a death-rattle, he always thought. All about them the fragile web of insect activity began to bring the air to life, and the nocturnal creatures stirred in their tree-holes, ready to begin their day as night fell.

Her cry when it came seemed to blend in with the night. 'Aaagh!'

'Yoshiko, what's the matter, what is it?'

'Oh Craig – there – look there!'

With the reflex action born of boyhood years in the bush, Charles was out of the car and running, flashlight in hand, before his conscious mind had had time to programme his actions. And realisation was still lagging seconds, even minutes behind as the probing beam cut through the falling dusk to focus on the huddled shape lying thrust between two rocks with its head twisted at an angle never known in life.

'Well, she's dead, no doubt about that!'

Trust the police to come up with the obvious, thought Jon. 'Sure!' he said, 'but do you have any idea who killed her?'

The large, thick-set state officer in his light khaki fatigues shook his head. 'Now that'd be telling,' he said regretfully. 'And if we could tell, we would, wouldn't we, Roscoe?'

'Sure would, George,' replied his companion amiably, another large, fair, beefy Australian who could have been the clone of his partner.

'Oh, for Christ's sake! I'm going back to the house!'

Jon gestured at Alex's departing back. 'I have to apologise for Mr Koenig,' he said awkwardly. 'He's under a lot of strain – got a visitor arrived tonight – important business—'

'Yeah, the Jap lady, isn't it?' said Roscoe with interest. 'The one we saw back at the house with her boyfriend, the one who found the girl?'

'With her financial adviser,' corrected Jon. God, if

these two clowns blundered in on Mrs M with cracks like that, Alex would kill the pair of them!

George sniggered. 'Oh yeah, "financial adviser." Good title, that.'

'Sensitive issue, George, sensitive issue,' advised Roscoe.

Jon had the insane feeling of being trapped in some kind of surreal double act. From the moment the 4WD had pulled up at Koenigshaus to disclose a steely white Mrs Matsuda and a speechless Craig Buckley, with Charles sweeping in like a tiger in their wake, the nightmare evening he had been preparing for had dissolved into another kind of nightmare indeed. 'So what happens now?' he demanded hollowly.

Roscoe sucked on his teeth and both men exchanged glances. 'Well, we got an identification,' he said at last. 'Don't seem to be any doubt that this is Ellie Hands.'

'Well, of course it's Ellie!' Jon cried in fury, 'we all knew her, we can all tell you it's her!' He had to avert his eyes from the pitiful bundle lying nearby. It seemed an insult to Ellie's remains to be dealing with her death like this. 'Who killed her, that's what we all want to know!'

'Killed? Did we say killed, George?'

'I didn't hear killed, Roscoe.'

Jon could almost supply the next line himself, he was really getting into the swing of this gruesome duo. 'That's for the doctor to decide, eh, guys?'

'The pathologist,' corrected George. 'That's the Flying Doc in a funny frock.'

'But in the meantime,' said Roscoe generously, 'I think we can give you murder. At least we can say that a little lady who finishes up with the back of her neck where her face ought to be probably didn't arrange it that way by herself.'

'Talking of arranging,' George chimed in, 'I guess we've

done all we can here tonight.' He nodded at the man on duty beside the body. 'Forensic and all'll be out here in due course. Keep an eye till then, OK?' He turned to Jon. 'Give you a lift back to the house?'

Among the huddled party in the dining room, no one was thinking of food. Rose's Shrimp Supreme and her Koenigshaus Surprise wilted on either side of the superb roast that Helen had overseen and the once-appetising mounds of vegetables prepared by Geena. Trisha had positioned herself by the wine on the trolley at the head of the table and was demolishing a fine Chardonnay as if it were mineral water, Jon saw as he entered. Beside her sat Alex, grimmer than he had ever been, while at the end of the table Helen, Geena and a grey-faced Ben huddled together for comfort. Mrs Matsuda and Buckley had gone to bed, whether separately or together, no one knew. Only Charles stood alone, bleakly staring through the window at the moon-washed bush.

'Any news?'

Alex was already regretting storming away from the scene of the murder, Jon could see, he liked to know what was going on. OK, he could tell him. 'Nothing.'

'Nothing?'

Alex was almost snarling. Something in Jon rose in spite of himself to take the bait. 'Don't snap at me, mate, I'm not in charge of this investigation!'

Anxiously Helen hurried to pour oil on the troubled waters. 'They won't be able to do much before tomorrow,' she put in. 'We'll find out more then.'

'Find him then, don't you mean?'

Why was it that even Trisha's voice was so harsh and discordant, wondered Geena angrily, she sounds like a bloody cockatoo! And why does she have to keep looking at Jon like that? The next thought speared her with jealous rage – *and if she does, why does he take any notice?*

Why does he keep looking at her like that too?

'Him?' Jon crossed to the drinks trolley as he spoke. 'Who do you mean, Trisha?'

She gave him a lazy, cat-like smile as he reached for the open bottle of wine. 'It's obvious, isn't it? Yes, fill me up if you're pouring, there's a beaut.' She accepted the drink with what seemed like a good deal of by-play, then continued. 'Surely she was killed by that husband of hers, the one you're always on about?'

'Who, Mark?' said Jon, who had entertained the same suspicion himself, but did not want to risk accusing an innocent man.

'Yeah, him or one of the others,' Trisha drawled. 'I guess it could have been anyone from that camp of theirs, they're all the bloody same, those blacks.'

There was a painful silence. Then Geena rose slowly to her feet. 'Excuse me,' she said very clearly. 'I'm going to bed. Goodnight.'

The small feet with their turned-out dancer's walk stamped defiantly off into the night.

'Well, I think Geena's said it all,' said Helen steadily. 'I'll say good night too.'

One by one the company melted away, leaving Jon, Trisha, and a preoccupied Alex, still clearly bent on trying to salvage what he could from the wreckage of his hopes. 'So did you tell them to hush it up?' he began without preamble.

'Tell who?'

Alex's face frayed with anger. 'Who d'you think? The police, that's who, we can still make the sale if we can persuade Matsuda that there'll be no scandal. That's all the Japanese care about, scandal.'

Had he gone off his head? Jon stared at him in mounting rage. 'Christ, mate, a woman's died here and all you can worry about is the bloody sale! A woman who's worked for this family since she was a little kid. A woman you—' He bit his lip and broke off. No point in dragging that up in front of Trisha – but if any man should have cared about Ellie, he should!

Alex was very pale. 'Don't you lecture me, Jon-Jon,' he said softly. 'Just you shape up and do your bit for this sale like a good little brother, and then we'll see about that place of your own we talked about, eh?'

Jon tried to laugh. 'You're overlooking one thing, *big brother*,' he said as sneeringly as Alex had addressed him. 'I don't want to sell Koenigshaus! I don't care if you're offering me twenty places of my own, this is the only one I want! This station's not just money to me, the chance of a quick buck, but a living thing, a piece of us all! And if you want some hired hand to convey your instructions to those two goons George and Roscoe, well, put an ad in *The Australian*, mate, because I'm not here to do your dirty work for you!'

'Dirty work, is it?' Alex had regained control now. 'I'd have thought that's all you can do, you aren't exactly cut out for anything else! And it's a good job someone can do the thinking round here!' He drew himself up with an almost snakelike glitter. 'If you'll excuse me,' he said politely to Trisha. 'I've just got to try to catch those two goons as Jon calls them before they get back to town and start opening their mouths. I should be able to get them on the car radio, though. Shan't be long.' He hurried out.

Jon balled his hands into fists and resisted the temptation to give himself a violent punch. What was the point of that stupid argument? He still holds all the cards, he still has Koenigshaus . . .

Christ, what an evening! First the discovery of his father's hidden files with their disgusting secrets, and then this.

And Ellie – what a way to go, what a way for that pathetic little half-life to be snuffed out—

He had to be alone.

He turned to Trisha, still lolling back in her chair, playing with her wine glass, that dangerous grin still on her face. 'Goodnight,' he said curtly.

She got to her feet. 'Yeah, time to turn in. Will you see me to the guest house?'

As they descended the steps from the front door into the cinnamon-scented night, she caught her high heel, stumbled and almost fell. 'D'you mind?' she said, taking his arm. As they walked slowly across the grass he could feel her full heavy breast pressed against him and in spite of himself his body responded. Against his sense of this animal, sensual woman, the memory of a small slight figure in a white shift pacing with unworldly dignity and a bowed head out of the dining room only minutes earlier made him hot with shame. But he could not deny that a more powerful source of heat was the woman at his side.

'Okay, here we are!'

His attempt to sound bright and breezy fell as flat as a bad joke, she ignored it completely. She took a step towards him, then another, until there were mere inches between them. 'Alex calls you the little brother,' she began in a soft murmur. 'But you know what? I think you're cute!'

He knew he should back off now, this instant. But the flattery was very sweet. 'Yeah,' he said sardonically. 'That's what they all say.'

In response she lifted her hand and drew one long enamelled nail down the length of his chest, just avoiding his nipple. His blood pricked with raw excitement. For the first time in his life he felt the call of an experienced woman, one who knew what she was doing. Now she was tantalisingly opening the top of his shirt, and slipping a hand inside to explore his upper body. With her other hand she reached up to his neck and drew his head slowly down to meet her upturned mouth.

Jesus, could she kiss! He noticed with amusement that

his mind still retained a tenuous control even as his body was raging like wildfire. He wanted her savagely, he could see why Alex lusted after her with his every glance.

But it isn't enough!

Oh God Almighty, he thought, half in laughter, half despair. The only time in my life when something like a scenario from one of the men's magazines comes my way, and that's all I can think of? But he knew he was lost – or saved.

He looked at Trisha, swaying a little in the moonlight. *She wasn't enough.* All this wonderful, womanly flesh, all her poise, all her panache, all her sophistication and drive, they weren't enough. Set against a small sinewy frame more muscle than fat, against a pair of Bambi eyes and a coil of black hair that owed nothing to the hairdresser, nothing was enough.

What had he been thinking of?

How had he allowed that dream to fade – of himself and Geena and their future together?

Did he think she was only interested in the master of Koenigshaus, that she could not love him if he was plain Jon Koenig, master of nothing but himself?

If that was true, she would have transferred her attentions to Alex the second he appeared. Which she had not, preferring to look at him with that lost, hopeful look of a young filly foal every time he appeared. And he had walked by her all this time, losing himself in useless efforts to play amateur detective, and trying to head off a non-existent relationship between his mother and Charles!

His mother—

And father—

He could never feel the same about either of them now. They had shown themselves all too fallible with their weaknesses, their pathetic secrets, in his father's case worse than weak, despicable even in this hateful spying on the women he was supposed to love. Well, what was it the Bible said – '*for a man shall turn from his father and his mother, and take unto wife . . .*'

Yes, it was time.

'Time I was saying goodnight!' he said cheerfully. Before Trisha had a chance to react, he gripped her with an iron grasp and half-steered, half-lifted her up the steps into the guest house. 'And here we are!' Throwing open the door of her suite, he switched on the light and ushered her courteously over the threshold. Then he withdrew instantly and closed the door. 'Goodnight!'

The guest house, although a bungalow, was a substantial dwelling with each of its rooms separated from the others by a wide hallway and corridor. With a light step and an even lighter heart he turned his back on Trisha's suite and set off down the carpeted passageway to what he knew was Geena's room.

Outside he drew a deep breath, then lightly knocked. A small frightened face appeared round the door. 'Geena?' he said gently. 'Still awake? Look, could you just come out for a walk with me? There's a few things I want to say to you.'

Chapter 28

For the rest of his days, Jon looked back on that night as one of the high points of his life.

When Geena slipped out through the door to join him, half fearful, half in awe, he was unable to credit the joy he felt surging through him in waves. When he led her down the steps of the guest house and out into the night, he could not believe he was still anchored to the earth, he felt he must be flying.

When she hesitantly gave him her hand as they walked beneath the shadowy cupola of great trees behind the house, he thought he was holding a rare bird so delicate that if he did not treat it like spun glass, he might break one of its fragile little bones. And when in halting whispers he drew from her the words of love they might have shared long before if he had not been so blind, and at last sealed their new-found understanding with a kiss, he tasted paradise indeed.

'Oh, Geena—!'

'What?'

'Nothing.'

'Jon – what's happening?'

'Oh – everything!'

They laughed together, quietly. Then he was suddenly serious. 'I need you, Geena.'

Her eyes were pools of longing. 'I need you too.'

'No, I mean – I really need you.' He broke off.

How much could he tell her?

She brought one of his hands to her face, and brushed it against her cheek. 'I love you.'

He stared down into her eyes, and read the truth in them. Oh, her eyes—

Gently he pulled her to him and kissed her again, softly at first, and then with increasing passion. He could feel her response in every inch of her quivering little frame as he explored her mouth. He felt a vast sense of wonder at her strange blend of child-like innocence and womanly passion, she seemed the perfect union of all his fantasies with the best of his real life, all in one sweet, gift-wrapped package.

They were deep in the hidden heart of the trees now, where no one ever came. 'Let's sit down,' he said softly stroking her shining face. Gently he drew her down to the soft, dry sandy earth beside him. The ground welcomed them in the gleaming dark, warm as a living thing. He stripped off his shirt and spread it out for her, as he laid her down and took her in his arms.

Her great eyes were fixed on his as round and solemn as a child's, filling him with absurd delight. 'It's all right, it's all right,' he whispered, covering her face with kisses, and was rewarded by the sight of her delicate veined eyelids fluttering and closing as she yielded to him.

Stretching out like a great cat he abandoned himself to the slow luxury of getting to know the little body he now could call his own. Beneath her plain, light shift he could feel her rounded shoulders, the contours of her ribs and the small hard angles of her hips. Slowly his hand approached her small but well-shaped breasts and a shudder gripped him as he found her ready for him, her nipples longing, straining for his touch. Awkwardly he caressed her, then in growing confidence circled each little breast, coaxing deep-throated cries from her, and low moans of desire.

As ever she wore only a simple garment of loose cotton.

Gently he coaxed it up over her hips and drew it over her head. Only the wisps of girlish underwear lay now between her and nakedness. Suddenly he longed to take her as he had never wanted anything in his life. Shrugging off his jeans, he fought to keep his surging impatience in check, giving himself heart and soul to loving her. From her warm forehead and moist upper lip to the hollow of her ankle he covered her whole body in a rainfall of kisses, each caress meeting and feeding her rising tide of desire.

Now her hands were fluttering for him, fondling his ears, his jaw, his breast. Tenderly he drew down the silky scrap of lace and exposed her breast, kissing the tip, pink as a sunburned rose, brushing the satin furrows of the aureole with wondering lips.

He could feel her breath now, coming hard and short. 'Oh, Jon!' she cried, 'Oh, Jon!' He held her for a moment in his arms, sheltering her as the night air struck suddenly expectant, even chill. Then with circling sweeps down from the hollow of her hips, he stroked on down, down till his fingers found the centre of her body, and the centre of her love.

She quivered like a bird and clung to him. 'It's all right,' he whispered again. Gently he readied her with tender reassurance then, when his senses told him that the time had come, he entered her and made her his.

Afterwards he cradled her in his arms, in a state of trembling joy too deep for words. Yet sooner or later he would have to speak.

How much to tell her?

As he looked at her he drew strength. New love meant the chance of a new start. He had seen for himself the legacy of lies and suspicion that his father had left behind. What was the point of a relationship if you could not be honest with the one you loved? He took a deep breath. 'Geena, listen. The reason I've been – well, a bit out of touch since Dad died – it was nothing to do with you. The thing is – I just can't accept that Dad's death was an accident.'

'What?' Her eyes widened in shock. 'You think it was deliberate? That he was murdered?'

He nodded heavily, still holding her tight. 'Yeah, I do.'

'But who—?'

'That's what I don't know.'

'But you think—?'

He had to be careful, even with her. 'I think Dad was murdered because he wouldn't do anything to save the business, save Koenig Holdings, he just wanted to keep Koenigshaus going and he didn't care about anything else.' He paused. 'I think someone wanted him out of the way, so they could sell the station and get the whole thing sorted out.'

She was blazing with horror and indignation. 'Jon, you have to go to the police!'

He laughed bitterly. 'D'you think I haven't thought of that? But I've got no evidence!' He shook his head. 'I've got nothing to give them, nothing to support what I say.'

'Nothing?' Already she knew him as well as he knew himself, he thought. 'You wouldn't just have suspicions with nothing to back them up. You must have something.'

'Oh . . .' He shrugged. 'Well, I've got Dusty's word – the word of an Aboriginal who can read tracks no one else can see. A flight plan, for a plane that no one saw,and one sleepy stockman thinks he might have heard, the plane that might have brought Dad's killers from Sydney. No witnesses at all.'

'Anything else?'

He brooded over the answer. 'My own instincts.'

She squeezed his hand fiercely. 'That's good enough for me.'

'But who else?' He swung to face her despairingly. 'Look at it, Geena, I'm just the loser round here, the kid

286

who's been put out of his inheritance and can't stand the idea of selling the station. I would make trouble, wouldn't I? And if I start crying murder, 'specially now, on top of another violent death last night – who's going to believe a single word I say?'

'I am.' Her soft husky voice was firm with purpose now. 'And I say that you still have to tell the police, just tell them your suspicions and let them do the rest, that's their job!' Her arms still round his waist, she hugged him urgently. 'And look, there isn't going to be a better time than now, now the police are here and already investigating the water-hole and all!'

God, she was right! And she made it all seem so simple. He swept her into his arms. 'Geena, I love you!'

She fought playfully against him. 'Just go and tell them all you know, get it off your chest, and you won't have to worry any more. You'll have done what you think is right and it'll all be out of your hands, you'll be free.' She glanced up at him with a wicked grin. 'Free for me. All for me!'

'You get through to the police?'

She was still at it, Alex thought as he took in the bottle dangling from Trisha's hand, did she never stop? Even her perfect skin was starting to show the ravages, she looked dragged out and nervy, not herself at all.

'Yeah,' he said briefly as he came into the suite, 'got them on the car radio as they were driving back. They'd probably have kept their mouths shut anyway, they're a couple of good ol' boys. But I just wanted to make sure.'

'Drink?'

'No.' He tried to smile. 'There's only one kind of night-cap I want now.' He moved towards her, feeling his senses stir.

But she pushed him away. 'Alex, listen, I've been thinking—'

Rage woke inside him like cold fire. 'Don't you mean

"drinking", darling?' he inquired.

She flashed him a furious glance. 'Listen, you bastard – the day that little bitch barged in on us, the morning I fired her, fired that what's-her-name—'

'Ellie—' he said mechanically.

'Yeah, her, well I saw something that night, the night she must have died—'

Oh, no!

He was not going to have this.

With the sale already trembling on the brink of extinction, and the only hope now a painless, silent, swift police enquiry ending in an open verdict as soon as it could be fixed, he was not going to have the divine Miss Trisha casting herself as the star witness in the murder hunt, going for her hour in court like a movie star playing her big scene.

He grabbed her and drew her towards him, throwing her on the bed. 'You didn't see anything,' he instructed her, taking off his jacket and loosening his tie, his eyes glowing with fire. 'Whatever you thought you saw, you didn't. That's right, isn't it? Have another drink.'

'Oh, what a beautiful morning, George!'

'It is indeed, Roscoe, wouldn't you agree, Mr Koenig?'

'Hey guys, call me Jon, OK?'

Striding into the house and almost into the arms of the two burly policemen, Jon smiled to find himself far more disposed to bear with their weird brand of humour than he had been last night. Happiness was a wonder drug, he thought, it changes your life overnight.

And goons or no, the two officers were on the job promptly enough today, arriving at Koenigshaus before the latecomers had finished breakfast, and before Mrs Matsuda and her assistant had appeared at all to calm the nerves of a furiously tense Alex. But it was Jon they had come to see.

'Had your breakfast, Mr Jon? Wonder if we might ask you a few questions afterwards?'

'No, it's OK, I'm not hungry, I don't want anything to eat.' Like all new lovers, Jon had no need of food. 'Ask me anything you like.'

They were moving him towards the door as they spoke, one on either side, talking across him more to each other than for his benefit, picking up each other's words.

'Wonder if you'd come down to the Blacks' Camp with us—'

'—help us interview a few people there—'

'—specially Markie—'

'—Mark Hands, that is—'

'—the dead woman's husband—'

'—the thing is, they aren't too helpful to the police down there—'

'—one or two brushes with the law here and there in the past—'

'—but they like you—'

'—and trust you—'

'OK, OK!' Jon held up both his hands. 'Of course I'll help, I'll do anything I can.' You talked me into it! he almost said. Just don't keep talking at me, OK?

Down in the village the same elders sat clustered under the same tree in the same positions and attitudes, he could swear, as when he was here last time. Same as they had been for twenty, forty years, perhaps longer, perhaps for ever.

If he loved anything about this land, it was this timelessness, this eternal, unchanging peace. Around the old people at the heart of the camp the life of the settlement went on, the women working, children playing, horses grazing, dogs scratching around, and up at the top, he saw with a lift of the heart, the pencil-slim figure of Geena working intently with her group putting the last touches to their show. But under the white-hot eye of the ever-blazing sun, the land simply endured, in divine disdain of the human insects scurrying fretfully to and fro on its uncaring surface.

Dismounting from the police land-cruiser, Jon was surrounded as always by a swirl of excited children.

'Hey, hello guys,' he greeted them ruffling a head here, exchanging a mock punch there. 'And gals! How old are you now, Kristy, twenty-one? Nah, you're never twelve, a big girl like you?'

The huge-eyed skinny girl-child could have been Geena at that age. 'I am, I am!' she giggled.

'You're not!'

'I am!'

Jon patted her stubby plaits, admiring her butterfly bows. 'Well, I just can't believe it, I'll have to check with your mum!'

Laughing, he broke away from the children and immediately noticed the change in the atmosphere. From the old people, watching the two policemen under lids hooded like lizards' to the younger men gathered warily near the campfire, the very presence of the strangers had brought fear and a guarded dislike.

'Hi, Frank! Hi there, Slim, James!' Jon greeted the stockmen. 'How y'doing? You heard about what's happened?'

It was not really a question.

'Sure,' said Frank awkwardly, avoiding his eye.

'Bloody bad business,' said Jon with more assurance than he felt. 'Just need to check up on a few details, ask a few questions, that's all.'

'You, boss?' said Slim pointedly, his normally merry face dark and set. 'Or them?'

There was no mistaking the hostile emphasis.

'Hello, hello, hello,' began George genially. 'What's all this, then?'

'They don't seem pleased to see us, George,' said Roscoe.

'Well, we haven't been round for a while, that's true.'

'That's true, and it's a shame. It's more than a shame, it's an oversight.' Roscoe turned to Jon. 'Used to come here a lot, when we were kids.'

George nodded. 'Haven't thrown a line into the water-hole for – ooooh, years and years.'

'Donkey's years.'

'Not since our school days.'

'Dear old golden rule days.'

'Yeah, we remember!' Slim broke in aggressively. 'We remember you two as kids at school – and all the rest!'

'Hey, hold on, guys!' Jon was bewildered, raking his memory for a clue to what was going on. Everyone round here knew everyone, there was only one school for all the kids for miles around, so it was no surprise that Slim and the others knew the two officers, he knew them himself.

Of course he'd always known of them rather than known them, they were not his age, more Alex's gener-ation, so they must have been at school with him. But was it at school or in their later career that these two had picked up what was clearly such a bad name among the Aboriginals? And however they had earned this hostility, it was not going to make this investigation any easier.

Not that it seemed to trouble George or Roscoe one bit.

'Just want to know where a few of you were, the night before last,' observed George pleasantly, smoothing back his light sandy hair with one ham of a hand.

'Specially old Markie,' continued Roscoe. 'Ellie's man, Mark Hands, anyone seen him?'

All they got for their pains was a solid wall of blank stares. 'His hut's over here,' said Jon with a heavy heart, turning away. He pointed across the compound. 'It's that

291

one.' He could not stand by and ask the men he counted as his friends to betray one of their number. But he took little joy in having to do the Judas deed himself.

'But Dad, I thought you'd be pleased!'

Not for the first time a young lover in the throes of first love was discovering that older, sadder heads were less ready to share their delight. From the moment that Jon had escorted her back to her room after their blissful night wanderings in the enchanted garden of newly-declared love, Geena had been longing for the time when she could share her news with Ben. So her father thought Jon was just playing with her, ignoring her and treating her as the Koenigs always treated their underlings, especially their women? She was dying to tell him just how wrong he was, just how right Jon was for her, for him, for all the family.

She knew she could not just spring it on him, even the best news needs a little stage management. So she had waited till he had made his usual desultory breakfast and walked with him over to the office where they would be alone. On this perfect morning with the sun rising new-minted like a golden guinea, with the fairy terns and fruit doves clucking and carolling in the trees, how could he not rejoice with her in her overflowing happiness?

But here he was, grey and withdrawn, that little vein that flickered up by his eye at the end of a day with his computer already pulsing, though it was still early morning.

'*Jon?*' He was aghast.

'Yes, Jon!' she countered in alarm. 'Dad, what is it?'

He was staring at the wall, at the floor, anywhere but at her. 'Oh, Geena!' seemed to be all that he could say.

'Dad, what's the problem?' she said urgently. 'Look, you didn't like him when he paid me no attention. Now you don't like it when he does!'

'Oh, Geena! He does, he doesn't – don't you see, it makes no difference?'

'No, I don't see!' she cried in desperation. 'For God's sake, Dad, what have you got against him?'

'He's a Koenig!' he shouted back. 'He's a bloody Koenig, and they're all the bloody same! Everything they touch turns bad, they're rotten and they make other people rotten too! And no one knows that better than I do!' Then he covered his mouth with his hand, turned his face to the wall and silently, hopelessly began to cry.

Inside Mark's hut the reek of beer and stale manhood could have been cut with a knife. From the darkness inside came the sound of a stertorous snorting, but the figure slumped at the back against the wall was not asleep. 'Y'don't come into my hut without invitation!' he screeched, erupting into violent life. 'Y'want to talk to me, I'll come outside!'

Several minutes elapsed before the thick-set, muscular body shouldered into view, clutching the perennial can. Mark flinched visibly at the sight of the two officers standing stark and accusing against the sun. 'I didn't do it!' he cried hysterically. 'It wasn't me, I never touched the bitch!'

'Bitch, was she, Markie?' said George with interest.

'Why's that, Mark?' Roscoe took it up. 'What did she do to make you call her that?'

To Jon's horror, the drunk suddenly turned on him, advancing unsteadily with a wavering, pointing finger. 'Ask him!' he screamed. 'Fucking ask him! He was fucking her!'

'Well, well, well!'

'Well, fancy that!'

The two pairs of pale eyes fixed on Jon struck him with even more shock and dismay than the first accusation. He felt himself flushing darkly as he gasped out his reply. 'That's ridiculous! I never – I never touched her!'

'Yes, well,' said George in the same tone of amiable interest, 'they all say that, don't they, Roscoe?'

'Yes, well, they would George, wouldn't they?'

'Yes they fucking would!' cried Mark in a drunken moan. 'I know he was, she told me he was. And his brother, he was fucking her too!'

The two police faces gleamed with stronger interest.

'Mr Jon's brother, Markie?'

'That'd be Mr Alex Koenig then?'

'Yes, both of them! All of them!'

'Both of them, y'say?'

'*All* of them, y'say, Markie?'

This isn't happening, thought Jon dimly, any moment now I'm going to wake up out of this and it'll just be a bad dream. But still the macabre double act went on, and suddenly he knew that it was only going to get worse.

'Both of them did he say, George?'

'*All* of them did he say, Roscoe?'

Both men leaned into Mark in unison.

'Yes, all of them,' the demented husband raged. 'The old man had her too, he had her first! He moved on to her after he finished with Rose, when she got too old! And then they all had her!'

'Well, well, well.'

'Well I never, did you, Roscoe?'

'Look—'

Jon's voice sounded as if it came from a million miles away. He broke off and tried again, he could not believe the bitterness he felt. 'He's talking rubbish, the lying bastard! I never touched his wife. Nor did my dad, I'll swear to that!'

'You'll swear!' Mark laughed in disgust. 'What did you know, sonny, what did you see? Ask Rose! She was the first Koenig tart up there at the house, she knows it all, ask her! And my Ellie was the last.'

The first.

And the last.

If Rose was the first and Ellie was the last, *who else was there*?

It did not take the ponderous double-barrelled inquisition of the two police goons to draw out the next taunt from the drunken wreck at their feet.

'She was a stunner, best of the bunch by a mile, any man'd've wanted her! And when Koenigs want, they take. Never mind if she was married to another man. Never mind if that man was his best friend.'

He fixed his drink-sodden gaze on Jon in violent accusation. 'He was the biggest bastard in the world, your dad! Made a fool of his own friend, and fucked his wife. Poor old Ben!'

He laughed, and the sound chilled Jon to the bone. The little eyes were gleaming now with malicious glee. 'Left a cuckoo in the nest too, not that he cared.'

He turned and almost in slow motion gestured up the compound towards Geena, hard at work and poised at a still moment of her dance like a figure outside time. Jon had a last desperate urge to hold back the turning of the earth, arrest this boulder before it rolled down on him, crushing him, crushing them both.

Mark chuckled, he could smell his distress. 'That's her, that's the little cuckoo your Dad put in Ben Nichols' nest, when he fucked his wife! Our Geena. Say hello to your sister!'

Chapter 29

If it could have been any other woman on Koenigshaus, any other woman in the world . . .

If Dad had to have affairs, if one woman was not good enough for him—

But 'Geena's mother?

Was there no end to what he had been capable of?

How Jon had got himself away from the Aboriginals' village he never knew. His last memory was of the bovine faces of the two policemen, alive with prurient glee as they took in Mark's tale.

'Don't – don't put this about, hey guys?' he'd muttered, burning with shame. 'Keep it to yourselves?'

He was saying this? – he who had sneered at Alex for wanting to hush up a Koenig scandal, sucking round the cops himself now? Then he'd walked stiffly away like a zombie, taken his horse, and ridden off into the bush.

And ridden, and ridden, going and going as all men do who have nowhere to go.

Now the flat and arid landscape of the outback, so hated by those who never find its gift of spiritual peace, seemed to echo his inner world completely: he too was drained and desolate, empty, burned and dry. The squawking flocks of parakeets, the mocking cackle of the brolga, the curlew's haunting mimicry of a baby's cry seemed like the sounds of his own heart-rendering loss. All he could think of was to stay away from the homestead till he had worked out what he was going to do.

Geena his sister?

Half-sister then, it made no difference.

He could not love her, could not marry her.

Pain claimed him like a scream, he rode for miles howling in silence. He would not have believed anything could hurt so much. And the person he thought he could have turned to in any crisis was now the one soul to whom he could not appeal.

Geena.

Her very name sounded like a lament to him now, like a cry of distress. And what was his distress against hers when he told her that it was all off now, all over before it had ever really begun?

And to break with her for no reason – for how could he give her a reason? – he could not possibly tell her that her mother had betrayed her father with his, that she was not the child of the man she had called 'Dad' all her life . . .

He groaned aloud. Every way he turned, some new and terrible angle presented itself. Yet what could he do to get out of this?

Nothing!

What if it wasn't true?

This was the first straw he had clutched at, and it came round again and again like the false promise of hope to a dying man. Mark was a drunk, and vicious with it – in his fury against the faithless Ellie he would say anything. He could have made the whole thing up to spite all the Koenigs.

And if the two policemen had not asked him to go down to the camp with them this morning, he would not have heard Mark's wild accusations, would probably never have known anything about this at all. Besides, if Mark was wrong about him – for Jon could swear with truth that *he* had never touched Mark's wife! – then couldn't he be wrong abut Dad too?

This was only gossip, rumour, there was no substance to it, no proof!

Why didn't he simply pretend he had never heard what the furious Aboriginal had said, go right ahead as planned and marry Geena anyway? Yet even as the thought was born, it died. He could not do that to her. He could not betray her trust, her faith like that. For however long it took, he would live all his life in fear – fear for himself and her – that one day the truth would come out.

Could he check up on it, then, establish once and for all that it was a lie?

Yet how?

The only two souls in the world who could tell him the truth, Phillip and Geena's mother, were both dead now, and well past the truths and falsehoods of earthly life.

Would Ben know?

How could he ask him? 'Hey, mate, is it true what they're saying down at the camp, that your old lady played away with my dad, that he was plugging her for years? That your Geena's a bit of his own hot stuff that he left sticking to your oven door?'

Could he ask Helen what she knew about it?

If he was embarrassed to ask Ben, how much less could he put it to her! 'Hey, Mum, did old Dad have a zipper problem? Heard he just couldn't help swinging his dangle at the ladies, 'specially the black ones. Did you know you were sharing his dick with Rose, Ellie, Ben's wife, Mary from the Dairy and anything else that had a hole between its legs?'

He knew he was growing foul, vicious and foul, as bad as Mark, as bad as his father, he just didn't care. As the day wore on his wanderings became more circular, he knew, his mutterings more crazed. Under the pitiless sun he sweated and grew cold. Though he stopped by habit to allow his horse to graze, and sought out water-holes to allow it to drink, he could not think of himself at all. In the parching heat he could feel himself losing his vital body fluids, but he could not care.

He had to stay away, that was all he knew.

Only long after he was sure that all the household would be safe in bed did he dare to turn his horse's head for home.

From the stables at the back of the house he could see a solitary light burning in the kitchen. Rose always kept strange hours.

Rose.

Ask Rose! the drunken Mark had mouthed. Well, why not?

She did not look at all surprised to see him as he came in through the door. For once her eternal Tarot lay unopened by her side, and her only companion was a bottle of cooking sherry. He grabbed roughly for a chair and drew up opposite her across the wooden table. He felt his life would turn on what she had to say in answer to his question. 'Is there a curse on us, Rose, a curse on the Koenigs?'

She stared at him, leaning forward on her elbows, hunched and unblinking as an armadillo. 'Don't know what you mean.'

'Did the old people – your people, the ones that Johann killed – did they wish us ill?'

She picked up her glass. 'They're all gone, dead and gone, years and years ago. They won't come back.'

She didn't believe that, he knew. 'Before they went,' he persisted wearily. 'As they died – did they curse us for ever and ever, make a promise that we'd never live on this land in peace?'

Rose gave a tight shrug. 'Don't know none of that stuff. I went to Mission school!'

He made a furious grab for the Tarot pack and gripped it menacingly in his fist. 'You didn't learn this at Mission school!'

'Mr Jon, no!'

Her resistance had crumbled at once, he might have been crushing her baby before her eyes. She reached out wildly to reclaim the battered pack. 'What do you want to know?' Automatically she began to fumble out the mysterious characters of the brightly-coloured deck, the Lovers, the Hanged Man, the Falling Tower . . .

'No,' he said huskily. 'No cards.'

Her jet-bead eyes were instantly frightened again, he could smell the fear coming from her in waves. 'What, then?'

'You know the history of this place, all the history round here.'

Again that flare of fear. 'Some.'

'A lot,' he insisted. 'And a lot more than you let on.'

She was still stubborn. 'Some.'

'OK.' He was not going to fight about it. Some would probably be enough. The pain grabbed him again. More than enough, most likely. 'I'm not asking you to go all the way back to the time when the first Johann came here.'

'OK.'

'But as far back as my father—'

She did not move, but as he watched her he could see every muscle in her body set like stone. He held the pause for a long moment, then said, 'What about him?'

'About him?' Her breath escaped like the whisper of a sigh and a dull glow lit the back of her eyes, growing stronger with every word she spoke. 'He was a proper man! He was a Koenig! All Koenigs eat like horses, drink like fish, ride like centaurs—'

'—and fuck like dingoes, eh, Rose?'

He did not know what had come over him, he would never use such language, even to another man. But the old woman did not turn a hair. 'Yeah,' she said calmly, but with a reminiscent glint. 'Like dingoes. Just like dingoes.'

'So you were his—'

He groped for the word. 'Mistress' was too old-fashioned, too bloody Pommie. And 'lover' she had never been in Phillip's cold and loveless use of her, his calculated exploitation of her for his own selfish ends. 'His—?'

'Yeah. His.' She looked the happiest he had ever seen her. She rolled the word around her mind, and savoured it silently. 'His,' she said again triumphantly.

And he had to destroy it, crush her moment with the one reminder she must hate above all. 'You and who else?'

Her face closed like a trap. 'No one else,' she said flatly.

He could not bear it, not on top of everything else he had endured today. 'C'mon, Rose!' he ground out, clenching his fists. 'I don't care if you're protecting him, me or yourself, but I'm going to know, if I have to beat it out of you!'

She gasped, and flinched away. 'Doan hit me, Mr Jon! Not like he did!'

Oh God. So he beat her as well? Jon's soul rose in revolt. And this was the man he had been proud to call his father? Was there no end to it? 'Just tell me,' he managed. 'There was you?'

She nodded.

'And Ellie?'

She hesitated, and her face crumpled with remembered pain. He waited. At last came the confirmation, one slow nod.

'And—?'

She sat, impassive as the Sphinx, her eyes like gimlets in her screwed-up face. It was like a deadly game of poker, he would have to play his card, show his whole hand, drag it out of her. 'And – Ben's wife? Geena's mother? Did he have an affair with her?'

She pursed her mouth and her eyes grew dim and in-turned, as if she was playing a video-tape in her head. She sat, watching the action. 'Yeah', she said steadily at last. 'She loved him, Yuni did. Like we all did.'

It was no more than he had been expecting. But it was a punch in the solar plexus, he could hardly breathe. Now it was her turn to wait for him to speak. 'Yuni?' he forced out.

'Yeah.'

'That was Ben's wife?'

'Yeah.'

'She – and my father – they were—'

She looked over his head. 'He had her – like he had me and Ellie.'

'Before she was married to Ben?'

'Yeah.'

'And – after?'

Rose's voice was strong now, she was herself again. 'Yeah!' she said harshly. 'And during!'

'When – did it end?'

Rose clenched her fists. 'Didn't never end! Till she went to Sydney, till she died, she was his black woman like I was before and like Ellie after. Alla time! Till she died!'

Alla time . . .

All the time Geena was conceived, all the time she was growing up—

All the time she thought Ben was her father, and all the time she thought she was free to fall in love with the son of Phillip Koenig—

All the time she was his sister.

And now he had all the time in the world to work out how to tell her. And after that, all the time it would take to find the way to start his life again, cold, dead and alone.

It was truly amazing how everything came together when a sale was right, when the business decision was the right

303

one. Mr Matsuda would be very pleased with this, he would be pleased with her. He was the first who had taught her that a little touch of disaster was a very helpful thing to the purchaser when a deal like this was in the offing. It made the vendor so nervous that it could take thousands off the price.

In this case, hundreds of thousands. Mrs Matsuda peered at her immaculate reflection in the mirror of her suite in the guest house, finished applying her porcelain liquid foundation, dusted a few grains of magnolia silk finish onto her perfect nose with a swansdown mini-puff and smiled at the result. Koenigshaus was dropping into her hand. They would make the sale.

The Koenigs could not get out of it, not now. Carefully she selected a burnt orange two-piece in a stylish batik she had found in Jakarta and had made up in New York, and brooded over the necklace and earrings to complete the outfit. No, they had no way out. With the heavy weapons against them that Craig had found in their own cleverly doctored but virtually criminal figures, with the horrible death of the father and now the brutal murder of the maid, Koenigshaus for the Koenigs had become a liability, not an asset.

'If we wait any longer, they'll practically pay us to take the place off their hands!' Craig had exulted this morning.

And he was right, as usual.

What a good boy.

'Craig,' she called.

He appeared from the adjoining suite, ready as ever to do her bidding. She smiled at his fresh, preppy, good-boy expression, like a dog waiting for its owner to throw a stick and cry 'fetch!' He knew this stick, she didn't need to throw it. 'One more day—' she said.

Buckley laughed unpleasantly. 'Which should bring Mr Alex to his knees good and proper, the way he's going! Old Ben's cracking up too, it's too much for all of them!'

'—sit through the corroboree tonight—'

'—and do the deal tomorrow.' He nodded triumphantly. 'They won't fight, Alex'll be so grateful you still want it, he'll agree to anything.'

'That,' she said, 'is my thinking too.'

He laughed again. 'Well, the chopper's ready at the airstrip, they can all fly it, Ben's offered to have us up and away at a moment's notice, he wants out so badly now it hurts, and no wonder! So I'll tell the office then, shall I? Back late tomorrow, with Koenigshaus in the bag!'

'The corroboree? There isn't going to be any bloody corroboree!'

Charles would not have come down for breakfast if he had known that the only other person at the table would be Alex. God knows where all the others were, though he had to admit he'd been avoiding every possible meal himself. But to have to sit through even a hurried cup of coffee and snatched piece of toast with his least favourite person on Koenigshaus, possibly in the world, was an ordeal he could well have done without.

He prided himself he had been doing OK so far – well, not bad, anyway – just getting through on the tried-and-tested, take-each-day-as-it-comes basis. But it had not been easy; it had been bloody difficult, often almost impossible to endure, living in the same house with her. He could not bear to see Helen looking so bleak and bruised, in fact he could scarcely bear to see her at all, he was so angry with her.

With her, with himself, with Jon, but above all with Phillip. Even in death the great, greedy shade of that selfish, domineering old bastard continued to ruin their lives. It's only because she doesn't want to upset Jon's cherished memory of his old man that she's insisting on playing the widow in perpetual mourning! he told himself fiercely. Watching her so closely in the last few years, Charles had seen how Helen's feeling for Phillip had withered and died, choked alive by his cruelty, his egomania, his sexual greed. *She didn't love him!* his soul cried. *So why can't she love me?* It was the question he spent all day trying to avoid, and all night trying to answer.

And now to be confronted with a pale and unsmiling Alex coldly demanding to know what he was going to do at the corroboree was the last straw. 'There isn't going to be any corroboree!' he repeated.

Alex's face went even paler, if that was possible. For a wild moment Charles almost fancied he could hear him grinding his teeth. 'What are you *talking about?*'

'Well, surely you're going to cancel it – God Almighty, man, I would have thought you had already!'

'Cancel it?' Alex was gripping his coffee cup as if he wanted to crush it between his hands. 'Why the hell should I?'

Charles almost laughed.'Why? For Christ's sake, a woman's been killed! A woman who belonged to the village, who worked in this house from the time she was five years old! We should cancel it as a mark of respect!'

Alex's face cleared. 'You could just as well say,' he said earnestly, 'that we should go on with it as a mark of respect. The corroboree only comes round once a year, Ellie wouldn't have wanted them to put it off for her. It's a big thing for the villagers.'

'And a big thing for the Koenigs?' demanded Charles sarcastically. 'One of them anyway – if you can pull off the sale to Mrs Matsuda?'

Alex shook his head. 'You've got me wrong, Charles,' he said with a reproachful glance. 'I'm only thinking of the people here. This year they've been working up this special dance with Geena, something about the history of Koenigshaus. I don't want to let them down.'

'The show must go on, eh?'

Alex gave a cold smile. 'Exactly!'

Charles could have punched him. 'Except that it's not a bloody floor-show to them! Corroborees are sacred – special—'

'I know that!' Alex cut in. 'But this will be special. Different.'

'Yeah, sure.' Charles could see he was losing. 'Do one thing for them anyway. Let them have their corroboree down at the village in peace, undisturbed. Get Geena to put on her dance up here at the house to wow the pants off the Matsuda woman, if that's what you want to do. Then at least the villagers can do what they want to do for Ellie, without us playing the white masters, breathing down their necks. OK?'

Alex considered, working out all the angles. 'OK,' he said at last. 'OK, I think we can do that.' He favoured Charles with a sincere look. 'And I can promise you it won't be in any way disrespectful – to the villagers or to – to the dead lady.'

The dead lady.

Charles thought of the poor damaged waif who had been Ellie, and gave up. 'Have it your own way,' he announced briefly, pushing back his chair and getting ready to depart. *You will anyway*, was his last silent thought.

'Yes', smiled Alex tightly. 'I will anyway.'

The corroboree.

Last one for me on Koenigshaus, thought Helen. Last one, after twenty-five years . . .

Well, everything changes.

Coldly, brutally repeating the phrase to herself she turned back to her chest of drawers. Through the window of the bedroom the warm morning air was gently lifting the curtains with their silly lacy frills inside that sour green-apple satin that made her think of unripe Granny

Smiths. She gazed at the blossom-sprigged wallpaper with its endlessly-repeating pattern of little pink buds of rambling moss rose. How had she ever thought this room beautiful? It was a teenager's idea of a boudoir, not a grown woman's place at all.

Well, the next one would be very different.

How about a stark black cube, black ceiling, black fur walls and floors, no books, no pictures, no television, no telephone, no windows, no doors?

Oh, shut *up*! And cut out these bloody tomb-like depressive fantasies, you're going to leave here and go to Sydney and get a job and find a room and live like any other normal woman who's changing her life and making a new start!

She paused, the froth of underwear frozen in her hand midway between the open chest of drawers and the suitcase lying gaping on the bed. *But I don't want a new start*, she wanted to cry. *I want my old life back.*

What, all of it? sneered a hostile inner voice. Including Phillip, with his hot hands, hot tongue, hot sex—?

With a swift reflex shudder she threw the tangle of Parisian lingerie straight into the bin.

A new start, she repeated to herself mechanically.

Just see the corroboree, then get on the chopper with the visitors when they go, and that'll be it. There's no place here for me now. And it's time for Jon to strike out on his own, a man of twenty-four has to get by without his mum!

What about the furniture? came another voice.

Dear God, what about it?

With eyes as bleak as the North Sea she scanned the heavy oak bed, scene of so many savage humiliations now, the massive old oak wardrobe, big enough to sublet, Phillip's heavy desk with the sad secret of his hidden illness, the black thing eating him up inside, the tumour eating his brain. This place was never hers, all these things never had been hers, it was nothing to her to leave this behind.

Now a new realisation dawned, bringing a new freedom, a sense of the ties breaking, allowing her to float painlessly above it all and away. It had never been Trudi's either, as she had feared for so many years. It was always the Koenigs', always the property of those domineering men, always imposed upon their women without any thought that a new bride might like to fix up her own home, that a grown woman had the right to determine her own way of living, choose her own style. Well, she would have that right now. At the age of forty two, she would be free at last, not Phillip's wife or Jon's mother but a woman in her own right. She only hoped that it was not too late.

In the mirror on the dressing-table she caught sight of a pale, worn shadow of a woman, one who had lost weight in her face and looked ten years older than she should. No fear of any interference with her plan to be a woman alone if she went on looking like that! she thought harshly. And that was fine, just fine. If she never saw a man again in all her life, she thought she could die quite happy.

But a job, now—

That was a worry, a big worry.

What was she to do in the city, what could she do? But again she crushed it down. Time enough to worry about that when you're sitting in a cafe in Sydney with the morning paper in your hand going through the Sits Vac. She turned back to her packing.

The footfall on the stair took her by surprise. No one ever came up here now except her. 'Rose? What's the problem?'

Impossible to try to read Rose's face. 'No problem, Miz Koenig. But them police here again and Mister Alex want everyone downstairs in the dining room.'

She had been expecting more bad tidings as she

stumbled downstairs in Rose's wake. Those two unsettling creatures George and Roscoe could never be good news. But she was quite unprepared for the cheesy grins and self-congratulatory tones in which they made their announcement to the assembled household, all present except Jon. 'Sorry to say folks, sad news—'

'—an unfortunate occurrence—'

'—unfortunate for him, anyway—'

'—body of Markie, Mark Hands that is—'

'—found dead in the bush.'

'No suspicious circumstances—'

'—still awaiting the pathologist's report, of course—'

'—but surrounded by spirits—'

'—massive alcohol intake—'

'—died of alcohol poisoning—'

'—or as we say in the police, drank himself to death.'

'Previously heard expressing remorse for his poor wife's death—'

'—before which, known to have threatened her on many occasions—'

'—and beaten her, George, don't forget beaten—'

'—so with that history—'

'—we think we can take it he killed the little lady.'

George smiled. 'So we're calling the case closed. Sorry you've all been troubled.'

Roscoe smiled the same smile. 'Glad we could sort if out for you like this. Any time we can be of assistance to the Koenigs—'

Alex bounded to his feet. 'Good work, great work, boys!' he enthused. 'I'll see the Police Commissioner gets to know of this! And I don't think the Police Widows' and Orphans' Fund will be disappointed in the size of the Koenigshaus donation this Christmas!'

He beamed round the group. 'Now I know it's still early yet, and the performance that Miss Geena has been arranging is not till this evening, but I hope we'll see both you boys later here at the house when she unveils her show for us!'

Chapter 30

He knew he was getting light-headed, he probably should have something to eat or drink but it was so hard to move . . .

And he certainly shouldn't have grabbed that bottle as he left the kitchen after his session with Rose, not a great idea to go without food all day, then make a slap-up late-night supper on a full bottle of whisky . . .

The truth was that he didn't want to go, didn't want to leave this safe refuge where they'd never find him, where they'd never even think of looking for him.

Because he still did not know what to do, did not know what to say to Geena when she came to hunt him down, as she surely must do. After a day in the bush and a night half waking, half dozing in the chapel here, he had a raging thirst, and his body had passed through hunger and tiredness into a kind of floating despair. So every time he thought of moving, he sank back into lethargy.

From his perch on a pew about midway down the chapel he could see all the brass plates marking the graves of the long-dead Koenigs stretching like shining stepping-stones the length of the aisle. He raised his head mournfully towards the first plaque by the door.

JOHANN.

Johann.

Dear, sweet old Johann, who massacred a whole tribe at the water-hole. 'You carved Koenigshaus out of the bush, Johann,' he murmured. 'But you took the water at the price of blood. Human blood. Not a fair exchange!'

His glance wandered on down the aisle to the next sad plate.

PHILLIP.

'So what was it all for, Johann? Your only son, killed in battle like that. Phillip, the first Phillip, the one they named Dad after, dying with a bayonet in his throat at the bottom of a trench?'

'Phillip Koenig, now there's a black joke. A German fighting Germans. Did he think of Koenigshaus, was that the last thing that went through his mind before he died, knowing he'd never see this place again? Did he even still call himself a Koenig? Or when he signed on, did he change his name to King as you wanted him to do?'

'And don't forget dear old grandfather,' he instructed himself portentously, 'grandfather John. Not Johann – we'd got a bit more Aussie by then. What did you do right, grandad? Must have done something! Nursed the old place through the Depression and saved us again in the bad years of World War Two, was that it? Lived here in peace, had two fine sons Charles and Phillip, died full of years in your own bed, nothing out of order – until—until one son killed the other – and killed poor Ellie, for all I know – and for all I'll ever be able to prove!'

Proof.

He ground his nails into his palms in fruitless anguish. For all his questions, all his searches, all he had discovered was more and more reasons why Phillip was murdered, not who it was who had brought him to his untimely end. Christ, for some of the things he'd done, he could have seen the old man off himself! He swung towards the unmarked flagstones where his father lay.

'Well, shall we have a little chat as I'm here, Dad?' he challenged. 'Do you believe in dreams? I did, and look where it got me! All I've found out is what a bastard you were!'

'Hello, Jon.'

The door was ajar, he had not heard her come in. She stood in the doorway against a halo of light wearing another of her plain white dresses, she seemed to scorch his tired, drink-worn eyes with her flame of white and gold. 'Who are you talking to?

'The dead. But they don't answer me.'

She raised a hand as if to brush his foolish response away like buzzing fly. 'Where were you last night?'

She was not angry, not even reproachful, just hurt and baffled, and alarmed, he could see that. 'I told Dad about us yesterday,' she began stiffly. 'And he wasn't pleased like I thought he would be, he was very upset. So it was vital for me to have you there at dinner, so he could see that you meant what you said, that you weren't just stringing me along. And when you didn't come, didn't show up or come back at all, he was sure of the worst. *Where were you, Jon?*'

'Ah.'

Now the moment had come, he felt quite hollow. He stared at her owlishly. 'Ah.'

'Answer me.'

'Yes.' He tried to clear his throat. 'Out. I was out. In the bush. Not here.'

Her calm demeanour slipped. 'Jon, what's happening?'

'Nothing's happening, why?'

'Don't do this to me! Have you forgotten – what's happened between us? One day you say you love me, and the next day you're running away, going missing, hiding in the chapel, getting drunk—'

He waved the bottle. 'Not very drunk.'

She was on the verge of tears. 'Jon, I'd like to talk to you properly – when you're capable of it. In the meantime, I've got the dance to get ready for tonight. Alex has moved the whole thing up here, so I don't know where to begin.' She turned towards the door.

He desperately did not want her to leave. 'Look, why don't you have a talk – while I listen.'

She looked at him in mingled anger and pain. 'Are you serious?'

He got up slowly and began to move towards her. 'Never more so.'

She shrugged in despair. 'It'll have to be later. After the show.'

'Why not now?' He caught her by the arm. 'While I'm still drunk?'

She flinched. 'Jon, I know you've been under a terrible strain—'

'Strain?' The chapel resounded to his hysterical laughter. 'Yes, well, you could say that!'

She bowed her head. 'And you know how sorry I am about – everything.'

'Yes, well, it's good that we can talk frankly and openly like this!' he sneered.

She stiffened. 'Don't laugh at me, Jon! You've just given me one of the worst nights of my life, and I'm trying to be understanding, trying to see things from your point of view. Don't make it any harder!' She wrenched her arm from his grasp. 'I'll see you later. We can go on with this then.'

'Before you go—' *before you go, my dearest, sweetest love, before you go and take my heart with you, now and for always* – 'let's at least try to divorce the emotional issues from the practical ones.'

She grew pale. 'What—'

He spoke very quietly now. 'I want you to go, Geena.'

'What?'

'Leave.'

'Why?'

'I can't tell you.'

316

She was desperately hanging on to every last scrap of her courage, he could tell. 'You've got to tell me why!'

How could he say this and not die screaming? 'It's over.'

'*No*! No, I don't believe you!' Her eyes were black pits of all the suffering of the world. Her arms flailed wildly around, she seemed to be trying to protect herself from what he had to say. 'You're just drunk!' she cried, clutching at straws.

He laughed again, with deep bitterness. 'Not drunk enough.' *I'd have to drink a river, drown an ocean* – 'I'll say it again. It's over. You have to go. I can't explain. That's all there is to it.'

She seemed to shrink under his gaze as in a diminishing mirror. 'You wanted me yesterday, I know you did!' she said like a child.

He steeled his heart. 'And now I don't.'

'What have I done?'

'Nothing. Just go.' He did not know how long he could go on with this, how much more he could take.

'No!'

He turned on her savagely. 'Still here?

'I have to know what this is about!'

He consulted his watch. 'It's about eleven o'clock.'

'Why are you doing this?' She brought her clenched fists to her mouth in another unconscious gesture of childhood. 'I want to spend the rest of my life with you, and you're sending me away?'

'Yes.'

She stood braced, flexing herself for her final throw. 'You need me!'

He leaned forward and spoke with great distinctness, right in her face. 'I – need – you – to – go!' He tried to reach for a patronising tone. 'Go and get your show on the road! Tonight's the night, isn't it? Go and play Margot Fonteyn with your little dancing chums down at the village. Then we'll all see what you can do.'

'Right!'

Quivering with anger she drew herself up. 'Right, you bastard! I don't know what you've been playing at with me, but I hope it's given you satisfaction, Mr Koenig! Oh, Dad was right all along! You bloody bastard Koenigs!'

She raised her fist as if she were going to strike him, then gave it up. But she had one more shot in her locker. 'If you come to the dance we've been working on tonight, you'll be able to see our tribute to the Koenigs. And I don't think you'll have much problem recognising yourself in what they do!'

By car, land-cruiser, trail-bike and even horse, dancers and celebrants had gathered from miles around to join the corroboree. In the sprawl of the vast red desert the majestic gum trees, gleaming a ghostly white in the fading of the day, marked out the Aboriginals' camp as their destination from the living wilderness all around.

Within the compound at the heart of the village, Geena's dance offering had already introduced the real business of the corroboree, ancient ritual ceremonies of love and death going back to the dawn of life on the island. Now up at Koenigshaus a special dancing area had been set up for a second performance in a clearing by the house, the hard-packed earth newly brushed and swept for the dancers' feet.

A few chairs had been placed ready in a semi-circle at the front, though some of the spectators, like the detached, sardonic Charles lurking in the rear, had made it clear that they preferred to stand. Kerosene torches, awaiting the full descent of night, described a horse-shoe shape around Geena and her team of dancers and instrumentalists as they stood ready to begin.

'I think you'll find it very interesting,' an earnest Alex was assuring Mrs Matsuda and Buckley as he ushered them to the two seats of honour in the centre.

Christ, he never stops working for this sale! thought Jon, standing as far away from Charles as he could contrive while still being able to see the dance. He was sick with disgust and also, as he hopelessly knew, from the effects of the liquid food he had begun with last night and had stayed with all day.

Beside Craig Buckley sat Helen, paler than ever to Jon's eye, though it was a toss-up whether she or Ben on her other side looked worse. From the long stare of furious, stinging rebuke that Ben had given him when he saw him here tonight, Jon knew that Geena must have told her father all that had passed between them during the painful exchange in the chapel. Now Ben avoided Jon's eye completely, huddling into himself grey-faced and impassive, but his inner turmoil still betrayed by his ever-twitching hands and face.

Ben, Helen, Rose at the back there, Buckley, Matsuda, and Alex . . .

Wearily Jon checked over the little row of spectators settling themselves for the dance to begin. Oh, and Miss Trisha – don't forget the divine Miss Trisha! Seated on Alex's other side from Mrs Matsuda but quite unabashed by his presence, Trisha, seriously drunk, was playing at lighting a cigarette as she flirted with the two policemen, Roscoe and George.

'Got a light, boys?'

It was the oldest line in the book, you could hear it on every street corner of every city in the world. Jon did not need to know what she was saying, her reflex use of sex like a scatter gun was clear from any distance. Yet Trisha too was not herself, she seemed strained and unnaturally wrought-up, her laugh too high, her voice too loud, her suggestive drawl like the hoarse call of a goanna.

Alex turned on her venomously. 'Shut up!' he hissed. 'They're starting!'

God, he was wound-up! Jon thought. He looked as if he was on some powerful drug! Still, hang on, big bro! he hailed him in silent hatred, don't lose your nerve! Come tomorrow you'll be a rich boy and I'll be less than nothing, and maybe then you'll be happy!

He turned his eyes to the dance area as one thin, grieving note of the didgeridoo rang through the air to attract their attention. Geena stepped forward into the expectant silence. Like all the women dancers she was simply and skimpily clad in no more than a length of scarlet cotton twisted round her like a sarong, her face and body marked with the grey-white ash-paste of the Aboriginals, her arms and legs bare. Pallid even beneath the white paint, she looked almost unbearably tense, and her voice cracked as she began.

'We'd like to show you our dance drama, it's a mixture of the work of all of us over the last few weeks.' She cleared her throat. 'We're trying to tell the history of the Koenigshaus station from the early days. We want to show you some of the things that have happened here – a few living pages from the story-book we all share. Thank you.'

She bowed slightly and fell back to the group, giving the sign to begin. Now the didgeridoo began a deep, rhythmic roaring, to be answered by the light clicking of the clap-sticks and the dull boom of the drums as the whole scene came to life in the fading light. Sound and spectacle erupted together as around twenty dancers emerged into the open space, running, skimming and leaping to the accompaniment of a wild burst of sound, with Geena in their midst.

In the universal language of dance, the story had the stark simplicity of all true drama and all tragedy. First came the days before the Koenigs, before even the first human inhabitants had trodden the land. As the compelling dawn-time sound of the ancient instruments filled the air with their musical calls and cries, the leading male dancers bounded centre-stage as kangaroos, lords of their wilderness world unthreatened by man. Around their powerful, muscular bodies the younger men and the women preened as emus, stalked as coyotes or slithered like snakes, keeping up the endless throbbing refrain with their own cooing, trilling, barking, clicking and roaring as they did so. Vividly brought to life through the stunning skill of the performers, it was a Garden of Eden, a pure world of beauty and peaceful co-existence.

And then came man.

From the glimmering, lengthening shadows stalked a band of warriors, the largest men of the group who in chilling mime tracked the kangaroos and hunted them down. Hissing youths acted as look-outs while the kangaroos were speared and killed, the dancers on the ground quivering so desperately in their death-throes that it seemed impossible they were not actually being killed.

From the rear the women approached now, led by Geena, to welcome home the warriors and prepare a feast. At the head of the men their young chief came forward to greet the women and make their offering of the kangaroo meat to feed the tribe. Timbo, by God! Jon thought in wonderment, watching Geena, as queen of the women, accept the chief's offering and invite the warriors to join them. Who would have thought the kid could dance like that, look like that?

Now each warrior claimed one of the women-folk and two by two each pair of dancers, heads together and arms round each other, melted away into the shining dusk, leaving the young queen and the warrior chief alone. As Geena and Timbo bowed and exchanged glances, delicately circled each other and approached shyly, step by step, reaching out for each other with bodies alive with passion down to their fluttering fingertips, the pulse of the music skipped up the register to become the heart-beat of love and life itself. In a mimed courtship, the boy won the girl and took her hand to claim her as his own. At the front of the audience, Jon could see Ben shifting in his seat in evident unhappiness. So he didn't like the mock-marriage, either? In a red mist of jealousy, Jon could have killed Timbo now, he wanted to smash the successful suitor of 'Queen' Geena into little pieces, and feed him to the dogs.

Suddenly the music darkened, the strange instruments like a chorus of animal spirits wailing and coughing and howling in distress.

Enter the Koenigs! Jon told himself sardonically, they're the only discordant note round here!

Now a flurry of kangaroo dancers leaped away into the falling dark as a group of slow-moving cow-dancers, heads down, hands simulating thrusting horns, drove them away and put them to flight. In the background, kept off the water-hole, the women and youths mimed starvation and slow death. His warriors massed around him, the young chief, the lead dancer Timbo, pledged his new bride Geena in poignant mime that he would save the tribe. A sudden foray brought two dead cow-dancers back in triumph as food for the people. But on their heels came the biggest and heaviest of the men coated in ash-paint, white as ghost gums in the gloaming, Koenig dancers now, white men riding for revenge.

It was almost dark now, and no one had moved since the show began. To his left Charles was rigid with concentration, his jaw clenched, his face white and grim. But Ben was still shifting in his seat, rocking like a catatonic, seemingly possessed by the overpowering rhythm of the music as the sound rose accusingly, winding up the tension to a wild scream of pain. Alex too was staring at the dance with a scarcely-controlled, rigid glare and beside him Trisha was breathing unnaturally fast, her breasts rising and falling in a clear sign of stress. Suddenly she began to sob. Well, thought Jon bitterly, it's not a pretty story! Only Mrs Matsuda seemed unaffected by the mood of the night, watching with close interest but never losing her usual impassive stare.

White-faced, their bodies marked as if with belts of ammunition, miming rifles and heavy weapons, cracking stockwhips against the Aboriginals' simple fighting sticks and spears, the Koenig dancers rode down on the village, shooting and killing and trampling and laying bare. As the chief, Timbo was seen to rally his men for one last heroic defiance, one last stand. Then as the women wailed on one side and the men formed up on the other, he took his leave of Geena, and the two slight, expressive forms shuddered with the grief of parting and the hopeless hope of ever meeting again.

For already the music was foretelling the outcome of the saga. As the chief led his warriors against the Koenig dancers, the women and children huddling in terror behind, they were slashed down man by man by the cruel whips and guns, the stragglers rounded up by the Koenig dancers and driven towards the fatal edge of the sandstone wall overhanging the water-hole. Mesmerised with horror, the spectators watched them one by one as they huddled at the brink, vainly resisted their fates, and then fell, fell, twisting and turning like leaves and in autumn till they crumpled at the bottom. For the rest of her life Helen would remember the pathos of that scene, the pile of broken bodies still twitching and moaning in pain as the victims breathed their last, and the didgeridoo screamed a final threnody of farewell.

They had timed it perfectly, arriving at the climax as the sun dropped behind the mountains, plunging the dancing area into gleaming dark. One by one the dancers all fell back outside the arena, melting into the night that had now fallen to blank out all the action.

Through the darkness now flitted a form pale as a moth,

a slight girlish figure running towards them, dipping and wheeling, fleeing from someone behind. As she reached the front, a torch in her hand flared briefly and died again, the brief flash lighting up a young woman's features torn with distress. Geena? It had to be! But unrecognisable in the fear and horror she now showed in her running gait, the wild glances she threw over her shoulder, and her madly streaming hair.

Now from the dark loomed her pursuer, an outsize male shape, huge and threatening in the gloom. The girl dancer ran this way and that, but always he stalked her, ever present yet unseen just outside her circle of vision. From the darkness came a sharp intake of female breath, and a low moan of distress. Trisha? Helen? It could have been any one of them, Jon knew. For this was every woman's nightmare, the night-stalker, the predator in the dark – no wonder they were all afraid!

And as with the massacre of the tribe, there was only one conclusion. Slowly, slowly, but with a sick inevitability, the pursuer cornered his quarry and ran her down. The circles he drew round her became smaller, her movements more frantic, till like a snake he was ready to strike. She was facing the audience now, her whole body shuddering with the acceptance of her doom. In the glimmering dark they could see the big burly figure of her enemy bearing down behind. As one great arm swung in a wide arc to encircle her waist, another white forearm grappling her throat, the music died, and the torch in her hand flared again to illuminate the finale.

The two figures stood etched against the blackness by the one flickering light in an eternal tableau of brutal male dominance. She was gripped now like a rag doll, her small bare feet swinging free of the ground in the Koenig dancer's powerful grip, her body loose and unconscious, her head dangling on one side. And the face that looked down in triumph on his prey was the face of Phillip Koenig.

'Aaaaargh! Aaarggh! Aaaargghhhhh!'

The screams sliced through the quivering air. It was the last cry of a woman who sees and resists her fate. But Geena had not moved. The only sound came from the audience where Trisha had risen to her feet and was screaming hysterically.

'Aaaaargh! Aaaargh! Aaaargh! It's her! It's that woman – it's her! Aaaaarghhh! Aaaaargh! Aaaargh!'

It was the cry of one who any second must crack, must fly from the attacking furies, and keep running to the ends of the earth. But the figure who staggered up haltingly from the midst of the group, broke into a stumbling run then set off at full pelt into the darkness was not that of Trisha, but Ben Nichols.

Chapter 31

'Aaaaargh! Aaaaargghh! It's her! It's her! Just like she looked on the night she died!'

Alex was on his feet before anyone else could stir.

'Lights! Lights!' he called hoarsely. 'Get those kerosene lamps lit, all of them, let's have some light on the scene here!' Then he was moving to silence Trisha with the speed of an uncoiled spring.

'No, it isn't Ellie!' he hissed in her ear as his hand slid round her mouth. 'She's dead, Trisha! This is Geena! And it's only a play, it's a dance, that's all, she's not dead, look!'

On the dance floor a stunned Geena had slipped from her partner's arms to the ground and lifted her head in alarm, staring out towards the cries in the dark, her large eyes dilated with fear. As Alex strong-armed her into silence, Trisha collapsed like a pricked balloon, subsiding into hysterical tears. 'Don't leave me!' she wept, 'don't leave me with her!'

Alex dumped her roughly into the nearest chair. 'Here, you two!' he shouted, summoning George and Roscoe with a furious wave of the hand. 'Come with me, quick, we've got to catch him!'

Together the three men raced off into the night towards the police land cruiser parked nearby. One by one the kerosene lamps round the arena were bursting into life as Timbo ran round with a torch, and they could see each other's drawn and shocked faces looming out of the fearful dark.

Geena burst up to the stunned group standing round their chairs and gripped the nearest arm. 'Dad, Dad!' she was screaming, 'What's happened to Dad, what's the matter, where's he gone?'

'Geena, pull yourself together!' Charles said harshly, stepping towards her. 'Ben'll be all right! Alex has gone to look for him, they'll find him and bring him back and then we'll know what all this is about! Everything's going to be all right, I promise you!'

From the back of the group came a loud incredulous laugh. 'You promise! Can you give us one good reason why we should believe your promise, Uncle Charles?'

From the darkness behind the lights Jon came sauntering forward, his face and eyes set in a dangerous glitter.

'Did you enjoy the show, Mrs Matsuda?' he demanded with a theatrical flourish in the direction of the impassive Japanese woman standing tensely nearby, the protective Buckley at her side. 'What, you thought it was old Koenigshaus history? Not a bit of it! People have killed for this place you know – over and over again – and the last occasion was only a couple of weeks ago!'

Charles had gone very white. 'For God's sake, pack it in, you young idiot!' he hissed. 'Think of—'

'Think of the sale?' Jon mocked. 'Oh yes, the precious sale!'

Helen could not bear it. 'Jon!'

Can't you see, darling, this sale must go through? It's Koenigshaus that's the cause of all this, the curse of all this, the curse on us all, the place is rotten through and through and it's making us all mad, we have to go, we have to let go, start again somewhere else, can't you see that?

With a shock of horror she saw that it had all been too much for Jon, he had cracked at last, his mind had gone.

'Don't listen to Jon, Mrs Matsuda,' she said unsteadily. 'He's a very disturbed young man, his father's death has unbalanced him, you know he lost everything in his father's will. My husband was not murdered! There's nothing at all in what Jon says—'

Another terrible laugh from Jon cut her off. 'If you believe that, Mother dear, I'm afraid that you're in for a dreadful shock – right now!' He turned to Charles, standing in the shadows. 'He knew all about it, didn't he?'

Charles tensed like a boxer at the sound of the bell. 'Who?'

'Ben, of course!' Jon took a threatening step towards him. 'He knew what you were doing! Don't play games with me!'

Around them the faces seemed carved out of darkness, shaped and reshaped by the flickering yellow flames of the kerosene lamps: Helen, Geena, Rose, Mrs Matsuda and Buckley trapped like insects in amber as the combat began.

Charles tried to laugh. 'Who knew about what?'

Jon felt very calm. 'Ben. He knew all about your chicanery – all the double-dealing that has brought this place to its knees. He's been busy covering up for you, hasn't he? Using all his creative accounting to make up for all your borrowing, making it look OK? No wonder he's been looking so worried lately now that other people have been going over the books! He must have been driving himself mad checking and rechecking his handiwork, in case he left the slightest trace of what you'd been up to.'

From where Craig Buckley was standing with Mrs Matsuda there came the lightest exhalation of a surprised breath.

Charles shrugged calmly, but his eyes were very bright. 'This is all nonsense, complete nonsense. We've made no secret of the difficulties the company's been in – that's why we've been seeking a buyer.' He managed a smile in the direction of Mrs Matsuda and Buckley, both watching the proceedings like gamblers at a race, then returned to Jon. 'You're out of your bloody depth! You don't know the first thing about the business! You haven't got a clue what you're talking about.'

Jon shook his head in stubborn rage. 'I know there's more! Even if you've come clean about one lot of difficulties, there's got to be more. I know that, I just can't prove it!' His voice rose. 'What have you done with the money? Was that your revenge, if you couldn't have the Kingdom, to make sure you bled it dry?' He knew he was cracking, but he had to hold on, see this through to the end. 'There's only one thing I don't know right now – *if Ben knew that you had killed my father, as well as cheating him out of his company and all his money!*'

'No!'

It was Helen. But Charles was not long after her, his voice scything through the silence. 'You are mad!' he said wonderingly. 'That's the most evil thing I've ever heard! Yes, I hated Phillip!' Suddenly his pale face was livid with passion. 'But I didn't kill him, he died in an accident!'

Swiftly he turned to the sobbing Helen at his side. 'Don't worry, Helen, we'll look after Jon, I'll get him medical help, the best in Australia, we'll get him well again, don't cry!' He swung back to Jon. 'I've just decided that you never said that! And in the meantime there's someone else who needs our attention a lot more than you do! I'm going to join the search for poor old Ben! God knows where he's got to. But when we've found him, we can sort all this out!'

Helen did not stay to watch him go. Crying and moaning, almost beside herself, she flew at Jon. 'I hope you're satisfied!' she attacked him in floods of tears. 'What was the point of that performance, just to hurt Charles, or to embarrass us all?' She gritted her jaw to stop her teeth chattering, she was shivering from head to foot. 'Look, Jon, I know you've been having a rough time. But so have we all!' It came out like a wail.

She had crumpled into a chair next to the stunned and silent Trisha, and he crossed to her, kneeling down and taking her hands as he looked into her eyes. 'It's more than a rough time, mother!' he shouted. 'Dad was killed, and Charles killed him! I found out that Charles was borrowing money against the company, he's bled it dry. His only hope was to sell up, and with the help of Ben, cover his tracks for long enough to wind up the mess and get clean away.'

'No, no,' she sobbed, 'it can't be true, not Charles!'

Jon surged to his feet, furious with anger now. 'For Christ's sake, mother, grow up, get it through your head! Yes, Charles! Yes, dear old uncle-brother-lover Charles! You might as well know, the only thing I can't decide is if he killed Ellie as well!'

A thought struck him like a thunderbolt. 'Jesus, while I'm standing here arguing, he's getting away! He's probably racing to the airstrip right now to grab the 'copter, and he'll get clean away while the police are with Alex looking for Ben! I've got to stop him!'

He raced off into the night as the slurred voice of Trisha broke the silence. 'No, he didn't kill the maid, what's-her-name. Not Charles. Gotta tell Alex though.'

Mrs Matsuda cast a mild eye at the drunken Trisha, then gestured towards the sobbing Helen sprawled across a chair. Her face was almost compassionate. 'Let's get them up to the house,' she said. Stiffly Geena and Rose moved forward to obey.

Mrs Matsuda looked up at Buckley and put a hand on his arm. 'For a boy who knows nothing but cattle, it's amazing how much Jon got right, no?' she said softly. 'But what a pity we could not help him with what he didn't know – and what he got wrong. I'm afraid he still has to learn that the man behind all this is the one he still respects so much.'

Buckley murmured softly, so that Helen would not

hear. 'But when the villain of the piece is none other than his own father . . . ?'

Mrs Matsuda smiled her thousand-year-old smile. 'What's a boy to do?'

God, they did things so badly in the uncivilised west! It was no wonder that Japan was sweeping the board as a world economic power these days, when this was the only opposition. And when the sleeping giant that was China finally awoke from the sleep of reason that was communism, let the barbarians beware! They would not know what hit them!

No, not even barbarians, merely children, Mrs Matsuda sighed. Now, just when this household needs a strong man in charge, and a stronger woman behind him to pull the whole thing together, where were they all? All the men had gone racing off into the outback in search of a failure and a weakling, who in Japan would have been left to take himself off and make sure he was no further nuisance to a single soul. Meanwhile, all the women had collapsed into hysterical tears!

Well, not quite all. Impassively she surveyed the little clutch of survivors huddling together round the kitchen table. She had to make an honourable exception for Geena, still bedecked in the scarlet slash of sarong and unearthly ash-white face and body paint, but sturdy as a tree, and Rose, eternal as the face of sandstone rock keeping watch over the water-hole.

But neither of them could cope with a grieving Helen and the unstable, hysterical Trisha. And apart from the Tarot, Rose had only one remedy. 'Have another drink.' She reached for a bottle. Mrs Matsuda sighed.

'No – no,' said Helen weakly, lifting the hair out of her eyes and pushing the glass away. 'No, nothing for me, that isn't the answer!' She looked at Trisha, sprawled across the kitchen table, snuffling to herself in drunken self-pity. 'And Rose, look, no more for Trisha either – we've got to pull ourselves together—'

And that means you! she told herself fiercely, feeling sick with shame at her violent outburst and exhausted by the wild threshing of her emotions.

Oh God, just let us get through the next twenty-four hours! she implored her unseen deity. Just let Mrs Matsuda buy this bloody place, and we'll all be free, and I'll be able to do what I have to do for Jon . . .

Rising to her feet, she moved round the table to Trisha and laid a hand on the other woman's shoulder. 'Shall I help you get to bed?' She raised her eyes to Geena, standing tense with anxiety at Trisha's elbow. 'If you take that arm—'

But as soon as they touched Trisha she came alive, struggling to sit upright. 'Don't touch me, I'm OK!'

Her ruined face, with its lacquered foundation and perfect finish now blotched and reddened, her mascara-ringed eyes and swollen lips gave the lie to her words of bravado, but she sat back in her chair as if intending to take charge of herself. 'And I don't want to go to bed,' she pronounced defiantly. 'I'm going to stay up till Alex gets back and I can tell him – tell him what I know.'

'Know?' said Mrs Matsuda gently, 'what do you know?'

The whole kitchen was silent, hanging on Trisha's words. Though it was hardly the time for dramatics, she still could not resist making the most of her moment. 'I saw Ellie the night she died,' she declared triumphantly. 'Alex thinks the last anyone saw of her was when she came into my room the morning I fired her. That's what he told the police. But I saw her that night when I came across from the guest house for dinner. I was the last to come in, so I know I was the last one to see her. And I want to tell Alex!'

Craig Buckley laughed incredulously. 'Jeez, you mean you didn't tell him already?'

'I never thought of it at first!' she protested truculently. 'I didn't give a damn when she went missing, and I didn't even know that was the last night she was still alive till afterwards!' She fumbled for her bag, trying to find a cigarette. 'When I realised, I tried to tell him! But he didn't want to know, he was too busy.'

Too busy screwing you, thought Mrs Matsuda. Aloud she said pleasantly, 'So what did you see?'

Trisha sat up straighter. 'I saw the maid outside the house, I was coming across the grass from the guest house, she was making her way round the back, I thought she was coming to help with the dinner. There was a man waiting for her in the dark before she got to the kitchen door. He grabbed her and they had a fight.'

'What kind of a man?' demanded Buckley urgently.

Trisha pouted. 'I couldn't see, it was dark. And I was going in the front door, I couldn't be bothered with a couple of squabbling blacks out the back!'

Mrs Matsuda leaned forward. 'He was an Aboriginal?'

'Yes!' Trisha said crossly.

'Thick-set, well-built?' put in Helen. 'Sounds like Ellie's husband, Mark.' She groaned. 'Oh, poor Ellie! It would be!'

Mrs Matsuda held up her hand and turned again to Trisha. 'You're sure it was an Aboriginal you saw?'

'Yes, of course!' snapped Trisha. 'Well, who else would it be? I—'

'She didn't see him!' Craig Buckley pronounced explosively. 'It was dark, and it was a good way away, if they were squabbling near the back door as she went in the front.' He fixed Trisha with his Dr Goebbels glint. 'You just assumed it must have been a black, because they were fighting!'

'Yes, well I—'

'So it could have been any man, white or black,' Buckley persisted. 'It could have been any man on Koenigshaus – or even one from outside!'

334

A baffled silence fell. Suddenly from the corner came the voice they least expected to hear. 'It was Markie.'

All eyes turned to Rose, clutching her bottle and huddled in the corner by the door.

'It was Mark she saw,' she said thickly. 'I heard them. Just before dinner. Him and that – that no-good bitch Ellie!'

Rose did not belong to the school which held that you should not speak ill of the dead. 'Little slut was turning up just as I'm getting dinner on the table!' she spat venomously. 'An' that no-good drunk of a husband of hers was waiting for her, he wanted to stop her comin', he'd had enough of her airs and graces. "You told me they fired you!" he started in on her, "What you doin' here now?" And she screeched right back, "What you doin' tryin' to stop me? I told you this morning I was comin' back as soon as I wanted, when I was good an' ready!" And they started to fight an' I heard him dragging her off, him beating her and her crying like a stuck pig.'

There was a heavy silence. Helen lifted her head. 'So it was Mark who killed her, just as the police said.'

'Must've been him, who else?' Buckley cut in. 'Ninety per cent of the time they can charge the last person seen with the victim as the murderer.'

Mrs Matsuda nodded. 'Like Mr Matsuda, Mr Buckley knows a lot about these things. If the husband was the last to be seen with the woman, that is very bad for him.'

' 'Cept he wasn't the last.'

There was no mistaking the satisfaction in Rose's voice at triumphing over the foreign visitors and the self-styled expert, Buckley.

'What do you mean, Rose?' Helen queried, praying for control.

The housekeeper's face was tight with self-importance. 'Miz Trudi's spirit came to call that night,' she announced in a flat sing-song. 'She came for Mister Phillip an' she came for that no-good bitch Ellie too.'

'Rose—'

Helen took a deep breath. 'Why should Miss Trudi come for Ellie?'

'Because she a slut! I heard her, I heard her with Markie, boastin' and cryin' to him, I heard her say "I slept with them all, they all had me, Mister Phillip and Mister Alex and Mister Jon, all of them, all!" '

Dear God, thought Helen, is there no end?

Mrs Matsuda stared. 'And was it true? Or did she just say it to provoke her husband and punish him?'

'Not true about Mister Jon,' said Rose judiciously. 'But true about the other two, Miz Trudi's two, her husband and her son. And Markie didn't now that, didn't know any of it, not for sure, until she told him, and laughed at him too! So he's slappin' her around and she's screamin' and I can hear Miz Trudi laughin', and I'm thinkin' Markie Hands is mad enough to do her in. But as he's knockin' her about and she's screamin', she's screamin' one thing over and over again to old Mark, before she got away from him and ran off into the bush. She said he'd better lay off or he'd find himself under a bush with his head round the wrong way, she would fix it tonight as soon as she saw—'

The tension in the room was unbearable now.

'So she had another date?' Buckley demanded roughly, 'to see someone else? Who?'

Rose shook her head. 'To see "him",' she said. 'All she said was "him".'

He must be here, there was nowhere else he could have gone.

Exulting, triumphant, Jon roared through the bush on the trail bike which was the first thing to come to hand as he raced away from the house, and felt that at last, at last, he had Charles on the run. He had called him out in front of too many people for that web of lies to be spun any longer. No wonder he had made a run for it! And there was only one place he could go.

It had to be the airstrip. Charles could handle a chopper as they all could, it was part of living on a huge isolated station, a necessary skill.

Charles had to run, he had to hide, and he had to get out fast. There was only one way he could do that. He was far too clever to take a car that could be tracked by the police from the air as easily as an eagle tracks a slow-moving bug. And after all his years in the city, he wasn't clever enough in the ways of the bush to take a horse and just melt into the landscape. No, only the airstrip would give him his chance of a getaway.

As he roared on through the soft black night, in the intervals of wrestling to keep the bucking bike on the rough dirt track so badly lit now by the pale gleam of the moon that every yard was a death-trap, it occurred to Jon to wonder if Ben might have had the same idea. But he dismissed it at once. Old Ben had not been making for anywhere when he charged out blindly into the night. He had no ice-cool plan of escape, no special destination in mind, he was just panicking, he could be anywhere.

And he needed help, that was for sure, whatever he had done. But that had to be for later! It was Charles's turn now! Jon gunned the motor and the bike leaped forward again. He was going to find Charles first. And then there'd be nowhere else for the murdering bastard to hide!

The airstrip lay dead ahead, now at the end of a long straight stretch of track. He had them in his headlights before he knew what he was looking at, a cluster of figures he could not identify, in a pose he could not understand. As he drew nearer he made out the body of a man lying full length face down on the ground. Another man knelt behind him, holding down his arms, and a second burly figure was between his feet restraining his legs, while a third man crouched beside him leaning over the prostrate form.

By Christ, they'd got him!

As the figures grew brighter in the headlights of the trail-bike and he saw first Alex, and then George and Roscoe, Jon's heart surged with joy and relief. They must have got here first, they'd come to look for Ben and they'd been here when Charles came! And they'd arrested him, they'd caught the bastard trying to make his escape, which was as good as a confession of guilt!

He stamped on the accelerator in a burst of manic glee, he couldn't wait to join them, he wanted to break Charles's neck, dance on his face! He laughed aloud. What there was left of Charles, that is: the bastard must have put up quite a fight from the blood on the head and what he could see of the face! But he didn't care, he didn't care if they'd killed him!

Because they'd caught him, they'd got him there pinned down on the ground, they were tying his arms and legs. It was over, it was over, he was free, he could start his life again, he could begin to live . . .

He drew the trail-bike to a skidding halt, and flopped forward almost hysterical with relief, leaning over the handlebars.

'Hey guys!' he called breathlessly over the throb of the engine. 'You got him, eh? Great stuff!'

'Jon?'

Alex lifted a white face towards the lights as he turned round from the prostrate form on the ground.

And suddenly Jon knew.

Chapter 32

And suddenly, Jon knew.

Knew beyond doubt, that he had been horribly, terrifyingly wrong, till now, till this very second. As he drew up, drew the trail bike to a stop in the swirling, choking sand, he tasted dust and ashes, the triumph of finding the truth at last curdling in his throat to the certainty of defeat. For now he had found the answer he had been seeking so painfully for so long, he knew too that the price of this knowledge had to be his life.

For now he knew how Phillip had died. As he saw the unholy trinity of men, caught in a rare unguarded moment, frozen like rabbits in his headlights, he could see it all.

One man on the ground, alone, prostrate, defenceless against those who walked the night with murder in their hearts.

Two men to restrain him, two big and burly men, men steeped in violence.

And one in charge – one man to do the deed, to bend over the gagged and pinioned figure on the ground and arrange a violent passage for him from this world to the next.

George and Roscoe the two heavyweights, the thugs.

And Alex – brother Alex – to administer the poison. In that second Jon knew that he was seeing the murder of his father as clearly as if he had been there.

And he was less than six feet away from the murderer.

'Jon?' Alex turned his face into the headlights of the bike and shielded his eyes with his hand. 'Come to give us hand?'

'Yeah – sure!' He had to carry this off, not let them know he suspected anything. But even to his own ears his croaking voice sounded pathetically unconvincing. There was a moment's silence as the three men registered what he said. Then he saw Alex stiffen imperceptibly as George and Roscoe exchanged a glance.

Now it was his turn to feel like a rabbit before a snake. He watched, panicking inside, the muscles of his arms and legs starting to twitch, his brain seemingly paralysed as the two men unhurriedly finished tying up Charles's unconscious body as he lay face down on the ground. Then all three rose casually to their feet, Alex at their head.

'Lucky for us you came along,' Alex said lightly.

'Yeah, the more the merrier,' volunteered Roscoe.

His partner leered. 'Always room for a little one.'

'Hey bro!' Alex was not smiling. 'What brought you out here anyway?'

Just answer them, act normal, play along until you can see your chance to get away . . .

He was almost choking. 'I – I was looking for Charles.'

'Charles?'

Alex was staring at him unblinking, his eyes cold as stone. 'Why would you be looking for Charles out here?'

'Because I – because he—'

Alex flickered a glance towards George out of the corner of his eye and still smiling, the big man closed up behind. On Alex's other side Roscoe imperceptibly echoed the movement of his partner without need of instruction.

'Say again?' queried Alex calmly. 'You were looking for Charles – for what?'

340

He moved forward casually, his two thugs hard on his heels.

They were less than four feet away from him now. A wild terror gripped Jon, and with it a surge of Dutch courage. 'I was looking for him because I thought he killed my father! But I'm not looking for Dad's killer any more! I'm looking *at* him! Because I know it was you! It was you!' Panting, Jon hurled his last defiance in Alex's flickering face. Only the two policemen seemed quite unperturbed. 'Well, that's interesting, Roscoe, isn't it?' opined one.

The other nodded slowly. 'Not nice – but interesting, yeah.'

'But I don't think we can let a bloke run round the Territory—'

'—repeating this kind of allegation—'

'—libel and slander—'

'—against the respected owner of a major cattle station on our patch—'

'—can we, Mr Koenig?'

Alex's eyes were hard, bright and merciless in his set white face. 'Certainly can't, boys. What do you suggest?'

They were drawing up on him inch by inch as they spoke. 'What d'you think, George? Preventive custody?'

'Preventing him from preventing us, as you might say—?'

'And then an unfortunate occurrence—'

'—resisting arrest—'

'—trying to escape—'

'—assaulting an officer—'

'—many ways to have an occurrence—'

'—a very unfortunate occurrence—'

'—for him—'

'—but not for us—'

Alex's command escaped his thin lips like a hiss. *'What are you waiting for?'*

They were on him now. Roscoe's huge hand reached

out to grab the handlebars of the bike as George leaned in towards him feeling for the handcuffs at his wide leather belt. Roscoe smiled like a kindly uncle. 'Now you aren't going to make trouble for us, are you, Mister Jon?'

The cold metal claw of the open handcuff was brushing Jon's wrist as at last he found the strength to act. 'Yes!' he screamed, revving the engine to its maximum power and throwing the bike straight into third gear. From a standing start it bucked like a horse, almost hurling him off. But as it leaped forward it tore into Roscoe and sent George spinning like a top with a wild roar of pain. Then he was off into the night, plunging into the darkness of the airstrip and racing madly, racing for his life.

Behind him he could hear the screaming of an injured man and a volley of recriminations and curses. In a mad panic he careered across the airstrip and plunged off the other side. Within seconds he had hit a sandy hillock of rough grass and with a sick inevitability knew he would fall. The next second he came careering off the bike. He seemed to hang in the air for a long, painful second before he crashed to the ground, slamming sideways into the rock-hard earth.

He lay winded for a second, before panic seized him again. Frantically he staggered to his feet, trying to think straight.

Think, before they caught him! He had fallen the other way from the bike and been flung clear, so it wasn't as bad as it might have been. And the bike seemed OK as he groped for it in the darkness, front wheel did not seem buckled, and thank Christ! the engine restarted at the first go. But his left arm felt quite dead, he had hit his shoulder as he came off, pray God it wasn't broken. And his head hurt, but that might have been the whisky, except for the sticky feeling in his hair . . .

Think.

Think!

Get away, that was the first thing.

Carefully he clambered onto the seat of the bike. He still had movement in his left hand, he could manage the controls if he went carefully. And with a trail bike he could get off the main tracks where they would look for him and cut across country where the police cruiser could not follow.

So what are you waiting for?

GO!

Slowly he set off. Within yards he had switched off the headlights, preferring to feel his way by the light of the moon than to present such an easy target to a long-distance rifle with night-adapted sights. They would still hear him, he knew. But once in their own vehicle they could not detect the sound of his engine above their own. *Go, go boy, just GO.*

Go where?

Not back to the house, that would be the first place they would look. And he could not risk endangering his mother and Geena, Rose and all the other inhabitants of the homestead. He had to find a place to hide from them till he could figure out what to do, till he could get to a radio transceiver somewhere and call for help.

A choking laugh gripped him.

Call for help?

From the police?

Who do you call when the villians *are* the police?

He tried to pull himself together. Enough! You can worry about that when you've got your hands on a transceiver! For now . . . just go.

Just go.

Go.

Like Charles running to the airstrip, there was only one place he could go. Ever since childhood there was one place he knew he would be safe, one place where no one

343

ever found him, one place where he could think and be free, possess his soul in secret and allow himself to grow into the peace that comes only with silence and patience and long solitude.

He would go there.

And there he would be safe.

But like an animal falling back to its secret den in the heart of the wilderness, he knew better than to go there directly. George and Roscoe were sons of this land, they had grown up here, they had spent their lives hunting men, they could track him down.

For they would be hunting him, they had to be. Roscoe he thought he might have taken out when he went straight for him with the bike. With any luck he had clipped George too. But from the noise they made as he roared away, they might both have been more frightened than hurt. And it took a lot to disable a pair of killers like them, big strong men in the prime of their evil lives.

And there was still Alex, he had not been hurt. And he would be desperate, he would spare nothing to run an enemy to ground. Alex had to kill him now, or Dad's murder would all be in vain.

And Ellie's?

And Mark's?

Forget it! he told himself.

Time to sort all that out later. For now, he was seeking cover as a fox seeks its earth, to lick its wounds and save its hunted life.

The pain in his head was worse now, it had a regular beat almost hypnotic in its intensity, thudding out some cruel kind of call and response with the pulsing pain in his shoulder. He tried not to listen to it, he feared it would make him fall off his bike. And he forced himself to track and back-track as a hunted animal does, seeking out little creeks to enter and exit in several different places to throw his pursuers off the scent. Describing a series of unconnected loops, crossing and criss-crossing, he rode on through the night.

Only as the soot-black bowl of the darkness began to tilt towards dawn did he permit himself to make for his refuge. Exhausted, grimed and bruised, his hair black with blood, he paused at last on the rim of the water-hole. Riding down the great bowl, he scattered and put to flight a covey of water-doves, who rose wheeling round his ears in great broken rings, cooing in alarm. Almost dead with fatigue, on the brink of tears with relief, he drove down to the water, along the edge of the pool as far as the mouth of the cave. Then with one last super-human effort, he drew the bike inside.

One last task.

Returning outside he tore off a branch of a gum tree and walking backwards from the edge of the scrub, care-fully brushed all tracks of the bike away. Then he with-drew into the black night of the interior, and dropped to the ground in the velvet darkness, completely spent.

But safe.

He knew he was safe.

Carefully he stretched out as comfortably as he could, nursing his injured shoulder, and lay back to relax.

No one could have tracked him here. If he had learned anything from Dusty, learned anything from his years as a boy in the bush, he had learned that. He had run like an animal, but cleverer than an animal. Even another animal, armed with its incredible gift of scent and eyes that could see in the dark, could not have tracked him here tonight.

Tonight he could rest in peace.

A few hour's sleep – or rest anyway, because he could probably only doze with this pain in his head – or was it his shoulder – a few hours – time to plan where to go, what to do.

First thing tomorrow he would get help.

Who to turn to?

Dusty?

Henry Suffolk better, get to Henry, go with him to his place, use their transceiver. They were nearer to town on their small station holding, the Suffolks, weren't they? How much petrol in the bike? Enough to get there? Probably.

Or was Golden Mountain the nearest, the neighbourhood station where Mum had worked? Mum. Oh, Christ.

Mum.

And Charles.

No he couldn't face it, not tonight, he'd make up for all that madness, all that jealousy, all that—

Tomorrow.

He'd make up for it tomorrow.

He stretched, too tired even to yawn.

Tomorrow was another day.

He lay in the deep night of the cave, almost at peace. Tomorrow he would sort everything out, start afresh with Mum, with Charles, with everybody. Now all he had to do was sleep.

He lay listening to the silence. Then from behind him in the blackness, he heard the whisper of a stir.

Next came a sound that bore the chill of death.

'Hello, Jon.'

Chapter 33

He did not move. But the hairs on the back of his neck rose in the first wave of the shudder that possessed his whole body.

'I'm sorry about this, I truly am,' the voice went on conversationally. 'You know, I like you, I really like you. And if you hadn't insisted on sticking your nose into this—'

'You'd have got away with it.'

'I already had!' The speaker was angrily indignant. 'I was home and dry!'

Jon could have laughed at the insane assurance, the terrible pride. 'The perfect crime, eh?'

'It was more than that! It was what everybody wanted! They all wished him dead!' There was a pause, pulsing with venom. 'And with bloody good reason!'

Was this to be Phillip's only epitaph?

Oh, Dad.

A wave of mingled sorrow and rage seized Jon. 'Except me.'

There was a light laugh in the darkness. 'Except you. Yes, well, I'm sorry about that. Because that's what brought you here. Unfortunately for you.' A sigh. 'Because I'm sorry to say, you're not going to be able to leave.'

It could have been a polite dinner party, Jon thought, with the guests' carriages unfortunately delayed by some minor setback. 'You're quite sure about that?'

'Oh yeah, I'm sure. Well, you've got to see my position . . .'

Jon tried cautiously to sit up. The pain in his shoulder was so bad now he could hardly stir.

'Don't move!' came the crisp command. 'I've got a flashlight here, and a revolver. I'll tell you when it's time to go.'

Time to go.

What a nice way of saying time to die.

Of all the questions bursting like fireworks in his mind, one was uppermost. 'How did you know I was here? You couldn't have tracked me, no one could've, how did you find me out?' If this was his last question on earth, he had to know how his bushcraft had failed.

Another laugh. 'I didn't even try. You're the bush-baby, Jonno, not me. But you were thinking like a bush-man thinks, acting just like an animal doubling and redoubling to throw another animal off its trail. I just tried to work out where you'd go, where the animal in you would try to hide. It's no secret round Koenigshaus that this has been your special place ever since you were a kid. Where else would you go?'

He had been thinking like an animal, his enemy had thought like a predator. He was defeated, outsmarted, by a stronger, crueller force. It was his doom to come here to this place, to meet this fate, at these hands who had claimed his father's life. Now the fear of death that had knocked the breath from his body at the first sound of this deadly voice claimed him for its own.

'And don't forget—' he heard a twisted sigh '– that I was once a Koenigshaus kid too. It was my special place before it was yours. I used to love it just as much as you do.'

'Then why – Alex, for God's sake, *why*, why did you kill Dad?'

There was a dreamy pause.

348

Jon felt himself slipping away, half-swooning with the pain in his shoulder, which seemed to be taking him over completely. But he must stay alert!

'So many reasons,' Alex went on in that same strange light voice, 'that it's hard to know where to begin. I wanted Koenigshaus, for one. The Kingdom was mine first, before you were born! And I wanted you not to have it, that was the second reason. Or even the main one.'

Two brothers, one keeping the other from his due. Jon could have laughed with bitterness. He had had the right motive. But he had been looking at the wrong generation! He tried to twist towards the unseen figure in the darkness at his back. 'How did you do it – the will and all?'

'Oh, it wasn't hard.'

Alex might have been giving lessons in murder and malpractice. 'I knew Dad kept one copy of his will in the safe. I knew the combination, he told it me himself when I was still the only son and heir, in the days before he got suspicious, and learned to hate his wives and sons. And of course—' he chuckled. 'You must have guessed I had a sleeper in the house.'

I'm losing it, Jon thought. 'A sleeper?'

'A spy inside the camp. Someone who worked for me, and told me everything I needed to know.'

Of course.

There was only one person it could be.

Jon could see the little face before him as he spoke, half-sly, half-fearful, all corrupt. 'Ellie.'

'Correct! Miss Ellie Hands!' He gave a deprecating cough. 'Or I should say "Mrs". Miss or Mrs, she'd have done anything for me, she's been stuck on me since she was five. It was no trouble to make contact with her when I was ready to stage the return of the Prodigal Son.'

Jon groaned. 'So she got the will for you, and you altered it, and then—'

'—had it delivered to Carey at his bloody bank, to

349

make sure it was safe and would turn up all correct on the right day.'

'And George and Roscoe?'

'The boys?' Alex laughed again. 'Chums since child-hood, those two psychopaths are, they're good lads, they'd do anything for me. Especially since they could see a big slice of the Koenigshaus cake coming their way.' He clucked regretfully. 'And they're both going to want your death to be a lot more painful than it's likely to be with this highly efficient piece of fire-power I've got in my hand. Because I'm sorry to say that you made rather a mess of both of them when you blasted into them with your trailbike. And even with their famous sense of humour, they were not amused.'

Jon could not even pretend to be sorry. 'They were one hundred per cent volunteers!' he said with passion. 'And I'd do it all again!'

'No, little bro, once is enough. Enough to hang you, anyway. I'm afraid poor Roscoe's in for an uncomfortable night, stuck out at the airstrip with two broken legs.' Alex was still maintaining the eerie tone of normal conver-sation. 'But George'll make it back to the homestead with the perfectly true story that you went stark, staring mad, and drove your bike at them for no reason at all, in the deliberate attempt to kill them. So when I bring you back with a couple of self-administered bruises on my head and a new ventilation system between the ears in yours, I'll be able to claim that I had to shoot you in self-defence.'

'Self-defence!'

Now it was Jon's turn to laugh. 'And is that why you had to kill Ellie?'

'Of course! I had to defend myself against her, she could have ruined everything! I thought she'd be OK, I promised her I'd see her all right. I was going to get rid of Rose and give her Rose's place, but she turned nasty when Trisha arrived. I had to get rid of her. I told her to meet me that evening out at the water-hole, we often met here before I came back. She was much easier to kill than I thought. I just got her on the ground, started fucking her, got on top of her, and then strangled her as I was kissing her. Her neck went like that!' There was a dry clicking of fingers in the dark. 'Snapped like a chicken bone.'

Jon fought to keep the shudder of dread out of his voice. 'And Mark?'

'Oh, the boys saw to him, he was easier still, a piece of cake, they said! They picked him up wandering round the bush, and simply sat him down under a tree and poured all the hooch down him he could drink. Kept it up round the clock till his liver packed in. The bastard couldn't believe his luck, he was in hog heaven, it was his idea of paradise.' He laughed. 'So was hers when I was fucking her! At least you could say they both died happy!'

Jon could take it no longer. 'Try and say that about Dad, you bastard!' he ground out. 'Are you going to tell me he died happy, with your two goons sitting on his arms and legs and you emptying a sack-full of King Browns on his face?'

'No, mate.'

Alex's voice changed completely. 'No, I'm not going to tell you he died happy. But then, I didn't want him to. I wanted him to die in agony. And I wanted him to know exactly what was going on, and who was doing it to him. I wanted him to look me in the face, and know that I'd come to get him at last.'

'But why? *Why?*'

'Oh, you still don't see, Jon mate, do you?'

The voice in the dark was as old as the ages, as young as new grief. There was the sound of a brief fumble, followed by the click of a switch. The light from a flood-lamp filled the small space of the cave, and Jon could see

Alex's hunched and brooding shape, behind him a huge evil shadow on the cave's painted wall.

'I wanted him to die in agony, and know who had killed him! I wanted him to know that the one person in the world who should love him and protect him and care for him was the one who turned against him. Like my mother! Like the way he turned against her!' He drew in his breath in a scream of hissing air. 'I wanted it because I wanted him to die the way he killed my mother!'

'Don't you think you ought to get some sleep?'

A rambling, nauseous Trisha had been led across to the guest house, Mrs Matsuda and Buckley had declined a late supper of coffee and cheese and biscuits and turned in, even Rose had retired to her quarters with her bottle of home comfort. There was still no news of any of the men. But somehow Helen had managed to regain enough control to deal with all of it and keep smiling through, however strained her smile had been.

But now she was craving her bed in what had to be her last night on Koenigshaus. She would not sleep, she knew – not till Jon or Charles or Alex or Ben returned and she knew what was happening – but she could do no more now, she had to be alone. She turned to Geena, still in her wisp of scarlet and traces of the deathly-looking paint she had worn earlier for her dance performance. 'I'm ready for bed. Aren't you tired at all?'

Geena shook her head. 'I want to wait up for the men.'

The words came out before Helen could stop them. 'All the men? Or just Jon?'

Geena threw up her head defensively. 'My dad – and Jon!' she said.

Helen sighed. 'Oh, my dear – I don't know what you're thinking – what you're hoping for – but I wouldn't place too much weight on Jon right now, if I were you . . .'

Her voice trailed away.

What could she say? *I think my son's gone mad?*

Not very loyal, coming from a mother! Yet this little woman-child with her skinny shoulders and wounded eyes called out the mother in her every bit as much as Jon did. 'I just think he's – not well,' she managed. 'And I don't want him to hurt you—'

Geena forced a smile. 'He already has.'

Helen wanted to take her in her arms. 'How?'

'Oh . . .'

She seemed to have trouble remembering without bursting into tears. A long pause elapsed before she went on. 'Last night he said he loved me. Then this morning he said it was all off.'

'That's not like Jon!' was Helen's involuntary retort. But the next thought came like a sick blast of fear. *Not like the Jon he was – but if he's gone mad . . .*

They stood there, sharing the fear. Then from outside the kitchen came a hoarse cry in the night, and the sound of a heavy, dragging weight. Almost by reflex Helen found Geena leaping into her arms, and they clung to each other in horror, not able to cry or scream.

Moments later, there was a violent thumping at the door and it swung slowly open against a dead weight behind. The body of a man covered in blood, blood pouring from a gash on his head, one arm swinging crushed and useless, one leg dragging behind the other, half stumbled, half fell through the door. With a cry he recognised Helen and came lurching at her like a creature from the nether world. 'Mrs Koenig!'

'Oh God!' Helen screamed. 'Roscoe?'

'It's your son!' he muttered hoarsely. 'He's gone mad! He's done for Ben Nichols, he's got the pair of us, and now he's after Alex. He's mad! He's gone completely mad!'

Chapter 34

He's mad, he's completely mad.

Was it his imagination, or had the sky outside the cave begun to lighten? If he could keep Alex talking, even this insane rubbish about Dad, maybe he'd think of something, maybe there'd be a glimmer of hope . . .

'You don't believe me, do you?' Alex looked almost amused. 'You know, your loyalty to the old man does you credit! I promise you, I felt the same. Until he killed my mother!'

Jon's nerves were fraying, even though he knew he should keep calm. 'Christ, man, why should he do that?' he challenged violently. 'She was his wife, he loved her!'

But even as he spoke, fragments and sentences of the secret report came surging back to mind: *'charges of prostitution and drugs involvement dropped for lack of evidence . . . good lifestyle, no visible means of support . . .'*

'He found out that she wasn't what he thought she was when he married her,' Alex said, his face contorting with rage. 'I was only a kid, but I heard all their rows. Some people wanted him to go into politics. He had her checked out just to see that nothing bad could come up. And bad things did. So he killed her.'

Jon could hardly move or breathe. 'How – *how do you know?*'

'I saw it,' Alex said simply. 'They went riding in the

bush. I was already out there, they didn't see me. They were rowing and she flew at him. He called her a whore, and she tried to hit his face. He hit her first. He knocked her flying, and she went spinning back and fell and hit her head.'

'So it wasn't – planned?'

'Deliberate? Oh no. He cried, d'you know the bastard cried? He tried to bring her round. Then he put her on her horse and led her back. I had to go a roundabout way back to the house. But I still got there first because I could gallop and he couldn't, so he never even knew that I'd been out. But I knew he'd killed her. And so sooner or later, I knew I had to kill him.'

'But if he didn't mean to—'

Alex was blazing with the unearthly light of madness. 'What difference did it make? Didn't make any difference to her or me! She was dead, wasn't she? *And now he is too!*'

He stretched back almost reflectively. Now the manic glitter in his eyes had sunk to a dead sleepy black and his face was empty of all emotion. 'And now you have to die as well, Jonno. Sorry about this. But you can see I can't leave any loose ends. Not having gone this far.' He stretched again and stirred. 'Up you get then. On your feet.'

Outside the last dawn he would see was streaking the black-grey gloom with finger-shafts of fire and rosy pink. In the gloom of the cave Jon caught the deeper gleam of gunmetal and felt the cold barrel of a gun laid against his temple.

'I think we'll do it outside, don't you?' Alex said cheerfully. 'Easier for me to get you a bit nearer the car. And maybe instead of taking you back I'll just lose you in the bush – where the dingoes and the kites will give me a hand with the disposal problem. On your feet then.' The gun caught a stray shaft of light as he waved it in the direction of the mouth of the cave. 'Outside.'

With a superhuman effort, Jon made it to his knees, wondering wearily at himself as he did so. Why make it easy for the bastard by walking out? If he had to die, why not just die here, lie down and die? Did he want one last glimpse of the world he had loved so much? Just to take leave of one last outback dawn? He stumbled towards the narrow opening and lifted his head to the air.

'Turn and face me when you get outside,' came the voice from behind. 'Or lie down on your back if you'd prefer, if this is self-defence, I'm going to have to shoot you in the front.'

You fucking bastard!

A wild spurt of rebellion seized Jon as he stared at the horizon. If he had to die, he'd die looking into the rising sun, and on his feet, he'd die fighting. And by Christ he wasn't going to lie down and and beg for it! Let the bastard shoot me if he likes, I'm ready now!

With a wild sideways lurch he threw himself against the wall of the cave, kicking out backwards as he did so. Almost before he felt his foot connect with flesh, he could hear the gun drop to the floor as the flashlight described a wild circle and went flying too. Madly he scrambled backwards in the dark, fists and feet flailing. As he felt both his feet connect again and again with Alex's body, his scrabbling hand closed over the gun.

'I've got it, I've got the gun!' he croaked. 'Stay where you are, I've got the fucking gun!'

There was a dead silence. Then his straining ears could hear an animal gulping noise, the sound of labouring lungs pumping in the dark. He grabbed for the flashlight where it lay against the wall. 'Alex, it's over, I've got the gun!'

He almost fancied he heard the suspicion of a laugh. Then as he reached the flashlight, turned it round and swung it in a wild arc, he saw a dark figure slip out of the circle of the light, out through the entrance to the cave. He was getting away!

Jon staggered to his feet.

I'll get him Dad, I'll get him . . .

Outside the cave the night was thinning with the promise of dawn. He could see a crawling figure carving his way up the hillside, hugging the wall of the great sandstone bluff which formed the rock face with the cave at its base.

'Alex, give in!' he shouted hoarsely. 'I'm coming after you, I've got the gun!' But even as he spoke his words died away uselessly in the rising air.

Doggedly he went in pursuit, driving himself on. Now his whole body seemed to be seized with pain, he was all pain from the wound on his head to the ache in his legs. But he had to get Alex, he had to head him off!

Like a bush animal he scrabbled frantically to make all the speed he could, he could see Alex more and more clearly now in the lifting light. He would not shout again, he needed all his breath.

Now his quarry was nearing the top where the great sandstone plateau led back to its bleak eminence brooding over the water-hole. But he was gaining on him, gaining every yard, once they reached the top, as soon as the ground was level, he could get him in his sights, hold the gun on him and—

The scrambling figure ahead had reached the top and broken into a run. A few steps and he was on the flat too. He could see Alex running across the level rock, making for the drop on the other side. Once there he could lose himself in the undergrowth, roll down the bank and make a getaway. Steadying himself Jon drew on his last reserves of strength. Then he called out in a voice he knew sounded as if it meant every threatening word, 'Stop where you are, or I'll blow your fucking head off!'

Twenty yards away, the fleeing figure of Alex froze in its tracks. With desperate wariness, Jon closed the gap. 'Alex, give in, you've had it, it's all over!'

His hands in the air, Alex swung round to face him.

He looked almost calm. 'So you win, eh, little brother?' he said softly, backing away.

'Stay where you are!' shouted Jon.

'Or what?' called Alex mockingly.

He was still backing away. Desperately Jon moved forward to close the distance between them. Or what? Alex had said. Could he shoot Alex in cold blood? It had been one thing to go for him in the cave, when it was purely life and death. It was another to blast a fellow human being out of existence, send him spinning to kingdom come.

Yet if he weakened now—

If he let Alex see that he could not do it—

I'll get him, Dad, I'll get him—

He surged forward viciously. 'Or I'll kill you, you bastard, like you killed Dad! I'm only sorry I can't kill you with my bare hands! I'd like to see you swing from the tallest tree on Koenigshaus, instead of going to prison for the rest of your blasted life!'

'Oh, no, mate.'

Alex was still backing steadily away from him. 'I'm not going back there, I'm not ever going back there!'

With a shock of horror Jon realised that Alex was moving towards the edge of the rock, to the sheer face of the precipice where the sandstone plateau dropped straight down to the water-hole below.

Devil Rock.

Alex was unnaturally calm, even exalted. 'You see, like any Koenig, I can't stand losing. And there's one thing I'd lose now that I can't bear most of all.' He laughed lightly. 'Give my love to Miss Trisha.' For the rest of his life, Jon never forgot the look of pain that passed over Alex's face with the mention of her name. 'No need to tell her not to mourn too long, she'll have forgotten me by the end of next week.'

'Alex, look—'

Alex even smiled. 'Yeah, I know you like history, Jonno, and those tales of all our ancestors. Will it make the spirits sleep more peacefully, d'you think, if a Koenig joins them here at Devil Rock?'

'Alex—!'

God, he had wished him dead, but now with all his soul Jon did not want him to die. 'Listen, listen, you don't have to do this!'

But he spoke too late. As the sun sprang over the horizon, Alex leaped silent as a bird in flight into the bursting pool of gold and fire, hovered for a moment, and was gone.

Chapter 35

'Roscoe? Oh my God!'

The figure at the door was the image of horror, blood matting his hair and caking his tortured face. One arm dangled uselessly by his side and he dragged one leg as he lurched into the kitchen. 'It's Jon,' he said hoarsely. 'We were at the airstrip looking for Ben Nichols – me and Roscoe and Mr Alex. Jon came up on a trail bike and just blasted into us! Roscoe's in a bad way out there, he's nearly killed the pair of us!'

He dropped into a chair.

'But where's Jon now?' cried Helen. 'And where's Alex?'

'Jon just went chasing off into the bush,' George rasped. 'Alex went after him. He'll – bring him back.'

Something in the way he spoke chilled Helen to the bone.

'Well, let's see what we can do for you now!' she said, crossing to the cupboard where the first aid box was kept. Mechanically she reached for cotton wool swabs and disinfectant. But as she set to work on the injured man with a mute Geena's help, her mind was seething.

I can't believe Jon would do this! He never hurt a soul in the world. He had no reason to attack this man. Something must have happened that I don't know about.

'Now that's better!'

With his head cleaned and the cut on his forehead

covered by a plaster, George seemed a lot more himself than the grim spectre who had staggered in earlier. He seemed to have regained the movement in his arm and leg too, refusing Helen's offer of a sling. He also refused to let her call the Flying Doctor to radio in an ambulance for Roscoe. 'Nah, we're going to have to wait a while anyways, for Mr Alex to bring back Jon. And I shouldn't be surprised if we won't be needing some more – medical assistance, then.'

Again Helen felt the creeping finger of a warning fear.

'Where's Rose, and the rest of them?' George demanded. 'All in bed?' Casually he loosened his belt and drew his gun from its holster, laying it on the table. 'Might as well make ourselves comfy while we wait,' he observed. 'Sit yourselves down, ladies. I take it you're going to keep me company while we hang on for the return of the wandering boys? Have a seat then.'

Afterwards Helen could not have pinpointed the moment when she knew they were in danger. But as the time wore on and George kept up his empty banter, little by little the faint whispers and murmurs of anxiety in her heart came together in a storm of fear. Why should George forbid her to get help for his partner? Why should Alex have gone chasing after Jon instead of simply coming back here and calling in the medics, if he was mad as they said? And above all, where, oh where was Jon?

Across the table she could see Geena's drawn face, greyer than the streaks of ash-paint she still wore. Poor girl! She was suffering twice over, for her father and for Jon. *Where were they all?*

The talk petered away. Geena sat like a ghost as Helen desperately tried to work out what to do.

What could they do except wait?

With half the household already chasing each other round the outback, the last thing they needed was another search party.

They could hardly believe the sound of the 4WD when it came, they had longed for it so much. Now they could hear the crunch of tyres drawing up and feet on the verandah.

'This'll be Mr Alex,' pronounced George with satisfaction. 'Now we'll know what's to do!'

But the figure swinging wearily through the back door was not Alex. 'I've looked everywhere for Ben, I just can't find a trace,' declared Charles as he came in. He looked exhausted, Helen saw. Seeing the group round the table, his face did not change. But as he entered, George's hand moved casually to his gun.

Geena swallowed. 'No sign of Dad?' she said huskily.

Charles paused in the doorway, his long length propped against the opening, his face grey with fatigue. He did not seem to notice George, still less the signs of his injuries or the gun lying under his hand. 'Not where I looked,' he said. 'Still, I could see the lights of the police cruiser making for the airstrip, so I didn't check there. Might be worth a trip out there when I've had a beer.' Casually he crossed behind George to the fridge. 'Beer anyone?' He opened the fridge door.

'Not for me, Mr Koenig,' said George with undeniable menace in his voice. 'I think we should all stay together here nicely, till Mr Alex gets back. Why don't you bring your beer to the table and just sit down quietly with the rest of us?'

'Not bloody likely!'

Slamming the fridge door, Charles attacked George from behind, throwing one arm round the policeman's neck while with the other he held something rammed into the small of his back. 'You aren't the only one with a gun, you bastard! Helen! Get his revolver!'

Almost before Charles spoke, Helen's fingers had closed on the cold metal and snatched it from George's grasp. With a completely steady hand she pointed it at

George's head and longed for the chance to shoot. 'Geena, gets some rope – quick!' rasped Charles. 'Helen, bring the gun round here!'

Only when he had the policeman's revolver in his hand and pressing on the back of his neck did Charles rise from his crouching position to reveal what he held in his other hand. 'You're the first crooked bastard to be arrested with a beer bottle!' he declared. 'And I'm just gambling that I haven't gone for a loop like you say Jon has. I don't know what the hell's going on here. But I do know a regular cop doesn't hold two women at gunpoint for any good reason. So we're going to get you tied up nice and tight, then I'm going to radio Police Headquarters for some help. And then perhaps we'll find out what's going on!'

He lay like a flying hero fallen from the sky, on the edge of the water. As Jon approached, he could see that he was dead. *Oh Alex*, his heart mourned, *did you have to die like this*? But even as he wept with the question, his heart knew the answer.

Clumsily he tried to rearrange the crumpled body as a last mark of respect, straightening the broken arms and legs. But the face he did not touch. Unmarked by the terrible fall, it was still Alex in all his fatal beauty, as they would all remember him, the skin gleaming as it had in life, his full dark eyes still open on the world that had betrayed him.

Now Jon's whole being coursed with love for this lost brother, born to so much, but inheriting not the kingdom he was promised but a bitter legacy of hatred and pain. Now at last the tortured spirit was perhaps at peace as he began the dream of all eternity. For a long time Jon kept vigil beside him, mourning the chance he had lost, the brother he had never had.

Now a new dawn was stirring, the day Alex was fated never to see. At last Jon rose stiffly to his feet and went in search of the car that must have brought Alex here. He found it hidden behind a clump of gum trees, the keys still in the ignition. Heaving himself up painfully behind the wheel, he set off for the airstrip.

He only hoped to God that Charles was still alive. If the figure he had seen prostrate on the ground, covered in blood, had spent all night trussed up like a chicken, he could be in a bad way. But even as he was urging the heavy land-cruiser forward as fast as he dared through the silvery shimmering dawn, he was considering another possibility. So when he came screeching up to the bound figure still lying on the ground, he was not surprised to see beneath its mask of blood and dust the face of Ben.

'How y'doing, mate?' he questioned anxiously. Ben stirred and groaned.

'He's still alive, he's been moaning all night! Which is more than I'll be if I don't get some fucking help here pretty soon!'

The shout came from Roscoe, lying nearby in the dust.

'Don't worry, mate!' Jon shouted back. 'We'll get you all the help you need! And where you're going, you're not going to have anything to worry about for a good long time!'

'He's going to be all right now, the doctor says that all he needs is rest.'

Shooing Jon and Charles before her, Helen left a pale and protective Geena beside Ben's bed in the guest bungalow and led the way back to the house. It was almost lunchtime, but still she felt as if she had not caught up with the morning yet. The whirl of events had left them all exhausted, and after a brief foray to find out the latest news of what was happening, Mrs Matsuda and Buckley had firmly withdrawn to their room. But that left the rest of the shattered household to carry on as best they could. 'Coffee, anyone?'

'I'll make it.'

A subdued Rose was doing her best to get everything back to normal, Helen noted with gratitude. 'Thank you Rose,' she said warmly. 'We'll have it on the verandah.'

Outside the sun was shining serenely as if the events of last night had never been. Gingerly Jon eased himself into a chair and shook his head disbelievingly as he marvelled at the course of events. From the time that he had roared back from the airstrip, things had moved so fast that they had spiralled out of his control. 'He's here!' he had called out to Geena as he stumbled into the kitchen, 'Ben's here, and he's alive!'

To his enormous relief, Charles already had both police and medics on their way, and only just in time. As Jon had guessed on the mad drive from the water-hole, the fleeing Ben had been struck down by Alex and his goons, fearful of disclosures that would spoil the sale of Koenigshaus. The plan had been, it seemed, just to disable him with a blow to the head, the blood from which had disguised his features from Jon in the dark.

'But he was still lucky that you came along,' Helen told Jon with a shudder. Jon too suspected that if he had not appeared, Ben's 'disability' might have been permanent.

The sight of Jon, Ben and the injured Roscoe, proved too much for George, who capitulated at once. In a short time he was relating his story to the highest police authority in the Northern Territory. And before sunrise a police helicopter had arrived to airlift him and his partner to the state penitentiary to await trial and conviction for their various crimes. The same team had also recovered Alex's body from the water-hole and removed it to the chapel to await burial.

The death of Alex hung like a pall over all of them. 'There's so much I still don't understand!' said Helen tremulously.

Charles frowned. 'It's not so difficult. He ran away to get free of his father. Then as he grew up, he began to see what he had lost, and he wanted it back. He wanted

Koenigshaus, and his inheritance.' He cocked an ironic eye at Jon. 'Men have killed for less!'

Jon groaned. 'Charles – I can't even begin to apologise— I don't know what to say—'

'Forget it. Just as long as you know who the real villain is now!'

'I think we can shed a bit of light on that for you too.'

It was the police inspector, heavy with the weight of the tragedy on his territory, as well as the shock of finding corruption among the officers of his force. 'We've got a few details on Alex Koenig now from the fingerprints we took – and it's an interesting story.'

Helen rose to welcome him. 'Sit down, inspector – coffee? And please – tell us what you know.'

'Alex Koenig, alias King, had a history of fraud,' the inspector began. 'On a grand scale. He set up phoney companies, and embezzled the proceeds. He was good at it too – enough to fund an international lifestyle. But somewhere along the line he slipped up, and we caught up with him. He went to jail for a long time.'

Jon could still hear Alex's last desperate cry – 'I'm not going back there . . .'

'He couldn't take it, seems to have driven him crazy – even though as a white-collar criminal he didn't have it so bad. In jail he shared a cell with a bent solicitor. Whether there or earlier, he managed to add forgery and legal chicanery to his repertoire. He knew from childhood that Mr Phillip Koenig kept his will in the office safe. That was a document that could never be committed to computer. All he had to do was get Ellie to purloin it for him, and forge the additions that gave him control.' He paused. 'We've yet to do the forensics on the will. But I'm certain it will prove to be a false addition by Alex Koenig's hand.'

'Yet he carried it all off so well!' said Helen wonderingly.

'Until the end,' Jon said slowly. 'Ben wasn't the only

one who cracked at Geena's dance performance. I didn't see it at the time. But now I know why the dancers got to him, the one made up as Phillip, and the others impersonating snakes, remember? They were painted with diamonds, and so lifelike as they slithered around – it must have made him think of the night he and the other two crawled down to kill Dad. He must have thought someone was on to him.'

'Well, someone was!' said Charles drily. 'You – in the end!'

'Well, if we learn any more, I'll be back to report,' said the inspector, getting to his feet. 'But you won't have to worry about those two crooks Roscoe and George any more, I can promise you. For what they've done, we're going to be able to lock them up and throw away the key!'

They watched him go in a silence that seemed hard to break. At last Helen spoke. 'What'll we do now?'

'Well, I'm going back to Sydney,' said Charles shortly, rising to his feet. 'I'll get the chopper with Matsuda and Buckley when they leave this afternoon.' He gave a wintry smile. 'I think they've grasped that there won't be any sale of Koenigshaus now the new owner is in control.'

'Hang on, mate.'

Jon turned to look Charles in the eye. 'Dad once made a will to leave Koenigshaus to me, and all the business side and the cash to you and Mum, didn't he?'

Charles stiffened. 'Yes, he did.'

'Well, as far as I'm concerned that still stands. All I want is this place. You and Mum can have the rest.'

'Jon!' Helen leaned forward, her face anxious. 'Are you sure about this, you're still not well from that blow on the head.'

Jon smiled. 'I'm about as sure as I'll ever be about anything!' he said cheerfully. 'I can't run a business, as Charles pointed out forcibly last night! And I don't want to. It's all yours. As far as I'm concerned, you're just taking a load off my back.' He looked back at Charles. 'Maybe you can sell all that stuff to Mrs Matsuda instead of Koenigshaus.'

Charles nodded, his eyes bright. 'It's an idea.'

'Then you can split the take with Mum.'

'Oh, but Jon, darling—'

'Hey, no more argument!' Jon reached over and squeezed Helen's hand. 'If I were you, Mum, I'd just take the money and run!'

'Yes, well, that's something we can't do.' Charles shook his head. 'There's no point in concealing it any longer. You were right about all the borrowing on the companies, all the madness that led to us cleaning ourselves out. You were right about Ben too, he was covering it up and presenting the books as better than we were to try to get this sale, and Craig Buckley found that out. But what you didn't know was who was responsible.'

Jon braced himself. 'I'm beginning to think I do.'

'It was Phillip,' said Charles painfully. 'He always used to let me run the business end, and then it was all square. But latterly some kind of madness seized him, a greed for money, power – oh, I don't know what. He was the driving force behind all this, he decreed it all, and the more he lost, the more he borrowed, I couldn't stop the banks throwing money at him. Some of his ventures were virtually fraudulent.' He laughed mirthlessly. 'Like father, like son. And the Matsuda duo found that out too.'

Jon let out a harsh breath. 'So there's nothing left? The companies are just shells?'

Charles shook him head. 'Not entirely. Now I can take control, we can salvage something. It won't be the fortune that Alex dreamed off, poor bastard. But we'll be able to have a clean slate and start again from scratch with something in the bank.' He lifted his head. 'I think I'll just go and have a word with Mrs Matsuda. I think she'll be interested.'

Helen waited until Charles had gone before speaking.

'There's so much I want to tell you,' she said huskily. 'Charles talks of Phillip's "madness" and his greed. But your father was ill! I found letters from a specialist in his desk. He had a brain tumour, he was dying of it. God knows how long he'd been like that, he wasn't responsible for his actions.'

'He was for some of them.'

There was no point in keeping secrets now, as Charles had said, it had all got to come out. 'Mum, I don't know what this'll mean to you,' he said gently. 'But I found out from Alex that Dad killed Trudi. He saw them fight, out at the water-hole. And Dad hit her and knocked her down. That's why Alex killed Dad, as much as for Koenigshaus.'

Helen sat very still. He thought he had pained her beyond bearing. But her voice when it came, though quiet, held no surprise. 'I always thought he must have.'

'You thought Dad killed his wife – and you still married him?'

'Oh, not before, of course not! Not when I first knew him. But afterwards, I feared—' She pressed her hands to her mouth. 'Trudi was a good rider, there was no reason why she should fall like that. And Phillip had dreams – he used to call and cry out – I knew, I just knew.'

'Didn't you think it might come out one day?'

'Of course I did! Especially when he died! I was terrified he would have left some evidence against her or himself – some proof of what he did – and I still wanted to protect his name, prevent you knowing, losing faith in him.'

Oh, the ways and means of mother love, Jon brooded in wonderment. So that was why Helen had been so desperate to get into the safe. She had no suspicion of finding anything against herself – her only thought had been to protect her husband's reputation for the sake of her son.

'And you just lived with that, you didn't think to go to the police?'

She smiled at him with infinite love. 'Jonny, by that time I had you! The most gorgeous little boy – and he was your father! How could I do that to you, I loved you so much.' Her eyes shadowed. 'And I loved him. I loved him and I felt sorry for him. Because he didn't get away with it, you know. He never stopped paying. All his life he paid. He never knew peace or happiness from the day she died.' She sighed. 'Well, perhaps they're all together now, the three of them – him, Trudi and Alex.'

Time to stop paying.

With tender love Geena smoothed the hair back from her father's forehead as she sat by his bedside, and patted his hand. 'OK, Dad?'

Ben raised a watery smile. 'Far better than I deserve to be!'

'Don't put yourself down!'

From last night's events and the morning's conversations, Geena had gathered that her father's role in Koenig Holdings had not been above reproach. But she had been suffering her own pangs of guilt for her father's breakdown – if she had not insisted on the 'Phillip' make-up for the Koenig dancer at the climax of her show as a way of taunting Jon, Ben would not have cracked as he did. And with her heart still sore from Jon's betrayal, she was more than ready to blame his dereliction on the Koenigs. 'You were just responding to pressure!' she said hotly. 'None of it was your fault.'

'Some of it was,' Ben said with a deep sigh. 'But it's all over now. Jon and Charles'll sell up, and with luck I'll be able to retire from the company and forget about it all.'

'That's the spirit!' said Geena firmly. 'And we'll soon be out of here! If not today, we'll get the chopper out as soon as you can. And we'll never come back again, eh?'

Her eyes were alight with tears.

'Not for anything?' asked Ben sadly. He hesitated. 'Not even for Henry Suffolk?'

'Henry?' Geena smiled hopelessly. 'Oh, Dad, I can't care for him. When I see him, I'm going to tell him, he's only got a crush on me, he'll get over it.' She stood up and moved across to the window. 'It's not the real thing.'

'I just wanted everything to be OK for you. It was all for you.'

Jon looked at Helen with tears in his eyes. How could he have been so cruel to her, so stupid? Seeing her now, tired and defenceless, he had never felt so close, so protective.

Helen too was sharing the same feeling of hopeless, helpless love. 'So what now, darling?' Suddenly, in the newfound openness between them she knew she could speak out. 'What about Geena?'

'Mum, it's no good.'

'Why not? You love her, don't you?'

He could not help it. Mum knew so much now, she had to know the rest. 'Yeah. But a man's not allowed to marry his half-sister!'

'His *half-sister*?'

Helen sprang upright. 'You mean – God, what have you been thinking now—?' He could almost hear her mind racing. 'If you mean Phillip had an affair with Ben's wife . . .'

'Yeah.' He could not keep the rage from his voice. 'That's exactly what I do mean!'

'Jon – I don't know about Yuni and Phillip, I'd have to think about it, work it out. But I remember exactly when Geena was born, I was involved with Yuni every step of the way.' Her eyes were bright with memory. 'Her birthday's before Christmas, she was born at the end of November.' She was making rapid calculations as she spoke.

Where was this getting them? 'So?'

'That means she must have been conceived in the February of that year.' She was picking up excitement with every word. 'And that year, it'll still be in the business diary, Phillip was away from before the New Year till early June. In those days there were no intercontinental flights, when he went travelling on business he had to go by sea, he'd be away for months!'

Jon could feel the tears of joy pricking the back of his closed eyes. 'So that means . . .'

'Geena can't be Phillip's daughter. She can't be your half-sister and you're free to go to her, love her, take her for your own.'

She could picture the scene as Jon went bounding off across the grass in the direction of the guest house, she almost felt she was there. A knock on Ben's door, a heartfelt plea for a moment of Geena's time, followed by a full confession and a bid for her forgiveness. Then the girl would put him through the gamut of her tears and reproaches, tell him he could never be forgiven, and then forgive him all the same. Then they would wander off hand in hand into the trees and lose themselves among the drifting hibiscus and marzipan-sweet frangipani shrubs.

And then they would emerge engaged to marry, or as good as, she felt sure. Where were they now, mid-June? Helen calculated in a haze. They'd be married before Christmas, she'd almost bet on it, probably in time for Geena's lucky birthday that had made their happiness possible against all the odds.

And then she would be out of a home again, giving way as all women must to her son's bride. No kitchen had ever been built big enough to contain two women.

Time for her to go then, as winter came down.

Time to find that room in Sydney, time to paint it black . . .

Because opportunity did not knock twice at their age, Charles had said. She had rejected him once, and he would not ask again. She had chosen her son over her lover, and she had to pay the price. And pay, and pay, and pay till the day she died.

'Helen?'

He was coming towards her out of the dining room, his face cold and withdrawn. 'Just come to say goodbye,' he said curtly. 'I'm getting the chopper with Mrs Matsuda and Buckley, we're taking Trisha too, so she'll be out of your hair. Mrs Matsuda says she's interested in taking the business if she can't have Koenigshaus, so I'll be in touch about that.' He paused. 'But I shan't be back. Goodbye, then. Take care of yourself.' He turned to go.

She seemed to be holding herself like a brimming glass, she felt if she moved, if she drew a breath, she would spill over with a cascade of tears, of endless grief and pain. 'Oh Charles,' she said. 'I—'

He turned back. 'Yes?' he said huskily.

'I don't want you to go!'

'What's this?' he stiffened.

'I don't want to say goodbye to you!'

Charles let out his breath in a light sardonic laugh. 'It's a bit late for this, isn't it?'

She could feel the tears rising like a tide. 'I don't want you to leave me, I can't bear to see you walk away!'

'Oh Helen!' he threw back his head in pain. 'We've been all through this before! And I'm too old to play games!' He turned to face her, his expression bleak and withdrawn. 'Look, let's just admit we tried it, it didn't work.'

Opportunity never comes twice at our age, he had said. She gathered all her strength. 'We can make it work.'

He was still watching her narrowly, suspicion in his eyes, 'What about Jon?'

'I've spoken to Jon. I've straightened it out with him, it'll be OK.'

'Who for?'

Never had she seen him look so cold, so distant. 'What do you mean?' she cried.

He covered his eyes with his hand. 'Helen, don't do this to me, I can't take it. I can't switch on and off when you feel like it. When I spoke to you before, I wanted to love you, I wanted to live with you,' he broke off and gave a defeated shrug. 'Well, that's history. It's all over now.'

'Only if you say so.' She had never felt so desperate. 'Because I love you and I want you more than anything I've ever wanted in my life.'

He was staring at her, caught between hope and fear. She moved towards him and drove on. 'I know I had my chance, and I missed it. I know I turned you away, and said goodbye. But I'm asking, Charles, I'm begging for another chance.'

She took his hand, almost blinded by tears. 'Not just for me, darling, you must see that. For both of us. Still he stood irresolute, his face a mask. 'Do you mean it?' he said trembling with suppressed tension.

'I never meant anything more in my whole life!' she wept. 'Oh Charles, I can make you happy, darling, I promise you, only give me a chance!'

'A chance?' Was he weeping too? His face was a blur through her tears. 'Only don't leave me!' she cried. 'Charles – please don't leave me!' She opened her mouth in a cry of anguish. 'I don't want you to go! I don't want to be apart from you! I don't want you ever to leave me! I just want to be with you!'

She could see a rainbow of emotions colouring his face. 'Helen, d'you really mean it?'

A moment later she was in his arms and he was pressing clumsy kisses all over her face, kissing the tears away. 'I won't leave you, darling!' he pledged passionately. 'I won't leave you! We'll be together now for the rest of our lives!'

More Compelling Fiction from Headline:

PATRICIA SHAW
RIVER OF THE SUN

When Perfection Middleton catches the eye of Darcy Buchanan, all hell breaks loose. Joint heir to the vast estate of Caravale in North Queensland, he's a catch all right, and far too good for a housemaid whose parents came over on a convict ship. That's what his family thinks, anyway, and his brother Ben dreams up an ingenious plan to prevent the marriage. It's a plan that goes tragically wrong...

Lew Cavour is very taken with Perfy, too, but he gets caught up in the gold rush and the race to stake a claim on the river of gold, as does Ben Buchanan, who sees it as the only way he can buy out Perfy's share of Caravale. But their journey to the river of gold is dogged by disease, madness and murder.

Diamond, an aborigine girl, has a profound effect on all their lives. Brought up by a kindly German widow, she feels she is at odds with both worlds: too intelligent to be content as the menial slave to which her colour condemns her; too sophisticated to return to her tribe.

Patricia Shaw's magnificent new saga celebrates the pioneering spirit of the men and women whose courage and ambition laid the foundations of modern Australia.

Don't miss Patricia Shaw's previous Australian saga *Valley of Lagoons* also available from Headline.

FICTION/SAGA   0 7472 3658 5

A selection of bestsellers from Headline